Lock Down Publications and Ca$h
Presents

THE
SINGLE
LADIES

Unconditional Love

I0564912

Written By
Christopher "Diesel" Hornezes

CHRISTOPHER "DIESEL" HORNEZES

Lock Down Publications
P.O. Box 944
Stockbridge, GA 30281
www.lockdownpublications.com

Like our page on Facebook: Lock Down Publications
www.facebook.com/lockdownpublications.ldp

Stay Connected with Us!

Text **LOCKDOWN** to 22828 to stay up-to-date with new releases, sneak peaks, contests and more...

Like our page on Facebook:
Lock Down Publications

Join Lock Down Publications/The New Era Reading Group

Visit our website:
www.lockdownpublications.com

Follow us on Instagram:
Lock Down Publications

Email Us: We want to hear from you!

Insert

"Are we really gonna' do this to her?" asked Katrina. "There's no comin' back from it."

"Hell yeah, we doin' it!" Onika replied, starting her car's engine. "You scared or somethin' now?"

"No! But it just seems . . . really mean."

Onika laughed again. "You soft as hell. I thought people from Chicago was some gangsters. How you a CO and actually have a heart?"

"Onika. Please stop," Whitney said. "Katrina, we are going to teach the girl a lesson, and that's that. Understood?"

Katrina sighed. "Okay, Whit. I just hope I can still get into Heaven after this."

PROLOGUE

"Oh, whoa, whoa, whoa! Hold up, lil' mama. You need somethin' here?" asked the big muscular bald-headed bouncer, who held his huge bear claw of a hand out to stop the girl from entering the dancer's entrance of the club.

Through the eye holes of her Mardi Gras-style mask, she scowled at him. "I'm a dancer, yo," she said, gripping the strap to the book bag she was holding extra tight.

The bouncer looked at her. She was wearing a black spandex bodysuit that showed no skin but most definitely revealed that she had one hell of a voluptuous physique. From behind her little shiny mask, he could tell she was caramel-complexioned and that her hair was platinum blonde, wrapped up in a bun on the rear of the top of her head. She looked to him to be about five-foot-five or six and was definitely young.

"Dancer, huh?" he asked, eying her suspiciously. "How come I haven't seen you before then?"

"Because I'm new," she said with a shrug, while her heart pounded in her chest, praying he didn't turn into super cop on her.

"New?" He chuckled at her. "What's your stage name?"

Yes! He's dumb! I'm in this biatch, yo! she thought to herself, her excitement coming back as it seemed that her mission for the night was still possible.

"*Mysterious*," she told him, giving him a flirtatious smile. "And it's very nice to meet you . . . um?"

"I'm Bruce. You know, whenever a new girl starts workin' here at *Jimbo's*, they gots to give me a lap dance before the night's over," he told her, with a sneaky cat-that-ate-the-canary smile.

In ya' dreams, fat boy, she thought, doing her best not to bust out laughing at his corny ass.

"Oh, okay." She stepped close to him, enough for her breasts to touch his stomach. He leaned down when she beckoned him to give her his ear. "I'll keep that in mind, handsome. Can I go in so I can get changed and ready?"

"Of course. Go ahead and get you some money, Mysterious. Welcome to Jimbo's, and if you don't leave with at least five grand tonight, you ain't shake that ass right."

She giggled at him. "Oh, trust and believe, Bruce . . . I am most *definitely* leavin' up outta here with *more* than five thousand dollars tonight."

CHAPTER 1

Cardi B's *"WAP"* blared from the speakers inside of Jimbo's, a very popular night club in Pittsburgh's Homewood area. The atmosphere was charged up with excitement, as people inside were getting lit, saying goodbye to a long week of hard work. Friday nights were the club's biggest nights. The dancers that hypnotized the crowds of ballers were at the top of their game. Using their voluptuous bodies, they all raked in thousands of dollars.

The lighting inside the massive establishment flashed different hues every five seconds. The people in the crowd whistled and cheered as the beautiful, voluptuous chick on stage performed her set of extremely seductive dances, utilizing the pole in the center of the stage.

Her skin was honey-gold. Her hair was long and brown. Her coke-bottle figure was flawless. Naturally, she had everybody's eyes on her. Her body was so perfect. The outfit she wore looked like a red shoestring that hung over her shoulders, V-ing down, barely covering the nipples of her succulent breasts, and ending down at her crotch, covering her coochie with just a tiny patch of red. Clear platform pumps were on her feet, giving her five-foot-four-inch-tall frame more height. The eyeshadow and lipstick she wore matched her outfit, as did her nails. She was whom most of the men—and women—came to see.

Putting on a show for all the ballers was what the dancer lived for. She was about that money. Everyone that knew her personally knew that for the right price, she was down to give *private* shows . . . or more.

WHITNEY

Uh uh! Hell no! thought Whitney, as she watched the dancer doing what she herself thought was way too much.

Whitney was a tall, beautiful, milk-chocolate-complexioned woman of West Indian descent. She stood five-nine without the stilettos on her feet. Dressed in a blue, form-fitting *FeFe* leather dress that had wool sleeves, stylish fishnet pantyhose with star patterns woven into them, and blue pointed-toe *FeFe* pumps that had chrome six-inch heels, she was looking like the chic boss that she definitely was.

People often said Whitney reminded them of the actress Gabrielle Union. The way she had her dark hair pulled back into a sophisticated bun, and her beautiful slim face, framed by the plain black Gucci glasses, gave her the sassy edge that anyone that encountered her could tell she was a businesswoman.

The only makeup she wore was black eyeliner, and blue lipstick. The white-gold Tiffany & Co. earrings that dangled from her ears, along with the matching white-gold necklace, and the Cartier watch on her wrist, were all gifts from co-workers at the fashion magazine production business that she owned.

Whitney watched the girl back her big butt up to the pole to where it went in between her cheeks. The club then filled with uproars as everyone inside that were attracted to women went insane.

"Maaan, why y'all bring me here for my birthday?" she asked the three ladies that worked for her. "I haven't seen a single guy get up on stage yet! I don't want to see no girls puttin' poles between their booty cheeks! How they know if it's been sanitized or not?"

Shaquayla, Riley, and Lanisha, all turned and looked at their friend/boss.

"Guuurl, this is 2022," said Shaquayla, who was an ebony-toned woman, with a bob-cut hairstyle. She was stacked like a brick house. Dressed in a wine-colored *FeFe* dress that fit her buxom, five-foot-ten-inch frame like a second skin, she looked like an African model. On her feet were *FeFe* pumps with zebra-prints. She, too, sported expensive jewelry on her wrists, around her neck, and in her ears. Sipping on a glass of Dom Perignon, Shaquayla had been enjoying her night out with her friends until their very own Gabrielle Union started with her old-worldly code of ethics. "*We* women, we do what we want now, and can't nobody say a damn thang to make us feel bad about ourselves. Hence, listen to this song. I mean, come on . . . the girls are rapping about wet ass p—"

"I know what they're rapping about, 'Quayla!" Whitney interrupted, before taking a sip of her Long Island Ice Tea.

"Okay, then," Shaquayla continued. "If we wanna' shake some ass for cash, we do. If we wanna' pop that thang for some change, we do. We some sexy Black queens, Whit! We run the world!"

"For real, Whit," agreed Riley, a five-foot-five-inch-tall woman that was so light-skinned with natural sandy-brown hair that most people thought she was white. She was rocking a peach-colored silk button-down *FeFe* top with a brown *FeFe* high-waist pencil skirt and orange pointed-toe pumps on her feet. "Cardi B and Megan Thee Stallion are doing exactly what they should be doing by dropping a song like this: representing for us! Women who aren't afraid to speak their minds and say how they are! *Major* props to them, yo!" she said, then also took a sip of her drink—*Sex on The Beach*.

"But," chimed in Lanisha, who was a café au-lait-brown-skinned, five-foot-eight belle, wearing a white *FeFe* dress with blue and turquoise rose prints all over it, with white open-toe stiletto pumps on her feet, and her dark brown hair braided in an intricate fishbone design. "What *you* need to be doing, *Miss 34-year-old Birthday girl*, is not be so worried about that girl up on the stage, but yourself. We ain't bring you here for the girl dancers, of course; there's plenty of male dancers that will be comin' up. And you need to be loosening up so you can snag you one, and get you some lovin'. It's your b-day, and you have been single for *waaay* too long, girl," she told her, picking up her Cîroc. "Sheeit, it *should* be *you* up there, poppin' ya' thang, havin' all these guys goin' crazy for you like they are for her little ass."

The ladies laughed, but Whitney didn't. She wasn't upset, but the idea of dating—or finding a good man—had been one of the worst things she could imagine. They all knew why, yet they constantly tried to hook her up with different guys, despite the physical condition that had plagued her since she was a baby. Because of it, Whitney had been single for more than six years. Even before that, she'd never experienced love, and she didn't believe she ever would. Whenever the idea of dating came up, she always thought: *Who could love a woman like me?*

She was blessed with an amazing job that paid her six figures, allowing her to acquire the newest fashion labels and mingle with celebrities and famous designers. Materially, she wanted for nothing. But love—love was what Whitney yearned for. She was approaching her mid-thirties, yet she wasn't even close to having a man in her life or the children she so desperately wanted.

Loneliness had become her norm, though she didn't welcome it. Nonetheless, Whitney had been single for so long that she had stopped believing any man could desire her. Her friends persisted in their attempts to encourage her, telling her that if she gave up on finding love, she would certainly never have it—and that she might miss out on the one good guy she'd been waiting for because of her fear that all men were the same.

●●●

Shaking her head at Lanisha, Whitney picked up her drink and took a sip before speaking.

"Nisha, you are *not* gon' mess up the night with that stuff. Mm-mmm. Not gon' happen, honey boo-boo. So I'ma tell you like..."

Whitney's words suddenly halted as she felt that familiar, uncomfortable bubbling sensation in her gut, accompanied by a squeezing pain. The pressure inside her built rapidly, causing her to double over and groan in discomfort. Her girls immediately recognized the look on her face. They knew about her *'condition'*, and the mood at the mall shifted to panic.

"Oh God! Whitney! Go!" urged Shaquayla, as she quickly stood to let Whitney out of her corner seat.

Riley and Lanisha jumped as well, watching Whitney bolt like a track star in her pumps. They silently prayed she'd make it in time.

Whitney cursed and groaned as she pushed her way through the thick crowd gathered about to cheer on the final performance of the golden girl on stage. She squealed in panic as gas escaped her, feeling her bowels threatening to explode. Instinctively, she cupped her rear as she ran, pigeon-toed, towards the restroom.

Come on, come on, come oooon! Not here, please, not here! she begged internally, the pressure in her abdomen mounting.

The women's restroom came into view, just feet away. Relief washed over her as she reached the door and pushed her way inside.

Grateful that the bathroom was clean and empty, Whitney quick-stepped towards one of the stalls, with only seconds to spare. But just as she reached the first stall door—

WHAM!

"AAAAAGGGGHHHH!" Whitney screamed in pain as a blunt object struck the back of her head, sending flying her forward. She crashed to the floor face-first.

At that exact moment, her bowels gave up, releasing uncontrollably. She cringed as the mess soaked her Victoria's Secret panties, the humiliation overwhelming her.

Ashamed and embarrassed, Whitney cursed under her breath, attempting to get up from the dirty floor. Suddenly, she heard the sound of the bathroom door locking, followed by approaching footsteps.

Looking towards the door, Whitney saw a person dressed in a hoodie, sweatpants, sneakers, and a ski-mask. A 9mm semi-automatic handgun was in their hand.

Gasping in fear, Whitney tried to scoot backward as the masked individual approached.

"Don't shoot! Please!" Whitney pleaded, her voice trembling.

"The only way I don't pop you is if you don't make a sound, and give up *all* ya' drip!" the figure demanded.

Hearing the voice, Whitney froze in shock. She couldn't believe that it was a female robbing her. The voice was unmistakable—a woman, with a thick East Coast accent, likely from New Jersey or New York.

"And once you come up off all that, you can go in one of them stalls and clean 'yaself up, 'cause ya' stink *real* bad right now," the stick-up girl added.

"Okay! Okay!" Whitney replied, hurriedly removing her jewelry.

Once she was bare of any shine, Whitney spoke again.

"I gave you what I had! Please, let me go! It's my birthday!"

Without another word, the stick-up girl stuffed her score into her pockets, tucked the gun away, and unlocked the bathroom door before slipping out.As the door closed behind the thief, Whitney broke into tears. Her hard-earned valuables were gone, and the shame of what had just happened crushed her.

This was the last time she'd ever step foot in a club.

CHAPTER 2

ONIKA

A Few Hours Later—
In the alleyway behind the club, Jimbo, the owner, reclined in his newly purchased Bentley Bentayga, groaning in bliss as he received some of the best oral pleasure from his top dancer. She was on her knees in the passenger seat, hunched over the center console, her head bobbing in his lap. The cocaine he had just given her had her going wild.

As his eyes rolled back in pleasure, Al Green played from his stock audio system. She deep-throated his length, taking him all the way to the back of her throat. The honey-gold beauty was working hard to earn them extra dollars her boss was paying for her to dome him up. Every night she worked, before she left, she orally pleased him to fatten her money bag up. And her love for the white powder fueled her willingness to do all the nasty things required that made the ballers pay top dollar for her explicit services.

Jimbo groaned loudly, reaching around to grab her rear end, caressing her phat, round booty through the shiny, black, skin-tight vinyl Rag & Bone skinny-leg pants. Her succulent breasts were freed from the skimpy Versace top and sexy Cosabella bra she'd had on. On her feet, she still wore her gold six-inch FeFe stilettos.

"Damn, Onika! Wooo!" the older man cursed, smacking her ass as she worked him like she was trying to suck his soul out of him. "Yeah, baby! You workin' for it tonight! Shit! Gon' get this money, baby!"

Onika used one hand to start jerking him while she sucked, knowing it would get him there faster. She didn't exactly enjoy giving a fifty-year-old man head, but when she did, she milked his pocket for as much as she could—because she knew he couldn't tell her no.

Jimbo bucked and kicked, his toes curling in his Gucci loafers. He felt his nut coming and cursed. Seconds later, he exploded in her mouth. Onika kept jerking and sucking him, until he filled her mouth up with hot semen globs. For her, it was all about the money, and her cocaine high allowed her to get *extremely* X-Rated. She put on a show for him, spitting it back onto his shaft before slurping it up again, swallowing it up like it was the tastiest thing ever.

"Mmmmm, damn, baby. You taste so good!" Onika purred, sitting upright in the seat. "Did you like that?" she asked, grabbing her bra and top.

"Hell yeah, I did! You's a beast!" Jimbo told her, stuffing his limpness back into his Italian-cut trousers. "All women need to learn how to suck cock like you do."

Onika giggled as she got her bra and shirt on. "I hear that."

Jimbo dug his wallet out and fished out two new hundred-dollar bills. He handed them to Onika, as a song by Luther Vandross came on.

"All you, baby girl", he said

Onika sucked her teeth as she took the cash. "Two 'hunnid dollars? Seriously?" she asked incredulously, sniffling as her nose began to run.

Jimbo looked at her with a raised eyebrow. "Well, *damn*, Onika! All you did is give me some dome! It ain't like you gave me everlastin' life or made me richer!"

"Uh, technically, I *did* make you richer tonight! Shakin' my ass on *your* stage—*I* make the hood come out to your club! They wanna come see *me*! Icey! So stop bein' cheap, yo!"

Jimbo muttered a curse under his breath, pulled out two more hundreds, and handed them to her.

"Uh-huh. I think one more will do," Onika then said, her hand still out.

"Girl, you killin' me now! It's bad enough Bruce's dumb ass let a dang on stick-up clown—a girl no less—up in my club! The little bitch dun' hit the woman upside her head with her gun, then robbed her on her birthday! *And* made her crap on herself in *my* bathroom! And now you chargin' me five hundred dollars for some neck? Ain't this about a bitch?"

"Naw, boo-boo. This about *money*! I need money! You own a damn night club, so ya ass should be used to the bullshit! And you *should* know that lettin' ya employees suck ya' dick can come with very bad repercussions, *if* one of them reports you!"

Jimbo sighed and handed her another hundred. "Get out, Onika."

"I need more coke, and you can at least drive me to my car," she said, tucking all the money into her FeFe handbag, with the rest of her cash.

"Don't got no more, and no. Use ya' legs. Now get out."

Her nostrils flared in anger. "Whatever, yo! Cheap-ass bastard!"

Angrily, she got up out of his SUV. Jimbo mashed the gas and peeled off, leaving Onika by herself in the dimly lit alley way. She screamed after his Bentley, flicking him off before stomping off towards her car, parked out on Frankstown Avenue, the main street in front of the club.

"Bitch-ass shit, yo!" Onika fumed, feeling the itch she always got when she needed some cocaine.

As she walked down the dark sidewalk towards her white 2015 Mercedes C300 coupe, she dug into her leather, diamond-stitched FeFe handbag, pulling out her key fob and pressing *unlock* and remote start. A couple of cop cars rolled past, riding slow—no doubt still looking for the robbery suspect who had hit Jimbo's club.

"How the fuck did my life get like this? So many good men out there, and a bitch gots to be shakin' ass on stage for some change? Suckin' and fuckin' on horny-ass dogs to come up! When am I gonna' find a man that can take me away from all this shit, yo?" she asked herself, wiping her nose as she reached her car's passenger-side door.

Just as she reached out to open the door, Onika heard that all-too-familiar sound behind her.

CLICK-CLACK!

She immediately froze as the barrel of a gun pressed against the back of her skull.

Oh shit . . . oh, my God . . . dammit! she panicked, trying not to pee on herself.

"Do me a favor and please don't poop ya' pants."

Onika heard a female's voice, tinged with a heavy East Coast accent. Inside her head, she cursed.

Goddammit! I'm getting' robbed by a bitch! This is crazy!

"Come on, yo!" Onika pleaded. "I'm havin' a *really* bad night—can you just rob someone else? Like you did earlier? You had to have just seen those two cop cars ride past, lookin' for you."

A hard shove from behind sent Onika stumbling into the side of her car.

"I didn't ask you all that, and I don't care about the pigs! Shut ya' mouth up and run me ya' purse, and the keys, yo! Or I'ma splatter ya' brains all over this pretty white car."

"Okay! Chill, yo!" Onika said, quickly handing the stick-up girl her purse and car key. "Happy now?"

"I am. Now walk ya' ass back to the club and go get that dumb-ass bouncer to come help you," the stick-up girl ordered. "And *don't* look back, or I'ma shoot you in ya' money-maker."

Onika sucked her teeth, but obeyed.

All that money I made tonight and this bitch just gon' take my shit? Ain't this about a bitch? she thought to herself, stomping off.

●●●

RUBY

Ruby watched as the dancer stormed off, cursing up a storm. She chuckled to herself, then she hopped into Onika's car. Headlights approached, making her duck down, in case it was the cops again. Once the lights passed, she put the car into drive, pulled out of the parking spot, and hit the gas, heading up Frankstown towards Penn Hills.

ONIKA

"Shit! My freakin' car, man! Goddammit!" Onika snapped as she, and three security bouncers, and two Pittsburgh police officers arrived at the empty parking spot. "I don't even have insurance on it yet, yo!"

"If you want, Icey," said Bruce, calling her by her stage name, "I can give you a ride to ya' house."

Onika whipped around so fast that the guys all jumped back, thinking she was going to swing on one of them. She stormed up to the gigantic man, fire blazing in her eyes.

"It's your fuckin' fault the bitch got inside in the first place, stupid! Now my car's gone, and all my money I made!" she screamed, so angry that tears filled her eyes.

Bruce, who had always been enamored with Onika, was well aware of her fiery personality. But he was so shocked by her outburst that he was rendered speechless. His two men said nothing either. They all knew the wrath of the young chick.

Just then, cackling on the cops' radios caught their attention. Onika barely made out something about a car crash

17

just up the road, near the border of Homewood, East Hills, and Penn Hills.

"Ma'am, we need to go," one of the cops said. "Just file a police report, and a detective will contact you."

The two officers rushed off to their cruiser, heading to the crash scene minutes away.

Left standing with the bouncers, Onika fought to keep from breaking down. Bruce stepped forward, attempting to comfort her.

"You're right, Onika. I apologize for all this. If you want, I can give you a ride home," he said, hopeful.

Onika nodded. She really didn't have a choice—her money was gone, her credit and debit cards were gone. She couldn't call an Uber, a Lyft, or even a jitney.

"A'ight, man," she muttered, then walked off with them, sulking as if the world had just ended. "I need to make a stop somewhere first, though, Bruce."

"Where?" he asked suspiciously.

"Don't worry about it! Just drive where I say, yo! Stop askin' so many damn questions!" Onika snapped, the monkey on her back making her irritation even worse.

KATRINA

"Ma'am? Hey, ma'am? Can you hear me?"

Katrina groaned as a sharp pain pounded in her head. A bright light shone against her closed eyelids, turning them red and making the pain even worse. Something wet and sticky trickled down her face. Wincing, she squirmed in her seat, attempting to move—then, suddenly, it hit her. The crash. The violent, horrific crash.

She was still trapped in her crumpled Dodge Charger SRT-8, her Allegheny County Sheriff's correctional officer uniform stained with blood. She was in such pain that she felt like her whole body was broken. As the EMT shined a light at her eyelids, she squinted.

She had been on her way home from work and made a quick stop at Giant Eagle, a grocery store that sat at the bottom of a steep hill, just seconds from the four-way intersection of Verona Road, Robinson Boulevard, and Frankstown Road. She had just crossed through the intersection when, suddenly, blinding headlights came hurtling toward her from the passenger side of her car.

A car ran the red light. The impact was brutal. The vehicle slammed into her so hard that the entire passenger side caved in, sending her car tumbling violently before landing on a grassy patch near a BP gas station. Katrina blacked out. Everything faded to nothingness—until she heard voices and saw flickers of light pushing against her eyelids.

"Hey! She's responding!" she heard the paramedic yell. "Let's get her outta' here! I need the neck brace—now!"

The jaws of life tore open the wreckage. Katrina then felt the paramedics secure the brace around her neck brace before they carefully lifted her out of the car and onto a gurney. Within seconds, she was loaded into an ambulance, sirens blaring as they and sped to the closest emergency room.

RUBY

Ruby limp-ran for her life the moment the cops spotted her crawling out of the severely damaged Mercedes she'd stolen.

She had been speeding like bat out of hell . . . she took her eyes off the road for just a second, as she approached the intersection, when her gun slid off of her lap and fell by her feet. When she looked up, it was too late.

The traffic light in front of her was red. A car was already passing through the intersection.

Ruby slammed the brakes, but she'd been going way too fast.

The impact was devastating. She T-boned the vehicle with such force that it went flying, crashing onto the corner of a gas station. Her own vehicle spun out of control, flipping before landing upside down in the parking lot of a small shopping plaza that housed a Family Dollar and a liquor store in it.

Ruby blacked out for an unknown amount of time, until sirens and frantic voices snapped her back to consciousness. When she came to, she realized her left leg was pinned under the seat, bent at an angle that nearly broke her bone. When she saw red and blue lights flashing, Ruby panicked. As fast as she could, she pulled her leg free, crying out in pain as she did. Then, dragging herself out of the car, she tried to stand. The agony that shot through her body when she attempted to run was unbearable, but she knew that if the cops caught her, she was done for. She already had a long criminal record.

The cops saw her, and started chasing her up Frankstown. And the worst part? She'd forgotten to grab the bag stuffed with the jewelry and money she'd ganked from the dancer and the other woman—and she'd left her gun in the car.

Ruby managed to limp her way up to Graham Boulevard, an old brick-paved street lined with houses and trees, shrouded in darkness. But the cops were right on her ass . . . closing in fast.

"STOP! I SWEAR I WILL LET THE DOG GO! STOP RUNNING!"

But she didn't stop. She couldn't. If they caught her, she was screwed.

Ruby pushed herself forward, limping as fast as she could. Her leg felt like it was going to snap off at any second. Then, just as she rounded a curve in the road where the lines of houses began, she heard it—heavy paws pounding against the pavement.

She turned just in time to see the German Shepherd charging straight at her.

"AAGGGHHHH!" she shrieked as the K9 lunged, taking her down hard. The dog's teeth sank deep into her right arm, mauling her.

"STOOOP! GET THE DOOOOG! PLEEEAAASE! I'M DOOOWN!" she wailed.

The cops arrived seconds later—but took their sweet time getting the dog off her. Despite her bleeding arm and mangled leg, they showed no sympathy.

Roughly, she was yanked up off the ground and handcuffed. A police car screeched to a stop next to her, and Ruby was slammed up against it.

"Please!" she cried as one of the cops yanked open the cruiser's rear door. "I need a doctor! My leg is broken, and your dog tore my arm up!"

The officer ignored her and shoved her inside.

Another cop stepped forward, sneering at her like she was the lowest form of life.

"Fuck you, your leg, and your arm, you piece of shit! Because of you, a woman is in critical condition!" he snapped. "And just so you know, she's an officer of the law . . . if she dies, you are *fucked*."

Ruby gasped.

Oh my God! That was a cop! she thought, horrified at the possibility of having a cop's death on her hands.

"GET HER OUTTA HERE! TAKE HER TO COUNTY! LET THEM TREAT HER WOUNDS!" the cop barked at the officer behind the wheel before slamming the door shut in Ruby's face.

CHAPTER 3

WHITNEY

Around one o-clock in the morning, Whitney entered her lavish home in the Wilkinsburg area. She lived on Laketon Street, one of Pittsburgh's historically brick-paved roads. Her house sat across from a school in a peaceful neighborhood. It was a luxurious 3,300 square-foot property with four bedrooms—two on the first floor and two on the second. Whitney had invested heavily in renovations, adding features that boosted its value tenfold.

As the boss of her own self-created fashion magazine— the hottest and most popular to come out of the Steel City— Whitney could afford the luxurious home with ease, along with several more if she wanted.

She shared her home with her best friend, a beautiful light-brown-skinned woman with fiery red hair from Chicago. Tonight, however, Whitney was extremely glad that her homegirl was not there.

Before leaving the club, her friends and co-workers had gotten her a change of clothes. To avoid any potential lawsuit, the club owner had allowed her to use the dancers' shower to wash up and had even offered her some *hush* money.

Whitney refused the money but took the shower.

When her girls dropped her off, she all but ran into her house, dying to take another shower with her own soaps. She hurried to the big marble-and-stone bathroom, stripped naked, turned on the shower, and got in.

Under the stream of hot water raining down on her from the custom ceiling shower head, Whitney broke into tears.

Just after her sixth birthday, a series of uncontrollable bowel movements had Whitney discover that she had ulcerative colitis. The inflammatory disease affected the large intestine and the rectum. Though both men and women could get it, but studies showed women were slightly more prone.

For Whitney, flare-ups always struck at the worst possible times. When the urge hit, she had no ability to hold it in. If she wasn't near a bathroom, she was out of luck. And worst of all, while the disease was treatable, it was incurable.

She hated that she was a woman in her mid-thirties still suffering accidents like this. As a prominent figure in the fashion industry, she had fought to keep her condition a secret, but slip-ups had happened, and a few people had found out.

She wore the sexiest, most expensive designer clothing on the market—many as gifts from designers featured in her magazine, the rest purchased with her enormous salary. She had ruined countless outfits simply because she couldn't make it to a toilet in time. The embarrassment was crushing.

And it was why Whitney couldn't keep a man, let alone find one who wasn't repulsed by her condition. She hadn't asked for this, but life wasn't fair. These days, the fear of rejection kept her from even trying to find love.

Her school years had been the worst. Teachers had refused to let her use the bathroom without a doctor's note. She had accidents in class, on the bus, and during field trips. She was bullied so badly that she had nearly contemplated suicide.

The names they called her still cut deep.

Even some school staff and security guards had mocked her, giving her cruel nicknames that stuck with her for years.

She didn't even want to go to her own graduation, out of fear of having an accident on stage while waiting for her diploma. She only went because the friends that she *did* have had promised her that if she had an accident and anyone talked crazy, they'd beat their ass until *they* pooped *themselves*.

As a teenager, Whitney had refused to eat at certain times, thinking that if her stomach was empty, it couldn't betray her. For a few months, it worked. But when she started losing weight rapidly, people noticed. Rumors spread that she had an eating disorder, and her concerned parents to put her in counseling.

After trying everything, Whitney had finally accepted that she would never live a normal life. She barely had any boyfriends growing up. The one guy she'd been insanely attracted to in high school seemed to not even want to come near her. So, Whitney bucked up, and just focused on trying to do something with her life. She had always loved fashion—the clothes, the shoes, the entire industry. That passion gave her direction.

She started out as a photographer, then became an article writer, then an interviewer. She climbed the ranks until she was running the show at the first magazine that hired her. Once she learned the ins and the outs of the business, she made the leap. With her connections to fashion designers, celebrities, and a keen eye for what people wanted, Whitney launched her own magazine. It took off so fast she couldn't believe it herself.

And yet, despite all her success, she was still plagued by her condition.

"Remission my *ass,*" Whitney muttered bitterly, fuming. She took IV infusions to ease her flare-ups and improve her quality of life, but the disease was incurable, and she was still having accidents.

"And that damn girl," she continued as she scrubbed her skin raw. "What the hell is wrong with her? I'm so tired of all this violence between our *own* kind! Oooo, I hope somebody catches her and kicks her little ass!"

Minutes later, she shut off the water and got out, wrapping a towel around her body, and another around her hair. She grabbed her throwaway clothes and carried them into her spacious master bedroom.

Turning on the lights, she tossed the ruined outfit straight into the trash.

She sat down on the edge of her bed and took a deep breath.

"Some birthday," she murmured, shaking her head. Then, suddenly, a thought struck her.

"Where the heck is Trina?"

Whitney got up and went to get her iPhone from the living room. Opening her messages, she scrolled to her last conversation with her roommate.

Hey? Are you with Jeff, or doing a double again? Let me know because I'm worried, Whitney typed before hitting *send.*

ONIKA

"Mind ya' business, Bruce," Onika told the bouncer, after taking another big bump of cocaine off her driver's license—her second in the last three minutes ago.

Bruce had just pulled into the parking spot in front of her house. She lived on Hamilton, at the top of a steep hill that connected to Oakwood Street in Homewood. Her crib was a modest two-bedroom with a sunroom in the front, a small front yard, and an even smaller backyard. A house on the left was connected to hers, with a few more houses attached in a row.

"I'm sayin, Onika!" Bruce persisted as he parked. "That shit is poison! You know you shouldn't be screwin' around with that!"

"I DON'T CARE!" Onika suddenly yelled, fed up with the bouncer's attempts to make her feel like a druggie. "BECAUSE OF *YOU*, I JUST GOT ROBBED AND MY CAR STOLEN! I DON'T GIVE FUCK ABOUT NOTHING!"

Tucking the quarter-ounce of powder she'd paid $200 for—discounted due to the sexual favor she'd performed on her dealer—Onika got out of the Jeep and slammed the door shut. Bruce stared at her, shaking his head.

"Onika, I'm sorry, yo. At least lemme' help you in ya' house. You don't got ya' keys."

"I'm good, player. Bounce."

Bruce continued to stare at her, with a burning hatred for her beginning to burn inside.

"I just wanna' make sure you're sa—"

"BOUNCE, GODDAMMIT! GET THE FUCK ON, YO!"

This time, Bruce got the hint. He maneuvered his Cherokee back out of the parking spot. He floored it up the hill and bent the corner, disappearing into the night.

Onika went up to her door. She reached into a small space behind her mail box, and pulled out a spare key. She let herself inside and locked the door behind her.

She turned on the light, illuminating her first floor. Directly in front of her, stairs led up to the second level, where her bathroom, a guest bedroom, and her own bedroom were. To the right was her living room, with an entrance to the window-walled sunroom. A 65-inch 4K HDTV was mounted on the main wall, facing her rented leather couch set and glass coffee table. To the left of the living room was her dining room, with a door leading to the basement. The dining area adjoined a small kitchen, which had a back door leading to the backyard.

Kicking off her high heels, Onika stomped upstairs, fuming. She had worked all night, and now she had absolutely nothing to show for it. In her bedroom, she flipped on the light and stripped naked, ready to shower. She grabbed a clean pair of undies and a bra and was about to head to the bathroom when her iPhone rang.

The number was unfamiliar, but she answered anyway.

"Hello?"

"Hi, is this, uh . . . Onika Temple?" a male voice asked.

"Yes . . . who's calling?"

"Hello, ma'am. I'm Detective Kavic with the Pittsburgh Police Department. Are you the owner of a white 2015 Mercedes C300?"

"Yes! Oh my God, did you find my car?" Onika sat on her bed, praying her baby was okay.

"Uh . . . yes . . . but your vehicle was involved in a bad accident near the border of Homewood, East Hills, and Penn Hills. It's totaled, ma'am."

Onika gasped, then cursed.

"The woman who stole your car ran a red light and hit another vehicle. The driver of that car is in bad shape."

"Oh my God! Will she be okay?"

"Well . . . we aren't sure, but she was a law enforcement worker, so you can rest assured that the suspect will be punished."

The detective gave Onika the name of the girl who had stolen her car and started explaining how to press charges.

Onika hung up on him without another word.

"Fuck I look like sendin' another Black person to prison?" she muttered. "It's already too many of us behind them walls now. Naw, yo. I know what to do. I'ma keep it hood and handle this shit like a bitch like me is supposed to."

She pulled out her cocaine, lined up four fat lines, and snorted them back-to-back. Then she got up to shower.

As she lathered her body up with body wash, the perfect plan came to Onika. But to make it happen, she was going to need money—real money.

Which meant she was going to have to put in serious overtime And some *off-the-books* work.

CHAPTER 4

KATRINA

Three Weeks Later—
Katrina was relieved to be cleared to leave the hospital. Her worst injury was a concussion, and the bruising on her face and body was mild. Knowing she was okay and wouldn't have to return to the hospital, Katrina sighed in relief as she signed her discharge papers and got a prescription for mild pain meds.

Around noon that day, her co-workers—who were her closest friends—arrived to get her up out of there. She was glad to see the three crazy ladies. They were all correctional officers like she was.

Twenty-six-year-old Shamika was a tall, six-foot, Queen Latifah-type BBW with peanut-butter-brown skin and neatly twisted dreads, currently styled into a crown atop her head. She was still dressed in her uniform, as was Andrea.

Andrea, a twenty-five-year-old dark-skinned beauty, stood at five-foot-four with a cute, round face and a nose ring. Her hair was shaved low on the sides and back, while the top was left long and dyed a vibrant purple.

Yvette, the oldest of the three at thirty, wore a white shirt—her sergeant's uniform. Her dark skin was the color of coffee with no cream or sugar. At five-foot-ten, she had a slim, toned physique, and her hair was styled in neat two-strand twists.

The three ladies were geeked to be bringing their homegirl home. Hearing the news of her crash had them all in tears. It'd been a long two weeks without her, but now that she was cleared to go, they had all called off work to come get her.

"Come on, *guuuurl*," sang Shamika, holding up a bag. "We springin' ya' ass from this joint, and we all pitched in and come bearing gifts!"

Andrea brought in a wheel chair for Katrina, as it was hospital policy for discharged patients to be wheeled out.

Seeing the designer name *FeFe* on the bag, Katrina knew that her girls had spent some real money. That popular Pittsburgh-born fashion brand wasn't cheap.

Katrina was a gorgeous redhead—a *red-bone*, as those from her hometown of Chicago always called her. She grew up on the *Wild '100s*, so she was no stranger to the crazy life. Despite her upbringing, she was a peaceful person.

At twenty-nine, she stood five-foot-six with a curvy frame. She was also a workaholic—something her friends constantly reminded her of. They always told her she didn't need to work as much as she did, that she should enjoy life more. But Katrina always found a reason to put in overtime at her job.

She was known for clocking nearly 90 hours a week.

Her bank account looked *real* nice because of it.

But it also meant she neglected the one good thing in her life—the one thing that, when she finally realized it, she didn't want to be without.

She had a man who loved her deeply—*did everything* to keep her in his life. And she loved him too. But she had been hurt so many times by men she swore were perfect for her. She had been cheated on, ghosted—she had even found out some were on the down-low.

Her biggest problem, though? She had grown up in poverty. She knew what it was like to go to bed hungry.

She had been adopted. She had suffered all kinds of abuse in her younger years. To say she was scarred was an understatement.

Her heart was guarded—protected by rabid pit bulls and a steel-reinforced wall topped with barbed wire.

As she got older and aged out of foster care, Katrina worked whatever jobs she could to keep a little food on her table and a roof over her head. One day, while at a job center, she saw a *Help Wanted* ad for correctional officers at the Allegheny County Jail in downtown Pittsburgh.

She saw the pay rate and applied immediately. She passed all the required tests and got hired.

Her first check was *more* money than she had ever made before, and after a few months, the benefits were *exactly* what she needed.

Being broke? Depending on government assistance? That was no longer a worry.

But without even realizing it, Katrina had become addicted to working. She rarely took a day off. Rarely took time for herself. Rarely took time for the man who was trying so hard to love her.

●●●

Smiling, Katrina appreciated her friends bringing her new clothes. "Thanks, y'all. I'll pay you back."

"We don't need you to pay us back, Trina," said Yvette. "You're our homie, yo. That's what friends do for each other."

"Real rap," agreed Andrea. "And just so you know . . . the little bitch that did that shit to you is in Tiffany's unit. Say the word, and she *accidentally* slips in the shower and busts her head open."

"Or falls down the stairs," Shamika threw in.

"Or!" Yvette added, coming up with another idea. "The little bit of money on her account disappears mysteriously.

Letters from her people—or her lawyer—never make it to her. And maybe, just *maybe*, some itchin' powder gets into all her panties and bras. Hell, she might even write a kite to the psych doctor sayin' she wants to kill herself . . . and ends up in the *naked room* for two weeks straight."

"Well, damn!" Katrina tried not to laugh, but her girls were crazy.

The others laughed with her.

"I thought close watch was only for, like, twenty-four hours?" Katrina asked just as Shamika and Andrea moved to help her off the bed and into the wheelchair.

"It is," Yvette confirmed. "But only if the doc feels like you're not a harm to yourself or others. If she deems it necessary, that bitch stays in that cold-ass, bright-ass room, hungry as hell, until she stops *bein'* suicidal."

"How about y'all stop abusing your authority—no matter how much the bitch deserves it."

The unmistakable voice made them all turn toward the doorway.

There stood Whitney, looking like *Deliver Us From Eva*-era Gabrielle Union.

The fashion magazine owner was wearing a tight, thigh-high mocha-colored leather Chanel skirt with a slit up the front of her right thigh. Nude-colored fishnet pantyhose emphasized her long, sexy legs. Her white Hermès blouse featured a ruffled neckline and flared sleeves, and the snake-skin Chanel stiletto boots she wore matched her skirt perfectly—knee-high with gold six-inch heels. Her hair was pulled back into a sleek, sophisticated bun, and she rocked gold double-C Chanel earrings. Her nails were fire-engine red with gold airbrushed designs, her delicious full lips painted the same bold shade. The moment she walked in, the scent of her expensive perfume filled the room.

Whitney was *stunning*. Nobody could ever deny that. But the scowl on her face right then made the ladies consider hauling ass up out of Katrina's hospital room.

"Uh-oh . . . Eva is in the building," Yvette joked, throwing back the *Deliver Us From Eva* reference.

Whitney shot the sergeant a look. "Eva my *ass*. Shame on you, Yvette. The color of your shirt means *you* of all people shouldn't be abusing your power. Stop getting down on your own kind. The bitch busted my head open and stole fifteen thousand dollars' worth of jewelry from me, but you don't see *me* tryna' make the girl go nuts and kill herself."

"You right, Whit'. My bad," said Yvette, not really wanting to hear any more of that ish.

Whitney ignored the others and stepped towards Katrina. "How are you feeling, sis?"

Katrina nodded. "Much better. I'm just ready to get up outta' here. Eat some *real* food. Watch me some '*Black Ink Crew: Chicago*', or Waka & Tammy."

"Have you called Jeff?" Whitney asked, one perfectly arched brow raised.

"Um . . . a few days ago. He came to see me," Katrina admitted. "He wanted to be the one to take me home, but . . . I just . . . I don't know why I didn't call him to."

Whitney shook her head. "Girl, you got a *good* man. You gon' lose him if you don't stop holdin' back. What did he do to you?"

"Nothing, sis. I just been hurt before. Jeff is too damn good to be true, and when that happens, someone gets hurt. And that someone is *always* me."

"You have to let the past go, baby girl. *Please*," Whitney urged. "Jeff is head over heels in love with you. Any man who barely sees his woman but still stays loyal? Stays strong for her instead of going astray? Girl, you gotta get yourself together. Not many good men like that left."

"Mmmhmmmm," the other ladies chimed in.

"She ain't never lied, Trina," Shamika said. "What I wouldn't do for a man to love me the way that man loves you. You better get it together, 'cause you don't know how much longer he'll be able to deal with havin' a woman who don't *have* him."

Katrina sighed. She knew they were right.

She was just *so* scared to let him in.

Her trust issues were damn near impossible to shake.

"I'll try," she finally said.

"That's all we ask," Whitney replied. "Now. I'm takin' you home." She turned to Katrina's co-workers. "Ladies, thank you for the clothes. I got her from here."

They looked at Whitney, then at each other, deciding not to argue.

"We'll see you later, girl," Andrea said.

Each of them hugged Katrina before heading out.

Whitney helped Katrina get dressed in the new outfit: a white ribbed, long-sleeved FeFe scoop-neck shirt, old-school tight acid-washed ripped skinny-leg jeans with *FeFe* graffiti painted in red letters, and a fresh pair of white low-top Air Force 1s with red Nike swooshes. She even had new ankle socks.

Once Katrina was dressed, Whitney wheeled her out of the hospital. The air outside was crisp, sending a slight chill through them as Whitney hurried to where she had parked her BMW truck. She helped Katrina into the front seat.

"I'll take the wheelchair back, then we can go get your prescription filled. Care for some gyros from Mike & Tony's?" she asked.

"Hell yeah! That sounds bomb as hell right now, *jo!*" Katrina exclaimed, her Chi-Town roots slipping into her speech.

"Cool. I need to make a stop downtown first," Whitney told her.

"To your office?"

"Not my office," Whitney said, shutting the door before heading off to return the wheelchair.

CHAPTER 5

ONIKA

Parking her rented Nissan Altima in a small pay-by-the-hour parking lot downtown, Onika hopped out looking like a straight-up diva. The cosmic silver leather *FeFe* handbag she carried matched the knee-high stiletto *FeFe* boots she had on. Her tight, dark-blue leather-and-wool sweater top was embellished with silver metal studs, and emphasizing her shapely bottom half was a pair of silver *FeFe* leggings with dark-blue stripes down the sides.

Her hair was braided in an intricate big-braid-little-braid design, swirling over her head in a style worthy of *Essence Magazine*. Silver earrings dangled from her ears, and metallic silver lipstick made her lips look like they had been dipped in chrome—just like her eyelids.

She was looking damn good, but she wasn't feeling good. Onika was pissed, yet happy at the same time. She was about to make her plan work, and get her payback. In her purse, she had mace, a box-cutter, and Vaseline. She had revenge on her mind, and she wasn't about to be robbed of it.

●●●

Approaching the entrance to the bail bonds office, Onika held her handbag close to her body. Inside, she had an envelope full of cash, ready to be handed over to the man that was behind the window. She got to the door just as it swung open.

A *very* large man of Hawaiian descent stepped out. He took one look at Onika and his eyes went wide in shock— his mind instantly filling with lustful thoughts.

"Yo, yo, baby what's—"

"SCUUURRRR!" Onika held up a hand, cutting him off before he could even try to holler at her. "You in my way, big fella! Move it!"

Not waiting for a response, Onika stepped around him and entered the building. She saw there was only one person in line, waiting for the current customer at the window to be done.

She got in line, shifting impatiently. Only *one* window was open, and the guy behind it was moving slow as hell.

Noticing the woman in front of her seemed to be feeling just as impatient as she did, Onika snickered to herself. Nosily, she took in the woman's outfit and had to admit— she was fly as hell. A nice white dressy shirt, a short stylish brown leather skirt, her legs encased in nude fishnet pantyhose, with knee-high stiletto boots that had shiny gold heels. Even the sleek old-lady bun on her head made her look sassy.

Onika couldn't help but feel a little jealous. The woman was gorgeous, and her expensive-looking outfit screamed *money*.

Absent-mindedly, Onika let her gaze drop to the lady's rear and saw a nice-sized bump, poking out from inside the tight skirt. She curled up her lip, then groaned, already tired of waiting.

Finally, the man behind the window called for the next person. The leather-skirt-clad woman stepped up to the window, setting her handbag up on the ledge, and pulled out a wad of cash.

Well, damn! That bitch is paid! I wonder what she does for a livin', Onika thought to herself, her eyes widening, seeing a lot of big face bills in the knot.

"Hi, I'm placing a bond for Ruby Baez Solice."

The second Onika heard *that* name, she immediately marched right up to the window next to the lady.

"Aye, yo! Hold up! Who is you?" Onika demanded, attitude *all* in her voice.

The woman turned her head and looked down at her. "Um . . . is there a problem, sister?"

"Yes! There is! Why the hell you bondin' that bitch out, yo? You family to her or somethin'?"

Onika prepared to take off on the woman if she said she was kin to the bitch that robbed her and took her car. Anybody associated with that *jack-girl* could get it.

The commotion drew the attention of the security guard sitting at a table in the corner of the lobby. He'd been watching 'Jerry Springer' but now groaning in frustration, he got up and went towards the women. *Damn. Now I gotta work.*

"Excuse me? I do *not* answer to you, missy!" the woman shot back, turning fully to face Onika. "Are *you* related to her?"

"NO, DUMMY!" Onika yelled. "WHY THE HELL YOU THINK I JUST ASKED *YOU* THAT?"

"Ladies?" the guard interrupted, as he walked up, his huge frame dwarfing both of them. His thick scruffy beard looked like a food trap. "Is there a problem here?"

Onika rolled her eyes and scoffed.

"Ain't nobody ask you to bring ya' big hot-dog-neck-havin' ass over here, yo!" Onika snapped, completely unfazed by the six-foot-seven-inch tall giant. "Bounce ya' big-ass back over to ya' muhfuckin' table before you get rolled up! *BYYEEEEE!*"

Onika dismissed him immediately, turning her focus back to Leather Skirt.

The woman was snickering at Onika, while the guard—*swole* as hell that he'd just been *treated* by such a small woman—retreated back to his table.

"The hell you laughin' at, yo?" Onika asked Leather Skirt.

"You. You are a funny girl. That was dope how you just based on Paul Bunyan."

That made Onika laugh. "Yeah. It *was* dope, right? Security guard my ass." She cast a side-eyed glare at the big man, who was now back at his desk, and watching some white girls get rowdy on stage.

"Hey, ladies? Are you bailin' this chick out, or what?" the older man behind the window asked, sounding irritated. "I ain't got all day here, ya' know."

"Uh-uh! Don't be rude!" Onika shot back at him, curling her lip up in disgust. "We decidin' about it right now, so hold ya' old ass up!"

The woman extended her hand. "I'm Whitney. What's your name?"

"Onika," she said, shaking Whitney's hand. "And I need to bond this bitch out so I can beat her ass for robbin' me and stealin' my car."

Whitney gasped. "Oh my God . . . was your car a *Mercedes?*"

"Yeah! It was!"

"Holy smokes! That was *your* car that hit my best friend!"

Now Onika gasped. "*Whaaaat?* Holy shit! This is crazy! Hold on . . . are *you* the one who was robbed in the bathroom and . . . um—"

"Yes." Whitney's face fell, still ashamed. "I'm the one."

They looked at each other for a minute, then they both spun around to the window.

"BAIL HER OUT!" they shouted in unison.

●●●

RUBY

Sitting at a table in the dayroom of her housing unit, Ruby couldn't help but frown. *Allegheny County Jail sucked.* It was not for her. She hated everything about it with a passion, especially the inmates surrounding her.

Some were playing cards, gambling in *Spades* or *Poker*. Others sat at tables talking, watching TV, or on the phone. Not a single one was in the shower. The unit held plenty of Black women, along with white girls, a few Hispanics, an Asian woman, and even a few Arabic ladies.

Old, young.

Fat, skinny.

Feminine, butch.

Lesbian, straight, non-binary.

Plain, cute, or ugly as hell.

Sitting with a leg brace on her left leg and her right arm bandaged heavily, Ruby was *fuming*—so much that she was practically radiating heat. Nobody dared sit at her table. She had the look of a *killer* in her eyes, and she had the other girls scared. Ruby was still pissed about how the cops had done her. They had made all kinds of threats, talking about having the COs put inmates on her. For that reason, Ruby had a sharpened piece of wood tucked into the waist band of her jail-issued pants. If anybody tried her, she was going to show them *exactly* how Jersey got down.

She had only got medical treatment *after* she got to the jail and found out they were legally required to provide care for her injuries. After she was booked in, she was cuffed to a wheelchair and put into a jail van, transported to the closest ER to the jail, and treated. Her injuries weren't as bad as she thought. Mostly superficial. She'd need time to heal, but nothing was broken or sprained. The teeth marks in her arm would heal in due time. Her *pride*, though? She wasn't sure that she would ever heal.

●●●

Still brooding, Ruby's thoughts were suddenly interrupted by a *foul* stench invading her nostrils.

She glanced toward her cell, where the window was halfway covered with paper—her cellmate's way of blocking peeping eyes.

The toilet kept flushing repeatedly.

Courtesy flushes.

At least the nasty bitch got some manners, Ruby thought.

She curled her lip in disgust.

Her cellmate was a *dope fiend,* and by the smell of it, the drugs were working their way out of her system—straight through her bowels.

It was one of the *worst* odors Ruby had ever smelled.

A few minutes later, the paper came down from the window, and the cell door swung open.

The unit *immediately* erupted with complaints.

Women groaned, waved their hands in front of their faces, and cursed out the heavyset, pizza-faced white woman who stepped out.

Nasty-ass, dope-sick-ass bitch, Ruby sneered to herself.

The woman's eyes were sunken in, her hair falling out.

She looked like she had hit the point of no return.

And from the vacant look on her face, she didn't even seem to *care.*

Ruby turned away, shifting her focus to the big 55-inch HDTV mounted on the wall—only to feel a set of eyes burning into her.

She looked over and locked eyes with a young Black CO sitting at the officer's desk, glaring *hard.*

She had long microbraids coiled on top of her head, dark skin, poison-green eyeshadow, and glossy lips.

Ruby sucked her teeth.

Grabbing the crutches she had been issued, she hobbled toward her cell so she could go lie down.

She was *over* today.

•••

Inside her two-person cell, Ruby stood at the sink, staring at her reflection in the dull metal mirror mounted above the stainless-steel sink-toilet combo.

The so-called mirror was actually just a polished sheet of metal, scratched up with names and gang slang.

But she could still see herself clearly enough, and what she saw managed to make her smile.

She was a very beautiful woman, without a doubt. Raised in the streets of Newark, Ruby had been surrounded by many gangbangers and hustlers her whole life. Her Cuban father was heavy in the streets. So was her African-American mother. Ruby had been raised in poverty, raised to be *tough,* and to *get it on her own*—by any means necessary.

Ruby stood 5'6" inches tall, with an amazingly voluptuous figure, creamy caramel skin, and platinum-blonde hair that cascaded down her back to her ample ass. Her arms were inked up with many tattoos, as was her chest, legs, and back. She had a *thug-miss* type of swag—fully capable of being feminine, but life had hardened her, sharpening her survival instinct to the core. She had locked that soft side of her away a long time ago.

She had been through many nights of grinding to keep a dollar in her pocket. Too many men had tried to pimp her, while other girls in her situation gave in and *laid down for money*. Not her. Ruby had *thugged herself out.*

She had been blessed with an eye-catching beauty that made people stare *whenever* she wasn't in *gangster mode.*

But despite her unparalleled beauty, Ruby was a certified beast. She could fight like a man, thanks to her father. She knew how to hustle—her mother taught her well. She missed them dearly. Every damn day. Her parents had met their fate a while ago, after relocating to Pittsburgh's East Liberty neighborhood, trying to get their daughter a better life away from the hood. But their past caught up with them.

One day, after school, Ruby came home and found that she was *alone in the world.*

●●●

Grinding her teeth, Ruby glared at her reflection.

Her lip was busted.

Her jaw was swollen.

Her left eye was blackened.

The K9 attack had her *ready* to shoot every German Shepherd she saw from now on.

The only thing keeping her from breaking down was the encouraging words from the old Black nurse who had tended to her in the ER.

"Bitch-ass cop dog!" Ruby cursed, hobbling over to look out of the little window that was in her cell.

Her view overlooked the Parkway running east and west behind the jail. Beyond that, the wide Monongahela River stretched out, and was across it—Pittsburgh's South Side, where all the clubs and bars lined East Carson Street.

"SOLICE!"

The sudden shouting of her name made Ruby jump in fear. She whipped her head to the left and saw two female COs there, blocking her doorway, smirking at her.

"What?" Ruby asked apprehensively, her fists instinctively balling up.

"Pack ya' shit up, yo," said the shorter one, a dark-skinned woman with purple-dyed hair. "Somebody *loves* ya' thievin'-ass."

"And hurry up, too!" barked a big light-skinned BBW with thick dreadlocks twisted up into a crown.

Ruby narrowed her eyes. *Man, forget all that.* She knew how COs moved. "Y'all can just jump me in here, yo. That sucker-ass shit y'all kickin' is for the birds. Ain't nobody bail me out 'cause I don't *have* nobody to do that!" she told them, thinking, *Plus my bond is more than a quarter-million dollars!*

"Look, you little bitch!" BBW stepped into the cell, and walked right up on Ruby, towering over her. "Pack up . . . *now* . . . or I'ma think you tryna go for my OC spray and that's gon' make me fall on ya' little ass! What's it gon' be?"

Ruby stood her ground. She knew she wasn't in the shape to fight—but she wasn't backing down either.

She nodded. "A'ight. Okay. Y'all bitches wanna' take me to a spot without cameras and beat on me. Cool. Just know I ain't goin' down like a punk!"

"Yeah, yeah, whatever you say," Purple Hair sneered. "Just so you know, *we* run this jail. We could kick your little ass *right here, right now*, and nobody could save you. *And,* we gon' beat the investigation, like all street or correctional officers do, Miss Jersey Bitch. You gon' learn *real* quick screwin' around in Pittsburgh, youngin'. Real rap."

"This my last time, tellin' you, bitch! Pack the hell up, or I'ma *beat* you the hell up!" BBW threatened, getting so close to Ruby that her breasts pushed Ruby back a little.

Ruby sighed. She was *so* not in shape for this shit. Complying, Ruby got her things packed up, despite struggling with her crutches. She stripped her bed of the ripped and stained bed sheets, and decided to leave the food items and hygiene she bought off of commissary during the two weeks she'd sat there.

Crutching herself out of the cell, with her sheets balled up and tied so she could wear it on her back like a book bag, Ruby took the equivalent of the walk of shame towards the unit's exit. The other inmates watched her go. Many of them glad she was gone; others were *swole* about it, wishing it was *them* getting up out of there.

Ruby prepared herself for a fight. She just knew the two COs were taking her to a dark corner to beat on her. She knew how COs got down. Jail and prison shows on National

Geographic *never* showed the reality of how guards really get down on detainees, when there are no cameras, and they had a personal vendetta against you.

CHAPTER 6

"Mmmm! Damn, I forgot how good these things are, yo!" said Onika, swallowing another bite of her gyro as she sat behind the wheel of her rental.

"Mhmm!" Whitney agreed, unable to speak with her mouth full of food.

Katrina sat in the back, *maxin'* her food too. "This is definitely *fi'*!" she said, her Chicago twang slipping out for a second. "But this ain't nothin' compared to a *Vicelord Burger.*"

"A *what*?" Onika asked, looking back at her.

Katrina was about to explain the combination burger—made with a beef patty and gyro meat—that a restaurant had named after a well-known Chicago gang, one she'd first had out west in the Chi, when Whitney suddenly shouted—

"THAT'S HER! THERE SHE GO!"

Onika and Katrina snapped their heads in the direction Whitney was looking and saw a girl with platinum-blonde hair limping out of the jail. Katrina had friends all over the jail. One was working in booking and had notified her that the girl was on her way out.

"You'd think they'd have given her crutches with how her leg got messed up in the crash," Whitney said, watching the young girl struggle to walk.

"They did," Katrina said. "But since they're *jail property*, they took them before she left."

Onika laughed. They all watched as the girl limped past the rental. She had no clue that she was being watched, and no clue she was about to get a taste of her own medicine.

"Are we really gonna' do this to her?" Katrina asked. "There's no comin' back from it."

"Hell yeah, we doin' it!" Onika replied, starting up her car. "You scared or somethin' now?"

"No! But it just seems . . . really mean."

Onika laughed again. "You *soft* as hell. I thought people from Chicago was some gangsters? How you a CO and actually *have* a heart?"

"Onika. Please stop," Whitney interjected. "Katrina, we are going to teach the girl a *lesson*, and that's that. Understood?"

Katrina sighed. "Okay, Whit. I just hope I can still get into Heaven after this."

●●●

Who the hell bonded me out? Ruby wondered, as she limped down the street, passing under a bridge that ran high above her, heading further into the downtown area.

She was *starving*.

She had $67.33 in her pocket, which *pissed* her off.

She had been up thousands in cash, with even more in jewelry.

Now?

She was *broke*, *hurting*, with a court date and a very *likely* prison sentence hanging over her head.

She didn't even have her gun anymore—so there was no way she could make a quick come-up.

Ruby ended up on 5th Avenue.

She stepped into Wendy's and ordered a *Baconator*, large fries, and a soda.

She ate like she hadn't had food in *days*, then headed back out, making her way to the subway entrance around the corner. A bunch of buses picked up passengers from there.

She knew which one would take her back to where she laid her head.

After waiting about ten minutes, she caught the last bus of the night going out to East Liberty.

●●●

Almost forty minutes later, Ruby got off the bus at the corner of Negley and East Liberty Boulevard.

She *limped* across the street, then made her way down Mellon, taking a left.

The street was lined with houses—some *actual* houses, others apartment buildings—on both sides, with cars packed in tight along the curbs.

It was *quiet*.

That block, between East Liberty Boulevard and Hays Street, was *middle class*.

The next block up?

That was the *hood*.

Ruby kept limping toward her spot.

She was so deep in thought that she wasn't even *payin' attention* to her surroundings.

Not until she passed a dark alley—

And heard the sound of car doors flying open.

She snapped her head to the right.

Two hooded figures in masks were sprinting toward her.

Her heart *dropped*.

"*OH SHIT!*"

Forgetting all about her injuries, she tried to *run*—

But the moment she pivoted, white-hot pain *exploded* through her leg.

She screamed.

Ruby *collapsed*, grabbing at her knee.

The two figures reached her, standing over her with their guns drawn.

Black pistols.

Fuck!

"Yo! *Hold up! Chill!*" Ruby pleaded, staring at the weapons.

Ironically, she now realized how it *felt* to be the victim of a game she had played *so many* times.

One of them kicked her—*right* in her bad leg.

"*AAGGHH!*" she *screamed*, the pain *blinding*. "*PLEASE! STOOOP!*"

The taller one stepped closer, pointing the gun right in her *face*.

"Get up," the short one demanded.

Ruby's eyes *widened*.

Ain't this about a bitch! I'm gettin' robbed by bitches!

She tried one last time to talk her way out.

"Come on, yo! I *told* you, I don't have—"

—WHAM!

A blow cracked across the back of her head.

Ruby's vision *blurred*.

Pain *erupted* through her skull.

"*BITCH! DON'T NOBODY WANNA HEAR THAT! GET THE FUCK UP!*"

Hearing the second one's voice, Ruby *realized* they were *both* females.

Taking too long, the two masked-up ladies *grabbed* her and *yanked* her up.

The short one's fingers *dug* into her injured arm, making Ruby *shriek* in agony.

"*Bitch, I swear on my dead raise, if you scream one more time, yo' ass is grass!*"

"*Wait! Please!*" Ruby begged, as they dragged her toward the trunk of a car. "*Please don't do this!*"

They ignored her.

Shoving her inside, they *slammed* the trunk shut.

They jumped back into the car.
The driver threw it into drive—
Mashed the gas—
And sped the fuck off.

●●●

Sometime later, Ruby felt the car stop.
She heard the engine cut off—
Then the sound of *three* doors opening.
Her heart pounded in her chest as she braced for what was next.
During the ride, she had *tried* to find that little emergency latch most trunks had.
If she could've popped the hatch, she would've jumped the hell out.
But it was *too dark.*
Too cramped.
Too late.
For almost a minute, *nothing.*
Silence.
Ruby was sweating so hard, she was *this close* to catching the bubble guts and shittin' on herself.
Another minute passed—
Then she felt something *wet* on her legs.
She wiggled, trying to adjust, and realized something was *leaking* through the trunk's hatch.
What the fuck?
She reached up, feeling around the roof of the trunk—
And her fingertips touched tiny holes.
There were a *bunch* of them.
Water was slipping through *easily.*
Seconds later, it got worse.
Then, just like that, it was *pouring* in.
Like the damn *Titanic* had just hit an iceberg.
Ruby *screamed.*

She banged on the hatch.

She *begged* for help.

"*HEEEELP! SOMEBODY PLEASE! HEEEELP MEEEE!*"

She was *picturing* it now—

The car sinking to the bottom of a pond or lake, turning into her *watery grave.*

She kept screaming.

Kept crying.

Her *bowels evacuated* out of pure fear.

She kicked and banged and screamed for help—

But nobody came.

The water kept pouring in.

In just five minutes, she was *submerged.*

Pissy and *shitty* water *all* around her.

Sobbing, she begged *God* to spare her.

She *pleaded* for His mercy.

She swore if He got her out of this—

She would *never* commit another crime *again.*

Then—

Suddenly—

The trunk *popped open.*

Ruby *gasped.* She wasn't sinking. She wasn't at the bottom of no damn lake. She was in a *garage.*

Three figures stood outside the back of the car—

Buckets at their feet.

Ruby's eyes *widened.*

She *recognized* them immediately.

"*Ew!* This bitch done *shitted* on herself in *my* car!" the short one—*the dancer*—spazzed, wrinkling her nose.

●●●

Onika was *furious* as she stared down at the girl.

She watched as the soaked and trembling—but still *shockingly* beautiful—girl tried to climb out of the trunk.

That pathetic-ass look on her face made Onika shake her head

"*You's a nasty-ass bitch, yo,*" she said as Ruby took deep breaths, trying to slow down her *racing* heart. "*You done pooped in ya' pants in my whip 'n' shit. I hope you know you gon' be the one cleanin' my shit out, bitch.*"

Ruby looked at her—then at the *other* two.

She saw the *tall* chick she had robbed in the club bathroom—

The *same* one she had *made* shit on herself.

And next to *her*—

The *redhead* she had *crashed into* with the dancer's car.

Whitney studied Ruby closely.

Honestly, she *felt bad.*

The girl looked *terrified.*

But a lesson *had* to be taught.

Katrina, though?

She didn't *want* to do this.

She *hated* that she had played a role in *breaking* Ruby.

●●●

Ruby looked at the three ladies. They looked at her. The tallest one then spoke.

"Any chance that you're going to say you're *sorry* for what you did?" she asked, grilling Ruby with pure rage on her face.

Ruby's eyes filled with tears as she clung to the edge of the trunk. "I . . . I don't wanna' die."

"Oh, naw? So thinkin' you was about to drown made you see how precious life is?" Onika asked her, hands on her hips. "You's a smart little bitch now, huh?"

Katrina just stared at the girl. She felt *bad* as hell. She couldn't imagine what Ruby had been thinking when she was trapped inside the trunk and they were pouring water on it to make her think the car was sinking into a body of water.

She hoped—prayed—that this was the lesson Ruby *needed* to leave the BS alone.

"We're *still* waitin' to hear an apology," Whitney said. "You can most definitely go back in the trunk. Maybe we *will* drive the car into a pool this time."

"I'm . . . s-s-sorry," Ruby whimpered.

"WHAT? WE CAN'T HEAR YOU! SHOUT THAT SHIT OUT LOUD, BITCH!", Onika snapped.

"I'M SORRY!" Ruby screamed.

"That's more like it. Good job, shitty butt," Onika said.

Whitney and Katrina *snapped* their heads toward Onika, *grillin'* her with venomous glares.

"Oops . . . uh . . . my bad, Whitney," she said, remembering Whitney's problem.

Whitney ignored her and turned back to Ruby.

"Well. Ruby. You need to get . . . uh . . . cleaned up. Come on inside. You can take a shower. I should have something that can fit you, then we can drive you home," Whitney offered.

"I'm cool," Ruby refused. "I can just walk from here."

"Bitch! You shitted on yourself and you refuse to take a shower!" snapped Onika.

She rushed Ruby and yanked her out of the trunk. Ruby screamed in pain when her bad leg slammed against the concrete floor in Whitney's garage.

Katrina and Whitney *jumped* in—

Pulled Onika *off* of her.

"*FALL BACK!*" Katrina yelled, pushin' Onika away.

Then she and Whitney helped the young girl up, and ushered her into the house, making a bee-line to the first-floor bathroom.

CHAPTER 7

After Ruby washed herself and her soiled clothes were disposed of, the ladies got into Onika's car. Onika drove back down to East Liberty, where Ruby lived. During the ride, the three introduced themselves officially. Ruby directed Onika back to Mellon Street and had her stop just half a block up from where they had snatched her. When Whitney asked which house, Ruby pointed.

When the three of them saw the boarded-up home, they all thought Ruby was joking.

But when they realized she wasn't, Whitney was the first to speak.

"Uh-uh! Hell no! You live in that?" she asked incredulously.

"Yes," Ruby said, feeling ashamed of her unlivable dwelling. "My mother and father bought the whole building and rented the bottom and upper apartments out while we lived on the second floor after we moved from Newark."

"Well . . . where're your parents now?" Katrina asked.

Ruby sighed. "They're dead."

Whitney and Katrina gasped in shock. Onika's eyes went wide.

"Oh my God . . . Ruby... baby girl, I am so sorry," Whitney said softly.

The other two women were speechless.

"I was at school one day," Ruby continued. "When I came home, I found them shot in their bedroom."

Tears filled her eyes. The horrible images of her mother and father, covered in blood, riddled with bullets, still plagued her sleep. It had been nearly a year since it happened.

"Did . . . the cops catch who did it?" Whitney asked.

Ruby snorted a sarcastic laugh. "No. My father was a Black Cuban man, and my mother was all Black. They don't care about us enough to solve murders they can just sweep under the rug and blame on a drug addict."

Onika shook her head. "That's crazy, yo. I swear on my raise, I can't stand cops."

Katrina stayed quiet. She was law enforcement, but she wasn't a fan of the actual police. She'd seen too many Black men and women come through that revolving door at the jail—it was sickening. Tears welled in her eyes as she thought about everything going on in the world—Black men and women getting killed by cops, brothers and sisters killing themselves. It was just nuts.

It all made sense to Whitney now—why Ruby was out there doing what she was. Such a young, beautiful girl, turning to crime just to feed herself. Whitney was glad Ruby wasn't selling her body, like so many girls did these days, but still, the young lady was living a life where the saying *Tomorrow isn't promised* was a harsher reality for her than for anyone else.

Onika understood too. She was still mad about her car, but she got it now. Ruby wasn't a bad woman. She was just trying to survive. She had to look at her own self at that point—shaking ass for cash, sexing different men for extra money. Who was she to judge?

Katrina had seen Ruby's type many times before. Where she was from in Chicago, it wasn't just the fellas carrying guns and making moves . . . ladies masked up and went on sprees too.

"Okay. Alright." Whitney took a deep breath, then exhaled. She turned back to Ruby. "You're coming to my house. I'm gonna help you get on your feet. There are gonna be conditions, but what I will say right now is—no drugs. If you partake in any, of any kind, they won't be in our home."

"In our home?" Ruby repeated, raising a brow.

"Yeah," Katrina spoke up. "We live together."

"Oh. Okay." Ruby looked up at Onika. "You too?"

"Nah. I live in Homewood, where it gets crackin'. I know a lot of people, too, who'll go find someone for me and beat 'em up."

"No stealing either, Ruby. No guns, no violence," Whitney added.

Ruby nodded in understanding. Then a thought hit her. "Um . . . was it one of you who bonded me out?"

"Yes!" Onika and Whitney answered in unison.

"I had no clue about that," Katrina admitted. "I was in the hospital when Whit came to get me. She made a stop downtown, then we met up with Onika, and here we are."

"Wow . . . y'all must've really wanted to kick my ass for what I did."

"Yeah. You could say that," Onika chuckled. "It's cool, though. We gon' give ya pretty little ass a chance. Don't screw it up, yo."

Ruby nodded again. "Why, though? Why y'all doin' this for me? After what I did to you, Whitney . . . and you, Katrina . . . I almost killed you. Onika, I stole and crashed your car. I don't deserve any of this."

Whitney smiled. "What you just said proves you do. You acknowledged you did wrong, and admitting it is the first step to recognizing your mess-ups. That leads to building yourself up, growing a conscience, which helps you become a better person. If I can help you become the beautiful Black queen you wanna be, goddamn it, I'ma go above and beyond to do so."

"Me too," Katrina agreed.

It took Ruby a minute to really process it. She was being given an olive branch—a chance to change her whole life for the better. Help—she couldn't even remember the last time she had that.

Living in a boarded-up shell that haunted her every time she entered it, versus living wherever Whitney and Katrina stayed—some nice house, Ruby was sure—was a no-brainer. But it made her wonder . . . could she really get herself together? Was she worthy of the helping hands being extended to her? Could she do right by Whitney, Katrina, and Onika for giving her this chance?

She knew that if she didn't, she'd be back out on the streets . . . or worse, in a grave.

And then, it hit her—these women actually cared.

A warm feeling spread through her chest, something she hadn't felt since her parents were alive. It made Ruby feel good inside.

"Yo, what's the hold-up?" Onika asked, looking back at her. "Did it take you this long to rob us? You either done with that bullshit, or you not. What's it gon' be, Ruby?"

Ruby spoke then. "I accept. I'm done. I wanna change," she told them, meaning it. "I swear on my parents, I won't make y'all regret this. I just hope when the judge sentences me, I don't end up doing decades in prison."

"Don't worry about that right now, baby girl," Whitney said, already having a plan in mind.

She knew someone who could help. She was glad to be able to contact him. But she was nervous to see him. It had been a while. And Whitney knew, the second she laid eyes on him, all those feelings would rush back and have her acting stupid.

But she had to. She wasn't about to let Ruby go to prison. She was gonna do whatever it took to stop that from happening.

"Worry about right now," she continued. "Getting yourself together." Whitney turned to Onika. "Can you take me back to get my truck?"

Onika groaned. "Goddammit. That is a long-ass ride back downtown, then I gotta come all the way back! Shit!" She turned back and looked at Ruby. "When you get ya' first job, and ya' first pay check, you owe me some gas money, yo."

Ruby couldn't help but chuckle. "My word, Onika. I will fill your tank up if I have to."

CHAPTER 8

Over the next few days, Whitney and Katrina got to know Ruby more and more. Katrina, being on leave from work, had more time to spend with Ruby. After work, Whitney always came straight home to be with them. They went out every day—whether to eat or to shop for clothes.

Whitney even got Ruby a pet guinea pig when the young girl saw the messy-furred brown baby scurrying around in a big tank with others, at a PetSmart out in Monroeville. Ruby named the female animal *Onika*, which made Onika mad, but Whitney and Katrina loved her reasoning.

"She's a funny-ass brown ball of energy, and always on the go," Ruby told them.

Onika waved it off and let Ruby have her fun.

●●●

As days went on, the Ruby learned more about the three ladies, who now called her their little sister. They all shared their backgrounds and upbringings. Ruby explained why she resorted to using a gun to get money instead of trying to get a job.

Most of it brought Whitney and Katrina to tears, hearing Ruby's truth and feelings about life. To be so young, with such horrible experiences growing up . . . many others had committed suicide for *way* less. They knew that they had to help Ruby get to a level where she could feel more confident

CHRISTOPHER "DIESEL" HORNEZES

in herself. Build her resilience. Guide her in the right direction. If they had to show tough love, then they would.

They knew Ruby was a very positive and ambitious young lady. She just needed to be able to see it herself.

●●●

Sitting at a table in the food court of Ross Park Mall, out in Ross Township, Whitney, Katrina, and Ruby were enjoying a day of leisure. They'd taken Ruby shopping again. A few thousand dollars' worth of name-brand clothes, shoes, makeup, hygiene products, and other accessories sat in bags around their table.

Whitney was chowing down on a chicken salad with a green tea. Katrina was grubbing on Lo Mein noodles, shrimp egg rolls, and grape soda; Ruby was eating some *Sbarro* sausage- and-cheese pizza, sipping on Sprite. She chuckled to herself, thinking about the last time she'd eaten Italian . . . she'd robbed an Italian woman for all her cash, then ended up at a pizzeria not even a block away from where she left the woman crying and screaming for help.

"So, I was wondering," Whitney said after taking a sip of her tea. "What exactly made you come up with the idea to pose as a dancer, then rob people inside the club?"

Katrina had wondered the same thing but wasn't sure if she should ask.

Chewing a bite of her pizza, Ruby hoped that her honesty was understood. Not everyone could handle hearing someone keep it real. She swallowed her food, took a sip of her beverage, then she looked at them both.

"The club is a really popular spot. Lots of ballers go through there—it's a lick-hitter's dream," Ruby said. "I didn't wanna rob no guys, though. Women are easy targets. Most won't fight back, especially if there's a weapon involved."

Whitney and Katrina listened as Ruby laid it all out. It bothered them, a little, about her logic—how she actually strategized. Anyone who worked *that* hard to do wrong could definitely do worlds of good.

"When I posed as a dancer, I knew most bouncers would wanna hit the new girl. I watched how those dudes hit on every dancer for a week while I was posted outside the club. I saw that one dude, always flirting with the girls. I figured he'd be the one I could bat my eyes at and get in on.

"For real, for real, I actually first thought about hitting the owner up—like DMX and Nas did in *Belly*—but I'm nowhere near their level."

Ruby remembered seeing the owner in a Bentley SUV, wearing flashy-ass jewelry, hopping out of the vehicle *without* security escorting him in or out. Even if he had a gun, he'd have been easy to catch slipping. Nobody but Shaolin monks would try to move when a gun was to the back of their head.

Ruby continued as the two listened. "So, I looked for women when I came out of the dressing room, like a dude. I saw you," she nodded at Whitney, "sittin' with your friends. Y'all definitely were a target's dream. I knew none of y'all would fight back once I pulled my gun. I watched y'all party and kick it, waiting. When you got up and started runnin' for the bathroom, that was my chance."

Whitney was overcome with embarrassment. "But . . . did you *have* to get me before I made it to the toilet? Like, come on now, Ruby. You saw I was in *distress*. I ruined a very expensive skirt suit."

Katrina knew her friend's UC was her one and only issue. She knew it hurt Whitney mentally and emotionally to have such a thing. It was a sensitive topic for her. And it often made her tear up.

Ruby felt horrible but kept it real. "I . . . I didn't know, to be straight up, that you were experiencing somethin' like that, Whitney. I swear. But . . . keepin' it real still . . . I didn't care. When I'm robbin' someone, the less they can fight back, the better it is for me. You havin' to . . . *go* . . . that was prime opportunity."

Katrina shook her head. "Wow."

Whitney sighed. "Well . . . I appreciate your honesty. But what about Onika? And her car?"

"The dancers make the most money in the club, of course. *Everybody* loves Onika. You *had* to have seen all that money rain down when she backed her booty up to the pole and pushed it into her crack."

Whitney laughed. "Oh, indeed I did."

"Damn . . . she doin' things like that on stage?" Katrina asked, a little shocked.

Whitney looked at her. "Guuurl, don't act like you don't like pole up your butt too. All them stories you told me about Jeff."

Katrina's eyes went wide. "Whitney!"

"Stop frontin', then," Whitney shot back. "Anyways, Ruby, continue."

"I was about to leave after I robbed you, but somethin' in me made me stick around. I guess I was bein' thirsty for more money. I saw Onika hop up in the Bentley truck with the owner and . . . do somethin' for him in the alley behind the club."

"Oh my . . . wow," Whitney muttered, shaking her head.

"When she got out, she was alone. More opportunity. Her car was for me to get far away."

Whitney and Katrina were amazed by Ruby's blunt honesty. It was crazy, but it made them realize they could trust her. She'd laid her cards on the table. Let them into her mind. Showed them her darkness. And it gave them a better way to bring her into the light.

"Ruby," Whitney said. "I know it wasn't easy telling us this. Hell, it wasn't easy *hearing* it. But I appreciate your honesty."

"And so do I," Katrina added. "I'm really happy that you see the error of your ways, but also that you trust us enough to reveal the thinking patterns you had back then. It shows you're ready to let it all go and be a grown woman."

"It does," Whitney agreed. "And what I see is . . ." She paused as sudden pressure in her gut built up. "Dammit! Excuse me!" She jumped up and ran toward the bathroom, her UC flaring up again.

"Damn." Katrina felt chills go up her spine. "That sucks to constantly deal with that."

"For real," Ruby agreed, feeling bad for Whitney. "Can it be cured?"

"No. All she can do is manage it. There's meds, and now there are shots that help put people with UC or Crohn's in remission. She got the shot, but it doesn't take full effect for, like, a month."

Ruby shook her head. "That's crazy."

Katrina took her iPhone out of her *FeFe* handbag and checked it.

"Where the hell is Onika? She was supposed to be with us today."

"Maybe she's at work?" Ruby guessed, biting into her last slice of pizza.

"In the middle of the day? Who goes to a strip club at one in the afternoon?"

"People with no life." Ruby laughed.

Katrina shrugged. "Maybe. But, um . . . I got a question for you. And I don't mean to offend, but it's been on my mind since I met you."

Ruby's eyebrow rose. "Uh . . . o-okay . . . what's up?"

"Do you like . . . girls?"

Ruby's eyes went wide. "What! No! Hell no! I like men! Why would you ask that?"

"Whoa, whoa, whoa. Calm down, sis. I didn't mean to make you mad. I only wondered 'cause you got a really . . . boyish . . . type of swag to you. I mean, the way you dressed now, it's not masculine at all, but you just got this macho-like thing about you."

Ruby looked down at her clothes. She had on a stretchy black long-sleeve shirt with a low cleavage line, *Calvin Klein Collection* written in gold letters across the front. She paired it with skin-tight, shiny black Calvin Klein Collection skinny-leg leather leggings and black Timberlands on her feet. Her hair was pulled back into a ponytail, and dangling from her ears were gold hoop earrings.

"Do *you* like girls?" Ruby countered.

"Hell no! Honey girl, I *gots* me a man, and a damn fine one, too," Katrina said as Jeff immediately popped into her mind. "He's everything I want and need in a man."

"Well, where he at? How come you never talk about him? And how come I ain't seen you get picked up by him, or him come over?" Ruby asked.

"Uh . . . I don't know."

"How you don't know? If you got a man, shouldn't y'all, like, be way more in tune with each other?"

Katrina sighed. "I'm sorta a workaholic, Ruby. I don't like not working. I had a really rough childhood growin' up in Chicago. I *despise* the thought of not having money," she explained. "And to be honest, I guess I feel like if I don't work every single day, as many shifts as I can, I'ma go broke, and I'ma be hungry and homeless again."

Nobody knew how bad that felt like Ruby did.

"I get it," Ruby told her.

"I haven't been the best woman to him," Katrina admitted. "I'm always doing double, triple, and quadruple shifts. He's always tryna link up, but I been puttin' work above him. Above *us*."

"Sounds like you recognize you need to do better," Ruby said.

Katrina nodded. "I do. I *have* to. I don't wanna lose Jeff. He loves me so much. He must if he puts up with how I don't make time for him and still stays patient with me. He could get any girl he wanted, with how fine he is and how he owns a *very* profitable business."

"Do you love him?" Ruby asked.

"I do," Katrina said, dreamy-eyed. "So much."

"Then yeah, it's time to show him that. Dudes cheat on their women for the dumbest reasons. A woman that don't give him the time of day? Yeah . . . that'll put you right in that category."

Katrina smiled at the young girl. "Well, look at you! Tryna give me advice. But you right, though, Ruby. I *do* need to show my man how much I cherish and adore him. He *is* my king, and I'm his queen. I'ma do that now," she said, grabbing her phone.

Whitney returned just as Katrina started texting her bae. She looked relieved, and it made Ruby smile.

"You ladies ready to go?" Whitney asked. "We still need to find a bedroom set for Ruby."

"Yep. Let's boogie," Ruby said.

●●●

After going to a few more stores, the ladies headed out. Katrina still hadn't gotten a response from Onika. Whitney tried to call and text her too, but no luck.

With the new iPhone that Katrina and Whitney pitched in and bought for her—adding it to their shared plan—Ruby tried to call and text Onika as well. But then her phone started going straight to voicemail.

"Well, I guess she's busy," Whitney said as they headed toward her BMW truck, dreading what could be keeping the dancer so preoccupied. "I hope she ain't doin' anything crazy. That job of hers . . . mm-mm . . . that needs to change."

"Dancers at popular spots like Jimbo's make a *lot* of money, though," Ruby said, hitting back on her whole reasoning for doing all the things that brought them together in the first place. "Dancing is how my idol got famous."

"Who's your idol?" Katrina asked.

"Cardi B! That is my *biatch*, yo! I love her so much!" Ruby exclaimed, so hyped you'd think she was about to meet the popular rap chick in person.

Whitney and Katrina chuckled at her.

"Cardi B, huh?" Whitney said, pointing her key fob at her SUV as they approached it. "The ladies I was with at the club that night, we was all talkin' about her and Megan Thee Stallion. How they got so many people talking about that song they made together."

"Yeah, and they all just some hatin'-ass bitches," Ruby replied, curling her lip. "They just mad 'cause Cardi and Megan don't deny they both got some wet-ass—"

"RUBY!" Whitney cut her off, then busted out laughing. "Girl, you do *not* have to say it. We *know* what 'WAP' means."

Katrina was cracking up.

Ruby giggled goofily. "My bad. But naw, yo, for real. I wanna be *just* like her. She so dope. I mean, come on! Did y'all see that McDonald's commercial? What other rap chick from the Bronx had that happen? Not even Jennifer Lopez, and she's the queen!"

"Wow!" Whitney laughed as she hit a button, making the rear hatch of her X7 open up. "Ruby, you are a *very* vibrant young woman. For real. We're gonna have *too* much fun living together."

"For *real*, Joe," Katrina agreed, her Chicago slang slipping out as she climbed into the front seat.

"Screw *Forbes* magazine. I want a McDonald's meal named after me!" Ruby said. "I want it to be called *The Ruby Burger*! Fat, juicy beef patties, cheese, bacon, barbecue sauce, onion rings, with gyro meat on it!"

"Damn. That *does* sound good," Whitney chuckled.

They loaded their bags inside the back, then hopped in with Katrina. Whitney started her engine, backed out of the parking spot, and headed to another spot she knew had good-quality furniture and home accessories.

During the ride, all three of them kept trying to contact Onika.

And all three of them kept getting voicemail.

CHAPTER 9

Face down, ass up, Onika moaned as the older dark-skinned man slid in and out of her anus repeatedly.

"OOOO, DARIUS! YES! OH, GOD!" she screamed, her face buried in the soft silk bedsheets of the luxurious hotel suite he had booked for them. "FUCK ME, DARIUS! FUCK ME HARDER, GODDAMMIT!"

Out near the Grove City Outlets, far from Pittsburgh, Onika was letting the older man have his way with her after he'd taken her on a *very* expensive shopping spree. She had so many bags of clothes, boxes of shoes, jewelry, shades, makeup—you name it. The man had easily dropped close to twenty grand on her. All for some of the phenomenal oral skills the beautiful dancer had, the goodness gracious between her legs, and how she let him enter through her back door.

Darius was one of Onika's sugar daddies. A dark-skinned man in his late 40s, he kept a fresh low fade, the salt-and-pepper color adding a distinct attractiveness to him. He stood six feet tall, with the physique of a young athlete. He owned a luxury car lot back in Pittsburgh—the same place Onika had gotten her Benz.

The skin-tight, *F*-monogrammed Fendi dress she wore was hiked up around her waist. Her brown fishnet pantyhose had a hole ripped open at the rear, letting Darius slide his thick ten-inch tool inside her from the back. She wore no panties or thong. Her Fendi pumps were still on her feet, and her hair was wild and loose.

Darius cursed as he felt himself about to blow. "Shit! Goddamn! I'm about to cum!"

Onika quickly pushed him out of her and got him on his back. She hurried onto her knees, hunching over him before bowing her head down and taking his cock back into her mouth, not caring that it had just been in her chute. She sucked him like a porn star, moaning and using her hand to jerk his shaft, smacking herself in the face with it while keeping her eyes locked on his.

Darius's whole body tensed up, seconds before his nut rose. Groaning gutturally, he exploded with such force that he thought his spine was about to snap.

"HOOOOLLLY SHHHHHEEEEIIIIIAAAAAT!" he shouted as Onika jerked and sucked all of it out of him, emptying him completely.

She swallowed it all, then sat upright next to him. "You gettin' old, baby," she teased, seeing how drained he looked after just fifteen minutes. "Lemme find out you can't hang with me no more."

"Please. I'ma always be able to hang. I just ain't get much sleep. My newborn daughter don't let me or my wife get no rest."

Onika curled her lips at the mention of his wife but knew better than to go there with him. She had to play her part if she expected to get that drop-top SL600 she'd been eyeing on his lot.

"Aw. She sounds so adorable. Congratulations again, handsome," she said, faking like she gave a damn about his family.

"Thanks, beautiful. You ready to get on outta here?" he asked. "I need to get to work. I got a shipment comin' in."

Onika nodded, then got up and fixed herself back up. As Darius got dressed, she took out her baggie of cocaine and cursed when she saw she barely had any left. She scooped a couple bumps onto her pinky fingernail and inhaled two up each nostril.

Darius shook his head. "Why you do that shit? That's poison, Onika."

She snorted back hard, making the sour-tasting back drip ooze down her throat, numbing her and making her feel electrified. Then she took the empty bag and licked the residue off. Her mouth went completely numb in seconds.

"Onika!" Darius snapped.

"WHAT?" she yelled. "Fuck is you yellin' for, yo?"

He shook his head. "You know what? Nothin'. I don't care. Do what you do."

Onika watched him get dressed, crossing her legs as her womanhood began to throb from the fresh coke in her system. She debated going another round with him. She had to admit—Darius was a fine-ass man, but she was more attracted to his *worth* than the actual man.

"Baby? When am I gonna get another car? I can't keep drivin' that punk-ass rental. That shit ain't for a high-class queen like me."

Darius chuckled as he stood, looping his Ferragamo belt through the loops of his Armani pants.

"When you choose a car that don't cost $74,000, Onika. I can't take that big a hit."

Onika sucked her teeth. "But I *love* that car! It's so sexy!"

"And it's so expensive. Pick another one—something for $20K or less. I can make it a tax write-off, but I ain't donating a car that's almost a hundred grand. *Especially* not for some ass."

She gasped. "*Ass?* That's all I am to you? Some ass?"

Darius looked at her. "Yeah. What you thought this was? That we was a couple? Come on now, Onika."

Her teeth started grinding. Her eyes burned red with fury.

"Take me home, yo."

"What?"

"TAKE ME THE FUCK HOME, YOU DIRTY-DOG ASS MOTHERFUCKER!" she yelled, trying her hardest not to cry in front of him.

Darius shook his head. "You got problems."

"Ya *momma* got problems, bitch! Take me home or I'll ruin you! *Hurry up!*"

● ● ●

Sitting in the back of Darius's new Rolls-Royce Cullinan, Onika ignored the calls and texts from the ladies. She sipped glass after glass of Dom, getting bubbly, feeling nice.

Finding another bottle in the champagne chiller built between the rear seats, she grabbed a crystal flute. After popping the top, she started pouring herself up.

Darius stomped it back toward Pittsburgh, *so* ready to get rid of Onika. He drove his $430,000 SUV like it was stolen, pissed that she was drinking his liquor like it was water.

Onika tried again, knowing that if she wanted a car, she had to play nice.

"Darius?"

She saw him look back at her through the rearview mirror.

"Wh-what about the B-BMW tr—" She hiccupped mid-sentence, then giggled. "My friend has one, and it's s-so—" Another hiccup cut her off. "So dope!"

He laughed. "You just called me a bitch. I ain't got shit for you. You lucky I'm givin' you a ride home instead of makin' ya ass walk! Stop talkin' before I kick ya ungrateful ass the hell up outta my ride!"

Then he grumbled to himself, "I don't even know why the fuck I was dealin' with a cokehead bitch like you."

"What?" Onika blinked hard, trying to focus. "What the f-fuck did you just—" She hiccupped again, then scowled. "Say?"

"I SAID I DON'T KNOW WHY THE FUCK I WAS DEALIN' WITH A COKE-HEAD BITCH LIKE YOU

ANYWAYS!" he yelled furiously. "YOU'RE A FUCKING FIEND!"

"STOP FUCKIN'"— *Hiccup!* —CUSSIN' AT ME G-GODDAMMIT! I'LL SMACK THE SHIT OUTTA' YOU!"

"BITCH! I WISH YOU *WOOOOUUULD*! SWEAR TO GOD I'LL MAKE YA' STUPID-ASS WALK! SHUT THE FUCK UP AND STOP DRINKIN' MY SHIT!"

"FUCK YOU! I'M DRINKIN' *AAALLL* THIS SHIT, BITCH!" Onika snapped back, then put the flute to her lips and took a long sip, mocking him.

"FUCKING BITCH!" Darius cursed, then slammed the gas pedal to the floor, driving like a maniac.

"HEY! SLOW DOWN, DUMMY!" Onika screamed as champagne sloshed over the rim of her glass and onto her dress.

"SHUT UP, BITCH!"

CHAPTER 10

"Perfect!" exclaimed the furniture store's supervisor after Ruby had turned in a job application for the open position posted on a billboard outside the store. "When are you able to start?" he asked.

Out at a home décor spot, all the way out in Monroeville, Whitney, Katrina, and Ruby had been shopping around, looking at bedroom sets for Ruby. The store was as big as a Walmart, with everything from plain no-name brand furniture, to designer pieces, both American-made and imported.

Ruby had found a set crafted from wood, painted black, silver, and charcoal. It included a queen-size bed fitted with a black acrylic headboard that had a mirror in it, a tall dresser, a short one, and a nightstand to match. Whitney agreed on it quickly, despite the hefty price tag, because the room she had given Ruby had black carpet, and silver walls.

Inquiring about the *floor-associate* position, which offered $18.00 an hour on a humbug, Ruby ended up filling out an application and turned it in to one of the other sales floor employees. They called the supervisor over their two-way radio, and the man came right out.

"I can start right away," Ruby said, geeked that she might actually get her first *real* job.

The supervisor nodded, but then pointed at her bandaged arm and leg brace.

"What about those, Ruby?" he asked. "You'd likely need to assist with inventory in the warehouse out back and maybe help carry pieces to the showroom floor. You'll need to be able to lift and carry at least 50 pounds."

"Oh . . . um . . . I go in for a check-up in a few days," she told him, looking at Whitney and Katrina, who were letting her handle this on her own.

"What happened, if you don't mind me asking?" the supervisor asked.

Katrina stepped in then. "Car accident," she told him, which wasn't a lie. "My little sister and I were hit by a delivery driver that ran a red light."

"Oh jeez! Are you two okay?" he asked, sounding legitimately concerned.

"Yes, we're fine. Thank you for asking," Katrina said. "My little sister gets nervous talking about it. It was a crazy day. But I can assure you she'll be ready to work after her doctor's visit, Mr. Gordon."

Gordon nodded. "I think so too, Katrina. She's got such a friendly face, and in this business, that's the number one requirement. Customers love a positive shopping experience."

"Well, Ruby is your girl then, Gordon," Whitney chimed in. "And there'll be no problem with her getting to work on time. I'll personally make sure she gets here."

"Great! Okay, how about this?" Gordon looked at Ruby. "I'm going to hire you, but I'm going to wait to start you until you get those injuries squared away. The day your doctor okays you to work, give me a call, and I'll get you up here to start. You'll have a one-day orientation, where you'll watch a video, take some notes, then the next day, you'll train with Brenda or Georgette out on the floor." He dug a business card out of his pocket and handed it to Ruby. "How's that sound?"

"Perfect to me, sir. Thank you very much." Ruby pocketed the card in her jeans' back pocket.

72

"Is there a specific uniform she'll need?" Katrina asked.

"Not specific. Just dark pants and a plain shirt. We do offer polo shirts with the store name on them, but we usually only wear those for special events, like blowout sales."

"Okay. Thank you again, Mr. Gordon," Ruby said. "I won't let you down."

"I'm already sure of that, Ruby. Thanks for applying." Gordon shook hands with all three ladies before heading off.

Whitney and Katrina congratulated Ruby for landing a job paying well above minimum wage—on the first try.

"Look at you, girl! Doin' it big already!" Katrina said as they went to find a sales associate to mark them down for the bedroom set.

"We're very proud of you, little sis," Whitney added. "And don't worry at all. You'll have no trouble getting to work, *especially* since winter is right around the corner."

Ruby nodded, grateful for it all. She knew this was the beginning of her new life, and she had to do it the right way. She was off to a good start. But now, she had to *keep* going.

It felt good to have people in her corner. People that genuinely cared about her.

She hadn't felt loved since her parents died.

●●●

After the bedroom set was paid for—with an addition of a 65-inch 4K HDTV and surround sound speaker system—a delivery schedule was set up. The ladies headed out of the store then and towards Whitney's SUV.

"Is there anywhere you wanted to go before we head back, Ruby?" Whitney asked.

Ruby did have a place in mind. Somewhere she'd been meaning to go for quite some time now.

"Yeah. Um . . . it's in Homewood . . . up Blackadore."

"On Blackadore?" Whitney asked, puzzled, as she pointed the key fob at her X7, and unlocked it. "A friend's house?"

"No." Ruby shook her head.

"That park?" Whitney tried again, thinking of the little tucked-away spot most people didn't even know existed unless they'd been there before.

"No."

"Well, the only thing that's on Blackadore, besides houses, that park, and that scrap yard, is the . . . oh." Whitney stopped walking and looked at Ruby.

"Okay . . . yeah . . . we can go there."

Katrina had to think about what Whitney had just realized. When it hit her, she sighed, feeling sad about what Ruby had told her regarding her parents.

"Are you ready for that, Ruby?" Katrina asked, knowing places like that were never easy to visit.

The young girl nodded. "It's been a while. I need to visit them. Show them the new me. I need them to see I'm doin' good now."

Whitney smiled admiringly. "They already do, baby girl. They know your heart. They're watching over you, every day, every night. We can go, but just know that they'll always be your guardian angels."

They got into the BMW truck, and Whitney pulled off.

Ruby sat in the back, feeling a little grief creeping in.

She was really glad Whitney and Katrina were there . . . because she knew she was about to cry her eyes out.

She just wished Onika was there too.

●●●

Onika stumbled into her house, sloppy drunk, trying to carry all her bags at once, though her boxes of shoes and other purchases still sat on the steps of her walkway.

Darius had dropped her off, tossed her shit out the back of his Rolls-Royce truck, and peeled off, leaving her hanging.

After making three more trips back to grab the rest of her things, Onika shut and locked her door. She turned on the lights in her living room, grabbed the remote to her TV, and plopped down on her long couch. Sighing in relief, she kicked off her high heels, wiggling her toes in her fishnets.

She had just turned the TV on when her iPhone started ringing. "Ugh, shit!" Onika muttered, realizing she'd taken it off *Do Not Disturb*.

She reached for her handbag, but as soon as she bent forward—

Hiccup!

She groaned, grabbing her phone and squinting at the screen.

Whitney.

Onika answered and flopped back onto the couch, laying the phone against her cheek.

"Thank you f-f-for calling I-Icey B-Baby—" She hiccupped hard, her words slurring. "C-Can I help—" Another hiccup jerked her body. "Take ya' order?"

"Well, *damn!* You sound like you dun' drank a whole bottle of Grey Goose or something." Whitney chuckled.

"Dom," Onika corrected, then hiccupped again.

"Hmm. Nice. Where you been at all day, girl? We been trying to call you all day."

"Ugh! Why you all up in my grill, yo?" Onika slurred, rolling her eyes. "Like you my raise or somethin', Whit—" She hiccupped, then groaned. "Damn . . ." Another hiccup jerked her body, making her swat at the air like she could shoo it away.

"I'm not sassin' you, Onika. I'm only asking because we made Ruby a promise that we would be there for her. She just got a job today—eighteen dollars an hour, full-time, with benefits after three months."

Onika opened her mouth to respond, but a sudden hiccup cut her off.

She swallowed, blinking lazily. "Good for her," she said, not even close to being interested at the moment, too busy trying to figure out her own life.

"What the hell crawled up your ass, man? You actin' real pissy right now."

"Um . . . about some tongue, and ten inches of asshole," Onika said, chuckling. "It's cool, though. I milked that son of a bitch for damn near twenty-five grand worth of designer everything."

Whitney sighed. "Wow, Onika. You *really* need to stop givin' these creep-ass men your body like it's the only way you know how to make money. They do *not* mean you any good. For real. You literally givin' away your soul for materialistic shit."

Onika laughed at that. "Maybe. But I be one sexy-ass bitch while I'm doin' it." She stretched, smirking. "Anyways, what's up? Y'all still in need of *Queen Onika's* presence?" she asked, perking up at the thought of a ladies' night.

Whitney laughed. "Sure, *Your Highness*. Please, tell me where art thou, so thy may cometh and scoopeth thee."

"I be's at my crib! I be's at my crib!" Onika sang, imitating a Nicki Minaj song.

She gave Whitney her address, then ended the call. Quickly, she got up, took all her things upstairs, and grabbed some clean undergarments and clothes before hopping in the shower.

●●●

Katrina held a sobbing Ruby in her arms as they stood in front of the young girl's parents' tombstones.

Ruby had spoken to her mother and father, trying to keep it together. But the floodgates opened, and her tears came pouring out.

Whitney walked back to join them, tucking her iPhone into her handbag. She saw Ruby crying in Katrina's arms, as her best friend whispered words of encouragement.

"It's okay, sis. We all here for you. Nothin' can hurt your mom or dad no more. You are loved, and you are cared for," Katrina told her, hugging her tightly.

Whitney joined the embrace and sent up a silent prayer, asking the Man above to give Ruby the strength she needed. After they said *Amen*, Whitney spoke.

"Okay, Ruby. No more crying. You a strong young Black Queen. You *will not* break. Your parents got your back from above in Heaven. And we got your back down here with you."

Ruby nodded, looking up at Whitney through tear-filled eyes. "Th-thank you," she said softly, as Katrina wiped her tears with her hands. "Thank you so much, Whitney, Katrina."

"Of course, little sister. Now let's get outta here," Whitney said. "We gonna have us a nice girls' night— movies, ice cream, pizza, and Onika's crazy ass."

"Oh, Jesus," Katrina chuckled. "Can't wait for *this*."

"Then tomorrow," Whitney continued, "we need to take a trip downtown to see your lawyer and discuss ways to keep you outta prison."

Ruby frowned. "But . . . I don't have a lawyer, Whitney. I couldn't afford one if my life depended on it."

Whitney exchanged a knowing look with Katrina before turning back to Ruby with a smile.

"I got an old friend who runs his own law firm. I reached out to him, told him about your situation. He agreed to take your case. Don't worry about paying for anything. It's handled."

Ruby gasped. "Oh my God! Whitney!" She ran into Whitney's arms, thanking her emphatically, bursting into tears again. "I *still* can't believe how much y'all doin' for me! This is crazy!"

"Well, start believin' it," Katrina said. "We told you—we got your back. Just do good, and you'll be okay. That's on my momma, Joe."

●●●

Showered and dressed in a *FeFe* sweatsuit, with *Nikes* on her feet and her hair up in a bun, Onika grabbed her overnight bag with a change of clothes inside. She had been told to pack something classy and sexy for tomorrow.

So Onika packed sexy, forgetting the classy.

She tried to sober up before the ladies arrived to pick her up, but that shit wasn't easy. She felt like being high or drunk was the only way to escape the constant shame of being what so many called a *drug-addicted whore.*

Those words had come from so many men's mouths that whenever she *wasn't* high or drunk, she kept hearing them on repeat.

But whenever she *was* high or drunk, the words meant nothing—because she was too gone to care.

●●●

Around eight o'clock, Whitney called and told Onika she was outside.

Onika gathered herself, then left out, locking her door behind her.

Whitney's BMW truck idled in front of her house, sitting next to Onika's Altima rental with the four-way flashers on.

Seeing Katrina in the front seat, Onika hopped into the back and immediately spotted Ruby—looking like a *sexy mama.*

"Well, *daaamn*, Ruby! Look at you, in a tight shirt and some tight jeans! You got some big boobies and thick-ass thighs on you, girl!" Onika said, pulling Ruby into a hug. "Lemme find out you got some ass, too."

Whitney and Katrina busted out laughing as Whitney pulled off.

Ruby chuckled, shaking her head.

She *did* feel sexy in her tight-fitting clothes. For so long, she had worn nothing but sweatpants, hoodies, jerseys, and boots, with her hair in a ponytail.

Now she was in a tight, low-cleavage *FeFe* top, with tight skinny-leg *FeFe* jeans, *FeFe* flats on her feet, and her hair flat-ironed, hanging loosely down her shoulders.

"Behave, Onika," Whitney warned jokingly as she made a left at the top of Hamilton, turning onto Oakwood Street to head down to Bennett.

"Behave?" Onika scoffed. "Uh-uh, girl! Oni' don't do no coochie-bumpin'. Strictly dickly, *yah mean?* She a sexy lil' thang, but not my cup of tea."

Katrina, Ruby and Whitney *busted out* laughing.

"IT STARTS!" Whitney shouted, knowing damn well this was about to be one hell of a *wild* night—because with Onika's animated, unfiltered ass in the mix, shit was bound to get crazy.

CHAPTER 11

The ladies' evening was eventful, even if they were just at Whitney and Katrina's house. They dined on pizza from Mineo's, out in Squirrel Hill, got cookies 'n' cream ice cream, and hopped on Hulu to watch movies.

They ended up watching *Girls Trip*, starring Tiffany Haddish, Regina Hall, Queen Latifah, and Jada Pinkett Smith—about a group of best friends dealing with drama, infidelity, and the kind of wild shit that tests friendships.

Ruby grabbed her guinea pig from her cage, holding the little ball of fur in her lap. Onika curled her lip at the rodent while Katrina and Whitney gushed over her.

After the movie went off, Whitney brought out a bottle of Chardonnay and poured them up some champagne glasses. She put on some R&B, setting the kick-it mood. As they sipped bubbly, getting tipsy, they vibed out and talked about all kinds of things.

And then, Onika got started.

She turned her attention to Ruby, hitting her with questions wild enough to make the girl's caramel skin turn pink. "Ayo, Ruby, you ever rode a dick before?"

Ruby's eyes widened in shock.

"Onika!" Katrina scolded as Jeremih's *Birthday Sex* came on. "Why the hell would you ask her something like that?"

Onika sucked her teeth. "She grown enough to put pistols to people's heads, she grown enough to answer a simple-ass question." She turned back to Ruby. "Now, Ruby, *yes* or *no*?"

Whitney cut in. "Ruby, you do *not* have to—"

"WHITNEY! LET HER TALK!" Onika shouted.

"It's okay, Whit'." Ruby exhaled, avoiding eye contact, softly stroking behind her guinea pig's ears. "No, I haven't," she said, shifting uncomfortably. "I am a virgin."

Onika nodded. "Uh-huh. So, you never had ya cherry popped, but have you ever gave a guy the neck?"

"ONIKA!" Whitney yelled.

"No, I have not, Onika," Ruby answered, getting frustrated. Even her guinea pig started squeaking.

"You do like guys, don't you?" Onika pressed.

Whitney and Katrina both shook their heads.

"Yes, I do, Onika," Ruby snapped. "I just never really had a love life, because I've always been in the streets, tryin' to eat and survive. Dick won't make that happen."

"Sheeeeeeeeeeeeeeeiiiiit!" Onika laughed. "You a *lie.*"

"Onika, you got *issues*," Katrina said, sipping her bubbly.

"Uh-huh, we *all* do. That's why we single." Onika shrugged. "But anyways, Miss Ruby, what made you resort to usin' a gun to get money instead of usin' that thang between ya legs? You'd get more pleasure out of it *and* have a lot of people willin' to put money in ya hands for it."

Ruby's face twisted in disgust. "Because I'm *not* a fuckin' smutt!"

"Oooo! She *do* get mad!" Onika teased, sipping her champagne. "Imagine how mad you made all the people you robbed."

"ENOUGH, GODDAMMIT!" Whitney shot up from her seat and marched straight up to Onika. "You gon' *chill out* with all them crazy-ass questions, or I *will* take your ass back home! Ruby does *not* need to relive the past! She's moved on! Her sex life has *nothing* to do with you! LET IT GO!"

"Straight up, Joe! Yo' ass trippin' now!" Katrina chimed in, throwing Onika a venomous glare.

Onika smacked her lips. Ruby stayed quiet, feeling embarrassed.

"Yo, I was just tryna see what she was really about," Onika reasoned. "I wanted to be able to teach her some things if she ain't got no experience. Y'all can teach her how to be successful and humble. *All I'm good at* is sex and encin' dudes—I feel like I can turn that into a positive by teachin' her how to spot good men from dogs. What's better than learnin' that crazy dark world from a bitch that *been there, done that*?" she asked. "Y'all want her to end up tryna suck some guy's dick with freaking grapefruits and make his ass *scream* in pain? Like Jada did ol' boy when she tried that banana-suckin' trick Tiffany showed her?"

Ruby, Katrina and Whitney couldn't help it then.

They *busted out* laughing at Onika.

Even Onika had to laugh, picturing Ruby makin' some poor guy *scream* in agony when grapefruit juice hit his urethra.

The crazy part?

Onika was actually *having fun* sober.

If she had it her way, she'd stay sober.

But she knew, eventually, real life would come knockin'—and she'd need something to help her cope with how screwed up her world was.

"Oh my God, this girl is *nuts!*" Whitney laughed.

"Yeah, you *definitely* got issues," Katrina added. "But aye, if you so well-versed in *sexology*, why yo' ass ain't got no man?"

"*Because!*" Onika shot back. "Same reason *y'all* ain't got no man! I'm fucked up! Crazy! Can't no man handle a bitch like me!"

Whitney stopped laughing.

Just like that, her insecurities about her UC kicked in, and it *stung*.

That *was* the reason she couldn't find and keep a good man.

"Onika, you should really watch what you say," Whitney muttered, then got up and walked away, needing a minute to herself.

Whatever, yo. With ya shitty-butt ass, Onika thought, watching Whitney leave.

When she turned, she saw Katrina and Ruby glaring at her.

"Why y'all lookin' at me like y'all tryna kick the fair one, yo?" she asked.

Katrina got up and stepped *right* to her. "I swear on my momma, Joe . . . if you don't chill the fuck out with that crazy-ass mouth of yours, I *will* punch yo' ass so hard you get a concussion. Try me."

Onika fell back, smacking her lips. But she ain't say *shit* else.

She ain't want no smoke with the redhead Chicago girl.

Instead, she just folded her arms over her chest and pouted.

●●●

The next morning, Katrina was the first to wake up. After showering and brushing her teeth, she decided to make breakfast for the girls. She got to work in the kitchen, preparing a smorgasbord of food—fried cheese eggs with chunks of bacon, hashbrowns, grits, and butter biscuits.

The heavenly smell pulled the ladies out of bed.

They drifted into the kitchen just as Katrina was setting the long dining table, laying out margarine, grape and apple jelly, and apple juice.

After filling their stomachs with Katrina's delicious cooking, they all went to get showered and dressed.

Up in her room, after feeding her guinea pig and giving it a drink, Ruby slipped into the *FeFe* outfit Whitney had picked for her—sexy and sophisticated, as the fashion queen called it.

It was like *nothing* Ruby had ever worn before.

A beige, ribbed, scoop-neck sweater dress with long sleeves, hugging every curve and stopping *just* below mid-thigh.

To make it look right, she took off her arm wrap. The bite wounds were healing fine, so she wasn't worried.

Also, upon Whitney's suggestion, she slipped into a pair of nude-colored fishnet pantyhose. To wear them, she had to remove her leg brace. Surprisingly, she felt *no* pain.

The pantyhose emphasized her thick thighs and long legs, giving her a chic edge. She liked the way they looked *so* much, she checked herself out in the mirror *without* the dress on.

Damn.

She was loving the way her body looked.

To match, she slipped on a pair of beige suede stiletto boots, zipped them up, then took a few test steps to make sure her leg was okay.

She ran some *Pink Lotion* through her hair, pinning it into an upswept style, then finished with matte beige lipstick, black eyeliner, and a spritz of Rihanna perfume.

After slipping on the gold Gucci watch from Katrina and the gold necklace Whitney had bought her, Ruby took one last look at herself in the full-body mirror—

And smiled.

She looked like a *beautiful* young woman getting her life together.

●●●

Onika donned a tight, *extremely* enticing *FeFe* bodysuit. It was all purple, covered in blue and pink roses. The long sleeves had cut-out shoulders, and over her breasts, three slits gave a teasing glimpse of the tops of her girls.

She paired her skin-tight ensemble with white pointed-toe *FeFe* pumps that had blue and pink roses all over them too.

She glammed up with blue eyeshadow, lined her lids in black, and put on glossy purple lipstick.

Pulling her hair into a high, cheerleader-style ponytail, she gelled her baby hairs down and styled them with a little brush, adding more emphasis to her beautiful face. She finished up her look with a gold necklace, a gold Versace watch, and a spritz of Yves Saint Laurent perfume.

Looking at herself in the mirror, Onika smiled.

She *loved* seeing the beautiful honey-gold girl that smiled back at her.

But deep inside, all she could think about was getting some cocaine and *blasting.* Getting *charged up.*

●●●

Katrina struggled to pull on a red pair of ridiculously tight leather *FeFe* leggings. When she *finally* got her shapely bottom half in them, they looked like they'd been *painted* on.

She stood in the mirror, checking out how thick her thighs looked, how plump her derrière sat.

"Eeeeee! *Red got ass, Joe!*" she said to herself, turning around so she could see her whole *44-inch booty.*

She made it wiggle a few times, giggling at how juicy it was.

Satisfied, she finished getting dressed, slipping into a black ribbed long-sleeve *FeFe* sweater top and black *FeFe* leather heeled ankle booties.

She parted her fiery red mane on the left side and let it hang loose, choosing to go *all natural*—no makeup at all.

A little *Guess* fragrance, gold hoop earrings, a gold necklace, and a pop of red lipstick, and Katrina was *ready.*

She grabbed her red, diamond-stitched *FeFe* tote bag and left her room, heading downstairs to meet the ladies in the living room.

● ● ●

Whitney gave herself one last look in her full-length mirror.

She nodded in approval.

She *was* the epitome of a grown, beautiful Black woman.

The sexy, wine-colored *FeFe* dress fit her body like a second skin. She paired it with black pantyhose, laced with intricate designs, and white *FeFe* pumps on her feet.

She had flat-ironed her hair and pulled it into a wrapped-around bun on the top of her head, combing her little bangs neatly over her forehead.

Some glossy lipstick—matching her dress.

Gold earrings dangled from her ears.

Two gold necklaces graced her neck.

On her left wrist, she rocked her new gold jaguar-head Cartier watch, matching rings on her fingers, with the matching bracelet on her right wrist.

She grabbed her *FeFe* handbag, which also matched her dress, and headed out to check on Ruby.

● ● ●

"Oh my God! *Ruby!* Look at you!" Whitney *gasped* when she stepped into Ruby's bedroom, her eyes going wide. She saw *perfection* in its rawest form.

"Wow! You look *so* beautiful, sis!"

Ruby smiled, blushing a little. "Thank you, Whitney. It's different for me, but . . . I feel like a woman for once."

"I *bet!* Wow! I *am* amazed! You really got it goin' on, Ruby! You are the *sugar-honey-ice-tea!*"

Ruby chuckled, turning to face Whitney and nodding in approval of her ensemble too. Then a thought popped into her head—something she had been wondering as she checked herself out in the mirror earlier.

"Um . . . Whit'? Do you think . . . like . . . maybe . . . I might attract a *good* man dressin' like this?"

Whitney smiled. "Ruby, you'd attract a *good* man in sweats and a t-shirt. You are a *seriously* gorgeous woman. That caramel skin, that bright gold hair . . . *guuuurl,* you *bad!*"

Ruby started laughing. "Thanks again."

"Of course. Now, come on. Let's get goin' so we can be on time for your appointment."

"You said the lawyer is a friend of yours from a while back?" Ruby asked, grabbing her *FeFe* handbag.

Whitney smiled to herself. "Yeah. He was . . . a *friend,*" she said as they walked down the hallway toward the stairs.

Ruby caught the look in Whitney's eyes.

There was *something* there.

Something that told Ruby this guy was *more* than just a friend to Whitney.

CHAPTER 12

Downstairs in the living room, Katrina and Onika waited for Whitney and Ruby. When they saw Ruby, both their jaws dropped.

"*Woooow!*" Katrina exclaimed, amazed by the complete transformation.

"Daaaaayuuum, girl!" Onika then shouted, taken aback by Ruby's new look.

At the bottom of the stairs, Katrina and Onika approached, checking Ruby out. Ruby felt a mix of embarrassment and excitement. She was going to have to get used to getting this kind of attention—because, truth be told, she was *smoking* hot.

"Yoooo, you thick as *hell*, lil' mama!" Onika moved behind Ruby, checking out her big round 43-inch booty poking out from her tight sweater dress. She smacked both of her cheeks, astounded by how they felt. "Wow! You got *butt*, yo!"

"Onika!" Ruby scolded. "Why are you pattin' my ass?"

"Yeah? I thought you liked men?" Katrina teased.

"I do. But any woman that says she doesn't look at other women's booties for comparison *is a lie*—and this little biatch got *ass!*" Onika again stated, playing patty-cake with Ruby's cheeks.

Whitney started laughing at Ruby's face.

"Onika, *leave my booty alone*, dammit!"

Katrina then noticed that Ruby wasn't wearing her arm wrap nor her leg brace.

"Hey, is your arm and leg gonna be okay, Ruby?" she asked.

Ruby nodded. "Yeah. They feel fine. I took my pain meds, too. Plus, I should get used to not wearing them. I have a new job I need to prepare my body for."

"Okay. As long as you're careful," Katrina replied.

"Well, let's get a move on, ladies," said Whitney. "Calvin's waiting for us."

As they all stepped out, Ruby walked close to Katrina and whispered to her, "Who is this Calvin guy to Whitney?"

Katrina chuckled. "A guy she's had it *bad* for since high school. Their history is a little shaky, though. You'll see."

●●●

They hopped into Whitney's BMW truck and got on their way.

Taking the Parkway to downtown Pittsburgh from the Edgewood-Swissvale area, Whitney cruised along with the steady flow of traffic.

Megan Thee Stallion's *Don't Stop*—featuring Lil Baby—bumped from the stock audio system.

Ruby sat up front with Whitney, lost in thought. Her past was about to come out—she *knew* it. A lawyer had to know *everything* so that once the prosecutor tried to paint an ugly picture of her in court, the defense could swerve around it and keep the fight strong.

In the backseat, Onika and Katrina were in their own worlds.

Onika was watching music videos on her iPhone, silently rapping along with Saweetie and Jhené Aiko—until her phone started ringing.

Katrina, meanwhile, was on the phone, getting an earful from the man she was *completely* gone over.

"I'm *for real*, baby! If I ain't care about you so much, you think I'd still be stickin' around for a woman that makes me feel like she don't *really* want me in her life?"

Katrina sighed. "No."

"*Okay, then!* Come on now, Trina! You *gotta* stop doin' this to me! I'm tryin' *real* hard to show you I'm *all in*, but you don't seem to be *all in* with me. I *need* to know what it is, right now. *Please!*"

"Jeff, I'm sorry, baby. I *promise*, if you can forgive me, I'ma do my damndest to be the woman you need. I swear to you. You *know* why I feel I need to work so much, but it's not an excuse. I'm just bein' honest."

"I understand, Trina. Look, I *love* you, baby. I *do*. But if you love me, you gotta *show* me. That's it, that's all. Can you do that?" Jeff asked.

"Yes, baby. I *swear* I can," Katrina said, her eyes welling up with tears. "I'm *so* sorry, Jeff. I ain't mean to make you feel like I don't care."

"It's okay, my queen. As long as we can move forward from this moment, we *gon' be a'ight*," he told her.

Katrina started smiling then.

The thought of *fully* giving her heart to such a *good* man—*That's* what she knew she needed to do.

At that moment, she swore to herself that Jeff was *it*.

He had *always* made her feel like she was his world. Now, she was about to do the same for him.

Jeff continued. "I miss ya beautiful ass so much. I *need* to see you, Trina. I wanna kiss ya lips and squeeze on that big ol' juicy butt. You be playin', though."

Wiping her eyes, Katrina chuckled. "Boooy, bye. I been injured. I *ain't* lettin' you give me an even bigger headache."

"If you take 'ache' out of that, then I *know* you wouldn't be so quick to shoo me away, punk."

Katrina laughed, making Onika look over at her.

"Behave, Jeffrey. I'm in the car with my girls, and I *don't* need you turnin' me as red as my hair."

"Then bring ya sexy ass to me and let me turn you *out* . . . again . . . and *again* . . . and *again*."

She laughed so hard, tears filled her eyes. To her left, Onika shook her head as she *again* had to stand her ground.

"No."

"Yo, why you so *petty* with it, Onika? What, I gotta be makin' *six figures* or somethin'?" Johnny, a guy who frequently came to Jimbo's just to see her, asked. "You let me smash twice already, but now you actin' like you too good for me."

"Yeah, you *got* to taste and feel it twice—but you a *roodie-poo*, yo. I ain't keepin' this cookie warm for no man that *ain't* a boss makin' at least six figures. Step ya game up, *player*, and *maybe* you might get to smell this *wet-wet* again."

"Bitch! You's a bi—"

Click.

"Shut up, clown," Onika muttered, hanging up on him.

Then, scrolling through her messages, she pulled up Darius's name and started typing.

So when am I gonna get my new whip? I'm tired of drivin' a rental. You need to get me a car or I'ma tell your wife about us.

Smirking, she sent the text.

She couldn't *wait* to see his response.

●●●

Getting off of the Parkway, Whitney drove through the cluttered streets of the downtown area. She maneuvered amongst the traffic, gliding along the little streets lined with towering sky scrapers. Less than ten minutes later, she'd reached her destination. Next to the law office was a pay-by-the-hour parking lot. She drove up to the security booth, paid for two hours, then found a spot to park. Hopping out into the crisp fall breeze, the four of them strutted toward

Herman, Nigel & Cleveland Law Offices—like they *owned* the damn city. Men broke their necks trying to get a good look at the gorgeous ladies. Even women couldn't help but stare.

●●●

Up on the 10th floor, the elevator doors slid open to a luxurious lobby. Speckled marble floors. Burgundy walls trimmed in gold. Sleek hardwood furniture. A framed photo of the three Black men who built the law firm hung on the wall.

Whitney's eyes locked on one face in particular. Her heart nearly leapt out of her chest. He was still so handsome. The epitome of Black perfection.

A few people were waiting to see different attorneys. Whitney checked in with the secretary, then they all took a seat.

Ruby's eyes landed on a *fine-ass* man with skin the color of cocoa. His bald-fade haircut was *fresh*, waves spinning up top. His beard and goatee were trimmed low, lined up razor-sharp. He was dressed in an expensive Amiri fit, and on his wrist, a sparkling Rolex, diamonds flickering just like the ones in his ears.

The guy looked up from his iPhone and *saw her.*

His eyes went *wide* in shock, making Ruby wonder if that was a bad thing.

She quickly looked away.

But she *felt* him still looking.

Onika's eyes were locked on the *light-skinned* man sitting next to the chocolate one. His dreadlocks were neatly twisted, his beard lined up *perfectly.* He rocked a light and dark brown monogrammed Fendi tracksuit, with black shiny leather Fendi boots to match. On his wrist, a diamond-encrusted Rolex *glistened*, and in his ears, diamond studs flickered like cameras flashing inside them.

That's my next sugar daddy right thurr', yo! Oooweee, Cash-App shawty! she thought, licking her lips as she waited for him to look up.

Katrina peeped Onika *ogling* the dreadhead and shook her head in disgust.

Whitney saw it too—but ignored it.

They were *here for Ruby.*

Not for chasing men.

●●●

Five minutes later, a *six-foot-two*, caramel-complexioned man with the *build of a linebacker* stepped into the lobby.

He was *clean as hell* in a Tom Ford turtleneck sweater, matching slacks, and designer shoes. His hair was freshly cut around the sides and back, while the top was slightly longer, waves spinning *out of control.* His beard and goatee were trimmed low, lined up razor-sharp.

On his wrist?

A *gold Hublot.*

Whitney's *heart started racing* the second she saw him.

At *thirty-seven years old*, Calvin Herman was *still* the man she had wanted for nearly twenty years.

His cologne filled the air, rich and intoxicating.

Goddamn.

She heard a whisper to her left.

"Gooooddamn!"

Whitney turned and saw Onika *eyeing him.*

Whitney's lip curled *instinctively.*

Onika caught the glare and immediately stopped *ogling.*

"Whitney?"

She stood up, an ear-to-ear smile stretching across her face as she stepped toward him.

"Hey, Calvin. Thanks for seeing us," she said, trying to *keep her nerves in check.*

"No problem," he said, his deep, smooth voice making a *rush* shoot through her.

He took her hand—and *kissed* the back of it.

"It's *very* nice to see you again."

Goosebumps *exploded* over Whitney's arms.

"I . . . I-It's nice to see you . . . um . . . too, Calvin."

Quickly taking her hand back, she turned and introduced the ladies.

"Nice to meet you all."

Calvin then looked at Ruby. "Are you ready, young lady?"

Ruby nodded.

"Follow me, then. We'll go to my office and discuss our strategy," he said, leading the way.

Onika, still trying to get the light-skinned guy's attention, huffed when he *continued* to ignore her.

The nerve! Onika thought, curling her lip.

Meanwhile, Ruby couldn't help but glance back at the *chocolate treat.*

He was *still* looking.

And when their eyes met, he smiled and nodded at her.

Ruby smiled back, then followed behind Katrina and Whitney—while Onika lagged behind, *muttering* something under her breath.

●●●

Inside Calvin's *plush* office, he offered refreshments.

Only Onika accepted.

He handed her a can of cranberry juice, then joined the ladies at the long table near the *floor-to-ceiling windows* lining the main wall of his office.

Opening a folder stuffed with paperwork, Calvin got straight to it.

"Well, I can tell you now, Ruby," he began, flipping through the file. "This isn't going to be easy. You already have a criminal record, consisting of other robberies and thefts."

Whitney and Katrina *snapped their heads toward her.*

"Ruby . . ." Katrina whispered, shocked.

Ruby's stomach *dropped.*

She hadn't told them that this *wasn't* her first time being arrested. She *kinda* hoped it was obvious.

Onika shook her head, but for once, *kept quiet.*

Calvin continued.

"So, the prosecutor on your case? She's a *hard-ass.* She doesn't like to wheel and deal—at least, not to anyone's liking. The judge, however, will go with her recommendation *if* we can reach a plea deal. *Obviously,* this is *not* a case that should go to trial."

Ruby swallowed *hard.*

"But," Calvin added, "I *am* very good friends with the judge presiding over your case. I've known him a long time. I'll be doing *my own* wheeling and dealing."

He leaned forward slightly.

"Whitney reached out to me and was *adamant* that you deserve a chance to reshape your life, Ruby. I've known her for a *long* time too."

He looked at Whitney.

She *tried* not to blush.

"In many ways," Calvin continued, "I wish I'd been a better person to her when I had the chance. So, if it's okay with you, I'd like to take this opportunity to do *right* by her."

Ruby spoke up.

"Am I . . . am I going to prison?"

Calvin locked eyes with her.

"We've got a *battle* ahead of us. I won't lie."

Then, softening a little, he said, "Let me work. Meanwhile, just stay out of trouble. You're *surrounded* by love now—show them that you *deserve* it."

Ruby nodded. "Okay. Thank you, Mr. Herman. I really appreciate what you're doin' for me."

Calvin nodded. "No problem. As long as you call me *Calvin*, I'll go *hard* for you."

Whitney smiled. "Oh, and Calvin?" she threw in. "Ruby just got a full-time job."

Calvin nodded, writing it down. "That's *huge*. If we can give the judge a *positive* image of you, Ruby, it'll help *a lot*. If all they see is *negative*, then prison *will* seem like the only option."

They spent the next thirty minutes discussing Ruby's background, putting together a strategy Calvin could present to the judge.

When they wrapped up, Whitney, Katrina, and Onika thanked him, then got up to leave.

But before Whitney could reach the door—

"Hey, uh . . . you got a minute? Before you go?" Calvin asked.

She froze. She looked at the ladies.

The ladies *smirked* at each other.

"We'll be outside," Katrina said, leading Ruby and Onika out, closing the door behind her.

Whitney stood there, seemingly *frozen* in place.

A ray of sunlight hit her just right, making her *glow*.

Calvin looked at her.

Damn.

She was *still* just as gorgeous as he remembered.

Inside his head, he'd been *mentally kicking his own ass* ever since she reached out for legal help.

He remembered how he treated her *back then*.

And he *hated* himself for it.

"Hey . . . um . . ." Calvin hesitated, then finally spoke. "I just wanted to *apologize* to you, Whitney. For how I saw you back then. I—"

She raised a hand, shaking her head. "It was a long time ago, Calvin. I'm *stronger* now. I don't hold grudges against you or *anyone* else. I've forgiven *everybody*."

Calvin nodded.

A *huge* weight lifted off his chest.

"Thank you. That really means a lot," he said. "Which makes this next part a little easier."

Whitney frowned slightly. "What part?"

He smiled.

"I'd really like to take you out, Whitney. *Dinner? Lunch?* Are you busy tonight?"

Her *heart pounded.*

Inside? She was *jumping for joy.*

On the outside?

She kept it *cool.*

"Well . . . I was just gonna hang out with the girls," she said, teasing. "Where *exactly* did you have in mind?"

Calvin's grin *stretched so wide*—Whitney *couldn't help* but laugh.

"I know a new spot that just opened up. A friend of mines owns it. It's five-star Dominican cuisine."

Whitney *loved* Caribbean food. And going out with *Calvin Herman* was something she never thought would happen.

Growing up in *Homewood*, Calvin had been *deep* in the streets. He sold drugs. He gangbanged. He'd been in plenty of fistfights—and *more* than a few shootouts. His name rang *bells* all around the way.

Whitney had always been one of those *good girls that loved bad boys.*

And *that* bad boy had been *Calvin.*

They'd had classes together from *sixth grade all the way to high school.* She loved that he was hood, that he had dudes ready to ride for him at a moment's notice. But what she *really* loved?

He was *intelligent as hell.* He never dumbed himself down to fit in. Calvin wasn't afraid to *show* how smart he was. And nobody clowned him for it. Because they *knew* they'd get their asses kicked.

Before Calvin had ever gotten in trouble with the law for his extracurricular activities on the street, he'd taken his dirty money and paid for his own college tuition. He'd taken business courses, then went into law. While he attended the University of Pittsburgh, Calvin had started a few small businesses of his own, generating clean money—slowly but surely legitimizing himself.

Whitney wanted to talk to him so bad. But her UC stopped her. It had plagued her so many times during school days, and in many other situations where Calvin or his friends were around. It got worse as she got older. Being a high school student with such a bodily malfunction had many people avoiding her, and teasing her. Calvin never outright teased her, but he avoided her too. Sometimes, the looks he gave her—*pity, disdain*—made her feel so low.

The one guy she was insanely attracted to, for as long as she could remember, was disgusted by her.

Fast forward a few years after high school, Whitney bumped into Calvin at a *Starbucks.*

At the time, she was working as a photographer for a small fashion magazine.

He was a public defender.

Calvin *instantly* recognized the *gorgeous* West Indian girl from school. The same one he had wanted to *holler at so bad* . . . but he'd been *scared* to get roasted for trying to date the *"poopy-pants girl."*

All grown up, Calvin approached her, praying that he didn't get a hot macchiato tossed in his face. To his surprise, Whitney was very forgiving, and even smiling like a woman who was seriously interested in a possible date, when he asked for her number. But she had to make it known that *she* had the power now. She simply flipped the script. So, instead of giving Calvin her number, she gave him her business e-mail. From then on, they stayed in contact. But Whitney had never agreed to go out on a date with him. She was terrified that her Ulcerative Colitis would flare up on her in the middle of their date, and it'd be over before anything even actually started.

●●●

"*Oh . . . um . . .*" Whitney was *speechless.*

"I know going out was something you weren't sure about since we ran into each other at Starbucks," Calvin said, stepping closer. "But . . ."

He exhaled.

"I really *want* to take you out. This isn't about *asking for forgiveness* for back then, Whitney. I've *always* wanted you. I was just . . . immature. And, being real? I didn't wanna have people talking about me."

"Cal—"

"No, please." He gently took her hands in his. "Let me say this."

Whitney's breath hitched.

"I *always* had the craziest attraction to you," Calvin admitted. "But it wasn't just how beautiful you were. It was *you.* Your *energy.* You were *the* sweetest girl in school. Your vibe was just . . . different.

"You were the reason I actually *liked* going to class."

Whitney chuckled, remembering all the times his boys would try to get him to skip.

"You *remember* how my guys stayed tryna pull me outta class?"

She nodded, laughing.

"I *stayed* because I wanted to hear *you* talk," he told her. "I used to *wish* we got partnered up in class. But somehow, you *always* ended up with *Anthony Benner's weird-ass.*"

Whitney burst out laughing. "Oh my God! I thought *I* was the only one that thought he was a weirdo!"

"No, I *couldn't stand* him," Calvin said, shaking his head. "That man *sniffed* the teacher's white-out for *God's sake.*"

Whitney *wrinkled her nose.* "That's *nasty.*"

"It *was!*" Calvin laughed.

Then, his voice softened.

"But . . . all that? That was just *kid stuff.* Those years shaped us into the people we are *now.*"

He looked into her eyes.

"I've been *following* your magazine. Social media. TV. I've seen reporters from *your* company covering fashion shows. I even saw *you* in *Paris* and *Africa.*"

He paused.

"Whitney, I'm *so proud* of the woman you've become."

Her heart *fluttered.*

"Not that you *weren't* already *destined* to be great," he continued. "But to *witness* it? To know that I went to school with a woman as powerful as *you?* It's just . . ."

He shook his head.

"A *blessing* . . . to *know* a woman of your caliber."

Whitney swooned.

The way he was talking, she wanted to *grab him* and *kiss the hell out of him*—like one of those *wild, horny* teenage couples back in high school.

But then . . .

Reality.

"I . . . *still* have UC, Calvin," she reminded him, voice barely above a whisper. "I know my disease ain't what men *want* in a woman. We're *friends* now. I don't wanna *ruin* that. I don't wanna *lose* you."

Calvin's brows furrowed.

"Lose me? *Because* you have UC? *Because* you're vulnerable?"

He tightened his grip on her hands.

"Whitney, I'm *not* shallow. Not *anymore.* If anything, I'm already *protective* over you," he told her. "You *are not* your condition. You think I care about having some *perfect life with a perfect wife?* Hell *nah.* I *prefer* real. *Flawed.* Because that's what's *realistic.*"

He met her eyes.

"I got a *past* I ain't proud of. That makes *me* flawed too. But I don't let it stop me from going after what I *want.*"

Whitney stayed quiet.

Then, Calvin spoke again.

"Your flaw is different from *mine.* I get that. But so *what?* I'm *standing* here, in front of you, asking you to let your guard *down.* Let me take you *out.* Hell, you can even come to *my* house and I'll cook for us. I just . . . I *really* wanna spend time with you, Whitney."

Her *heart melted.*

His words were spoken with *so much* sincerity.

She could *feel* it. She saw it in his eyes.

"Okay," she finally said, after thinking it through. "We can go out, Calvin."

Lord, she prayed, *please don't let me regret this.*

Calvin grinned. "Text me your address. I'll pick you up at *seven?*"

She nodded. "It's a date."

As she headed for the door, she looked over her shoulder and smiled.

The second she left, Calvin jumped in the air, *hyped as hell.*

Finally.

After *all* these years, he had his *shot.*

He shook his head at himself.

All those wasted years . . .

Better *late* than never, though.

CHAPTER 13

Inside the elevator, on the way back down to the street, Whitney felt eyes on her. She looked and saw the three ladies staring at her.

"Is there something I can help you all with?"

"Uh uh. *Guuuurl*, you better tell us *somethin'*, yo! Real rap!" Onika demanded, putting a hand on her hip, craning her neck in that well-known ghetto girl manner.

"For real, Whit. That man is *obviously* gone over you!" Katrina added with a chuckle. "Tell us, what happened? Did he ask you out or what?"

"He did." Whitney started smiling her ass off.

Onika and Katrina screamed in excitement. They both gave her props, hugging and congratulating her.

Ruby was skeptical, though. "I know he's my attorney in all, but if you've known him for so long . . . why are you just now about to go out with him?"

The elevator dinged as they reached the lobby floor. The doors opened, and Whitney answered the question as they stepped off.

"We have a . . . past. Not the greatest, but we established a friendship a little while ago." They exited the building, stepping onto the sidewalk and heading towards the parking lot. "He's a good guy. Just . . . things that we go through, or are influenced by as kids, shouldn't determine who we become when we grow up—unless someone just doesn't get it."

Ruby digested the words. "Okay . . . as long as you feel like he's good for you. I don't wanna' have to pop my own attorney over my sister."

"Ruby!" Katrina scolded. "Girl, you don't need to be talkin' like that! Stop it!"

"I'm just sayin'."

"No! Don't be *just sayin'* nothin' like that! We are on a different path now. Whitney would not put herself in the position to be hurt by any guy if she didn't feel he was worth her time. At least *now* she wouldn't—being a grown intelligent woman."

Whitney agreed but said nothing more on the topic. Her stomach was full of butterflies, seemingly building by the second. She hadn't even gotten home to get dolled up for her date, and she was *already* sweating.

●●●

They ended up walking to get something to eat.

Ruby had yet to taste one of downtown Pittsburgh's *famous* gyros, so Whitney suggested *Mike & Tony's* on Liberty Avenue. They all agreed and headed over to the little spot, their stomachs growling.

As soon as they entered, Ruby *immediately* saw the handsome guy from Calvin's law office, standing at the counter, ordering food.

Onika *silently gasped* when she spotted the *fine-ass dreadhead* next to him.

Okay, then! Round 2! His ass is comin' up off that phone number and all social media accounts, she thought to herself, as they all got in line.

"Looks like Ruby's developing a *crush*," Katrina whispered in Whitney's ear, clocking the way Ruby was staring at the same dude she had been lowkey thirsting over earlier. "And Onika's about to do some *sugar-daddy shoppin'*."

Whitney shook her head. "They better *quit* all that *fast-ass* mess."

The two young men grabbed their food and drinks, then stepped aside as the ladies moved up to place their orders.

The dark-skinned one saw Ruby *again.* This time, his eyes *lit up* with excitement.

And *infatuation.*

Ruby was *stuck* on his.

Time seemed to *stop* as they locked eyes.

Meanwhile, Onika was still *eyeballin'* the dreadhead.

And this man was still actin' like she was invisible.

She curled her lip up.

"Ahem!" she said, as if clearing her throat.

He *finally* looked up at her. "They got water in here if something's stuck in ya' throat, *lil' mama,*" he told her, then went right back to doing whatever he was doing on his iPhone.

Whitney and Katrina *busted out laughing* at how *Onika's face hit the floor.*

"*Queen Onika ain't used to that shit,*" Whitney teased as the man behind the counter waited for their orders.

"You *a'ight,* ma?" the man asked Ruby, noticing how *stuck* she was.

She nodded quickly. "Yeah . . . um . . . just . . . *hungry,*" she hesitated.

And horny, Onika thought, watching the exchange from just a few feet away.

"Yeah, *me too.*" The dark-skinned guy grinned. "Nice to see you again in such a short time."

Ruby *froze.*

"Y-Yeah . . . um . . . we *were* um . . . hungry, so we came to . . . uh . . ."

"Eat?" he finished for her.

"Yeah. That."

He *chuckled* at her. "My name's Darrell. What's yours?"

"R-Ruby."

"Hmmm . . . suits you. *I like it.* You are *amazingly gorgeous.*" He extended his hand. "Nice to meet you, Ruby."

She took his hand . . . and *felt a spark.*

Like, literally.

A *shock* zapped through her fingers, making her *snatch* her hand back.

"Sorry 'bout that," Darrell said with an easy smile. "I'm *full* of energy, I guess."

"Hey, sis! What do you want to eat?" Whitney called, looking back at her.

Off to the side, Onika pointed at Darrell.

"She wants to eat him!" she *clowned.*

"*Onika!*" Ruby shouted, *mortified.*

"*Girl, stop!* We *all* can see ya' heart *poundin'* in ya' *lil'* chest, yo! Ask the man if he wants some damn *company* while he eats, which he *does,* then take y'all asses to a table and get to *rappin'! Simple!*"

Ruby *groaned.*

Whitney and Katrina shook their heads.

Darrell chuckled.

So did his friend.

"I would *most definitely* enjoy your presence, Ruby," he told her. "If your sisters don't mind?"

"*We her sisters, honey boo-boo,*" Onika told him. "Naw, we don't mind. Don't be tryna' talk her up out her *panties,* though. Save that shit for the third date."

"*Oh my freakin' God, yo!*" Ruby groaned, feeling her face *turn red.*

● ● ●

Ruby and Darrell ended up sitting at a table toward the rear of the restaurant, together with Darrell's friend.

Dreads introduced himself as *Bagz.*

Ruby shook his hand after introducing herself.

Onika, of course, *invited herself* to the table, still *lowkey* thirsting over Bagz.

But he barely acknowledged her.

She stared at him.

Hard.

Finally, Bagz looked up.

"You got a reason you keep starin' at me like that?" he asked.

She shrugged. "You don't like *bad bitches* like me lookin' at you?"

He *chuckled*—but didn't answer.

Instead, Darrell turned to Ruby.

"So, Ruby," he said after swallowing a bite of his gyro.

She looked at him. "Yes?"

"Where you from?"

"Newark, New Jersey."

"Oh, okay. What brought you to Pittsburgh?"

"My mother and father. I been here since I was a kid."

"You still live with your parents?"

Before she could answer, Onika *cut in.*

"Damn, dude, you askin' a whole *lotta* questions right now."

Bagz interjected. "You got a real smart mouth, *lil'mama.*"

"Bagz, *come on, bruh,*" Darrell spoke up.

Onika snapped her head toward Bagz.

"Yo, *yellow boy,* who you think you talkin' to like that?" she *snapped.*

"Onika! Chill out, man!" Ruby begged. "He just defendin' his homie!"

"And I'm defendin' you, Ruby!" Onika shot back.

"Ladies, ladies, hold up." Darrell waved his hand. "Look, I apologize. I didn't mean to pry. I was just curious about you, Ruby. I can tell you ain't from Pittsburgh. I like what I see, and I'd like to get to know you better."

"Without ya chaperone," Bagz added, eyeing Onika suspiciously.

Onika curled her lip, ready to jump across the table at him.

"Bagz, bro, please. Onika ain't doin' anything wrong. She just makin' sure her people ain't in the company of a clown. Right?" Darrell looked at her.

She nodded. "Yes. One out of two fits that assumption," she replied, still glaring at Bagz.

"I understand. I'm not a threat, though, ma," Darrell told her.

Onika looked at him. "So what are you then, Darrell?"

Darrell looked at Ruby. She looked at him. Their eyes met, and they both smiled at each other.

"I'm a man who took the negative and made it a positive—same as my bro Bagz. What I'd like to be," he said with emphasis, "is Ruby's friend, for starters. I'm single. I don't partake in shmutts or groupies. I enjoy the company of a good woman, and I can see that quality in Ruby."

Ruby couldn't help but smile even harder. She'd never had a man say that about her.

"I'd like to be friends too, Darrell."

Onika still felt Bagz's eyes on her. She looked at him again and curled her lip in disgust.

"Yo, my man, what the hell is ya malfunction?" she asked him, ready to throw her soda in his face, then smack him with her half-eaten gyro. "A bitch been tryna see what's good with you, but you actin' like you too good. Sup with that, yo?"

"First off, lil' mama," Bagz started, finally giving Onika eye contact, "any woman that refers to herself as a bitch is automatically a clown to me. If you degrade yourself like that, ain't no tellin' what you'd allow other people to do to you. And I'm a one-woman type of man. My wife is the only woman I need and want in my life."

Glancing down at his hand, she saw he was wearing a wedding ring. Onika hadn't even been paying attention to his hand. She'd been too busy looking at his handsome face, his expensive clothing, thinking about how much money he might be willing to part with.

"Okay? So? You're married. That's good, but what that gotta do with me?" she asked.

"Onika! Come on now, yo!" Ruby scolded. "The man is showin' you his ring because, obviously, he loves and respects his wife! Stop actin' like that!"

Onika curled her lips again and threw her hands up, frustrated with the whole thing.

Just then, they heard a woman's voice from behind.

"Hey, baby."

Onika and Ruby turned and saw a beautiful, voluptuous woman walking toward their table. Her skin was as white as fresh snow, with a slim, model-like face and blue eyes. Her raven hair was swept up in a stylish updo. She wore a tight-fitting, above-the-knee blue *FeFe* bodycon dress with yellow roses all over it. Blue pantyhose made her sexy legs look even better, and yellow high-heeled pumps with belt-buckle ankle straps completed her outfit. A blue diamond-stitched *FeFe* handbag hung on her arm.

Her bright smile was focused right on Bagz. Onika looked at the woman, noticing the big, shiny rock on her wedding ring. Envy instantly filled her.

"Hey, beautiful." Bagz stood up and kissed the woman, making her gush. "How are you this evening?"

"I'm wonderful, now that I'm with my loving husband," she replied. Then, turning to Darrell, she said, "Hey, D! What's up?"

"Nothin' much, Ericka. It's good to see you, in-law," Darrell replied, standing up to greet her like a gentleman.

Ruby was wowed by the gesture of respect Darrell displayed. She found him even more intriguing.

Onika snorted in disgust, growing more frustrated just looking at the woman.

"Another Black man just had to go get a white chick. What the hell is wrong with these brothers, yo?"

"Baby, this is Darrell's new friend, Ruby," Bagz introduced.

Ericka smiled warmly at Ruby and reached out her hand. "That is a really lovely name. It fits you, too."

Ruby shook her hand. "Thank you, Ericka. It's nice to meet you."

"And this is . . ." Bagz paused, looking at Onika. "Uh . . . what's ya name again, shortie?"

"Ugh! It's not no damn *shortie!* My name is Onika!"

"Hi, Onika. Nice to meet you." Ericka ignored the girl's obvious attitude and reached out to shake her hand.

Onika refused. "Sorry. COVID is still a thing. Nothing personal," she capped.

"Oh . . . none taken. You are right," Ericka said, choosing to stay humble. Then she turned to her husband. "Well, are you still coming with me, babe, or do you want me to just go ahead?"

Yeah, leave, you goddamn piece of Wonder Bread! Onika thought, praying Bagz's wife would leave so she could keep trying to get at him.

"I am most definitely comin' with you, my love." Bagz dapped Darrell up, then shook Ruby's hand. "You two have a good evening." Then he looked at Onika. "Um . . . Ashely?"

"ONIKA!"

"Right . . . *Angeliq* . . . You have a good evenin' as well, shortie."

Bagz took his wife's hand and headed off, leaving behind a steaming Onika.

"What the hell makes Black men want white bitches so much now?" she asked, watching them leave the restaurant.

"First off," Darrell said, impressing Ruby even more, "many Black women are so scarred by us Black men that when most of us try to talk to y'all, y'all automatically assume we're just like the others who did you wrong. Now, I can admit, the way many of us treat our women is horrible. It makes y'all build walls around ya hearts so tall we don't stand a chance. Secondly, Ericka ain't white. She ain't Caucasian in any way."

Onika raised an eyebrow. "Then what the hell is she?"

"Half Israeli, half Argentinean," he told her.

"So she's a mutt that ain't Black!"

Darrell shrugged. Ruby shook her head.

"She is mixed, but would you like to know what else she is?"

"Oh, do tell me, please," Onika said sarcastically.

"She's a trained MMA fighter." Darrell eyed her, seeing if Onika caught his drift.

Onika sucked her teeth. "You know what, yo? I'm out. Y'all play nice."

She grabbed her food and drink and walked toward where Whitney and Katrina were sitting.

"Your sister is crazy," Darrell said to Ruby.

Ruby laughed. "Tell me about it. But, hey, we're all a little crazy."

He chuckled with her. "True. So, will I end up getting a face full of orange soda"—he exaggerated the word like people from Jersey and New York do—"if I ask why y'all were at Calvin's office?"

"Not if you tell me why you and Bagz were there first."

"Well, Bagz and I started an event-planning and catering business together. A customer felt that we got over on them, so they called the cops on us. Unfortunately, one of our cooks had drugs on him and got arrested. We were there to discuss his case, and make another payment for his defense."

"Oh . . . dang. Is he gon' be okay?" Ruby asked.

"Well, you reap what you sow, but he should be. I know if he thinks he's gonna' come back to work for us, we're demoting him to kitchen helper—with trash duty after every event. And he gets a pay cut."

"Harsh."

"Not really. He was in a good position, but chose to be dumb. Punishment is deserved in this situation."

"I guess."

Ruby then told him about her drama. She kept it all the way one hundred with him. "And so, my sisters are trying to help me beat this."

"Are you done?" Darrell asked, looking in her eyes, searching them for the real answer that her mouth might not give.

"Done explaining?" she wondered, with furrowed brows.

Darrell shook his head. "No. Are you done with the street stuff?"

"Yes. A situation where I thought I was about to die changed my whole mindset. I don't want to take life for granted anymore; I want to earn a good life and be able to live it. I want to be a real man's wife one day and have kids with him. I don't want to be in prison or dead."

Nodding, Darrell could tell she was being serious. The passion in the way she was talking, the way her eyes misted up as her emotions threatened to get the best of her—nobody could fake that.

"I wasn't always on the right path, Ruby. Me and my boy Bagz used to get it in, but you can't keep winning on the streets without suffering losses. And some of those losses? You might not come back from. It was time for us to grow and boss up, ya' know? So we did what smart people should do, before the law gets involved: We went legit. Shit, we had people at all our parties anyways, so why not make that a legit business where we actually make legal money doing it?"

Ruby nodded in agreement. "I agree. I know I just met you and Bagz, but as a Black woman, I am proud of you two for changing the game. Not many brothers can do that and stay with it."

Darrell smiled at her. He found that he was really feeling the beautiful girl in front of him. He was enamored with her already. She had that hood chick vibe that he loved, but he could see she was growing up.

"Can I take you out sometime, Ruby?" he asked then.

"Oh . . . uh . . . like on a date?"

He nodded. "Yes. I really like you, ma. Real rap. We can do whatever you want. I just want to get to spend more time getting to know you."

That made Ruby smile from ear to ear. "Yes, Darrell. I'd like that very much. What are you doing after this?" she asked, ready to continue on with him.

"Makin' you smile and laugh," Darrell replied with a warm smile of his own, then got up from his chair and took Ruby's hand, helping her up so they could get out of there.

●●●

I need some dick. Can you come get me?

Onika sent the text she'd just typed to Darius, hoping he would come get her.

"Onika? Did you hear me?"

She looked up at Katrina, who was looking at her with a raised eyebrow. Whitney was staring at her as well.

"What?" Onika asked.

"Who was the woman that the cute guy with the dreads left with?" Katrina asked.

Onika's lip curled up. "A shmutt."

A reply from Darius came just then.

Bitch, you really seriously are out of your mind! You just threatened to tell my wife about us, which she already knows! Why would I do that? Why do you still have my number? You were just so ass to me! You are not worthy of having a real man in your life! You'll never be more than a drug-addicted whore! Stop contacting me!

Onika felt her temperature rising as she read the disrespectful text. Her eyes began to fill with tears. She was crushed.

Whitney and Katrina saw the hurt in her eyes and immediately grew worrisome of what the heck was going on with her.

●●●

"Onika? Girl, what is going on with you?" Whitney asked.

"Talk to us, baby girl," Katrina pleaded.

Unable to form words, Onika snatched her handbag off the table and got up, storming off as the tears began rolling down her face.

"Onika!" Whitney called after her, but in just seconds, Onika had violently pushed out of the restaurant's door and disappeared.

Just then, Ruby and Darrell walked up. They saw Onika march out of there and were concerned.

"What happened?" Ruby asked the ladies.

"Don't know. She got a text and just lost her cool," said Whitney, looking at Darrell, as was Katrina.

"Who's this?" Katrina asked Ruby.

"This is Darrell. He owns an event-planning business with the guy that had the dreadlocks. Darrell, these are my older sisters, Katrina and Whitney."

Darrell nodded respectfully at them. "Nice to meet you, Katrina and Whitney."

"Nice to meet you, too, Darrell. You were in Calvin's office. Are you in trouble?" asked Whitney, giving him a suspicious-mother eye.

"No, ma'am. One of my employees had narcotics on him on the job, and a discrepancy between a customer and my business prompted the cops to be called. My business partner and I were at Calvin's to discuss the case, and to make a payment for his defense."

Whitney nodded. "Oh, okay. Well, Calvin's law firm is one of the best in the City of Pittsburgh. Your employee is in good hands."

"Most definitely. I've known Calvin since I was a youngster. I'm very confident in him."

"Hey, um, Whitney and Katrina," Ruby chimed in with a little shy smile. "Do you mind if I meet up with y'all a little later? Darrell and I want to go hang out for a while."

"Hang out where?" Katrina asked.

"I was thinking about goin' to a park or somethin' . . . to walk and talk, then a little later on, I'll take Ruby to *Dave & Busters*, out in Homestead," he told her.

"How old are you, Darrell?" Whitney questioned.

"I'm twenty-eight." Just to appease either of them on any more questions of his identity, he got out his driver's license and handed it over.

Taking out her iPhone, Whitney snapped a flick of it. "If my little sister does not return home by three in the morning, or, if I was to call to check on her, and she doesn't answer . . ."

"We comin' fo' yo' *ass*, boy", Katrina finished for her, looking at Darrell with narrow eyes. "I'm a correctional officer at the jail, *right* down the street, and I do have *plenty* friends that are cops. I am *very* protective of the girl you are trying to take out, and I am from Chicago . . . do *not* fuck with me. Got it?"

Darrell nodded. "Understood. I'll have her home by midnight, though. My partner and I have an event that we'll need to attend personally at one in the morning."

Whitney and Katrina both nodded.

"You're already suspect number one, if anything goes wrong, Darrell. While she is with you, she is your number one priority," Katrina added.

"Agreed," Darrell said, as Ruby blushed.

"Have fun . . . and *no sex!*" Whitney added.

"Whitney! Okay, man!" Ruby was beyond embarrassed now. "See y'all later."

She took Darrell's hand and hurriedly pulled him out of the restaurant before they could drill him further.

Whitney chuckled to herself. "Think we got through to him?" she asked as she forwarded the photo of Darrell's license to Calvin, asking if he knew the guy well.

"Oh, yeah. No Black man wants the cops on his ass over no woman, sis," Katrina told her before taking a sip of her Sprite.

Whitney got a reply not even a minute later.

Very well. He's a stand-up guy, and will treat Ruby right. I vouch for him, Calvin told her.

Whitney nodded to herself. "Got plans tonight for yourself?"

"Um . . . maybe." Katrina smiled mischievously at the thoughts of her plans with her boo later that day.

"Ooooo, girl, I see that smile. You gon' get you some *boom-boom* love tonight, huh?"

"No. We just gon' have a nice respectable evening," Katrina capped, still cheesing her ass off.

"Yeah. Okay! Keep lying through your teeth like that and they're going to fall out."

Katrina laughed. "Anyways! Don't worry about me, honey. What are *yooouuuu* going to do with Mr. Esquire tonight?"

"Talk."

"Liar!"

Whitney laughed. "No I'm not. What do you expect? I'm not sleeping with a guy I haven't seen in years."

Katrina twisted her lips up at her best friend. "Whitney, you may not have physically seen him in years, but every night, yo' ass sees that man in yo' dreams. So stop BS'n and allow love into your life. That man is so gone for you."

"I could tell you the same thing about Jeff, Trina," Whitney countered.

"Okay. Touché. How about this? *I* go for it. *You* go for it. Let's let love into our lives and be happy ladies, not single ladies."

Whitney nodded in agreement. She raised her Root beer up then. "Bet."

Katrina raised her Sprite. "Bet."

They touched their cups together, then sipped, hoping to God that they weren't choosing to open their hearts for the wrong men . . . again.

●●●

"WHAT! WHAT THE FUCK YOU MEAN I'M FIRED, YO?" Onika snapped.

As she had been making her way towards the bus stop to catch the bus back to Homewood and go to work, Onika called Jimbo to let him know that she was coming in. But the reply she got was not what she'd been expecting.

"Exactly what the hell I just said, goddammit! You are *fired!* You cause *waaay* too much drama around here! You dun' got my top bouncer havin' to see a damn psychiatrist because he in love with you and you bruised his whole ego!"

Onika almost gasped. *Bruce? . . . in love with me?*

Jimbo continued. "I'm cuttin' ties with you, Onika. You're bad for business. I got another chick that's so damn bad that she already makin' people forget Icey, and get this . . . she goes by the name Spicey . . . HAHAAAA! HOLLA!"

The call ended then, leaving Onika infuriated.

"I should burn his shit down, yo!" she growled through clenched teeth.

Reaching the bus stop, which was right outside a trolley station, Onika sat on a cold metal bench and leaned against the brick wall of the building behind her. She looked up at the sky, asking *why, why, why?*

She heard someone talking to her seconds later.

"Hey, lil' mama? Why you lookin' so upset?"

She lowered her gaze down and saw a random guy standing in front of her. She looked at the heavy-set man. He was dark brown with braids, wearing an Adidas sweat suit, with Air Force Ones on his feet.

"Yeah, a gorgeous chick like you should never be frownin'," another guy said. Onika realized he was waiting at the bus stop with the guy in Adidas.

He was skinnier, with high-yellow skin, and he had braids, too. He was wearing a black and blue Nike with *'Gucci'* in white letters across the chest, jeans, and Timberland boots on his feet.

"Uh-huh," Onika replied, twisting her lip up. "Game don't work on me, yo."

They both chuckled at her.

The heavier man said, "Ain't nobody tryna' spit game at you, ma." He pulled out a pack of grape swishers from his pocket. "But what I *am* tryna' do is make you smile. Purple Kush *always* makes *me* smile, especially when I'm havin' a bad day. Feel me?"

"Me, too," said the other guy, pulling out a knot of cash. "And havin' enough money in my pocket to whatever I want helps."

Onika saw all the hundred-dollar bills in the wad of cash and immediately perked up.

"What do you say, lil' mama? Tryna roll with us and go blow some of this good shit?" Adidas asked with a *cat-that-ate-the-canary* smile.

Fuck it . . . get high for free . . . get some money out these chumps? I'm down, Onika thought to herself.

She grabbed her handbag and got up from the cold concrete bus stop bench. "One of y'all got some powder?" she asked them.

They both grinned.

"Yep. If you talkin' about cocaine, I got that fire!" Adidas told Onika.

"Cool Where we goin'?" Onika asked, not needing to hear anything else but where they were going to go and party.

With a shit-eating grin, Gucci shirt said, "I know a spot we can go, and won't nobody bother us at all. Let's gon' ahead and get up outta' here, gorgeous."

"Lead the way," Onika said, ready to get high and make a few dollars.

CHAPTER 14

Ruby was amazed by how good Darrell was riding. The sleek 2018 Autobiography Edition Range Rover Supercharged was the fanciest vehicle she had ever been in. It sported a glossy ruby-red paint job, and a slick black leather interior. It glided along on big, expensive rims that matched the color of the leather, as Darrell crossed a bridge that ran over the Monongahela River, heading towards East Carson Street.

"So how long have you actually lived in Pittsburgh?" Darrell asked as he came to a red light where Carson Street was.

"Since I was twelve," Ruby told him as he waited in the left turn lane. "I really like Pittsburgh. It's eventful, and I love the hood, yo."

Darrell chuckled to himself. It was still amazing to him to have such a sexy thug-miss riding shotgun. She was the perfect mix of hood and woman, but in the back of his mind, something was telling Darrell that Ruby had yet to discover how much *woman* she actually was. Not to take advantage of her, but Darrel found himself desiring to be the one that showed her. He wanted to be the one to teach her. To mold her. But he knew he needed to take his time. He could also tell she had a lot of pain in her past. He wanted to be good to her. He wanted her to know that no pain would ever come from him.

●●●

Later on, just after seven in the evening, Katrina finished dolling Whitney up for her date with Calvin. Still sitting in a chair in Katrina's room, Whitney was nervous to see how she looked. Katrina, however, was confident that Whitney would love what she'd done to her.

Katrina had flat-ironed Whitney's hair and parted it down the middle. Then, pulling it back, she styled it up in an upswept do.

She kept Whitney's makeup as natural as possible. A little blush, blended in just right, enhanced Whitney's creamy milk-chocolate skin. Katrina added burgundy shadow to Whitney's lids and lined them in black. The glossy burgundy lipstick she applied matched the burgundy leather, above-the-knee *FeFe* skirt Whitney had on. She paired it with a matching, ribbed, long-sleeved *FeFe* sweater top.

To spice up the sexy outfit even more, Whitney had put on a pair of nude-colored pantyhose. She knew the average man was a fiend for a sexy woman in stockings—even plain ones. And on her feet, the expensive burgundy Christian Louboutin pumps had Whitney standing over six feet tall.

In Whitney's right ear, the gold earring she had in spelled **C-H-A**; the left one said **N-E-L**. The gold choker chain around her neck wasn't something she would normally wear, but Katrina made her put it on. Katrina had also given Whitney a manicure and painted her nails gold. By the time she was done, she swore she was looking at Gabrielle Union in her *Deliver Us from Eva* days.

"Guuuurl, you bad!" Katrina was extremely impressed with herself as she admired the sexy milk-chocolate queen. "On my momma, Joe, yo' ass finna have dudes tryna fight Calvin for yo' hand tonight!"

Whitney chuckled. "Have you ever noticed that when you get excited, that Chicago-hood-chick in you comes out?"

"Yahp! And? I'm from the hood, and I'm proud of it, biiiiatch!" Katrina took Whitney's hand and pulled her up from the chair.

She ushered her over to the full-length mirror and watched as Whitney gasped in shock.

"Oh, my God! Trina! Yo, you . . . wow!"

"I know, I know. I did dat!"

"Yes! Most definitely!" Whitney loved what she saw. "Oh . . . wait! I can't go out with Calvin looking like this!"

Katrina's eyebrows furrowed. "What? Why?"

"Because! He's gonna wanna . . . kiss me . . . and touch me . . . and . . ."

"Hit it?" Katrina guessed.

"Yeah! That!"

"Um . . . duh! Whitney Wright, you have been abstinent since you was twenty-eight years old. You thirty-four now! You need some lovin', 'cause shouldn't no beautiful, successful woman like yourself have had such a long dry spell!"

"It's a choice I made, Trina. Sex is great, don't get me wrong, but only if it's with someone who makes me desire them. My UC has made me undesirable to nine out of ten men! Like, really! What man wants a woman who, from time to time, can't hold her bowels and . . . ruins panties?"

Katrina shook her head. "A man that knows it ain't your fault and knows you still a beautiful queen," she said, her tone softer now, showing she truly understood Whitney's fears. "And," she added, "since Calvin knows all about your condition and still been tryin' to get with you, I'd say *him!* So get happy! Smile! And expect to have a great night with a great guy! Or Ima beat you up!"

Whitney's iPhone started vibrating on the table next to where she'd been sitting. She reached for it and saw Calvin had texted her to say he was on the way. She sighed, looking down instead of up.

"Come oooon, Whit! Please, can you be happy for me?"

"I'm worried about Onika, Trina." She turned her phone completely off. "I have no clue where she is, and with the amount of hurt in her eyes, there's no telling what she went to go do."

The thought of how young, angry women got into crazy situations due to not using their heads gave Whitney the sickest feeling in the pit of her stomach.

Katrina had been feeling the same thing in hers. It had her wanting to reach out to her cop friends, give them a description of Onika, and ask them to help find her. But she knew that unless Onika was actually missing, none of them could do that.

"She's probably at home, Whit. Try not to worry about her, okay? I'm sure she'll be fine by tomorrow," Katrina told her.

Whitney wasn't at all sure about that. And truthfully— neither was Katrina.

●●●

Megan Thee Stallion's "B**CH" blasted from the old stereo system in the ratty motel room.

Onika was high and drunk out of her mind, off a concoction of marijuana, ecstasy, cocaine, and Hennessy. She was so out of it that, as the two men ran a train on her on the motel bed, mentally, she was barely there.

The light-skinned man, who told Onika his name was TY, had himself in her mouth as he stood in front of her. The darker, heavier-set guy, who went by Byron, was behind her, pounding into her like there was no tomorrow.

Onika barely felt any of it. She couldn't stop hearing what Darius had said to her. His words echoed in her mind.

"You were just so ass to me. You are not worthy of having a real man in your life. You'll never be more than a money-hungry whore."

Tears welled up in her eyes as she continued being the object of the two men's pleasure. She felt exactly like what Darius had called her. Nothing more than a whore.

She thought about what she was doing at that moment—and was revolted with herself.

Suddenly, pain exploded in her rear.

Onika snapped out of her dazed state, realizing that Byron had just forced himself into her anus—and he wasn't being gentle about it.

She tried to get away, but TY grabbed her head and held it so she couldn't spit him out.

"Naw, shorty! We ain't done with you yet! You gon' finish me off, yo!" he demanded, refusing to let her go.

Byron got rougher, causing her so much pain that Onika tried to scream. He ignored her and kept going, stuck in a frenzy. She tried to buck loose, but they held her down and continued assaulting her.

When they finished, they released her.

Onika rolled off the bed and hit the floor. Blood seeped from her rear, and her stomach felt like it had a cheese grater inside it.

Bursting into tears, she sobbed loudly.

"Aye! Shut that shit up, yo! What chu cryin' for? Don't act like you ain't want that!" snapped TY as he stepped toward her.

Onika looked up at him. Byron stepped over too, malice in his eyes.

"I don't know about you, bro, but I'm not done with her," Byron said.

"Me neither," TY agreed.

"OOOOWWW! STOOOOOP! PLEASE!" Onika begged them to leave her alone as TY grabbed her by the hair and yanked her off the floor.

He threw her on the bed and punched her in the face.

"I told you to shut that shit up! Now, when we get our money's worth, you can go!"

Onika tried to jump off the bed and run for the door.

Byron caught her by the hair and flung her against the wall.

"HEEEELP! SOMEBODY HEEELP MEEEE!" she screamed, scratching and clawing at whoever she could—quite literally fighting for her life.

TY and Byron lit into her then, treating her like a side of beef hanging on a hook while a professional boxer went to work. They savagely beat her, mercilessly.

Onika could only take so much . . . before everything went dark.

●●●

Out in Homestead's Waterfront shopping area, Ruby was having a ball with Darrell. They both quickly discovered that they had a fiercely competitive nature. Neither of them played a single game without trying to best the other.

Darrell couldn't remember ever having this much fun in his entire life. Every time he looked at Ruby—her infectious smile, her unparalleled beauty—his desire for her grew tenfold.

Man, this girl is dope for real! Why am I just now meeting someone like her? he wondered as Ruby picked up on his pause in her peripheral view.

She used it to her advantage, scoring a couple of three-pointers in the Hot Shot basketball game they were playing.

Darrell realized what she was doing and tried to catch up, but the game ended before he could.

"YES! YEAH! OH YEAH! WHAT!" Ruby shouted at the top of her lungs, feeling triumphant. "WHO'S THE BEST, HUH?" She held an invisible microphone toward him. "LET'S HEAR IT, DARRELL! WHO IS THE BEST SHOOTER?"

Darrell chuckled and shook his head. "You got it, ma. You won fair and square," he admitted.

"OOHH, YEAH! Y'ALL HEARD THAT?" she shouted, looking around at the small crowd that had gathered, cheering them on. "I MADE A MAN ADMIT I AM THE SHIT!"

Darrell and the crowd burst out laughing as Ruby started doing a little dance. But in the middle of a spin—forgetting she was in six-inch heels—Ruby's ankle went sideways. She screamed in pain and was seconds away from hitting the floor when Darrell reached out and caught her.

Pain exploded from her ankle, like fire under her skin. Though the crowd applauded him for the incredible catch, Ruby burst into tears as her ankle throbbed. Darrell scooped her up in his arms and held her.

She shrieked. "Oh my God, please don't drop me!"

Darrell chuckled. "I wouldn't do that, beautiful. I got you for as long as you'll allow me to."

His words nearly made her pain disappear. She looked up into his eyes and almost melted from the warmth they held.

"Are you okay?" he asked.

"My leg—I messed it up a few weeks ago, and now I just screwed my ankle up! I'm supposed to be startin' a job on Monday!"

"Don't panic, Ruby. It's gon' be okay. I got you," he told her, heading toward the restaurant section. "You probably just twisted it, but it's not broken."

"How do you know?" she asked, looking up at him.

He smiled warmly down into her eyes. "'Cause you'd be screamin' so loud that everybody in here would hear you."

He sat down with her in his lap at a table. Gently, he unzipped the side of her stiletto boot and took it off. Looking at her ankle, he could see through the fabric of her pantyhose that it was swollen, but definitely not broken.

He lightly caressed it, massaging the tenderness. Ruby felt a sting for a few seconds, then it turned into bliss. She found herself experiencing something she had never felt before—she was getting aroused.

Her nipples got hard; she felt moisture building between her legs. Her heart pounded in her chest. She looked at Darrell, watching how hard he was concentrating on soothing her pain.

He looked up then, his eyes meeting hers. "How's that feel, Ruby?" he asked, his voice a little lower, sending goosebumps over her skin.

She nodded. "Good. Really good, actually. Lemme find out you a masseuse on the side, Darrell."

"I went to school for massage therapy while I was takin' Business 101 courses," he told her.

Oh wow . . . what haven't you done? she wondered.

Darrell looked up into her eyes and flashed one of his prize-winning smiles.

"Kissed you," he told her.

Ruby's breath caught in her lungs as he gazed at her with the eyes of a man falling hard. The next thing she knew, she was moving forward, toward him.

"Not yet, ma," Darrell told her, stopping her as her lips came within inches of his. "Let's take care of your ankle first. Then maybe we can get back to our evening."

"But—"

"Your sisters clearly stated that if something happens to you while you with me, they on my ass. I like my ass, so I ain't puttin' you down till your ankle feel better."

Ruby smiled bashfully. "What if it don't?"

"Then I'll never let you go," he told her, giving her a wink before getting back to her ankle.

Ruby bit her lip as he worked magic with his hands. She could only hope and pray he let her down soon—before she ended up soaking through her dress onto his lap. Her arousal was growing so fast, it felt like she was sitting in a sink full of water.

CHAPTER 15

"Wow . . . Whitney, you look so . . . damn!" said Calvin, his face full of pure astonishment.

Whitney enjoyed how godsmacked he looked. That told her she definitely looked damn good. When he glanced down at her legs, she could tell she was right about Calvin being a fan of a sexy belle in pantyhose.

"Well, thank you, Calvin. You're lookin' very nice yourself tonight," she told him, nodding in approval of his beige, tight-fitting, leather wool-sleeved Ferragamo shirt, paired with brown Ferragamo pants. On his feet were beige and white casual-style Ferragamo sneakers. He looked so fresh and clean. His *Versace Eros* cologne wafted into her nostrils and nearly made her mouth water. As she took him in, Whitney found herself getting excited in ways a man hadn't excited her in a very long time.

The Bentley Breitling Tourbillon on his wrist—she knew for a fact—cost more than $100,000, having seen the same type in a DuPont Registry magazine once. His whole demeanor screamed man with class and stability. Whitney's nerves were instantly calmed by how warm his smile made her feel.

"Thank you," Calvin replied as she invited him in.

He saw Katrina as he entered. She was wearing a sexy black, turtleneck-topped leather dress with long sheer sleeves. The black lace pantyhose with rose patterns and the red pumps she'd chosen to wear? Yeah, those were for Jeff. She knew he had a fetish for pantyhose and heels.

Katrina had on red lipstick, her eyes done up in a smokey style. Her fiery red hair was flat-ironed bone straight and left to hang loose after being parted up the middle.

"Wow. You must be goin' out tonight too, huh?" Calvin asked with a chuckle.

She nodded. "I am. My king's been in need of his queen's presence. I must do my job and give it to him."

"Glad to hear it. We all need our queens," Calvin said, then looked at Whitney. "Those of us that have queens," he added.

Whitney smiled bashfully at him.

Katrina shook her head but smiled as well. "Well, ya never know, Calvin. Good things come to those that wait. Maybe—just maybe—if you play your cards right, you'll be the next king to have a beautiful queen."

"I surely hope so," Calvin replied, reaching his elbow out for Whitney to loop her arm through. "May I escort this beautiful Queen of the Steel City out to my chariot?"

"You may, Kind Sir," Whitney replied, peeping that the vehicle Calvin was referring to was a far cry from a chariot. "Later, sistah girl!" she told Katrina as Calvin led her out of the house, down the walkway to where his newer-model Mercedes-Benz G550 4x4 Squared truck sat at the curb.

Katrina watched what felt like the perfect couple head toward the very expensive SUV. She sighed to herself.

"TAKE CARE OF MY SISTER, CALVIN! I'MA FIND YO' ASS IF YOU DON'T!" she suddenly shouted. "AND SHE BETTER BE BACK BY SIX IN THE MORNIN' WITH A VIAGRA MAN SMILE ON HER FACE!"

She heard them both laughing at her.

Calvin opened the passenger door for Whitney to get in. Holding her hand, Katrina stayed in the doorway and watched him help her up inside. Once she was in, he closed the door, went around, and hopped in behind the wheel. The engine started up, and seconds later, Calvin pulled off, crawling away from the house with precious cargo inside.

Just then, Katrina heard her phone ringing. She shut the door and hurried into the kitchen to grab it off the table

"Hey, handsome dude," she answered, catching it before it went to voicemail.

"Whassup, lovely lady? You ready for big daddy?" Jeff asked.

"Very. Hurry yo' ass up. Where you at?"

Katrina then heard a mean-sounding engine revving up outside.

"That answer your question?" Jeff asked with a chuckle.

She giggled. "Don't make my neighbors mad revvin' up yo' lil' putt-putt."

"Putt-putt? Yo, stop playin' and bring ya butt-butt outside."

Katrina busted out laughing. "Yes, daddy. Here I come!"

She hurried back upstairs to grab her *FeFe* handbag and a denim mini *FeFe* jacket. By the time she got to the door, Jeff was right outside of it, waiting for her, looking as good as ever in all-white Balmain—with the leather jacket to match.

Jeff was a thirty-year-old man, standing six feet tall. Katrina loved his deep chocolate-brown skin tone. He had the physique of a professional athlete. He rocked an old-school high-top fade, the sides and back of his head cut perfectly. His goatee was sharp and trimmed low. The white-gold jewelry he wore? Katrina knew it cost some money.

He hadn't always been riding on the right side of the street, though. Over time, getting to know him while they'd gone on dates, Katrina learned that Jeff had been a major heroin dealer around Pittsburgh. That wasn't uncommon—not in any way—but what was uncommon, at least in her opinion, was that Jeff had willingly gotten out of the streets before he ended up with a criminal record . . . or dead.

He had a college education, paid for by dope money. A degree in electrical engineering. An Automotive Service

Excellence certification in auto technology and diesel. He used his credentials, the money he'd stacked up, and—along with his love for anything that rolled on two, four, or more wheels—his hands-on experience in auto shops to invest in his own business.

Now, as the owner of a very successful towing and recovery business, Jeff did very well for himself. He worked hard and earned what he had. He even made charitable donations to children in need and animal rescue organizations. He was one of the most selfless men with big money that Katrina had ever met. She absolutely loved the fact that he was a Black man making his own way in the world, never letting anything take him off his square.

"Wow . . ." Jeff took in the sight of her and had to shake his head. Then he started singing: "Baby, *you're!*" paraphrasing a Gerald Levert song, "so beautiful," he added, biting his bottom lip as his eyes traveled down her sexy pantyhosed legs to her red stilettoed feet.

His manhood began hardening at the very sight of what he loved seeing her wear.

Jeff took her hand and pulled her to him. Katrina instantly smelled his Dior cologne. It made her mouth water. His smile hypnotized her. She had to actually wonder to herself if he looked even better than the last time she'd seen him.

"Thank you, Jeff. You look so good tonight. I see you swaggin', baby," Katrina told him, diggin' the Balmain fit. "You sure you lookin' this good for me and not no other woman?"

"Nah. If it was another woman, I'd just wear Gucci," he told her, making her laugh. "Where's my kiss at?"

Katrina looked up at him. His eyes were full of desire. They made her swoon.

She stood on her tippy toes as he leaned down. Their lips met. Fireworks instantly began going off inside Katrina. She felt little jolts tickle her lips as Jeff sent her on a journey out of this world.

"Mmm-mmm!" Jeff shook his head when they parted a minute later. "You messed up for makin' me wait so long for that, Trina."

"I'm sorry, baby. You deserve way better than how I've been toward you. If you'll allow me to, I promise things will be different. That's my word."

"So what do I get if you break your promise?" he asked, folding his arms, raising an eyebrow.

"I'm not gon' do that, Jeffrey."

His eyebrow stayed raised.

"Okay! If I mess up . . . I'll cook you a fat, juicy steak with cheese eggs and sausage."

"And grits?"

She scoffed. "Grits? Really?"

"Take it or leave it," he told her.

"Okay. Deal. But I'm not going to break my promise. Now all this talk about food has me hungry. Where we goin' to eat?"

"Wherever you want, love," he replied, stepping aside so she could see his brand-new, all-black Hellcat Hemi-powered Jeep Trackhawk parked at the curb. "Our *Putt-Putt* awaits."

Katrina laughed. "Okay. So it's not a *Putt-Putt*. Anyway, where's mine at?" she asked as she stepped out and shut the door.

"That thing might be a little too much for you," he told her, taking her hand to lead her to the $110,000 SUV. "How about a Ford Explorer?"

Katrina stopped in her tracks and gave him a narrow-eyed glare. "I wish you *would* try to put me in a damn Ford."

Jeff busted out laughing. "Keep on makin' it so I only see you once every time a meteorite flies through, and I'ma pop up on you with a Ford Pinto."

●●●

"How does it feel now?" Darrell asked, watching Ruby's face relax.

Her expression shifted to displeasure. "Why'd you stop? It felt so good."

"I can't massage your ankle all night, ma." He chuckled.

"But whyyy? Your hands feel so good, Darrell."

"Thank you, but I gotta get you home at a certain time. That's why."

Ruby pouted, crossing her arms over her chest.

He busted out laughing. "Don't pout. You makin' me feel like I just said we can't see each other again."

"Might as well have," Ruby mumbled.

"Huh?"

"Nothing. So, um, are you having fun?" she asked as she reluctantly scooted off his lap and grabbed her Sprite.

"I am. I really appreciate you puttin' some trust in me. I can tell you have a past where trust isn't easy to give. I haven't had this much fun *ever* in my life, Ruby."

She twisted her lip. "You just sayin' that, Darrell."

"Naw, for real. Bein' honest, I've always ended up with women who expected me to stay thuggin', instead of just bein' the man I am, ya' know?"

Ruby nodded. "So . . . what type of man are you?"

"I'm a man who wants a good life and will work hard to get it. I'm also a man who made a successful life from a bad one. I take nothin' for granted. I appreciate everything, even my failures, because I learn from them."

"Wow . . . are you human or a humanoid?" Ruby asked, completely shocked again.

He laughed. "I'm human for sure. Want me to prove it?"

"How?"

Darrell smiled. "Come here, and I'll show you," he told her. Then, to assist her in fulfilling his request, he took her hand and pulled her back onto his lap. He kissed her.

Ruby immediately felt her libido go into overdrive. Her whole body felt like she had touched a battery, and the current flowed through her. His lips were so soft. His hands cupped her face with a gentle but masculine grip. His scent invigorated her, making her feel like she wanted to smell only him forever.

Darrell felt it too, the instant their lips met: smitten, gone, stuck. He didn't want to pull back, but he didn't want to overwhelm her either. After nearly thirty seconds, he pulled back.

Darrell tried not to laugh at Ruby's stupefied expression, but it was obvious as a cow in a pig pen. He busted out laughing, earning a face-muff from her.

"It's not funny, yo. Turnin' me into mush on ya' lap," Ruby playfully scolded. "Why you do that?"

"Do what?" he asked, feigning ignorance.

"Kiss me."

"Because you wanted me to."

"So! You sayin' you didn't want to kiss me too?" she asked, raising an eyebrow.

"Not at all, because I most definitely wanted to see how them lips felt against mine," Darrell told her.

She twisted her lips for a few seconds, then started smiling. "I really appreciate you bringin' me here. I'm havin' fun."

Darrell nodded. "Me too. I just want to know why you doin' that to me."

Her eyebrows furrowed. "Doin' what?"

"Making me want to make you my woman on the first date."

Ruby let out a little giggle. "I ain't doin' nothin', though."

"Sure you not, ya' lil' liar. You tryna' make me strip you naked, lay you down, cover you in BBQ sauce, and lick you clean."

At the visual, Ruby felt herself getting hot. She began blushing hard, feeling shy and excited all at the same time.

"You ain't 'bout that life, Darrell," she told him, trying to put up a tough act, though she was beyond nervous and giddy.

"Oh, I'm not?" Darrell pulled her to him and kissed her again until she was breathless. "You can keep cappin', but real talk, even if you makin' it hard to walk away, outta respect for your sisters—and you—you ain't gettin' no play tonight."

Ruby leaned back, shocked. "Oh naw? Okay. So who's to say I can't get some action from another dude, since you tryna cap and act like you don't want some of this goodness gracious?"

"First off, you don't want action from another guy," Darrell said knowingly, looking into her eyes, which made Ruby eat her idle threat. "Second, I didn't say I didn't want it, but I'm a real man. I'm not gonna treat you like a thot. We just met today. You not a shmutt, so experiencing each other like that right now? Not gonna happen."

Ruby found it hard to contain herself. The man seemed perfect. She'd practically thrown it at him, and he didn't bite. He could've—and if she was honest, she would've gone for it—but Darrell had proven himself to be a gentleman, as she'd hoped.

"But," Darrell spoke again, smiling. "I'll tell you what I will give you."

"Oh yeah? What's that, Darrell?" she asked, hoping for something good, hot, and physical.

"Another kiss."

And he pulled her back to him and kissed her, with that red-hot passion TLC had once sung about. Ruby literally went limp in his lap. She just felt so right at the moment.

On the flip side, she was making it sooo hard for Darrell to keep his word to Whitney and Katrina.

CHAPTER 16

Whitney groaned in frustration as she put her phone back into her handbag. She still couldn't get in touch with Onika, and she was growing seriously agitated. Calvin could see the worry lines in her face, and it made him feel for her.

Sitting together at a table out at Mad Mex in Monroeville, the two had been enjoying dinner and conversation until Whitney gave in to the urge to try contacting Onika again. The restaurant was packed, full of people enjoying the company they were with. It was a nice spot to grab Mexican food and drinks while unwinding and catching a good vibe.

"Does she normally pull disappearing acts like this?" asked Calvin, feeling concerned himself.

Whitney shook her head. "I can't honestly say," she admitted, since she and Katrina had only met the young wild dancer a few weeks ago. "I just know the type of trouble that a young angry woman can get herself into when she feels like the world is against her."

Calvin nodded in agreement. "That's very true. My firm, unfortunately, has seen many misguided young ladies get themselves into binds that come from them acting off emotion instead of using their heads. I hope she'll be okay," he said solemnly, praying that he wouldn't hear that Onika ended up like lots other young girls that spiraled out of control.

"I . . . um . . ." Whitney grew hesitant as a thought that had been swimming in her head for a while resurfaced.

Calvin's eyebrows furrowed. "What's up? Talk to me."

She looked him in his eyes and saw the most soothing passion in them. "I . . . I think Onika is doing drugs, too."

He looked at her, shocked. "Drugs? She looked so healthy when I met her. What type of drugs are you thinking?"

"I don't know. She's always on the go, and . . . she's very promiscuous, with many partners."

"Sounds like cocaine to me, or pills—maybe both," Calvin said, familiar with how *uppers* affect people. "The fentanyl people put in everything these days, people are overdosing left and right, all over the country. This is *not* good at all, Whitney."

Her eyes filled with tears at the thought of Onika's body being discovered. She couldn't stand it anymore. She started sobbing. Her heart ached for Onika at that moment.

Calvin got up and came around to her side of the booth spot. He pulled her into his arms and held her.

"It's okay, Whitney. We can't let it get to us. Onika can't be that crazy to put herself in danger like that," he said to her, praying the young girl was smarter than that.

Whitney's emotions overwhelmed her, and she cried into Calvin's chest. A few people sitting nearby noticed and hoped everything was okay.

"Come on," Calvin said, feeling the need to get Whitney somewhere where she could gather herself. "I have somewhere we can go to relax a little."

Whitney did her best to calm down. She lifted her face from his chest and nodded. Calvin asked for everything she knew about Onika, and she told him. He sent a text with Onika's info to a good friend of his, then assured Whitney that Onika would be found. He just prayed it would be before she did something irrational and ended up paying for it with her life.

●●●

"Ssssss . . . mmm! Oooo, Jeff! Ooooh God! Damn!" moaned Katrina as Jeff's lips and tongue worked wonders between her legs. "Yes! Yes! Jeffrey!"

Holding her legs open as wide as they would go, Jeff sucked on her clit, lapping up her juices as Katrina constantly leaked. He'd ripped a hole in her pantyhose and slid her thong to the side. He had full access to her goodness gracious and was taking full advantage of it.

In the parking lot of a Jamaican restaurant in East Liberty, Jeff had Katrina laid out in the back of his SUV. Katrina, on her back, moaned and cried out his name as he pleased her. It had been so long since she'd felt his oral skills. She'd forgotten how good he could make her feel.

"Jeff! Jeff! Ooh, baby, I'm about to cum! Ooooo, God!" she hollered, feeling it coming on strong.

Jeff slid two fingers inside her and kept pleasuring her clit. Less than a minute later, Katrina exploded, drenching his face.

"Dammit!" she shouted, trying to catch her breath. "Holy freakin' crap!"

Jeff lifted his wet face from between her legs and laughed. "Lemme find out you forgot how I get down, baby."

"No!" she lied, avoiding eye contact.

Jeff twisted his lips. "Whenever you lie, you look to the left. Stop cappin'."

She sucked her teeth. "Okay, maybe I did. Now what?"

"Now we go inside, get some Curry Chicken and Oxtails, have a good dinner, then I take you home and make love to my woman like I know you want me to."

Katrina's mouth opened to respond, but she was speechless.

"Words ain't needed. I know you better than you think I do, beautiful," Jeff said with the smile that always got Katrina hot.

He fixed her thong, though there wasn't much he could do for her pantyhose.

"You ripped my stockings, Jeff," she said, feeling a slight breeze between her wet thighs.

"So? I always rip 'em. Stop complainin' when I just made you see Venus and bring ya' beautiful butt on. I'm starvin' like Marvin!"

"After all that you just ate, you still hungry?" Katrina asked as he opened the door for them to get out.

Jeff smiled. "Yup! You been neglectin' me for so long, you forgot I have an insatiable appetite. But now that you realized I'm your man, I'm gonna remind you every day and every night, my beautiful Black queen."

"Oh, is that so, Jeffrey?"

"Yes. You don't believe me?"

Katrina looked deep into his eyes and saw sincerity. It made her smile, feeling tingly all over. She appreciated that there were no dull moments with Jeff.

"I do, baby. I really do," she told him.

"Good, because I'm ready to be everything you need in a man so you feel comfortable enough to give me your heart all the way. I been prayin' hard that one day you'll open up. I'm thinkin' He's answerin' my prayers at this very moment."

Katrina laughed. "You sayin' God gave you permission to slurp me up in the back of yo' Jeep?"

"Yup! God knows what I need, and I needed to satisfy my sweet tooth."

She laughed harder. "Okay, it's time for some Curry Chicken or Goat. Let's go, Jeffrey."

"Right behind you, my beautiful Black queen," Jeff replied. As they got out, his eyes fell on all that juicy, round booty she had squeezed into her tight dress. "WOO! Goddamn, Trina! That ass is phat!"

●●●

Minutes away from Mad Mex, Calvin took Whitney to a ducked-off bowling alley tucked under the rear of a Big Lots store. Plenty of people were there, taking up most of the lanes. Whitney hadn't expected this, which was exactly Calvin's point. He figured that if she was like most women, fun was the number one cure to make her smile.

He was right. Whitney seemed to be having a ball, even though she hadn't hit a single pin during any of her turns.

"Dammit!" she cursed after trying hard to roll the ball straight down the lane without guttering it again. It curved left and went straight into the gutter.

Sitting at the desk, Calvin tried hard not to laugh. Whitney turned and saw how red his caramel face was from holding in his laughter.

"Go ahead. Laugh it all up, Calvin. I will kick your ass," she told him, scowling playfully.

He held his hands up in surrender. "I do not want no smoke with evil sister Eva."

Whitney raised an eyebrow. "Wha—? Oh . . . let me guess," she said. "Gabrielle Union, when she played in *Deliver Us from Eva*?"

"BINGO!" Calvin shouted and clapped his hands.

She put her hands on her hips. "So who does that make you? Ray?" she said, referencing LL Cool J's character, the hired player paid to distract Eva so her sisters' men could be dominant without big, sexless sister looming over them.

"Hell naw. I got hair." Calvin grinned and winked.

"Whatever. Maybe I like bald. How about that, smart guy?" Whitney teased, taking a seat next to him and crossing her legs.

She hated how goofy the bowling shoes looked on her feet.

"Just like Eva, too—mean as hell," he told her, taking her right hand into his. "But it's all good. I love me a feisty Black queen."

Whitney stood and went to mush Calvin's face, but he caught her hand and pulled her down onto his lap.

"You missed!" he teased with a taunting smile.

Whitney tried to wiggle free, but to her, it was like trying to escape a grizzly bear.

"Calvin Herman, if you don't let me go, we are going to fight."

"That's fine. As long as I get a kiss, I'll take one or two to the jaw."

Whitney screamed as one of his hands slid to her side and started tickling her. She tried even harder to get away, but he was just too damn strong.

"Okay! Okay! You win!" she shouted, surrendering as she laughed so hard that tears filled her eyes.

Calvin laughed with her. He released her and watched as she hopped up, making an "X" with her fingers to ward him off.

"I think it's my turn, ain't it?" he asked with a sly smile as he rose from his seat.

Smirking mischievously, Whitney walked up behind him as he reached for his ball.

"Actually, it's my turn," she told him. Grabbing him, she made him turn toward her, pulled him down by his collar, and kissed him.

Ooooos and *ahhhs* filled the bowling alley as the two got lippy in front of the crowd. People clapped and cheered. The ladies shouted for Whitney's bold move, and the fellas hooped and hollered for Calvin to scoop her up.

His lips were so soft against hers. His hands caressed her sides, giving her goosebumps. The feeling of kissing the man she had always wanted was like nothing else. Whitney was gone, and she didn't want to come back.

After a minute-long kiss, Calvin pulled back. They gazed into each other's eyes, reading each other's thoughts. He smiled at her, and she smiled back.

"I have wanted to do that since I first saw you," he told her. "I'm mad you beat me to it."

Whitney giggled. "Ya' snooze, ya' lose, big boy. Now let's finish our game before we end up doing something we might regret."

Calvin chuckled. "Nothing—and I mean nothing—will I ever regret when it comes to you, baby," he told her. "Now, yes, let's get back to me kickin' ya' butt so you can buy me my ice cream when you lose our bet."

Whitney scoffed. "Game on, mister. Now your ass is mine," she challenged as she grabbed her ball.

Calvin stood back, watching as she carefully lined herself up with the middle of the lane. She took three steps and rolled the ball.

Gutter ball.

Calvin busted out laughing. Whitney folded her arms and pouted, watching him roll so hard that tears streamed down his face. His laughter made her crack up too.

Soon, they were back in each other's arms, locking lips again. Bowling was over—other things were now on their minds.

CHAPTER 17

Right at midnight, Darrell pulled into the driveway of Whitney and Katrina's home. Ruby saw the BMW truck still parked in front of the garage door, but none of the lights were on. She knew they were both gone from the text Whitney had sent, which included a reminder of the entrance code to unlock the door and disarm the alarm.

Darrell put the Range Rover in park, got out, and walked around to open her door. He took her hand and helped her out. Ruby stepped down, gently applying pressure on her ankle, trying not to hurt it again. Hand in hand, they walked up to the door.

"I can't even describe how much fun I had with you this evenin', Darrell. I can't wait until we—"

Darrell cut her words off with another deep, sensual kiss. Ruby instantly went limp in his arms. He wrapped her up, holding her close as he got him some more of her.

His hands slid down her sides to her wide hips and landed on her juicy booty. He squeezed it, feeling how soft and perfect it was. His manhood grew hard in his pants. Backing Ruby up to the door, he lifted her slightly. Ruby lifted her left leg and wrapped it around him, feeling his tool poking out. It drove her crazy. She found herself wanting to know how he would feel inside her. She longed for it.

The way his lips and tongue explored her, the way his hands caressed her ass—it felt like Darrell was staking his claim on her, and she was with it because she was staking her claim on him, too.

"Um . . . so . . . this is going to sound a little crazy," Ruby said, flustered as their lips parted. "Do you have a girlfriend? Any groupies? Baby mommas?"

"Well, you are a girl, and you are my friend," he teased, chuckling.

Ruby sucked her teeth. "Come on, Darrell, don't play. I can't be messin' with no man that's boo'd up, yo."

Darrell laughed. "Naw, ma. I'm not in any sort of relationship. I don't have a 'hoe,' a friend with benefits, or a lesbian friend that's not really a lesbian behind closed doors."

Ruby's eyebrows furrowed. "Who would even think about all that?"

"You'd be surprised how many insecure women have crazy thoughts about what role every woman plays in a man's life." He kissed her again. "Am I gon' be able to see you tomorrow?"

"You better," Ruby told him, really not wanting him to leave at all.

She turned and entered the code Whitney gave her. The door unlocked, and she opened it. Turning back to Darrell, he kissed her once more.

"God, why do you have to go?" she asked.

"Because if I don't, we'll move too fast. I don't know about you, but I believe in takin' our time to build. There's no rush—I'm rockin' with you the long way."

He made her smile again.

"I'm rockin' with you, too, Darrell. Thank you for so much fun. Enjoy your event."

"Thank you, Ruby. I will. Sleep tight, and hit me when you wake up, a'ight?"

She nodded, staying at the door to watch him walk back to his Range Rover and hop in. After backing out, he pulled off, heading down Laketon towards Robinson Boulevard. In seconds, he had disappeared.

Ruby stepped into the house, closed the door, and leaned against it. She sighed, feeling like she was stuck in a dream she never wanted to end.

"Please let him be real," she said softly, looking up.

With that, Ruby headed to her room to grab some night clothes and hop in the shower.

●●●

Just past one o'clock in the morning, Calvin pulled up to Whitney's house. He hadn't known it, but Whitney's UC had flared up horribly as he exited the parkway in the Church Hill area. She'd clenched and done everything she could to hold her bowels, praying to God she didn't ruin her new outfit—or her night with Calvin.

But now that she was in front of her house, she had to go!

"Okay! Bye!" Whitney nearly screeched the words as she grabbed her handbag and frantically opened the door to jump out.

"What? Hey? What's—" Calvin's words fell off as she jumped out like her ass was on fire.

"Gotta' go! I'll call *me*! I mean *you*!" she yelled over her shoulder, running as fast as she could in her heels to the door. She tried not to cup her rear, knowing Calvin would see and it would only add to her embarrassment.

She quickly entered the code and pushed the door open. Without a second to spare, Whitney ran inside without even shutting the door. She made it to the bathroom just in the nick of time.

Relief washed over her as she finally let go. But seconds later, tears filled her eyes, and she started sobbing. She just knew Calvin would never want to see her again.

"Whitney?"

She gasped, realizing she hadn't even closed the bathroom door. Grabbing the *Febreze*, she sprayed all around.

"Hold on a sec, Ruby!" Whitney called, reaching for the box of baby wipes.

"Are you okay?" Ruby asked.

"Yes! I'm good! Just give me a second, Ruby! Please!"

"I'm sorry . . . I was just letting you know Calvin's in the living room, waiting for you."

Goddammit! Why-why-why-why-whyyyyyyyy! Whitney screamed internally, filled with worry and panic.

"O . . . okay. I'll be right . . . out," she told Ruby, now so nervous she didn't even want to come out of the bathroom.

●●●

"So, did you two have fun?" Ruby asked Calvin, sitting across from him in the living room with Onika, her baby guinea pig, on her lap.

Calvin chuckled as the guinea pig squealed. "I believe so. I've never had so much fun with any woman I've gone out with in the past. Whitney seemed to be having a ball until . . . just now."

They both heard the bathroom door slam shut, followed by the shower turning on. Calvin's excitement died down right before Ruby's eyes. She felt bad for him, but also for Whitney. It didn't take a rocket scientist to figure out that Whitney's UC had flared up.

"I heard you went out with Darrell?" Calvin asked, trying to change the subject.

Ruby smiled then, and the dreamy-eyed expression told Calvin everything he needed to know.

"Yeah." Ruby picked up Onika and nuzzled her tiny nose. "We went to the Dave & Buster's out in Homestead. I'd never been to one until tonight."

Calvin admired the affection Ruby showed the messy-furred animal. It confirmed again that the Jersey girl wasn't a hardened criminal.

"Oh, naw?" he asked. "I know y'all had a lot of fun."

"Most definitely, yo. He's so cool and fun to be with." Ruby sighed, wishing she were with Darrell right then.

Uh oh . . . Young Darrell got this girl gone already. He better not hurt her. Hold up . . . what am I saying? Youngin' is a good and respectable guy. Ruby's in good hands with him, Calvin thought, noticing how entranced Ruby looked.

"He's a good dude, Ruby," Calvin told her, snapping her out of her daze. "He turned his life around and made something of himself. He's every bit a boss, and you'd do great rockin' with him."

"Yeah?" Ruby smiled hard, definitely liking how Calvin was advocating for Darrell.

Calvin nodded. "My word."

●●●

Half an hour later, Whitney entered the living room wearing a large shirt, leggings, socks, and her hair down. She felt clean now but still embarrassed. She saw Ruby, baby guinea pig on her lap, keeping Calvin company. It made Whitney smile a little, but the smile quickly fell away as she anticipated hearing Calvin say he didn't want to see her again.

Ruby noticed Whitney enter before Calvin did. She stood, said goodnight to Calvin, hugged Whitney, and took Onika upstairs to her bedroom.

Calvin stood as Whitney approached. He could tell she was beyond embarrassed but felt relieved she'd come back out instead of locking herself in her bedroom. She stood near the kitchen entryway, so far from him, arms crossed over her chest, eyes on the glossy white oak floor.

He made his way to her, hoping she wouldn't let her flare-up make her think he found her repulsive.

"I had the best time of my life this evening, Whitney," he told her seriously. "I'm really hoping to do it again sometime soon."

Stopping just inches away, Calvin paused and took her hands into his. Whitney looked up into his eyes and managed a small smile.

"You're just saying that to make me feel better."

"I'd do anything to make you happy, Whitney. But I'm being honest. Being with you today confirmed what I've always thought about you."

"And what have you always thought about me?" she asked.

Calvin gave her a warm smile. "That I really, really want to be more than a friend to you," he said, his eyes full of passion and sincerity.

"Calvin, I—"

"Wait, Whitney. I know you're afraid because of your UC. I get it. But doesn't tonight prove I care enough that it doesn't bother me? Or make me see you as any less of a woman?"

She shook her head, struggling to believe him. "You say that now, but what about next time I don't make it to the bathroom? What if we're out somewhere extravagant and it happens? What if we're stuck in traffic? Or if we're with your friends and their women, and it happens? What then? How will you treat me then?"

"The same way I'm treating you now," he told her. "I know it's tricky, and I know you remember a crazy past filled with evil-mouthed men. I know your heart's fragile. But words don't mean anything—I'd rather show you that your UC doesn't bother me. I will stand with you, not against you. I swear that on my mother's grave." Calvin brought her hands to his lips and kissed them. "Actions prove sincerity. I'm a sincere man, and you know that."

"I . . . I do, Calvin. I just . . . you deserve a woman better than me."

"Whitney, you're an intelligent, successful, sexy, beautiful Black queen. What could be better than you?"

"An intelligent, successful, sexy, beautiful Black queen that doesn't have Ulcerative Colitis."

Calvin shook his head. "Let's be real for a minute, okay?"

Whitney nodded.

"Be thankful UC is all you have. It could be gangrene, or blindness, or cerebral palsy. What if you had cancer? Diabetes? Or a disorder that made you tremble uncontrollably? Or epilepsy? Or were missing a limb—or two, or three?"

Hearing all of that floored Whitney. She'd never thought of it like that. People suffered from all kinds of things. As she thought about more than what Calvin mentioned, she actually grew thankful. Indeed, all she had was a bowel disease. She was in fashion. What if she were blind?

"So," Calvin continued, "maybe if you think about that, you can stop feeling so inferior. I remember you told me about the IVF treatment. What happened with that?"

"It's once a month, and remission's supposed to happen in a year. It's been a year. My doctor told me to be patient, but I'm in fashion, Calvin. I can't keep sneaking off to the bathroom during video shoots or interviews. People might not think I'm worthy to represent their fashion lines."

Calvin sympathized. "I understand. You're such a good woman. You'll excel no matter what. Listen to your doctor; trust him. And trust that I'm for you."

Tears filled Whitney's eyes. His words made her heart race. She wished her heart wasn't so fragile. Calvin was steadily proving to be the epitome of her king. But the thought of it all being a ruse terrified her.

"Whitney, baby, please, don't cry."

Looking into his eyes, she saw something that shocked her. She saw love.

"Let me in, Whitney. Please."

She saw Calvin's eyes watering. No way this was fake.

"I'm sorry for what you went through, and I'm sorry I was immature. But you can't let the past dictate the future. I'm here, begging for a chance. I will cherish you, protect you, shower you with affection. I'll love you the way you deserve. Trust me."

Conflicting thoughts battled in Whitney's mind. But her heart begged to open. Calvin's eyes displayed truth. And love.

"Okay," she said, barely a whisper. "Okay, Calvin. We can try. Just . . . please . . . don't hurt me."

"I won't." He wiped her tears, tilted her face up, and pressed his lips to hers. "Give me your worries." He kissed her again. "And your problems." He kissed her once more. "I'll carry them for you."

Calvin kissed her again, this time with so much passion that Whitney's temperature rose so high she felt like she would spontaneously combust. Her nipples grew hard, and moisture built between her legs. She was aroused to no end by the man.

She moaned as his tongue entered her mouth. As he explored her, Calvin's hands slid down her sides, landing on her perky booty. He cupped it just as Whitney wrapped her arms around his neck. Calvin picked her up by her rear and carried her over to the couch where he'd been waiting. Sitting down, he positioned her on his lap and continued kissing her.

Hungrily, Whitney kissed him back, cupping his face with her hands. Feeling his hands lifting her shirt, Whitney raised her arms and pulled back just long enough for him to slip it off.

She wore no bra underneath. Her perfect 32 C-cup breasts were so full and perky, aching for him to taste the chocolate tips. Calvin's mouth watered at the sight of them.

Whitney bit her lip and moaned when he leaned forward and took her right nipple into his mouth. He sucked lightly, skillfully swirling his tongue around the sensitive bud.

"Mmmmm . . . that feels good, Calvin," she moaned, throwing her head back, eyes closed as she focused on the feeling.

Calvin suckled her right breast for a minute, then gave the left the same attention. Whitney was hot and ready for him, but he wasn't done showing her what his foreplay was all about.

He stood with her still in his arms, then set her down on her feet. Kissing her again, he trailed kisses down to her chin, chest, and flat stomach until he reached the waistband of her leggings. He pulled them down and discovered she was bare beneath. She was completely shaved and smelled so fresh.

He kissed just above her womanhood. Whitney gasped sharply from the feeling of his lips so close to her bliss. Calvin helped her step out of the leggings and then sat her on the couch.

He took her right foot into his hand and kissed her toes, then trailed kisses up her leg to her thigh. He repeated the same with her left leg, stopping at a sensitive spot between her thighs, mere inches from her wetness.

Calvin pushed her legs wide and inhaled her scent.

"Mmmmm, baby, you smell so good to me," he said, his deep, raspy voice making Whitney even hotter and wetter. "Can I taste it?" he asked, kissing the inside of her left thigh.

"Yeessss," Whitney hissed, biting her bottom lip. "Please, Calvin. Please."

Calvin ran his tongue up her slit, lapping at her liquid desire. He drank her in, smiling at her taste. He opened her up, parting her swollen lips. Putting his lips to her clit, he sucked.

"Ooohhh, Calvin! Oh God, baby, what are you doing to me?"

Pausing from French-kissing her clit, Calvin said, "I'm showing my woman how I'll please her every chance I get."

He got back to it, determined to please her like he promised. Focusing on Whitney's clit, he listened to her repeatedly call out his name, moaning in bliss. She rubbed the top of his head, running her hands over his neat waves. Whitney started seeing stars from the phenomenal attention he gave her.

Calvin turned up the intensity, inserting two fingers inside her. Slightly curling them, he stroked her walls, finding her G-spot in seconds.

By the way she started bucking and crying out, he knew he'd found it. Calvin took full advantage, wanting her to know he was the man she needed in her life. He knew there were a few ways to prove himself: treat her like a queen, always be there, and when it came to pleasure, make her feel *damn* good.

Whitney's toes curled as Calvin ate her and stroked her at the same time. She couldn't remember oral sex this good, and it blew her mind.

A couple of minutes later, her orgasm hit hard. She cried out that she was about to cum. Calvin intensified his efforts on her clit and stroked her faster. Whitney started shaking uncontrollably before she exploded, soaking Calvin's face.

Whitney shrieked, horrified when she saw him. "Oh my God! I'm so sorry!"

Calvin chuckled. "Sorry? For climaxing?"

"For . . . that! Wetting your face. I've never done that before."

"Sooo . . . you've never been made to feel so good that you squirted before?" Calvin smiled triumphantly.

She shook her head no.

"Well, now you have," he told her. "And believe me, baby, we are far from done."

Calvin stood and stripped completely naked. Whitney's eyes widened, nearly popping from their sockets. The man was a muscular god. She licked her lips as her eyes traveled down his wide shoulders to his barrel chest. His flat, toned stomach boasted a six-pack.

Then her gaze fell to the 10 inches of rock-hard bliss pointing at her. Her mouth watered as she imagined herself wrapping her lips around him, sucking until he filled her mouth with sweetness. She attempted to slide to her knees, but Calvin stopped her.

"Naw, baby." He took her hand and pulled her to her feet. "Tonight, it's all about you and your pleasure."

Calvin laid her on the couch and climbed between her legs. Just as he prepared to enter her, Whitney spoke.

"Please . . . be gentle. It's been a while," she said nervously, her heart pounding.

"I promise," he told her. He slowly, gently guided the bulbous tip of his length into her wetness.

Both of their eyes rolled to the backs of their heads. Whitney felt him stretch her out. The pain quickly gave way to pleasure. Calvin felt like he'd entered paradise. Her womanhood fit him like a glove, as if she were made just for him.

"God, you feel so good, Whitney," he told her, kissing her while slow-stroking her.

Whitney thought of all those old '90s love songs and figured this was what ecstasy felt like. Her entire body responded to Calvin's touch. His gentleness showed he wanted her pleasure first. She loved that.

"Oh, Calvin! Oh my God, baby, yeesss! Yes, baby!" she cried out as he went faster, feeling her getting wetter and more adjusted to him.

Her legs wrapped around him and squeezed.

"More! Faster! Give it to me, baby!" Whitney demanded.

Calvin obliged, diving deeper into her abyss. He pinned her wrists to the armrest above her head and whispered sweet words in her ear as he went faster, deeper, and harder. Whitney felt like she was on a trip through outer space. Calvin was her spaceship, taking her to oblivion and beyond.

●●●

From the top of the stairs, hidden by the darkness of the shadows, Ruby watched the hot lovemaking session unfold in the living room. While lying down with *Onika*—her guinea pig—Ruby had heard Whitney moaning. Unable to resist her curiosity, she crept through the hallway and perched at the top of the stairs. When she saw Calvin with his face buried between Whitney's legs, her eyes went wide.

By the looks and sounds of it, Ruby was sure the two didn't care about anyone else but each other and the pleasure they were giving. She silently cheered Whitney on, happy that she had opened up enough to be getting it on right in the living room.

Ruby couldn't help but keep watching. She felt wetness building between her legs, and her nipples grew hard. Soon, she was imagining that the steamy session before her was her and Darrell. Her clit throbbed the second she pictured Darrell naked on top of her, sliding deep into her love tunnel.

Ruby stayed frozen, listening to Whitney moan and scream Calvin's name. She could tell the big man was really working her. Minutes later, Whitney announced she was cumming and exploded with another orgasm. Ruby saw Calvin stand and pull Whitney onto his lap. She slid down on his length and began riding him, gyrating her hips like she was dancing for him. As she got more into it, Whitney started bouncing up and down like she was a 1964 Chevy Impala Low-Rider. Ruby bit her lip to keep from giggling as she watched Whitney get her freak on.

Whitney came again soon after mounting Calvin. They switched positions—Whitney turned Reverse Cowgirl and bounced on him with her booty facing him. Ruby could tell Calvin was enjoying every second of it. His groans and moans were deep, like a mating grizzly bear. Before Whitney could reach her next climax, Calvin switched things up again. He bent her over, had her place her hands on the couch, and entered her from behind. He worked his lower back and pounded into her like a human jackhammer. Whitney buried her face into the couch cushion and screamed in sheer bliss before coming again.

Ruby couldn't move. She was stuck, transfixed. Calvin was going apeshit on Whitney, and it was such a turn-on for her. She hadn't realized she'd started pleasuring herself until she felt her hand inside her leggings, her fingers stroking her clit. Ruby bit her lip to keep her moans quiet. She closed her eyes and imagined Darrell hitting it from the back, grabbing her hips, and smacking her ass just like Calvin was doing to Whitney at that moment.

"OH! CALVIN! YEESSS! HARDER! FASTER!" Ruby heard Whitney cry out.

Their skin slapped so fast and loud it sounded like applause. Ruby's hand was soaked as she kept playing with herself. Seconds later, Whitney screamed that she was about to cum again. Ruby leaned back, feeling her own climax about to hit.

"OOOHHHH, CAAALVIIIIIN! I'M CUUUMIIIIIING!" Whitney shouted, then came so hard it seemed like she had a Super Soaker water gun inside her.

Ruby climaxed right after Whitney, coating her hand with her hot juices. Out of breath, Ruby pulled her hand out of her leggings and took deep breaths. She could still hear Calvin grunting and moaning. When she looked again, she saw Whitney now on her knees in front of Calvin, taking him in her mouth. Calvin roared like a wild animal as Whitney finished him off. Ruby saw his muscles flex as if he were lifting something way too heavy.

She watched Whitney jerk Calvin's shaft while sucking everything out of him. Ruby took mental notes on the grand finale and smiled, already plotting on knocking Darrell's socks off very soon.

CHAPTER 18

Bright and early the next day, Katrina woke up in Jeff's arms, in his big, comfortable bed. The sun shined through the luxurious master bedroom's wall of floor-to-ceiling windows. The deluxe room looked like something out of an A-list celebrity's mansion. Jeff had done quite well for himself with his towing and recovery business. His house and vehicles were proof that he was definitely making a great living.

Laying there for a good minute, Katrina's mind replayed the night they'd shared, and it made her smile. He'd taken her up to the Overlook on Mount Washington to admire the beautifully lit-up downtown Pittsburgh area after they enjoyed Jamaican cuisine together. They stayed at the Overlook for a few hours, then went to a movie. Afterward, they got ice cream. Keeping the promise he'd made after tasting her in the back of his Jeep, Jeff took her to his big, 3,700-square-foot home out in the Penn Hills area.

Katrina then remembered how hard Jeff had gone so hard on her when he got her naked and into his bed. He'd kissed all over her, licked and sucked on her feet and toes, and devoured her sweetness. When he made love to her, it was the perfect mix of rough and gentle—something many men couldn't do. Either they were too hood or too lame. But Jeff? He was what she called a *Top Gun*. He'd made her climax more times than she could ever remember any man making her cum.

● ● ●

She turned over onto her left side and looked at her handsome brown king sleeping peacefully. She bit her lip in pure lust. He was as naked as she was, lying on his back with his chest rising and falling steadily.

Katrina couldn't help herself. She scooted over to him and started rubbing his defined six-pack abs. She kissed his stomach, then moved up to his chest, licking around one of his nipples.

"Mmmm." Jeff chuckled, eyes still closed. "You must ain't get enough last night, huh?"

Giggling, Katrina slid her hand down his stomach, under the fluffy blanket that covered their lower halves. She gripped his tool, excited to find he was already hard as a steel pipe.

"I did not," she told him. "How about you make me cum a few more times? I start back to work today, and I'd love to walk up in there looking like I just got hit off right, and make all those sexless female CO bitches jealous."

Jeff groaned in frustration. "Back to work? On a Friday? I'm never gon' see you now since I know you gon' feel like you gotta make up for all the days you missed."

"Aww! Look at you! Poutin' 'n' shit!" Katrina leaned down and kissed him. "I promise you, Jeff. Things are going to be different. Can you trust me?"

He looked up at her. She was so beautiful, and her eyes showed no lies. He nodded.

"Yeah. I trust you, Trina."

"Good. Now gimme some of this good-good so I can walk up in there smilin' like that dude that can't get hard without pills."

Jeff busted out laughing. "You want me to hit it so you can go to work with a Viagra Man-smile?"

"Yup!" she told him and climbed on top of him. "Got a problem with that?" she asked, sliding her wet center back and forth to get him ready.

"Mmmm . . . shit . . . not at all," Jeff said before flipping her onto her back. "You want to make people jealous? I'ma have you walkin' into your job pigeon-toed, lil' mama."

"I hear you talkin'. Let's see if you about that life," Katrina challenged. She reached down, gripped his length, and guided him to her entrance, ready to feel that thick nine-inch magic wand he'd used to make her do tricks last night—all over again.

●●●

Whitney cursed under her breath as she tried to call Onika for the hundredth time. She kept getting voicemail, and none of the texts she sent were being read. Whitney felt something was very wrong.

"Onika, where are you, little sis?" Whitney asked herself, praying to the Man above that she wasn't hurt . . . or worse.

"You think we should call around to the hospitals?" Calvin asked, sitting on her bed beside her. "I've got a few friends on the force that I could ask to keep a lookout for her."

"Yes. And please, yes. Her name is Onika Temple."

Whitney then sent a text to Ruby: *Hey, little sis. I hope you're ready.*

After she sent it, a reply came back in less than a minute: *I am . . . I like this outfit, but I think people will think I'm a thot.*

Whitney stood up and gave Calvin a description of Onika so he could pass it to his cop friends. Then she left her bedroom to go see Ruby.

●●●

"Wow." Whitney admired Ruby in her outfit, swearing for a second that Ruby could be a model featured in her magazine. "Ruby, baby girl, you are so damn gorgeous. Do you know that?"

Ruby turned to look at Whitney, smiling but still feeling a little unsure whether she looked good or slutty.

The tight, wine-colored Valentino dress hugged her voluptuous body like a second skin. It had long sleeves, gold V's monogrammed all over it, and a bustier top that made Ruby's breasts look even bigger than they already were. The flared hem stopped at mid-thigh, and wine-colored pantyhose enhanced the look of her sexy legs. She wore metallic gold Valentino pumps with shiny, mirror-like six-inch heels. Her hair was pulled up into a high ponytail, and her baby hairs were gelled down around her gorgeous face. Gold hoop earrings with "FeFe" inside dangled from her ears. A gold, herringbone-patterned choker adorned her neck, and gold bangle bracelets covered both wrists.

Ruby had applied a little makeup, following a few tips from Katrina. Her eyelids matched her dress, and her lips complemented her pumps and jewelry.

Whitney marveled at just how seriously beautiful Ruby was. It made her shake her head, thinking how all that beauty had been hidden under baggy clothes and represented by guns.

"Do I really?" Ruby asked as her smile began to grow.

"Yes! Hell yes!" Whitney replied, making her way up to her.

"You are a very beautiful woman too, big sis," Ruby said, appreciating how professional yet sexy Whitney looked.

Whitney had chosen a gray, black, white, and charcoal-colored checker-box business dress from the Donna Karan New York line. It had an above-the-knee hem, elbow-length sleeves, and a low cleavage line. She paired it with black pantyhose and black pumps. Her hair was flat-ironed bone straight and left hanging loose. She completed the look with a black blazer jacket and accessorized with white-gold Bvlgari jewelry, red lipstick, and black eyeliner.

"Thank you, Ruby. It's my sexy office woman look." Whitney struck a sassy pose, then giggled.

Ruby chuckled. "I bet Calvin loves that look on you, huh?"

Whitney started smiling so hard her cheeks ached. She could still feel Calvin's hands, lips, and tongue all over her.

"Calvin approves," she told Ruby, choosing to stay modest.

Oh, I bet he does more than approve, sistah girl, Ruby thought to herself.

"Mhmm," was her only reply.

Seeing Ruby wiggling her eyebrows suggestively, Whitney pursed her lips, feeling like she'd just been caught in a doggy position, getting pounded by a minor.

●●●

"See you later, love." Calvin kissed Whitney's lips through the open window of her BMW truck, tasting the spicy cinnamon gum she was chewing.

"Bye, baby," Whitney replied, feeling shy and turned on at the same time.

"Oooooooo, Whitney and Calvin! Sittin' in the tree! You two are bunny rabbits! Bad influences on me!" Ruby sang teasingly.

Calvin busted out laughing. "You are somethin' else, Ruby. Yo, you two be safe. And baby, give me a call when you're free. Maybe we can all go have lunch?"

"That sounds nice, handsome. I'll call you."

Calvin hopped into his Mercedes truck and pulled off. As her engine idled, Whitney sighed, grabbing the steering wheel and staring straight ahead with the biggest smile on her face. She then heard Ruby clearing her throat. Turning to look at her, she saw Ruby wearing the cheesiest smile.

"Don't say it, Ruby," Whitney chuckled as she put the car in reverse and started backing out of the driveway.

Ruby started laughing. "Why, whatever are you talking about, big sister? How I woke up hearing, 'Oh, Calvin! Oh, my God, baby, yeesss! Yes, baby!'" she teased.

Whitney gasped. "Ruby!"

She shifted to drive and headed toward the Laketon and Robinson Boulevard intersection.

"Aww, don't get your panties in a bunch," Ruby replied. Then she added, "If you're even wearing any."

"Oh, my word, Ruby! What has gotten into you?"

"Definitely not what got into you, guuurl!" Ruby said, sassily snapping her fingers above her head.

Whitney shook her head. "Keep talking like that, and I am going to a church to dunk you in some Holy water, young lady."

Ruby started laughing again. "Dunking me in water, huh? I still wouldn't be as w—"

"RUBY! Stop it before I put you on time out!"

Ruby immediately fell silent, but the mischievous smile curling her lips gave her away. She knew she was toeing the line—and loving every second of it.

●●●

Half past seven in the morning, Jeff dropped Katrina off at home. He escorted his beautiful queen to the door, kissed her breath away, and, wishing her a good first day back at work, hopped back into his Trackhawk and pulled off.

Katrina entered the house with a big, satisfied grin on her face. She fanned herself to cool down, then hurried to get showered.

●●●

Fresh and clean, Katrina went to her bedroom and got dressed in her Allegheny Sheriff Correctional Officer uniform. She pulled her flaming mane up into a ball-bun on top of her head, applied a little black eyeliner and some strawberry-flavored lip gloss, and skipped perfume to avoid enticing any of the detainees she would encounter.

Just as she finished putting the final touches on herself, her Galaxy started ringing. Seeing her friend and co-worker calling, she answered it.

"What up, 'Mika?" she asked.

"Hurry ya' butt up, Lisa Raye!" Shamika shouted jokingly. "I'm ready to see my biatch back in uniform!"

Katrina sucked her teeth and ended the call. Looking at herself in the mirror on the back of her makeup counter, she shook her head.

"I do not look like no damn Lisa Raye," she told herself, though plenty of people said she did.

●●●

Outside, Shamika sat in her brand-new Jeep Wagoneer, dressed in her CO uniform, wearing a leather headband while her dreads hung loosely. Katrina hopped in up front, and Shamika pulled off.

"Thank ya' for pickin' me up, girl," Katrina said, digging out a $20 from her handbag. "I know I'm outta your normal route from home."

"Trina, I do not need your money," Shamika said. "You my girl, so why would I charge you gas money? I'm ballin', honey girl!"

Katrina chuckled as they approached Laketon and Robinson Boulevard.

"What they gon' do about your car, though?" Shamika then asked.

"They gots to cut me a check. I had full coverage on it. I thought about getting another STR-8, but after Jeff let me drive his Trackhawk, Mika . . . I want one of those!"

Shamika laughed as she made a left turn at the intersection and headed toward the business district of Wilkinsburg.

"Uh oh! You was with ya' boo last night?" she asked Katrina, grinning. "That's why ya' ass look all shiny 'n' shit! You got some good lovin' last night!"

Katrina started laughing. "Hey, I was due, okay? Don't be tryna act like I don't give my man no attention. He's been very patient with me. I love him for that."

Shamika nodded as she passed a used car dealership lot. "How long did y'all actually date for before you both became official?"

"Like, three years. We were kind of off and on with it. You know what I'm sayin'? Like, he was mine, I was his, but we saw other people . . . sort of."

"Sort of?"

"Yeah. I actually didn't go out with anybody. I don't know if he did or not, but I just wasn't in the mind-state to see any other guys. Hell, I only wanted Jeff, but my head just couldn't get right."

"And it is now?" Shamika asked, stopping at a red light on Penn Avenue.

"Yes. My man is good to me. He loves and cherishes me. How dumb would I be to screw that up? The number of eligible men out here who are amounting to something and not dope heads or creeps is so low you'd think there are none left."

"Girl, you ain't never lied. I'm still tryna find me Mister Right and not Mister Right Now."

"Last night, though, Mika, Jeffrey Palmer was all mine! His ass was like a lion! No . . . like a tiger! He was going crazy!"

"Oooo, you freaky little red-neck shmutt!" Shamika teased as the light turned green and she hit a left turn to head up a steep, curved hill toward the Parkway.

Katrina shot her a look, lips twisted. "Mika, you and I are the same color."

"No the hell we not! I am brown! You's a bright girl! Don't they call y'all redbones in Chicago?" Shamika asked as she stayed to her right, merging onto Ardmore Boulevard and maneuvering the narrow, curvy road toward the tip of Forest Hills.

"Naw, boo-boo, they call me the Sugah'-Honey-Ice-Tea in Chiraq, biatch. Betta act like ya' know, joe," Katrina said, switching to her true Chi-Town accent. "We gets it bussin' out in the land, shorty."

Shamika busted out laughing as she ascended the hill toward the Parkway on-ramp.

"Uh huh. I hear ya' talkin', lil' mama, but you better remember that you are now in PITTSBUUUURGH! We gets it crackin' out here, yo!"

Shamika turned up the music and blasted Wiz Khalifa's "TWEAK IS HEAVY," rapping along with the verse where the tatted Pittsburgh rapper said exactly what she had just told Katrina about Pittsburgh.

●●●

"Well, you already are tatted up like Che Mack, Ruby," Whitney said as she cruised along the Parkway toward downtown Pittsburgh. "You really think you need more tattoos?"

"Who is Che Mack?" Ruby asked, glancing over at Whitney.

"A chick who's been featured on *Love & Hip Hop: Atlanta.* She was friends with that sleezeball dude who's a producer for Bad Boy."

"I never seen it."

"Oh, it's a dope show. I really like Kirk Frost's wife, Rasheeda. Now that woman is the epitome of Black female perfection. She's a boss, and she has thick skin. You don't see many strong Black women like her."

Fifteen minutes later, Whitney got off the Parkway and made her way through downtown to the building where her magazine's studio office space was. It wasn't far from Calvin's law firm. As they reached the entrance to the subterranean parking garage, Ruby Googled the show Whitney had mentioned and found a bunch of episodes and cast biographies. She ended up finding the Che Mack girl and checked out one of her social media pages.

"Wow. She's beautiful . . . and bad!" Ruby said, looking at the tatted-up, light-skinned girl with short hair and braces. "This is a man's dream woman right here, yo! Straight up!"

Whitney chuckled as she paid for parking. "All the women on those shows are beautiful, Ruby. There's no such thing as ugly, unless you're talking about ugly on the inside."

●●●

Taking the elevator up to a lobby, they exited into the space and walked through glass double doors to the outside. Walking and talking, Whitney and Ruby tossed around different ideas for photo shoots Whitney was still deciding on for future fashion articles.

As they reached Whitney's building, a car horn beeped. They turned to see a couple of guys in a clean Dodge Charger, eying them lustfully.

"Aye, yo! What up! Can we come slide with y'all?" the dread-head in the passenger seat shouted through the window.

"No, thanks!" Ruby replied. "We both taken!"

"What that mean?" the guy shouted back.

"It means buh-bye!" Whitney told them before she and Ruby entered the building, leaving the two guys looking swold as hell.

•••

Up on the 16th floor, the gold elevator doors opened. Ruby immediately noticed the *Steel City Queens* Magazine sign hanging above a wall, featuring a photo of Whitney and three other women, all looking like divas.

Stepping off the elevator, Ruby took in the industrial chic-looking space teeming with activity. All 2,800 square feet of the area featured an open-studio concept with a warehouse feel. Exposed brick walls and pillars contrasted with the imported Italian marble floors. Gold-trimmed windows and custom-made Italian furniture added a touch of luxury.

Sections were set up for photo shoots, with racks filled with articles of clothing, shoes, and fashion accessories. Photographers captured models in designer labels with perfect flicks for the upcoming issues. Design techs worked on editorials, and makeup artists prepped the models.

Ruby's excitement grew, especially knowing that Whitney owned it all.

"Yooo, Whitney! This is so dope!" she said just as a robust woman with creamy-brown skin, orange-dyed natural curly hair, and a tiger-striped Gucci headband walked toward them with a big smile.

The woman wore a long, tight-fitting tiger-print Gucci dress with orange pumps and hoop earrings. She reminded Ruby of the woman who played Elroy's chick in *Next Friday.*

"HEEEY, LOOK WHO'S BACK IN THE BUILDING, EVERYBODY!" the woman shouted, making the twenty-odd *Steel City Queens* staff stop what they were doing.

Cheers, whistles, and clapping filled the space as Whitney's employees excitedly acknowledged her. Appreciating the warm welcome, Whitney waved.

"Hey, Lanisha," Whitney said, hugging her friend like it'd been ages since they'd last seen each other, even though it was only a few weeks ago at Jimbo's.

Just then, two more women approached with warm smiles.

The taller one had super dark ebony-toned skin and a bob-cut. She wore a bright banana-yellow Dolce & Gabbana pantsuit with a white silk ribbon tie around her neck and white high-heeled booties.

Her companion had sandy-brown hair in neat two-strand twists, skin so bright that Ruby wondered if she was white. She wore a zebra-print blouse, black leather skirt with a triple-ruffle hem, black pantyhose, and zebra-print pumps.

"Ladies!" Whitney greeted her friends, happy to see them.

"What's up, Miss Whit-Whit!" the dark-skinned woman said, hugging Whitney. "We missed you here, girl! Glad you're back!"

"Yeah, boss lady," the super-bright chick said as Whitney gave her a hug. "You're all the way back in action now, right?"

"I am. Ladies, this is Ruby," Whitney introduced.

The three women turned to Ruby with less-than-pleasant expressions. They knew who she was as soon as Whitney said her name.

Ruby realized they were the ladies with Whitney at the club the night she'd robbed her, Onika, and crashed into Katrina.

Fear instantly overtook Ruby. Her nerves went haywire, and the room seemed to shrink. The stares made it feel like she could barely breathe.

"So you're Miss Thief, huh?" the ebony-skinned woman said, stepping toward Ruby with anger in her eyes.

166

"The one that likes to hit people with guns?" added the tiger-dress woman.

"Then robbed them for what they worked really goddamned hard for?" the super-bright girl added, scowling at Ruby.

"Hey, hey, hey! Enough!" Whitney stepped in front of Ruby. "The past is the past. Ruby is a brand-new woman with a good job. If I can forgive her, so can you!"

"I . . . I'm sorry," Ruby said, looking at the ladies. "I wasn't living right. I'm a changed woman now. I swear."

"Mmmhmm. Tell ya' story walkin'!" the tiger-dress woman said, crossing her arms. "Everybody says they changed when they're in front of a judge—or some women that'll beat their asses!"

"Shaquayla!" Whitney narrowed her eyes. "I said stop!"

Shaquayla fell back before she pissed off her friend and boss.

"I brought her here to show how things can turn out for someone who takes their time building their life up the right way. So, instead of getting ready to attack, let's show this young *Steel City Queen* how us Black women work so well together."

"We can do that," the super-bright woman said, taking a deep breath. She looked at Ruby and extended her hand. "I'm Riley. It's good to hear that you're trying to be better. I support that. I'm the head makeup artist here at *SCQ Magazine.*"

The woman in the tiger dress reached out next. "And I'm Lanisha. I'm the head photographer. I hope you know I'll be keeping a close eye on you, young lady, so you better not screw up, or my foot's going in your—" She stopped as she felt Whitney's glare boring into her. "Keep yourself clean, and you'll have a friend in me. Okay?"

Ruby nodded.

Shaquayla introduced herself last. "I handle Public Relations and head our Human Resources department."

"Whitney, I have the spreads for Olivia's shoot ready, and Shatrice's too," Lanisha told the boss.

"I've got Paul and Jake scheduled for their trips to Paris for shoots," Shaquayla added, pulling out her iPhone. "And Mrs. Royce has agreed to let us officially showcase *Steel City Billionaire,* her new men's line."

"Great! I hear it's getting a lot of attention on social media," Whitney said. "Have we gotten in touch with Cardi B's and Megan's people to set up a feature?"

Ruby gasped.

"I did!" Shaquayla said. "They're penned in for one week from today, boss lady!"

Oh my God, Cardi B and Megan Thee Stallion are coming here! Ruby thought, doing everything she could not to go bananas.

"Perfect. Thank you, ladies," Whitney said.

"Hey, Whit. I'd like us to use more natural tones for the next issue," Riley said. "I've been seeing a huge interest in natural beauty. It's always been a thing, but more women are realizing they don't need to be all dolled up to feel good. Alicia Keys helped with that."

"I agree. Natural is always better," Whitney said. "Do it. You have my support."

"There's a present on your desk, Whit," Shaquayla added with a sly smile.

"Uh . . . okay." Whitney wondered what it was.

●●●

The ladies followed as Whitney took Ruby up to her deluxe office, which was located on a loft floor above the work area. Ruby loved how chic Whitney's office was. It looked like something Beyoncé would have a scene in for a bossy music video, with her stiletto'd feet up on a custom-made titanium and glass-topped desk.

Two big flat-screen computer monitors sat on the desk, alongside stacks of previous *Steel City Queen* issues. Behind the desk, a wood bookshelf filled with fashion magazines and books stretched across six shelves. The walls were adorned with blown-up photos of models featured in the magazine, along with shots of celebrity visits to the studio. On the wall across from Whitney's desk hung a massive 88-inch HD screen, used for both video calls and TV. Ruby loved the whole aesthetic, but what caught her eye most were all the African art pieces—paintings and statues that added rich character to the space.

●●●

Whitney shrieked with excitement when she spotted a box of donuts on her desk. She instantly knew they were from her favorite bakery, Dana's, which had been a staple in Homewood since she was a kid.

"Heeey!" she said, opening the box and grabbing a big glazed cinnamon roll donut. "Ruby! You've got to try one of these, baby girl! Krispy Kreme and Dunkin' Donuts ain't got nothing on Dana's!"

Ruby peered into the box and grabbed a pretzel-shaped glazed donut. She took a bite and immediately cheezed up.

"Whoa. Okay, why isn't this Dana's bakery everywhere?" Ruby asked, taking another bite. Then another. And another.

"It's like a flavored orgasm, isn't it?" said Riley as she grabbed a maple-iced long john from the box.

The ladies laughed as the other two reached for donuts.

"Leave it to the white girl to make donuts a sexual thing," teased Lanisha.

Riley shot her a narrow-eyed look. "Lanisha, I am not white! My dad is half Scandinavian and half Black! My mother is all Black! Do the math!"

"Whoa, whoa, whoa . . . calm down, killer. Get back to orgasm land with your donut," Lanisha laughed as the other women joined in.

"Hey." Whitney finished the last of her donut and immediately went for another. "I want Ruby featured in a shoot. Who do we have available?"

Ruby gasped at Whitney's declaration.

"Um . . . I think Pierre is," Riley said, glancing between Ruby and Whitney. "But . . . are you—"

"If you ask me if I'm sure about something I just said, you'll regret it, Riley."

Damn, Whitney is a boss for real! Ruby thought, impressed by how big sis wasn't shy about making her commands heard.

"Okay!" Riley said quickly, shifting focus. She grabbed Ruby's hand. "So! Ruby! Let's go see how much the camera loves you!"

She tugged Ruby out of the office, heading for one of her makeup stations.

Shaquayla and Lanisha remained behind, exchanging glances as Whitney stood at her floor-to-ceiling window, enjoying her donut.

"If either of you question me, you're both fired," Whitney said, not needing to turn around. She could feel their eyes on her.

CHAPTER 19

"Ten-four," Katrina said into her radio, responding to a call from an officer en route to her unit to escort one of her detainees to bond court.

She yelled out, "HILL! BOND COURT! GET READY!"

Sitting at her desk in the unit, Katrina kept her eyes on everything. Her post was in a male unit for the day, one of the easier ones to run. Many detainees were sitting at tables—some playing poker and dominoes, while others talked, drank coffee, or watched TV. Katrina knew plenty of them were looking at her. Being a voluptuous, light-skinned woman with red hair, she figured she was like Beyoncé walking into the unit, completely naked. What she didn't like was the number of perverts gawking at her, trying to undress her with their eyes. It came with the job, and she ignored it, for the most part.

A tall, beefy, light-skinned detainee sitting at a table playing bones smiled at Katrina. She shook her head and refocused her attention on the computer in front of her, replying to an email that Yvette had sent from her sergeant's office.

"Aye, Miss Rose?"

Katrina looked up and saw inmate Hill walking toward her desk, licking his pink lips like he was eyeing a steak dinner.

"Are you ready to go, Mr. Hill?" Katrina asked, ignoring the lustful look in his eyes.

"Yeah. But I got a question for you, though," he said.

"What might that be, sir?" Katrina asked, still not giving him the satisfaction of eye contact.

"Why you always lookin' so mad? Like you don't have no fun in ya' life. You too beautiful to not be smilin' every day."

She looked at him and put on a fake smile. "Better?" she asked, with obvious sarcasm.

"Because it was me that made you smile, of course. Now check it. I'm 'bout to bond out this joint. You should let me take you out to dinner or a drink, ya' mean? I'll make sure you get home safe."

Katrina looked at the 22-year-old, who was in for his fourth domestic violence charge. Seeing he was dead serious about hollering at a correctional officer, as if fraternizing was legal, she wondered how many times he'd been dropped on his head as a child.

"Mr. Hill. Please step away from my desk and wait by the sally-port door. I actually do not want to send you to the hole, but that type of talk will not be tolerated. It's fraternizing."

Inmate Hill's eyebrows furrowed. "Fraternizin'? Man, come on with that, yo! You ain't allowed to talk?" His tone grew aggressive, and the look on his face hardened. Katrina's hand moved toward the pepper spray on her hip. "I'm just tryna' put you in a good mood, Ms. Rose! You buggin' right now, yo! Homiez!"

Katrina's eyes narrowed into slits as her blood began to boil. Other inmates heard Hill getting loud and could tell he was close to getting out of pocket. They feared for him because they knew how Officer Rose got down.

Katrina stood, ready to spray him. Before she could snatch the canister off her belt, the sally-port door opened, and six feet of dreadhead Shamika entered the unit. Sensing Katrina was close to snapping, Shamika walked right up to inmate Hill and smiled.

"Hi, Mr. Hill!" she said, sarcastically. "How are we doing today, sir?"

Her snide tone made Hill immediately fall back. Everyone knew Officer Rose was about that action, but Officer Fricks was a certified bone-crusher.

"I'm . . . I'm cool, Ms. Fricks," he said, taking a step back.

"Oh, great! I'm so happy to hear that, because ya' see"— Shamika took a step toward him, getting in his face, putting her hand on her hip where her high-powered, correctional-issue taser was holstered—"I gots me a new little toy today. To get this toy, I had to receive a demonstration of how effective it is in takin' someone down. Boooooy, this muthafucker hurts! But I'm a strong woman, so I recovered fast. I ate them volts up, ya' mean?" She got so close to Hill her breasts bumped him backward. Katrina stifled a laugh while the other detainees were dying to see Hill get fried.

"But you," she continued, her smile fading into a frown, "a little punk-ass bitch like you that loves hittin' women, you'll fold up like origami if I pop ya' dumb-ass with this thing. So here's what's gon' happen. You gon' fall ya' shmuck-ass back up off my officer and take ya' dumb-ass over to the door! Now!"

Hill wasted no time complying. He all but ran to the sally-port door.

Every dude in the unit howled with laughter. Katrina could no longer hold it in and busted out laughing. Even Shamika chuckled at herself.

"You good, girl?" Shamika asked.

Katrina nodded and sat back down. "Oh yeah. I'm Gucci. If you hadn't come when you did, I was gon' add a little spice to his life. I wish we could've recorded that."

Shamika laughed. "You must've forgot where we are." She pointed at all the cameras monitoring the unit, including one above the desk.

"Oh yeah! I don't know how I forgot about that! Aye, when you come back, bring some popcorn!"

"If I return," Shamika replied with a devious smirk. "Mr. Hill might try to smack my booty in the elevator that doesn't have cameras, and I might have to shoot him in his nuts with my taser."

Katrina busted out laughing again.

"If I do gotta fry him, you gon' hear me calling for some fresh Fruit of The Looms for him," Shamika added.

Katrina was in tears from laughing so hard.

●●●

"Wooow! . . . this girl has exactly what we need," Pierre, an American-born African man and Lanisha's top photographer, said in awe.

He was stunned by how photogenic Ruby was. Dressed in a silver, skin-tight, ribbed Italian wool dress by Saint Laurent (designed by Anthony Vaccarello), with pointed-toe stilettos on her feet that looked like they were dipped in chrome, her hair and makeup done to perfection—he couldn't believe how incredible she looked in every photo.

"Where did you find this one, honey?" Pierre asked, turning to look at Whitney, who stood beside him with Lanisha.

"Let's just say . . . she found me," Whitney told him, not feeling the need to explain how they'd met.

"Ain't that the truth," Riley commented, raising an eyebrow.

Whitney shot her a look that shut her up immediately. Pierre noticed the exchange but didn't question it. He returned to his job and encouraged Ruby.

"Okay, baby girl!" he said, snapping ten more headshots and full-body shots. "It's a wrap! Good job!"

Ruby felt so much emotion at that moment that her eyes began to water. Never in her wildest dreams had she imagined being the object of a potential modeling position for a major fashion magazine—especially one owned by someone so dear to her.

As the photo shoot went on, everyone in the studio stopped working to watch her. They were stunned—entranced by everything about her. Even Whitney's top three ladies had to admit Ruby was a straight-up dime piece.

● ● ●

The photos from Ruby's shoot were printed out and handed to Whitney. She took Ruby to her deluxe office, shut the door, and laid the photos across her desk so they could review them together. Whitney was astounded.

"Ruby, I think this is what you were meant for, baby girl," she told the Jersey girl. "That ol' Hollywood term 'The camera loves you' is an understatement in this case."

"Thanks, Whitney." Ruby smiled as she admired herself in the photos. She felt like a real model with how she'd posed and made her eyes look sultry, like a beautiful vixen. "I really like them. And that dress was so soft on my skin. I can't even imagine what it cost."

"A pretty penny, that's for sure."

Knock! Knock! Knock!

Whitney called for the person at the door to come in. Both women turned around to see Calvin step in, wearing a big smile.

Whitney's heart leaped as she drank him in. He was dressed in a sky-blue, wool-knit Hugo Boss sweater, denim Hugo Boss jeans, and extremely rare Christian Dior-edition Air Jordan 1s. A vintage white-gold Presidential Rolex adorned his wrist—the only jewelry he wore—and his hair looked freshly faded, though it had already looked fresh that morning.

"Good afternoon, you two beautiful Steel City Queens," Calvin greeted. "Am I interrupting?"

"No, no, not at all," Whitney said, trying to hide her excitement while eying him like he was a caramel-coated snack she wanted to devour. "We were . . . uh . . . damn." She looked at Ruby. "What were we doing?"

Ruby burst out laughing. "Checking out the pics from my shoot."

"Yes! That!" Whitney turned back to Calvin. "What she said!"

Calvin chuckled. "I'd like to see how baby girl killed the camera, if that's okay?"

"Yes! Come on over, babe! Come see the next Steel City Queen!" Whitney said, elated to have Calvin be the first outsider to check out Ruby's photos.

He joined them at the desk and reviewed the shots. Calvin was beyond impressed.

"Whoa. Ruby, you most definitely had the wrong profession, youngin'. This is your calling," he told her, pointing at one of her full-body shots.

Ruby blushed. "Thank you, Calvin. It was really fun. I've never done anything like this before. Never even imagined it."

"Well, today," Whitney chimed in, "you can add this to your accomplishments, Ruby, because you just became SCM's next model."

Ruby gasped. "Oh my . . . are you serious?"

Whitney nodded with a big smile. "Yes. What I'm going to do is figure everything out for you. While you're working your job, I'll create a portfolio for you. Once everything is ready, I'll have a contract for you to review and sign. I'll also pay for a lawyer to represent your interests."

"A lawyer?" Ruby's eyebrows furrowed. "Why do I need that?"

"So you'll feel secure signing the contract. Since you'd be working for me, it's best if someone represents you that doesn't know me. No conflict of interest."

"She's got a point," Calvin chimed in.

"I know Whitney would never take advantage of me, or else she wouldn't have done everything she has for me," Ruby said. "I trust her—hell, I live with her."

"How about this," Calvin suggested. "I'm not just a criminal defense lawyer; I'm also well-versed in business. Since I know you both, I can represent Ruby and renegotiate any terms if she doesn't like them."

Whitney nodded. "Agreed. But, Ruby," she said, turning to the young belle, "you need to learn that no matter how well you know someone, snakes are everywhere in business. I don't care if you're going into business with your boyfriend, husband, best friend, or family—always have legal and professional representation so no one can get over on you. A business lawyer is trained to recognize shady deals and contracts. Never just trust someone because you know them. That's who will dupe you first. Understand?"

Calvin's respect and admiration for Whitney grew tenfold. He was all about teaching the next generation the right way to be successful. Far too many people of color fell victim to bad business deals because they simply trusted a friend or family member to be honest.

Ruby nodded. "I understand. Calvin's representing me, so I'm good then, right?"

"Yes. You're in good hands, little sister," Whitney said.

"Good. Now that that's settled," Calvin said, "Ruby? Do you mind if I get a few minutes alone with my woman? I need to talk to her about something."

Ruby grinned. "Suuuuure, Calvin." She wiggled her eyebrows goofily and headed for the door. "Take all the time you need. I'm gonna go see the other models bein' fly for the camera."

She left and closed the door behind her. Calvin walked over and locked it. Whitney felt a flash of heat as he turned back, a mischievous smile on his face.

"So," Whitney said as he stepped toward her, "what brings you by?"

Calvin walked right up to her, pressed his body against hers, and wrapped her in his arms. Leaning down, he kissed her. Whitney moaned as he parted her lips with his tongue, exploring her. His hands slid from her sides to her hips, then down to her ass. He gave it a squeeze before pulling back from the kiss.

"I had to come see you. You got me feenin' for you right now," he said, then kissed her again with a hunger that had Whitney's temperature skyrocketing.

Whitney was overjoyed. He wanted her so badly he came to her office just to get some of her. She was hot and ready to please him.

"You want me?" Whitney asked, getting aggressive as she kissed him and pushed him around her desk toward her chair.

"Yes! I need you!" Calvin groaned, his cock throbbing in his boxer briefs.

Whitney pushed him into her chair. Before he sat, she undid his pants and yanked them down, along with his boxer briefs. His hardness stood erect, pointing at her. She pushed him into the seat and dropped to her knees.

Calvin cursed as she gripped his tool with one hand and placed the tip to her lips. Whitney stuck out her tongue and licked around it. She ran her tongue down the shaft to his balls, making circles with her tongue before taking them into her mouth.

"Shhhiiiit!" he cursed again, loving every second of it.

Calvin's eyes rolled back as Whitney pleased him. After releasing his nuts from her mouth, she ran her tongue back up to the tip, opened wide, and engulfed his entire tool like it was nothing. She took him to the back of her throat, sucking harder as she pulled back. When she let her lips go, a loud *pop* echoed.

"Holy shit, Whitney," Calvin groaned, his toes curling in his Jordans. "Goddamn!"

Whitney acted like she was shooting a porno, determined to please him to no end. There were no limits to what she'd do to satisfy him. He was hers now, and she intended to make him never forget it.

She started sucking him slowly, gradually picking up speed. Every so often, she released him and spit on it before slurping it back up and sucking again. Using one hand, she jerked his shaft while she worked his cock with her mouth. Calvin could barely contain himself. Whitney was going crazy!

He wasn't ready to be finished so soon. There was a fantasy he'd been waiting to play out, and he wasn't the type to leave plans undone.

Stopping her, Calvin took his tool from her and stood, pulling her up from the floor. He spun her around and made her grab the desk. Lifting her dress, he exposed her pantyhose-clad derrière. He marveled at it as Whitney wiggled enticingly.

"I love how your booty looks in pantyhose, baby," Calvin told her, rubbing on it before smacking it. "Hope you ready for this," he added, sinking to his knees behind her.

Whitney gasped as he ripped her pantyhose. "Hey! These are Wolfords, Calvin!" she protested, though she was turned on like crazy.

"I'll buy you more. Now hush and let me handle my business," he told her, pulling her skimpy thong out of her crevice and shifting it to the side.

Spreading her cheeks, he put his face in and ran his tongue up her crack. Whitney squealed with sheer ecstasy. She'd never gotten her ass ate before—only heard about it and how good it supposedly felt.

"Ooo, Calvin! Oh, my God! Whoa!"

Calvin licked up and down, around and around, making her head spin. He didn't care about her bodily issues—she was his woman, and she deserved to have a freaky man. There were no doors between what he'd do to please her.

He moved down and ate her from the back. Slurping her up, he made her cum within minutes, causing her to squirt all over his face.

"Holy crap!" Whitney exclaimed, feeling Calvin lick her clean.

He stood and turned her around to face him. Placing her on the desk, Calvin laid her on her back. Their eyes locked as he slid inside her. Whitney put her legs over his shoulders, letting go of all restraint as he started making love to her right there on her desk.

Calvin's powerful thrusts created delicious sensations inside her, making Whitney bite her lip and repeatedly call out his name. He took her to the same place he had the previous night—and she was thrilled to be back so soon. She had missed it.

"Whitney," Calvin groaned. "Damn, baby, you feel so good."

She moaned and cried out in bliss. Minutes later, she came again, blasting him with an intense orgasm that left her legs numb.

Calvin pulled out and put his face between her legs again, licking her clean before making her cum with his phenomenal oral skills. Once she climaxed for the third time, he had her grab the desk again and hit it hard and fast from behind. Whitney laid her face on the desk, reaching back to hold her cheeks open for him. Calvin went deeper—so deep she swore she could feel him in her chest.

She came again in less than seven minutes. Soon after, Calvin was ready to explode. Whitney felt him pulsating inside her and knew what was coming. Turning her freak all the way up, she took him out of her, spun around, and dropped to her knees.

Opening wide, she took him back into her mouth. Calvin groaned gutturally as Whitney used one hand to suck him while jerking him with the other. Seconds later, he exploded in her mouth.

Whitney kept sucking and jerking until he was completely spent. Putting on a grand finale for her man, she spit all his jizz onto his cock, then slurped it back up before swallowing.

"Whoooaaa!" Calvin felt lightheaded. His legs nearly gave out, and he started laughing suddenly. "Goddamn, baby! That was crazy!"

Whitney kissed the tip of his manhood before rising to her feet. "I know. I've been wanting to do that for so long."

"With me, or whoever you felt comfortable with in here?" Calvin wondered as he pulled up his boxer briefs and pants.

"With you, silly. I can't think of any man I'd feel so comfortable doing such dirty deeds with. Like, you just ate my booty in my office, and I just sucked your cock twice in a row. Then I gave you the goodies on my desk."

"I guess that means I'm special then, huh?" he asked, grinning.

"Yes. You most definitely are." She stood on her tiptoes and kissed his lips. "You shouldn't even need to ask that, Calvin."

He crouched down and helped her fix her dress. Her pantyhose, however, were done for. "Sorry about your Wolfords, baby."

"It's fine." She leaned in close to whisper in his ear. "When I look at them later, I'll have replays of how good you just made me feel. And I might end up calling you to make me feel like that again."

"Oh, trust and believe, I can definitely do that . . . anytime you want."

Whitney looked at him with eyes full of insatiable desire. "I'm going to hold you to that, so make sure you stock up on Wheaties. Now let's go get Ruby before she starts texting everyone about what I'm sure she assumes we're doing in here."

Calvin laughed. "Lead the way, my beautiful Steel City Queen."

CHAPTER 20

Ruby sat on a long chaise chair by a tall floor-to-ceiling window, looking out over the busy street. She smiled at the text message she had just received from Darrell. She couldn't stop herself from re-reading it repeatedly.

I miss you already, Gorgeous. I don't know why you have such a strong effect on me, but I do not hate it. As soon as I'm done with this wedding, I would like to come get you and spend the rest of the day with you. How about it?

Ruby read the second sentence four more times before replying:

I would really like that. I'll be waiting for your call. XOXOXO.

The loud click-clacking of high heels made Ruby look up. She saw Calvin leading Whitney towards her. Both of them had cheesy grins on their faces and looked like a twister had scooped them up, blown them across the country, into a gas station bathroom, where they'd tried to fix themselves up and look presentable. They had failed miserably.

With a comical smirk, Ruby opened her mouth to speak, but Whitney quickly stopped her.

"You better not start, young lady", she warned.

Ruby busted out laughing at her. "Whatever are you talking about?"

"Mhmm. Are you ready to go?" Whitney asked as she and Calvin stopped in front of her.

"Uh huh." Ruby smiled even harder, looking at Calvin.

He tried his best to look normal, but ended up busting out laughing his ass off.

Whitney elbowed him in his side. "Hush! Don't feed into her nonsense, Calvin."

"It's hard not to. She's a funny girl, yo."

"Whatever. Let's go," Whitney said before stepping off in front of them, heading towards the elevator.

Ruby looked at Calvin, whose eyes were fixated on Whitney's perfectly round derrière.

"You better have used a condom, unless you plan on marrying her," she told him.

Calvin looked at her. "Both," he replied before walking off to catch up.

Ruby chuckled to herself, then hurried to join them as the elevator opened up, and the two stepped onto it.

●●●

"Oh wow . . . that's nuts." Katrina shook her head. "Why put yourself in that situation to lose a good career, with great benefits and longevity?"

She was sitting at a table toward the rear of the break room with Yvette and Andrea, eating lunch.

"Because she's dumb and horny," Yvette replied, wearing her pressed sergeant-striped shirt proudly. With her long hair, now free of the two-strand twists, flat-ironed and pulled up into a tight bun, the beautiful dark-skinned queen looked very official—yet enticingly sexy.

"Personally," she continued in a low volume, so others in the break room wouldn't hear her, "to me, it's not what you do, but how you do it. Do you know how many female staff members are in some type of relationship with inmates? Not just here, but in jails and prisons all over the country?"

Andrea chuckled as she sipped her Mountain Dew. "I can only imagine."

"Too many to count, I'd bet," Katrina said, replying to a text from Jeff attempting to get her all hot and bothered.

"Precisely. People move smart, keep their mouths shut, and things can happen," Yvette said before taking a forkful of Caesar salad.

Katrina narrowed her eyes at Yvette. "Why does it sound like you might have personal knowledge of this, 'Vette?"

Andrea snickered.

Yvette looked at Katrina. "Because I'm a sexy chocolate queen, and everybody wants a taste of what I got," she said with the confidence of a woman who knew she was just the baddest chick on the planet. Katrina and Andrea busted out laughing, drawing attention from other officers and a few nursing staff in the room. "And," Yvette added, "because I didn't always have these stripes on my arm, I had me a little fun. But now that I do, I fly straight. You feel me?"

"So what if you ran into somebody you let taste that chocolate before you got those stripes, and they wanted another taste?" Katrina asked, dying to know the answer.

Yvette pulled out her taser and held it up like she was going to shoot the sky. "I'ma cook his ass," she told Katrina.

Andrea pulled hers out next and held it up. "Extra crispy!"

Katrina howled with laughter at the two trigger-happy women. She pulled out her can of mace and held it up.

"And I got the sauce for that extra crispy ass!" she added since she hadn't yet been certified to carry a taser.

Their radios squawked as an officer shouted for assistance to break up a fight in one of the female units.

"ACTION! DEUCES!" Andrea yelled before shooting up out of her chair and out of the break room like she'd never been there.

Yvette shook her head and took another bite of her salad.

"You not going to go help?" Katrina asked.

"Nope. I'm on my lunch break, boo-boo."

Katrina laughed at her friend. Just then, a text came in from Jeff. She opened it and burst out laughing as she saw he'd made his own version of a Bobby Womack song.

IF YOU THINK YOU'RE HORNY NOOOOW . . . WAIT UNTIL TONIGHT, GIIIIIRL! WOOO! YOU GETTING' PREGNANT, YO! TWINS!

Yvette noticed Katrina's more cheerful, content demeanor. She knew something had changed while Katrina had been on leave.

Katrina typed a reply:

As long as there's a ring on my finger, I don't mind some babies that look like a little of you and me. But would you really be up for that, Jeff?

"That man has you smiling like you feel that thang in you from when he worked you out on ya' time off, Trina," Yvette said.

Katrina gasped. "Sergeant Yvette! You's a nat-nat!"

Yvette busted out laughing. "What the hell is that?"

"I heard that's how girls down in Atlanta say 'nasty chick.'"

"Oh. Well, screw it. If I'm a nat-nat, then so are you, ya' red-head nat-nat."

Jeff's response came seconds later:

Making you my wife would be better than winning the Powerball. With you, I'm actually rich—not just because you're in my life, but because of the joy you add to it. Without you, I'm poor. Real rap.

"Aww! My baby is so sweet! God, I love him!" Katrina gushed.

Yvette chuckled at Katrina's googly grin.

I feel the same way, baby. So what are we going to do about it? Katrina sent the text and waited.

Ten seconds later, his response came back:

☺, was his reply.

●●●

Ruby screamed excitedly inside her head when Darrell entered the restaurant. Calvin had taken her and Whitney to a spot down in Station Square, very close to the docks where the *Goodship Lollipop* and the *Gateway Clipper* riverboats were. Ruby had told Darrell where they were, and ten minutes later, he was walking through the door.

Darrell smiled when he saw her, and it made her light up like a Christmas tree. Overwhelmed with joy, Ruby jumped up and ran to him, throwing herself into his arms and kissing him like it had been forever since they'd last seen each other.

"Daaamn!" Whitney was surprised at how much her baby sis was into Darrell. The PDA she and Calvin—and others in the restaurant—were witnessing was astonishing, yet it was also reassuring that love was real. "She is really into him."

Calvin chuckled as he munched on a honey-barbecue rib tip. "He's really into her."

Ruby lip-locked with Darrell for damn near an entire minute, though to them it felt even longer. When she pulled back, her eyes suddenly welled with tears.

"Ruby? Yo, what's wrong?" Darrell asked, taking her hands into his.

She shook her head. "I don't know. I'm just . . . I don't know, Darrell." She wiped the tears from her face. "I guess I'm just really happy to see you."

Darrell wrapped his arms around her and planted a soft kiss on her forehead. "I'm happy as hell to see you, too. You look beautiful, baby."

Ruby gushed at the way he was looking at her. "Thank you, baby. You're looking very good, too," she told him, admiring the white, silver, and crystal-blue Christian Dior sweater top, the dark-blue denim Dior jeans, and the same Dior edition Air Jordan 1s Calvin had on. His long white-gold Cuban link chain and white-gold Audemars Piguet watch flossed hard, and his diamond studs sparkled in his ears. "You are a very fly guy, Darrell. I think I'ma have to start fightin', 'cause I know you be having eyes on you everywhere you go, and I am not with sharing my man."

Darrell chuckled. "The only eyes I care about are yours, Ruby," he told her, giving her hands a gentle, reassuring squeeze. He took a step back to get a good look at her. "Goddamn . . . you are bad! I know you killin' it in a t-shirt, jeans, and sneakers, but yooo, I love how you look in that dress!"

Ruby did a slow spin for him, and Darrell felt his manhood responding to the sight of her plump, round rear. He had to bite his lip to keep from losing control.

"I'm glad you like it. You hungry?" Ruby asked.

"I actually ate some Chipotle before I came, so I'm good. What's your plans for the day, though?"

Over at the table, Whitney saw the two still talking. "I know Mr. Darrell is not gon' come kiss my little sister up and not come say hello to us!" she shouted.

Hearing her, Darrell took Ruby's hand and led her back to Whitney and Calvin's table. He dapped Calvin up and gave Whitney a hug.

"I'm sorry, Whitney. No disrespect to you or Calvin," Darrell said as he pulled out Ruby's chair for her and pushed her up to the table. "I just honestly lose sight of everything and everyone when it comes to Ruby."

Ruby beamed, her eyes full of giddy joy.

Calvin chuckled.

"Mhmm. I hear you talkin', Darrell. But one thing I'm going to tell you, young man, is you better not just be kicking game on her. She doesn't need any interferences in her life."

Darrell sat next to Ruby. "I understand. I swear to you, on my raise," he said, invoking his mother as those from the Homewood area do. "What I feel for her is real. I can't honestly narrow down the exact reason why I like her so much already, because there are many reasons. She's like . . . a colored diamond."

"Meaning, she's expensive?" Whitney asked, testing him with her eyes.

"Well, money isn't a problem for me," Darrell said, keeping it real while staying humble. "My homie Bagz and I do exceedingly well with our business, but no, I don't mean expensive. I mean, Ruby is a once-in-a-lifetime type of blessing. One a smart man holds onto and thanks God for every day and every night. Real love, affection, growth, being able to actually be a team—that's what I feel a real relationship should be. Bagz and his wife are a team, even though they're not business partners. They always involve each other in new thoughts, goals, desires, and they keep motivating each other.

"You can't rush love, but when you do find it and know it's real, you embrace it." Darrell took Ruby's hand and kissed it. "It only comes once."

Calvin smiled at the young man's words. He reminded him so much of himself. Calvin couldn't have had more respect for Darrell in that moment.

Whitney, too, was taken aback by Darrell's words. They felt authentic, passionate, and sincere. She saw it in his eyes—he was dead-ass serious about Ruby. She glanced at Ruby and saw the expression on her face. The Jersey girl was gone over the smooth-talker.

"Well . . . alright then." Whitney nodded and took a sip of her sweet tea. "I believe you. Just don't forget what you just said, and we'll be fine."

"No doubt, Whitney. That's word," Darrell promised.

Ruby was blushing so hard that she was the color of the baked salmon on her plate.

CHAPTER 21

After lunch, Whitney, Calvin and Ruby parted ways from Darrell, temporarily, and headed back to Whitney's office. Before leaving, Darrell promised Ruby he'd link up with her after his last meeting with a new client. He left her with a kiss that stole her breath away.

Calvin drove them back to Whitney's studio for about an hour, then with a check-up scheduled for Ruby's arm and leg, he took them to Presbyterian. Ruby was a little apprehensive when she saw the same nurse that had treated her when she was brought there as a detainee, in a jail-issued clothes, cuffs, and shackles, escorted by correctional officers. This time, however, the nurse was the one doing her check-up.

Surprisingly, the older woman was very happy to see Ruby. She had the warmest smile on her face that put Ruby at ease.

"Hey, Ruby!" the nurse said, with a slight accent. "Wow! You look so . . . oh my word!" Nurse Louis Hornezes, a dark-skinned grandmother originally from the south, was old-school and pro-Black. She didn't play no games when it came to making people act their age. When she first met Ruby, she hadn't been a fan. But now, seeing the transformation of the Jersey girl from hoodlum to beauty queen, she was pleasantly surprised. "Now *this* is you, young lady! You are gorgeous!"

Ruby gave the woman a gracious smile. "Thank you, Mrs. Hornezes. I've been getting myself together. My big sisters have been there for me. By the way . . ." Ruby looked at Whitney. "This is one of them, Mrs. Hornezes; this is my oldest sister, Whitney Wright."

"Hi, Mrs. Hornezes. It's very nice to meet you," Whitney said, shaking the woman's hand.

"Likewise, Whitney. Good job on getting Ruby's head together. She was definitely heading for the great fires of the underworld, the way she was going."

Standing off to the side, Calvin's eyebrows rose in shock at the comment, but he stayed silent. After being introduced to him, Nurse Hornezes was ready to take Ruby back for her exam.

"Can my sister come, too, Mrs. Hornezes?" Ruby asked, feeling the need to have Whitney there.

"Of course. Come on back, you two, and let's see how well you've healed up."

●●●

In one of the examination rooms, Nurse Hornezes had Ruby sit on the table in the center of the room. Whitney sat in a chair off to the side, near a tall poster displaying the human body's inner workings.

"Alright, Ruby, I'll start with your arm. Let's see now."

Ruby pulled up the sleeve of her dress and showed Nurse Hornezes the dog-bite wounds, which had healed perfectly.

"I see you took your bandage and leg brace off early," Nurse Hornezes said, inspecting the barely visible marks. "Any pain at all?"

"No, ma'am. I took them off because I didn't feel I needed them anymore. Plus, it would've made me look goofy wearing high heels with a leg brace on."

The nurse chuckled. "Like a woman just weeks away from giving birth, still trying to walk around in six-inch heels."

Whitney laughed at that.

"I took my pain meds as directed too," Ruby added.

"And she was very responsible with them, Nurse Hornezes," Whitney confirmed, just in case the nurse asked. Prescription pain meds were widely known to be abused.

"That's great news. Now, Ruby, I'm going to check your leg. Are you wearing pantyhose to hide the scarring?"

Ruby laughed. "No, ma'am. I'm wearing them because my sister made me." Ruby shot Whitney a playful look, which made Nurse Hornezes laugh.

"Hey. It's fall time, Ruby," Whitney said, defending herself. "Plus, stockings are stylish and convenient for women who wear dresses and skirts year-round. And I'm a fashionista, so to me, they're very trendy and sexy."

"I agree, and so does Darrell," Ruby said.

"Oh lord." Whitney shook her head.

Nurse Hornezes busted out laughing. "Sounds like this young lady has also found love, huh?"

"Too fast," Whitney said. "But he's a good guy, and he's been adding positivity to her life, so I'm for him."

The nurse had Ruby lay back on the exam table and extended the leg rest. She asked Ruby to pull her tights down so she could check the leg injured in the crash.

"It's definitely healed a great deal since when I first saw it," she told Ruby. "Warms my heart to see you doing so much better. Any pain?" she asked, lightly squeezing around the area with gloved hands.

"No, ma'am. None at all."

"Good. I hope to never see you in cuffs or hurt again. Just this morning, a young lady was rushed in here in horrible shape. She was barely clinging to life. I seriously don't know how she's even alive with the amount of cocaine found in her system. She was beaten so viciously that her face swelled to double its size, and she was . . . abused . . . severely. They found her in an alleyway, left for dead. Just twenty-three years old."

"Oh, my God. That is so messed up!" Whitney said, deeply saddened.

"For real." Ruby shook her head. "Will she make it?"

"Only time will tell. She's got a broken leg, broken ribs, a broken arm. Her head trauma was so severe that her brain swelled. The emergency surgery she underwent to relieve some of the pressure before her brain exploded is what saved her life. It reduced the swelling significantly. Without it, she surely would've died. Such a beautiful girl too. Light-skinned, almost gold, like honey. Long brown hair and very curvy—a dancer's body."

Whitney's eyes shot wide open. A thought popped into her mind, and Ruby immediately noticed. For a nanosecond, Ruby was puzzled by the way Whitney was looking—until the same thought hit her.

"Uh . . . Nurse Hornezes! What is this young lady's name?" Whitney asked urgently, ready to jump out of her chair.

Ruby sat up on the exam table, praying to God that what they were thinking wasn't true.

"Hmm . . . well, she didn't have any identification on her. She was completely naked when they found her and rushed her in."

"Can we see her? Please! We may know her!" Ruby said, hopping off the table and pulling her pantyhose back up.

"Oh . . . yes! Sure! We've been trying to figure out who she is! Follow me! She's in our ICU."

●●●

Katrina was elated when her shift ended. A call over the radio, addressed to all officers that were soon to be clocking out, asked if anyone was interested in overtime. Normally,

Katrina was the first to respond and request extra hours. But now, with her promise to Jeff in mind, she didn't even make a move towards her radio.

"Officer Rose? Do you copy?"

Katrina chuckled as she heard the shift-commander call to her personally, knowing that she was always down for overtime. She was known for exceeding the legal amount of hours an officer was allowed to work. She'd pushed eighty to ninety hours Monday through Friday for over a year.

She grabbed her radio and responded. "Yes, sir. I'm good. Thank you."

"Wow . . . okay," she then heard, and chuckled.

She had a life to begin living. And in her life was Jeff. She was now going to put in her overtime with him.

●●●

"See ya', girl!" Katrina said to Andrea, waving at her friend as she passed by the locker room section where she was changing.

"Be bad, Katrina," Andrea replied with a mischievous smile, knowing Katrina's man was waiting for her in the parking lot.

Katrina laughed and made her way out of the jail.

Powering on her Galaxy as she exited the building, she saw Jeff leaning up against his Trackhawk Jeep. He looked fresh in a tight-fitting Balmain shirt with fitted biker-style Balmain jeans. On his feet, he rocked extremely expensive Virgil Abloh x Nike low-top Air Force 1s.

"Look at you," she said, gushing over his rich-man swagger. "Comin' up to my job lookin' so good that ol' girl in the control room's probably salivatin' over you enough to drool into the control panel and cause a short in the electrical system. The towin' and recovery business must be boomin'!"

Jeff busted out laughing as she walked straight into his arms and hugged him. "You got a whole lotta people that suck behind the wheel and need to get pulled outta ditches or off a center median. My company is one of the top towing businesses called to emergencies. And now, with the four big wrecker tow trucks I just bought to get into the heavy-duty towing and recovery game, my company has expanded its portfolio times ten."

"Ooooweee. Damn, I should come work for you, Mister Baller Shot Caller!" she joked, as her phone started ringing.

Kissing Jeff's lips, she looked at her phone and saw Whitney calling. "One sec, babe. Whit's calling me."

Jeff nodded and stepped back while she answered.

"What up, what up, whaazzzuuuuuup!" Katrina answered excitedly, mimicking Martin.

"Trina!"

Hearing the urgency in her best friend's voice immediately took the smile off Katrina's face. It sounded like Whitney was crying. Jeff noticed the rapid change in her expression and could tell right away that something was very wrong.

"Hey? Why do you sound like that? Is everything cool?" Katrina asked.

"N-N-No! We f-found . . . Onika!"

Katrina froze. She could literally feel her heart drop. Just from the way Whitney said "found," Katrina was already thinking the worst.

Her eyes started filling with tears as the thought became like a real-live film in her head.

"Where? Is she . . . is she . . ." She couldn't even get the words out.

"No . . . she's alive, but . . . oh, God, Trina!" Whitney began sobbing loudly. "Someone really hurt her! She's in a coma!"

"Oh my God! Where are you?"

"Presbyterian!"

"I'm on the way right now!" Katrina ended the call and turned to Jeff. His franticness matched hers. "Jeff! I need to go to Presby, baby! Right now!"

"What happened, Trina?"

"JUST TAKE ME! PLEASE!"

"Okay, okay! Come on!"

He opened the passenger door for her and helped her in, then ran around and jumped behind the wheel. He started the engine, slammed it into drive, and peeled off, forgetting they were in a parking lot filled with law enforcement vehicles.

He laid down rubber tracks nearly all the way out of the lot and jumped straight onto the highway to get to Oakland. Katrina's tears fell like water from a broken faucet as she sobbed in her seat. She was terrified to see Onika. Jeff had no clue what was up, but he said a silent prayer for whoever they were about to go see.

●●●

Ruby ran to Darrell as he rushed into the ICU wing. "DARRELL!" she cried just before reaching him.

"I'm here, baby! I'm right here! What happened to her?" he asked, dread filling his chest about Onika.

As Whitney had called Katrina, Ruby had called Darrell. He had immediately dropped what he was doing and hurried to the hospital. He knew she needed him, and he would never deny her when she did.

"She got beat up really bad!" Ruby cried in his arms. "And she . . . she got . . ."

Ruby couldn't say it.

Darrell figured it out in seconds. His heart dropped. "Oh my God . . . Ruby . . . I am so sorry." He held her tightly. "Please tell me this didn't happen after she stormed out of the Gyro spot."

Ruby didn't answer, confirming it.

He felt horrible. Like a monster. Darrell cursed under his breath as his heart felt like someone was squeezing it.

He saw Calvin holding a seriously distraught Whitney, who was crying her eyes out.

"Any idea who did this?" Darrell asked as Calvin approached with Whitney at his side.

The pure rage etched in Calvin's face said he was ready to relive his wild younger days and go find the creeps who hurt Onika.

"It was two men," he told Darrell. "They . . . they found two different strands of DNA inside of her. Cops are looking for the guys now. They have criminal records, so they popped up in the database right away."

"This is my fault, man," Darrell said as his own eyes began to well up with tears. "I shouldn't have let things get heated like that at the Gyro spot."

Calvin was puzzled. Whitney, though, knew exactly what moment Darrell was talking about. She explained what had gone down at Mike & Tony's after they'd left Calvin's office. Calvin was shocked. He looked at Darrell for a moment. Darrell braced himself for a punch.

"It's not your fault, youngin'," Calvin told him. "Unfortunately, Onika's anger led her to act irrationally. By the grace of God, she's okay, but this isn't on you, Darrell."

"I agree," Whitney said. "Onika has been wildin' for a really long time. It finally caught up to her. I just hope to God that when she wakes up, she realizes this crap has to stop!"

Ruby nodded, too upset to speak. She was just thankful Onika was alive and could make a full recovery. But the road to mental recovery was going to feel like *Mission Impossible* for all of them.

"Where did they find her?" Darrell asked.

"In an alley, up in the Hill District. Right where heroin and every other drug flows like the Three Rivers," Calvin told him.

Darrell swallowed hard. Once upon a time, he and his homie Bagz had moved a lot of dope up on the Hill.

"I know people up there. I can put word out to find them dudes and have 'em dealt with, yo," he said through clenched teeth.

"No." Whitney reached out and touched his shoulder. "No, Darrell. Let the cops do their job."

"They won't, Whitney!" Darrell snapped. "They don't give a shit about us! For all we know, they probably think Onika was a drug whore and chalked it up to prostitution gone wrong!"

"I understand, Darrell, but I don't want you resorting back to the streets! You've worked so hard to accomplish what you have!" Whitney argued. "You just got done talking about how well you've done for yourself! Don't throw it away!"

"But Onika is family to you and Ruby! That makes her family to me, too, and I protect my family, Whitney!"

"I swear to you, Darrell, I understand your anger. I'm furious! But just let it go. Ruby needs you with her, not in jail facing murder charges! Please, Darrell, let it go!"

Calvin watched Darrell intently, seeing the wheels turning in his mind.

Darrell looked down at Ruby. Her arms were folded over her chest. Her tears still fell. She looked up at him, feeling his eyes on her. As if she could hear him mentally asking if this was her wish, too, Ruby nodded, telling him to let it go.

"She's alive. That's what matters most," she told him.

Frustrated at being told not to ride for his people, Darrell could only nod.

"Okay. A'ight. I'll let it go. Y'all have my word," he said.

Calvin nodded. He was glad Darrell cared enough to want to avenge Onika but also cared enough about Ruby to realize how easy it was to get locked up, which would crush her.

"You wanna go get some fresh air, bae?" Darrell asked Ruby.

She nodded. "Yes. Just let me go check on her once more before we go out there."

Together, Ruby and Whitney went into Onika's ICU room.

Darrell squeezed the bridge of his nose, trying to stay calm. Truthfully, he was livid. He didn't know Onika well, but he despised men who abused women. He lived by his own motto: *We all came out of a woman, so what gives anyone the right to abuse the ones who give life?*

"Aye, youngin'?" Calvin walked up, bringing Darrell out of his thoughts. "I know how you feel. I'm proud of you for keeping it together. You have to be strong for Ruby, 'cause right now, she's weak. This is where you become the rock she needs. Someone tried to break their circle up. They're gonna need us for support, lil' bro."

Darrell nodded. "I know, big homie. I just wish I could find them perverts and let Onika get 'em back when she recovers."

Calvin chuckled. "Don't worry about it, cutty. It's handled."

Darrell frowned. "What do you mean?"

"I mean, it's *handled*." Calvin gave him a serious look. "I know a lot of people from my days of runnin' around all the hoods. None of them like creeps. Especially certain friends that now carry badges but wear regular clothes. You dig?"

Darrell picked up what Calvin was putting down. He grinned.

"Enough said, big homie. I dig what you sayin', yo," he replied, dapping Calvin up, hoping that soon, results of what he knew Calvin was capable of would satisfy the wrong done to a young innocent woman that had lost her way.

CHAPTER 22

Ruby and Whitney stood next to their battered and broken, comatose sister. Onika looked so bad. Their hearts ached for her. They couldn't believe they were looking at her in this state. It was devastating, to say the least. She was breathing on her own, but learning there was no telling when she'd wake up—if she would—scared the ever-loving crap out of them.

"I'm so sorry, Onika," Whitney cried, touching Onika's cold hand. "I should've come after you, baby girl. You wouldn't be here if I did."

Ruby couldn't contain her emotions at all. Tears flowed down her face. She could barely breathe.

Just then, the door flew open, and in ran a distraught Katrina, with Jeff behind her.

"Onika! No!" Katrina lost it as she rushed to Onika's side. "Oh my God . . . oh my God!" she cried, stunned to see the young girl in such a state.

It was murdering her mental state.

Whitney and Ruby let the redhead get next to Onika.

Katrina gently took Onika's hand and rubbed it. "We're here for you, baby girl. We're all here."

Ruby turned and, nodding at Jeff, left the room. She couldn't take it anymore.

Whitney stayed and tried to fill Katrina and Jeff in. Jeff put his arms around his woman to comfort her as Whitney gave her the details of what had happened.

●●●

"I know this isn't a good question to ask, but are you okay?" Darrell asked, hugging Ruby as soon as she came out of Onika's room.

Calvin walked in as she was leaving to go back and be at Whitney's side.

Ruby shook her head as she sobbed. "No . . . I need to get out of here, Darrell! Please!"

"Okay. Come on. Let's go," he told her. Taking her hand, he led her out of the hospital to the lot where his SUV was parked.

●●●

Twenty minutes later, Darrell reached the top of Mount Washington. The last bit of daylight was fading. The sun was tucking in for the evening, creating a brilliant orange and purple hue in the sky. Ruby almost smiled at the picturesque sight.

He parked in a spot and got out, going around to open the door for Ruby. He took her hand and helped her out. Together, they crossed the little street and went to one of the Overlook's big circular viewing pads that looked out over downtown Pittsburgh.

They were the only ones there. It was quiet. Peaceful. The only sounds were traffic traveling east and west on the Parkway, which was visible across the wide Monongahela River.

It was cool out. Being so high up, the air was much colder. Ruby caught chills and crossed her arms over her chest to stay warm.

"You cold, bae?" Darrell asked, seeing her rubbing her arms to create heat.

She nodded.

Darrell pulled off his Dior sweatshirt and helped her put it on. She immediately felt at ease when the scent of his cologne filled her nostrils. He wrapped his arms around her from behind and held her tightly. She felt so secure and safe in his arms. She felt cared for. It made something inside of her start heating up like coal in an old locomotive's firebox.

"This view is so dope," Ruby said, taking it all in.

It was her first time at the Overlook. She'd heard about it, but it was her first time experiencing the breathtaking view. It was mesmerizing. Being up there with Darrell had her feeling a lot better, though Onika was still very much on her mind.

"It is, right? I love comin' up here," Darrell said. "It was always me and my homies' spot when we was younger. My mans Bagz, our homies Perry, City, the twins Cee and Dee, my boy Macho, his older brother Tool, and our homegirl Lacey. We used to come up here every Friday evening before we threw a party in the hood. We had some real good times up here, bae."

Ruby turned to face him. Looking into his eyes, she smiled, happiness shining through her tears.

"It's most definitely relaxing. You keep calling me 'bae,' though, and you gon' have to make that a reality, Darrell."

"Is that what you want . . . bae?"

She nodded. "Yes. I do. I really do, Darrell. You mean a lot to me already. I know we haven't known each other long, but I feel a connection with you that can't be faked. You feel like...like you're mine. And like I'm yours."

"I feel like that, too, Ruby." Darrell leaned down and kissed her lips. "So be mine, officially, and I'll be yours, officially."

Ruby smiled so hard she thought her cheeks would tear.

"Period. I am your woman, and you are my man. It's you and me, Darrell."

"I love how that sounds, baby," he told her, then kissed her again. This time, with so much passion, Ruby felt like they had taken a trip to outer space, entering a whole new world. She was instantly turned into mush.

Pulling back, she told him, "Oh, my God. The way you make me feel when you kiss me is . . . incredible." She stared into his glistening eyes, then traced the line of his jaw with a finger.

"I don't know how, but you make me feel things no other woman ever has, Ma. You dun' put a spell on me."

Ruby started laughing. "Naw, yo. I'm just a sexy-ass Black and Cuban Steel City Queen with a nice smile, tattoos, and a—"

"Big ol' juicy booty," Darrell finished, running his hands down her sides and squeezing her plump rear end.

"Well, I was gonna say swag, but what you said is fine, too," Ruby said. "But!" Biting her bottom lip, she added, "I can feel what I'm doing to you, Darrell, and it feels like heaven. I would like to see what my man is working with now."

Without waiting for a response, Ruby slid one hand down into his pants, entering his boxer briefs. Darrell smirked, looking down at her face. As soon as she gripped him, her eyes went wide with excitement.

"Oh, damn." Ruby was surprised. She was sure he was packing, but she hadn't thought it was going to be like *that.* "Yeeaah . . . um . . . hmmmm."

She squeezed and softly gave it a few jerks.

Darrell groaned. "T-T-Too much for y-you?"

"Uh . . . well." Ruby realized Darrell had no clue she was a virgin. Nonetheless, she had no plans of letting his size scare her off. "Nope. Not at all, boo-boo. But just so you know, I am coming back to your house, and we are spending our first night together."

"Oh, you think you ready for that? To consummate our relationship?"

"If that means am I ready to give you my . . . body . . . in exchange for yours," she said, grabbing his collar and pulling him down to kiss him again. "Then hell yes, I am."

Darrell laughed so loudly they were sure the people walking around downtown could hear him.

"I definitely am, baby. I been wantin' it, but I wanted to wait until you did, too. Let's enjoy bein' on top of the world a little longer, then we can go. Cool?"

"Definitely." Ruby nodded, finally releasing his hardness. Darrell leaned in for another kiss. Ruby took his bottom lip between her teeth and nibbled.

"Mmmmm . . . tonight, I'm making you fall in love."

"How you know I'm not already there?"

"Because I haven't put the woo on you yet."

Darrell laughed even louder. "Heeeell naw! She said she gon' hit me with the woo! Yo, this girl is wild as hell!"

"Yup! So you better be ready. I hope you ate the breakfast of champs this morning," Ruby told him, turning back to face the city.

"Can't remember what I ate this morning," Darrell said, resting his chin on her shoulder. "But I'll tell you what I'm gonna eat tonight."

Ruby trembled in anticipatory bliss when she felt his lips on her neck. He sucked on it, swirling his tongue around. The insides of her thighs were drenched.

●●●

Katrina and Whitney hugged each other goodbye. Their men, meeting each other officially for the first time, dapped each other up. After giving silent prayers to Onika, they all headed out of the hospital to their SUVs.

At first, Whitney had no intention of ever leaving Onika's side. The doctor told her it wasn't the best idea because there was no indication of when Onika would come out of her coma. The doctor gave her word that the second Onika woke up—God willing—she and Katrina would be the first to be notified. That got Whitney thinking . . . *did Onika even have any family or friends?*

As they were leaving, Whitney, Katrina, and their men saw a massive man sitting outside Onika's room. He was weeping, head bowed, hands clasped with his arms resting on his thighs. When he heard the door open, the man looked up. His eyes were bloodshot, and it looked like he'd been crying all day.

He shot straight up out of his chair and towered over them as he stepped closer.

"Please. Tell me how she's doing!" he begged. "Please! I heard about her being found, and I came as fast as I could!"

Whitney swore the guy looked familiar, but she couldn't place him. Katrina looked wary of him, wondering if he was one of Onika's sugar daddies or a creepy stalker. The men stepped close to their ladies, picking up on the nervous looks on their faces.

"Who are you?" Calvin asked, standing almost as tall as the six-foot-seven-inch, twenty-eight-year-old giant.

"My name is Bruce Diggs. I was a bouncer at the club Onika used to work at."

"Why are you here? She is not hoeing herself out to nobody!" Katrina snapped, glaring at him evilly.

Jeff's jaw muscles clenched as Katrina's words made him think Bruce had ill intentions. He was seconds away from swinging on the bouncer.

"I thought I recognized you." Whitney now remembered the man from the front door of Jimbo's the night she was robbed.

Bruce looked at her. "You . . . you were the lady who was robbed in the bathroom, right?"

Whitney nodded. "Yes."

"Did they ever catch the punk that did that?"

"She is not a punk! She is our little sister, and she has made significant changes to her life! Watch your mouth!" Katrina demanded angrily.

"Before I put my fist in it," Jeff added, stepping in front of his woman and siding next to Calvin.

Bruce took a step back. "I have no ill intentions for Onika. I promise. I . . . I have always had feelings for her. The night her car was stolen, I kind of took her somewhere to get something she shouldn't have gotten. I didn't know at first, but when I found out, I tried to take it from her. She bucks against me all the time, so I let it go. I never wanted her to go down the path she'd been heading down, but it happened. And now, I feel like this is all my fault. I just . . . I came because . . ."

He paused. Tears filled his eyes again, and his voice began to break as he tried to speak.

Whitney could hear how hurt the man was over Onika's tragedy. Even Katrina could see he was broken. Those were not fake tears.

Calvin and Jeff immediately fell back. As men, they knew real pain when they saw it. They were looking right at it.

"Bruce?" Whitney stepped around Calvin and touched his arm. Bruce looked at her. "Onika has been seriously hurt, but with time, she'll recover. If you really are a friend, then you can do nothing at this moment except pray."

Bruce nodded. "Can . . . Can I see her?"

"Not tonight, bro," Calvin said. "She's resting. Give me your number, and when we come back, I'll give you a call so you can join us."

As Bruce gave Calvin his number, Whitney had a thought pop into her mind.

"You said 'was' a bouncer?" she asked.

Nodding, Bruce clarified. "I quit. Jimbo took advantage of all the women. He's the reason why most of them have drug habits or are alcoholics. He makes them perform sexual favors for a few extra dollars. It's just despicable to me. So I quit. I have plans to help young drug-addicted women and start my own security firm soon."

"That's noble of you. There should be more of that," Calvin told him.

"Definitely," Jeff agreed. "Give us a call. We may be able to help you, Bruce. We need to stick together more—if not for each other, for our women."

Bruce nodded. "I will. My word. I am so sorry for anything I've done or didn't do that contributed to this. She didn't deserve this. Have they caught whoever did it?"

"Working on it," Calvin said. "They're on limited time, is all I'll say, Bruce."

He sighed in relief. He didn't know why, but Calvin's words felt serious, like they were laced with a power only a humble former gangster would have.

"Okay. Please, give me a call. I'll drop what I'm doing and get here fast. Thank you for listening to me," Bruce said, then turned and headed toward the exit, disappearing from their line of sight.

●●●

Jeff took Katrina to his three-bedroom, lavish home out in Penn Hills after stopping by her and Whitney's house so she could pack a bag. He parked his SUV in the one-car driveway, nosing up to the garage, and killed the engine. Carrying her bag into the 2,950-square-foot home, Jeff led Katrina inside through the door to the living room.

It'd been a while since Katrina had been there. She'd almost forgotten how nice his house was. Glossy hardwood floors stretched across the main level, while the upstairs was carpeted. Fancy leather furniture and an expensive audio system were set up in the living room. Over the stone fireplace, a big 72-inch 4K HDTV was built into a section of the wall.

The house smelled so fresh and clean that Katrina smiled. In her mind, it felt like home whenever he brought her there.

"Right this way, ma'lady," Jeff said, leading her up the carpeted stairs to the second floor.

●●●

Up in the lush master bedroom, Jeff turned on the recessed ceiling lights. Katrina stepped in behind him and wrapped her arms around herself, feeling completely relaxed. The cream-colored carpet was soothing to her eyes, as were the beige-painted walls. The windows lining the rear wall, behind the big four-post bed and dressers, looked out over his spacious backyard.

Built into the main wall across from the bed was a massive 88-inch 4K HDTV, with an expensive audio system wired for top-tier sound quality.

Katrina noticed the African art portraits and statues still in the same spots as the last time she'd been there. She loved how Jeff embraced African culture.

The aroma of potpourri wafted into her nostrils, further easing her mind. Jeff sat her bag on the bed, grabbed the remote to the sound system, and turned on some mood music. Usher's "Superstar" started playing. He then turned to face her and reached his hand out, beckoning her to come to him.

Katrina went to him, and he wrapped his arms around her tightly.

"Can I get you anything, baby?" he asked, kissing the crook of her neck before resting his chin on her shoulder. "Something to drink or snack on?"

She pulled back so she could look up into his eyes. "All I need is you, Jeff," she told him.

Jeff smiled. "You already have me, my queen, but I'll enjoy reminding you of this," he said. Then he leaned down and kissed her until Katrina felt so hot that she was sure she was baking like a cake in an oven.

CHAPTER 23

Calvin lived in an upscale area of West Mifflin, in a quiet cul-de-sac with only seven homes. They were all large and luxurious, costing no less than half a million dollars.

His own home spanned 4,000 square feet, with five bedrooms and three bathrooms. It had a double-wide driveway and a two-car garage located at the rear, next to a big, professionally maintained backyard. The house's exterior was painted a soothing Caribbean Sea blue, accented with white trim and shutters. The front porch was made of imported stone, giving it an extra touch of elegance.

As Calvin turned into the driveway and hit the button on his built-in garage door opener, Whitney gasped when two English Bulldog puppies tumbled out, running toward the SUV.

"Aww! Calvin! You didn't tell me you have puppies!" Whitney said as he put the car in park and killed the engine.

Calvin chuckled as he opened his door. Whitney could hear both puppies whimpering, begging for attention from their human.

"Come and meet them, my queen," he said.

Whitney hurried out, making her way around the front of the Mercedes. The pups saw her and immediately abandoned Calvin, running full speed to meet her.

"Oh, my God! You two are so *cuuuuute!*" Whitney gushed as the pups went wild with excitement, trying to climb up her legs.

Calvin watched her, smiling admiringly. He knew they'd take to her.

"The bigger one's name is Gucci," Calvin said, pointing to the steel-blue, tiger-striped, white Alpha male. "The other one is his little brother, Dior." He motioned to the slightly smaller, nearly identical pup. "They're both four months old. Got 'em from one of my mans out in New York a couple weeks ago."

Whitney picked them both up and received a flurry of sloppy puppy kisses. She giggled from how much their little tongues tickled her face.

"Didn't anyone tell you if you bring your woman home and you're expecting some booty, having cute pups like this might make her want to play with them all night long?"

Calvin laughed. "I've got all the time in the world for you to give me some booty, baby." He kissed her on the forehead, then took Gucci, who had started wiggling free. "Come on, let's go inside. I'ma clean up after them and get 'em settled. You can grab a bottle of wine or champagne, then we can watch a movie or something."

"Oh!" Whitney shouted suddenly, startling Dior into barking. "Oh, I'm sorry, Dior!" She held him up and kissed his wet blue nose. Turning to Calvin, she said, "I want to watch *Fashionably Yours*! It's this dope-ass Hallmark movie starring Kat Graham. She plays Lauren, a fashion organizer, and there's this moving company owner named Rob. He's hired to help her move back home, but she ends up falling for him and—" She stopped herself abruptly. "Oh, crap! Sorry!"

Calvin busted out laughing. "It's all good. Sounds like a good movie. Right up your alley."

"Yes! I loved it when I watched it alone. Watching it with you is gonna be magical!"

"Sounds good to me, beautiful. Go on and get settled in, and I'll be right in."

Whitney kissed Dior, then set him down and grabbed her bag from the SUV. After Calvin told her the back door's security code, Whitney headed inside. Dior tried to follow her, but Calvin called him back.

"Ah ah! Dior! Get ya' little butt back here, lil' dude!" he shouted, stopping his pricey pup in his tracks. "You and ya' brother ain't gon' get to cuttin' up tonight. Both of y'all better be on your best behavior, or you're sleepin' in the garage in y'all's kennels. Understand me?"

Dior looked at him with wide, innocent eyes.

Still cradled in Calvin's arms, Gucci looked up and grunted.

"Grrrr to you too, you lil' cream puff," Calvin replied.

He set Gucci down and went to clean the garage. He scooped after them, hosed the floor, and used the app on his iPhone to control their automatic food and water bowls.

Once the garage was clean, Calvin brought the pups into the expansive chef-style kitchen. They ran straight to their iFeeder bowls and started chowing down on Blue Buffalo puppy food, gulping down vitamin-infused distilled water alongside it.

Now that they were good for the moment, Calvin headed off to join his woman, ready to relax and enjoy her company.

●●●

Darrell put on some music as Ruby sat on his big luxury Maree bed. His one-bedroom studio, located in a high-rise along the Monongahela River, reminded her of Whitney's magazine studio. Ruby fell in love with it as soon as they walked in.

The concrete floor had a smooth, shiny finish that resembled marble. The interior had wood trimming and exposed brick walls. Stainless steel furniture with leather cushions or inserts added a modern touch. A wall of floor-to-ceiling retractable glass windows provided a view of Station

Square. Ruby could see the Good Ship Lollipop and the Gateway Clipper riverboats moored there, their lights glowing like something straight out of New Orleans.

Kelly Rowland's *"Motivation"*—featuring Lil' Wayne—played from the surround-sound system wired around Darrell's bedroom. Custom recessed ceiling lights cast a deep red hue over the space, setting the mood. Ruby felt hot, ready for passionate love. She was falling for him hard and fast, but she wasn't sure if it was love yet. She was dying to find out.

Onika, Ruby's baby guinea pig, sat in her cage atop a long dresser. Ruby couldn't leave her alone overnight, so when Darrell swung by to help her pack a bag, she brought Onika with her.

Darrell turned to Ruby, walking over with slow, deliberate steps. He took her hand and gently pulled her up from the bed. Tilting her chin up, he lowered his lips to hers, intensifying the heat between them. Ruby tasted like Jolly Ranchers from the candy she'd been sucking on. Their tongues danced, and a competitive streak hit Ruby. She pushed Darrell onto his back with surprising strength and straddled him, kissing him with a hunger that left him breathless.

Darrell raised his arms so Ruby could strip off his shirt and tank top. She sat up, removed his sweater from her body, and tossed it on the bed above his head.

He muscled her over onto her back, kissing her deeply as his hands traced down her body, caressing her sides. Slowly, he pushed her dress up to her chest. He helped her sit up, lifted her arms, and pulled the dress off.

"Wow. Damn, Ruby," he said, drinking in the sight of her.

She wore a pearl-colored Cosabella lace bra and panty set, along with pantyhose and her heels still on. Her tattoos added a tough, sexy edge. To Darrell, she was perfection.

Ruby beamed so hard that her cheeks ached. The way he looked at her, his eyes filled with desire, made her feel like the most beautiful woman alive.

"You see me, now lemme see you," she requested, eager to take in all of him.

Darrell didn't make her wait. He stripped down to his Dior boxer briefs. Ruby's eyes roamed over his chiseled body. His defined muscles and tattoos told a story of a troubled past that had blossomed into a bright future.

"Mmm, mmm, mmm." Ruby licked her lips. "You are so damn fine, Darrell."

TLC's *Red Light Special* came on. Ruby, filled with mischief, told him to sit. Darrell obeyed, watching as she stepped to the center of the bedroom floor. She closed her eyes, tuning into the sensual music. When she opened them again, pure desire gleamed in her gaze.

She began to dance. Her hips swayed, her hands glided over her body, and her eyes never left his. She moved like a woman who knew exactly what she wanted and planned to devour it.

Ruby reached behind her and unsnapped her bra. Tossing it at him, she freed her 34D breasts. Darrell caught the bra, but his eyes stayed glued to her. His cock throbbed painfully, hard as steel.

I think I love her, he thought, mesmerized.

Ruby hooked her thumbs into her pantyhose and panties, tugging them down while kicking off her pumps. She stood, bare and unashamed, continuing her seductive dance. The slow turn she did broke Darrell's restraint. He jumped up and claimed her.

Dropping his boxer briefs, Darrell revealed himself. Ruby's mouth watered at the sight.

"You are so damn beautiful, Ruby," Darrell said, pulling her into his arms.

In his embrace, Ruby felt wanted and cherished. She marveled at how they'd only just met at a Gyro restaurant, yet here she was, sure she'd found her equal.

"Thank you, baby," she said, blushing. Her body was drenched with need. "You, my delicious chocolate king, are the most handsome man alive."

"Why, thank you, ma'lady. Now, let's make some beautiful love, because you got me feenin' for you so bad I'm about to go blind."

Donell Jones's *"I'm Gonna Be"* started playing.

"Make love to me, then, Darrell. I want you so bad."

He scooped her up and laid her down on the bed.

"Wait . . . I need to tell you something," Ruby said as he began kissing her breasts.

"Tell me, baby," he murmured, his lips finding her left nipple.

Ruby moaned. "Mmmm . . . Darrell, I . . ." She arched off the bed. "I'm . . . I'm a v-virgin."

Darrell froze. He released her breasts and looked her in the eyes.

"Oh . . . oh." He paused, stunned.

Ruby's anxiety spiked. Did this change things?

"I'm sorry. I should've told you," she said.

"There's no need to apologize, baby. You didn't do anything wrong. I'm just shocked that a woman as beautiful as you is still . . . untouched. Have you ever experienced . . . anything?"

She shook her head. "No."

"Okay. Well, you're about to."

Ruby smiled, her nerves easing. "I'm ready for you, Darrell. Just . . . give it to me. Make me your woman for real."

Darrell grinned with admiration. "I'm glad you told me."

"Why?"

"Because I was about to go apeshit on you."

Ruby laughed. "It's not like you can't."

"Naw, baby. Your first time should be slow and sensual. The second time is for wild and crazy."

"Mmm." Ruby kissed him. "So which time do I get to give my man head for the first time?"

"After I taste you," he said. "And then I'll give you the woo."

Ruby laughed again. "Woo me, then. I'm ready."

Darrell moved back to her breasts, teasing her. He sucked on her right nipple while his hand slid down to her core, playing with her clit. Ruby felt like she was on fire.

He kissed down to her stomach, then her thighs. Parting her legs, he marveled at her glistening folds. "Bottoms up, baby. Here comes the woo."

He dove in, licking and kissing her with dedication. Ruby trembled and moaned softly, her head spinning out of control.

When Darrell sucked on her clit, she almost lost her mind. "Oh my God, Darrell! Whoa!"

He worked her love button expertly, determined to make her first time unforgettable. Swirling his tongue, he felt her legs shaking.

"OOOHHH! DARRELL!" Ruby cried out, climaxing hard. "HOLY SHIT!"

Darrell lifted his head, laughing. "I guess I don't need to ask if you liked it."

"That was amazing!"

"There's more," Darrell said.

He rolled over to the nightstand, grabbed a box of Trojans, and sheathed himself.

"You ready?"

"Yes. More than ready," Ruby said, opening her legs. "The kitchen is open for business, zaddy."

Darrell chuckled as he positioned himself. Slowly, he slid inside her. Ruby winced, but the pleasure outweighed the pain.

"Are you okay, baby?"

"Yes . . . keep going . . . please," Ruby begged.

Darrell took his time with her. Once he'd broken through her virginity, Ruby's freak-mode came out of her. She wrapped her legs around him and pleaded for him to put it on her. He was more than ready to do so.

CHAPTER 24

Katrina, Ruby and Whitney woke up to delicious breakfasts in bed the following morning. Their loving men had gone the distance to wake their women up with their skillful cooking. Each man silently vowed to always show appreciation for the queens in their lives. They'd gladly become their personal servants if it meant seeing their smiles.

Darrell made love to Ruby again—this time, even better than the night before. After going three rounds back-to-back, Ruby was overcome with so much emotion that she cried tears of joy.

Jeff took his red-headed queen to heights that rivaled the Overlook. He filled Katrina with such bliss that she was convinced no other woman alive reached as many climaxes in one sex session as she had.

Whitney's head spun as Calvin loved her like a giant version of the Energizer Bunny. She was astounded by how high his sex drive was, but no less turned on by how much he loved making love to her.

●●●

After showering, Ruby and Darrell got dressed for the day. Ruby slipped into a new red *FeFe* turtleneck sweater and shiny, red, latex-like skinny Rag & Bone pants. On her feet, she rocked red suede thigh-high Chanel boots. She pulled her hair into a high ponytail, gelled down her baby hairs, then spritzed herself with peaches-n-cream body mist.

Darrell chose a green Ralph Lauren polo shirt with an orange horse-and-rider logo on the left chest, paired with khaki Ralph Lauren cargo pants and a matching khaki beanie. On his feet, he wore fresh wheat Timberlands. He added a long white-gold chain and a white-gold Rolex. After brushing oil sheen into his waves and rubbing on some Versace cologne, he grabbed his wallet and Range Rover key fob. With Ruby by his side, the two headed for the elevator to go down to the lobby.

•••

Katrina slid into a form-fitting, purple-and-white striped *FeFe* maxi-dress with slits up both sides, reaching all the way down to her ankles. On her feet, she wore fresh footie socks and new white Gucci sneakers with purple shell toes and Looney Tunes characters on the sides. She topped off the look with a purple Gucci mesh trucker hat featuring Donald Duck.

Jeff dressed in a black and charcoal-gray long-sleeved Louis Vuitton sweater with black Louis Vuitton jeans. He paired the outfit with low-top Louis Vuitton shell-toe sneakers that matched his sweater. A black ceramic Cartier watch and a dab of cologne completed his look. Grabbing the key to his Trackhawk, he turned to Katrina.

"Ready, bae?" he asked.

"Not yet," she told him, walking up with a mischievous glint in her eyes. "I got something I need to do before we go."

"What's that?" Jeff asked, his smile widening as he caught her vibe.

Katrina stopped in front of him, smiled seductively, and undid his pants. She freed his tool and dropped to her knees.

"Oh . . . I see," Jeff groaned as her warm mouth enveloped him. "Do ya' thang, then, baby . . . wooo! Goddamn!"

Katrina deep-throated him with ease, going so far that her tongue flicked his sack. Jeff's eyes rolled back as she went crazy on him, using both hands to jerk his shaft while she sucked. In just six minutes, he exploded so hard that his knees almost buckled.

"HOLY MOTHER OF GOD! GODDAMMIT, GODDAMMIT, GODDAMMIT!" he shouted as she milked him dry.

Katrina swallowed every drop, then stood up, pulled his pants up, and tucked him back in.

"Now, I'm ready to go, babe," she said with a grin, taking the key fob from his hand. "*I'll* drive, by the way."

Rendered speechless, Jeff could only nod.

Katrina giggled and walked off. Jeff's eyes immediately dropped to her big, round booty, watching as her cheeks bounced with each step.

●●●

The mixture of Whitney's giggling and moaning was music to Calvin's ears as he hit her with his XXX-rated oral skills. Her hands were planted firmly on the crème-colored marble top of the kitchen island. She was bent over, reveling in the feeling of his tongue in her butt.

"Calvin! Oh my God, you are so nasty!" Whitney cried out, her voice filled with bliss as his tongue swirled around. "Haaahaaa! Oooooo! Oh my G-G-God! Haaahaaahhh . . . Mmmmmmmmm . . . GOD!"

The moment Whitney entered the kitchen dressed like the sexy boss chick she was—in a tight white ribbed Chanel turtleneck sweater, a snug, coffee-brown leather Chanel mini-skirt, nude fishnet pantyhose, and white six-inch Rene Caovilla pointed-toe pumps—Calvin couldn't resist getting another taste of her.

Whitney held on tight as Calvin's tongue traveled from her ass to her gooch. He knew the space between her anus and vagina was her sweet spot. The second his tongue hit it, her cries of ecstasy grew louder, sounding like the roar of a crowd when the underdog team made a miraculous comeback.

Calvin worked his way back to her asshole, slipping his tongue inside her sphincter. He repeatedly thrust it in and out, tongue-fucking her as if it were her pussy. Whitney squeezed her eyes shut and cried out, consumed by pleasure.

Minutes later, Whitney exploded, erupting like a volcano. Calvin slurped her clean, savoring every drop of her juices.

"Good God, Calvin!" Whitney gasped, as Calvin gave her ass a playful smack. "Why are you such a booty freak?"

He laughed as he stood up. "Because I love booty—your booty. And I'm not afraid to get nasty to please my woman."

Without another word, he spun her around. Knowing exactly what he wanted, Whitney fell into sync with him. Calvin picked her up and sat her on the counter. He stepped between her legs and slid inside her. Whitney's eyes rolled to the back of her head. His did too. They went at it right there on the counter.

"Calvin! Oh, God, baby! Yes! I love it! I love it, baby!" Whitney cried out as he hung her legs over his shoulders and pounded into her like a jackhammer breaking concrete.

Calvin grunted and cursed, feeling her walls clench around him. She was so wet, tight, and warm he swore he could live inside her forever.

Whitney came again, drenching him. He took her off the counter, placed her on her feet, and turned her around. She braced herself on the countertop as he entered her from behind. Calvin laid it down so good that in just seven minutes, she exploded again. Once he reached his climax, Whitney gave him a grand finale. Dropping to her knees, she took him into her mouth, letting him face-fuck her until his cum oozed down her throat. She swallowed every drop, savoring the taste of her man. The freedom to be this nasty and dirty with each other turned her on more than anything.

"Good God almighty," Calvin panted, out of breath.

He took her hand and pulled her up from the floor. He was still astounded that she was finally his in every way. Whitney saw it in his eyes and felt the same.

Calvin helped her adjust her tiny white La Perla thong, which was swallowed up in the crack of her ass, then pulled her pantyhose back up. He straightened her skirt and turned her around to face him.

With a shy smile, Whitney said, "You're nasty."

"So?" He chuckled, shrugging his broad shoulders.

Whitney mustered up the courage to look him in the eyes. She smiled, feeling warm and fuzzy all over. He was just too damn fine in his Tom Ford polo shirt, Tom Ford jeans, and leather Giuseppe Zanotti design zipper sneakers. He was the epitome of Black perfection.

"Make sure you stay like that, okay?" she requested.

"Oh, you definitely don't have to tell me." Calvin grinned. "I made a personal oath to keep it super-hot, erotic, and spontaneous while I please my sexy, beautiful boss lady." He paused and leaned close to her ear, dropping his tone so deep that Whitney felt it between her legs. "And I'll be there to catch her when her legs give out from cumming so hard."

His words made Whitney's lips tremble. Her entire body burned with heat. She felt like the only way to avoid melting into a puddle would be to crawl inside the freezer.

"You are . . . too much, baby," she managed to say, just as Gucci and Dior came running into the kitchen with goose-down feathers stuck to their faces.

"Aww, come on, maaan. I know y'all ain't up there tearing up my pillows, yo," Calvin said, eyeing his pups, who both looked guilty—and amused.

Whitney couldn't help but laugh at the goofy Bulldogs. They were too cute for their own good.

"After we go see Onika, can we come back and take them to a park?" Whitney asked.

"Sure. They can tear up tree branches or whatever instead of my expensive pillows and blankets." Calvin shot the pups a warning look. They took off running upstairs, barking the whole way. Whitney laughed again.

"Let's go check on baby girl," Calvin said, grabbing the key fob to his AMG truck.

"Let's," Whitney agreed, silently praying Onika would wake up—when they got there—as they headed out of the house.

●●●

3 Weeks Later—

Spending so many days at the ICU, everyone had grown much closer to each other. Whitney, Katrina, and Ruby had gotten to know Bruce better and saw how deeply he cared for Onika. The men supported the ladies while also ensuring there wouldn't be any hospital care bills left unpaid. Bruce shared the story of his life, and once he earned their trust, they allowed him to visit Onika without them being present. Not a single day went by that Bruce didn't spend countless hours by her side.

In the first week of November, during Onika's fourth week in a coma, the three couples met Bruce in the parking lot. He held a gift bag with a stuffed teddy bear clutching a heart and a bouquet of roses. The gifts instantly made Whitney, Katrina, and Ruby smile. They began to realize Bruce's feelings for Onika went far beyond mere concern. The fellas were warming up to him more, but, being aware that snakes came in all shapes, sizes, and colors—and knowing some were masters at faking sincerity—they still kept a watchful eye on him.

Inside Onika's room, the doctor overseeing her care explained her latest condition.

"The swelling in her brain has gone down significantly, and through scans, we can see she's thinking." He explained that a specific part of her brain showed activity on the CAT scan. He went on to say it was likely she could hear them and might be close to waking up. "It is now safe to say that your sister is out of the woods," the doctor concluded.

Elated, all seven of them cheered. The ladies teared up and thanked the Man above for His grace, while the men dapped each other up, embracing like the Steelers had won another Super Bowl.

"But," the doctor said, drawing their attention back to him, "I still want her resting. I don't need her stressed in any way—no adrenaline from celebration, nor recollection of the trauma she endured. Her body needs significant healing, and her mental state will be fragile for a while."

"Oh, that's normal, doc," joked Katrina, drawing a chuckle from everyone.

"I . . . heard . . . that . . . red . . . head . . . wanch."

"ONIKA!" Whitney shrieked, realizing Onika had just come out of her coma.

All seven of them turned and saw Onika's eyes fluttering before they finally opened.

"SIS!" Ruby ran to her side and grabbed her hand. "Oh my God! You're awake!"

Katrina and Whitney crowded her other side, tears of joy streaming down their faces. The men stood back, trying— and failing—to hold back their own tears. Bruce silently thanked God, his eyes welling as his emotions threatened to break free.

"Baby girl! I'm so happy you're back! Don't you ever do that again!" Whitney exclaimed, tears pouring down her face.

A weak smile formed on Onika's dry lips. "I'll try," she croaked.

Katrina grabbed a Pedialyte drink from the mini-fridge, opened it, and held it to Onika's lips. The cool liquid soothed her parched throat, making it a little easier to talk.

"Ain't no tryin', baby girl," Calvin said as Onika sipped. He nodded at Darrell to get the doctor, then continued. "We're all family. We lean on each other when times get rough. Nobody judges, nobody shames; we love and cherish each other. Right, everybody?"

"Right!" they all said in unison.

Onika noticed Bruce then. Her eyebrows furrowed. "Why . . . is . . . he here?"

The doctor walked in just then, Darrell following behind. "Good to have you back, Ms. Temple." He was happy to see such love and support surrounding her. "How are you feeling?" he asked, stepping to the side of her bed with his stethoscope around his neck.

Still eyeing Bruce, Onika answered, "Beat up."

"Well, you will heal. That's a promise I'm comfortable making. You've got a lot of love and support from these wonderful family members of yours—and this very big man too. Cherish that. I need to run some tests, so I'll get Nurse Hornezes."

With that, the doctor left.

"He's been coming here every day," Whitney whispered to Onika, noting the conflict in her sister's eyes. "He really cares for you. Don't brush him off."

Bruce met Onika's gaze but didn't speak. He silently vowed to wait on her hand and foot, helping in any way she needed. All he wanted was to show her how much he loved her.

"You look like hell took over," Katrina said, noting the bandages and casts covering Onika's battered body. Her swollen, bruised face, broken arm and leg, and rib brace made her almost unrecognizable. Both eyes were blood-red from burst vessels. "But you're still so beautiful," Katrina added with a warm smile.

Onika twisted her lip. "If I could move, I'd muff you."

Everyone burst out laughing.

"Still feisty," Darrell chuckled, holding Ruby by the waist.

Onika turned to them, her lips curving into a knowing smile. "You two had sex," she said, looking at Ruby.

Ruby gasped. Whitney and Katrina shot her looks. Calvin and Jeff turned to Darrell.

"Ruby!" Whitney scolded. "Y'all better have used protection!"

"We . . . um . . . did," Ruby replied with a shy smile. "A lot of it."

Darrell ducked behind Ruby, trying to hide.

"No wonder you're glowing like that," Katrina teased, leaning against Jeff's chest as he rested his chin on her shoulder.

"Don't encourage her, Trina!" Whitney snapped. "She needs to focus on her job and court! She's lucky her boss allowed her to push back her start date and the judge postponed court because of this."

"I'm good, Whitney," Ruby promised. "The love in my life now isn't worth losing. I care about Darrell, and he cares about me. It felt like the right time . . . to make love all over the place."

Darrell sank lower.

Katrina burst out laughing. "Get 'im, guuuurl! Heeey!"

Whitney shook her head. "Just be responsible. Please. And stop hiding, Darrell! You're way bigger than her, so you look silly!"

Calvin, Jeff, and Bruce laughed as Darrell stood up, looking sheepish.

"I promise we'll be responsible," he told Whitney, resting his chin on Ruby's head.

Ruby reached behind her to stroke his chin, smiling like a woman crazy in love.

The doctor returned with Nurse Hornezes. "Alright, Ms. Temple. We're taking you for another CAT scan and MRI. I'd like to run more tests before giving your family any updates, okay?"

Weakly, Onika nodded.

"We'll be here when you get back," Ruby said.

"Y'all better be," Onika replied as she was wheeled out, casting one last look at Bruce.

CHAPTER 25

A couple of hours later, Onika was brought back with good news about her condition. She had a concussion, which could last for a few hours, days, weeks, months, years, or even forever. Her broken ribs and bones would heal with time. However, what Whitney, the ladies, and the men were more concerned about was Onika's mental recovery. She had become the victim of one of the most horrific acts a human being could endure.

The doctor wanted her to rest, so he allowed the seven of them to stay just ten more minutes before asking them to leave.

Bruce stayed back for a moment. He stepped up to Onika's bedside and looked at her.

"I'm so sorry, Onika," he told her. "I feel so much guilt about this. If I had just been more of a friend instead of someone who seemed like he was trying to control you, maybe you wouldn't be here."

Onika didn't know what to say. As she looked up into Bruce's eyes, she started feeling something she never thought she could for a man who wasn't pulling in six figures or more. She admired Bruce. Over the past few weeks, she had gotten to know him better. He was a good guy—kind, patient, and sincere. As time passed, Onika couldn't help but notice how handsome he was. His infectious smile made her smile, and he was actually funny. When she heard about his plans to start his own business and help young women avoid what she had endured—or help those who had already suffered—her respect for him grew, flourishing like grass after a summer rain.

"I know you need time to let me in—if you ever will—but I swear I'll show you I'm a good guy to have in your life," Bruce told her. "I'll be back. The doctors and nurses have my number in case you need anything."

He leaned down and kissed her forehead, then gave her a warm smile before heading out, leaving Onika completely astounded.

●●●

Calvin drove back to the house and got his pups. Whitney was just as excited as Gucci and Dior to be going to the park. Calvin packed little go-bags of treats and water while Whitney put the pups in their soft cotton harnesses and leashes. Once they got Gucci and Dior up into the Mercedes truck, they headed off to meet Katrina and Jeff at Frick Park out in the Point Breeze area.

●●●

Darrell parked his Range Rover behind the new maroon Cadillac Escalade. Bagz sat behind the wheel, with his wife in the passenger seat. They were waiting for Darrell and Ruby in the parking lot of a 13,000-square-foot building on Verona Road. It was on the back side of Penn Hills, near a Dairy Queen. The building was formerly a strip club that had shut down due to excessive drug activity. Bagz was waiting for his business partner to arrive so they could meet with the real estate agent, who was showing them the building. It was up for sale by the owner, who wanted nothing more to do with it. The asking price was a steal.

Seeing Ericka, Ruby smiled, happy to have a girl to hang with while the men handled business. They all got out of the SUVs and greeted each other with hugs and daps.

Bagz, his dreads freshly re-twisted, was swagged out in Balenciaga from head to toe, diamond studs in his ears, and a Ferrari Hublot on his wrist. His beautiful Arabic-Latina wife rocked a sexy black-and-white flower-printed *FeFe* wrap dress with black suede knee-high *FeFe* stiletto boots. Her hair was styled in a sophisticated bun, and big *FeFe* earrings dangled from her ears, shining like the necklace around her neck. She carried a black alligator-skin *FeFe* tote bag that was more popular than the latest Chanel bags.

The real estate agent pulled up a minute later in a black Audi SUV. She stepped out, dressed in an Armani business pantsuit with heels, her hair in a bun, and a cheerful smile on her face.

"Hi, everyone!" the milky-white Italian woman greeted. "My name's Emma, and I'll be showing you this beautiful, dirt-cheap property today!"

Darrell and Bagz introduced themselves, then their ladies. They all shook Emma's hand.

"Okay! Let's head inside and check out this place!" Emma said with spunk.

"We're right behind you, Emma," Darrell said.

Emma grabbed a leather briefcase from her SUV, then unlocked the front doors of the establishment and led them inside.

●●●

"They are just too cute, man!" Katrina said, sitting on Jeff's lap in the park. She, Whitney, Calvin, and Jeff watched Gucci and Dior go wild with a tree branch in the children's play area of Frick Park.

Gucci, the bigger and stronger alpha male, dragged his little brother around, but Dior wasn't a punk. The smaller

Bulldog pup had heart and determination. He outsmarted his big brother by pretending to let go of the branch. Gucci dropped it for a second to adjust his bite, but as soon as the branch hit the grass, Dior snatched it up and took off running. Whitney and Katrina awed at the scene while Calvin and Jeff laughed their asses off.

"Why don't I have a puppy?" Katrina asked Jeff.

"Because a Chihuahua isn't a real dog," he replied, earning himself a face-muff from Katrina and laughs from Whitney and Calvin.

"I never said I wanted no lil' apple-head Chihuahua, Jeffrey. I want a Boston Terrier," Katrina corrected him.

"Heeeelll no! Them dogs are weird, yo!" Jeff exclaimed. "With them big-ass eyes that just stare at you! No!" He stomped his foot to emphasize his disgust.

"I didn't ask for your permission. I can buy my own puppy, wit'cha punk-ass," Katrina snapped at her man.

"Get one of those French Bulldogs," Whitney suggested, watching Dior shake Gucci like Christian McCaffrey running through defenders.

"Those are too expensive, sis," Katrina replied. "I'm not payin' five grand for a dog."

"Ya man will buy you any dog you want," Jeff said, patting her thigh. "But I'm not getting no punk-ass yipper."

The ladies laughed at him.

"What about a Doberman Pinscher?" Calvin suggested.

"OO! How about a Rottweiler!" Katrina shouted, her eyes lighting up.

Jeff thought it over and nodded. "Now that's a good dog. And I know some brothers with a real prestigious breeding and training business specializing in purebred Rottweilers. I can give my mans a call right now," he said, pulling out his iPhone.

Gucci, tired of trying to catch his little brother, plopped down on his belly. Dior teased him by running circles around him with the branch, flailing his head around and hitting

Gucci in the process. Laughing, Whitney scooped Gucci up, and Dior followed, still carrying the branch.

She sat down with Gucci on her lap and cradled him like a baby. Calvin smiled at how happy Whitney looked. Knowing her for twenty years and now finally being with her had him feeling conflicted. He was in love with her, but would she believe him if he told her? He just wanted to give Whitney the unconditional love she deserved.

"Yessiir!" said Jeff's childhood friend, City, when he picked up the phone. "I got a litter due any day now, another litter that's a month old, and one that's three months old and ready to leave momma whenever. Those pups are already temperament-tested and trained for standard obedience. You and your lady are welcome to swing by anytime, Jeff."

"Cool. Thanks, City. We'll be on our way in a few," Jeff said.

"Period. See you soon, cutty," City replied, then hung up.

Jeff set his phone down and patted Katrina's thigh. "Got some good news, lovely lady. My mans got three picks of litters for us. We can head out to West Miff' right now if you ready."

"West Mifflin? You talkin' about that Royce K9 spot, up on Route 885?" Calvin asked.

Jeff nodded. "Right across from the Port Authority bus garage and that GetGo station."

"Yeah, yup. I been knowin' the Royce Boyz for a real long time," Calvin said. "They used to be on that Steel City Mafia time real heavy; them, two Dominican dudes, and a white girl."

"Her name's Lacey," Jeff said. "Aye, so you gotta know Perry then, right? He the youngest, but bro like six-foot-five or somethin'."

"I met him before. He owns a dump truck company that runs out of Oakmont," Calvin replied. "The youngin' is gettin' serious money around Pittsburgh."

"Indeed, he is. His homeboy Macho has an older brother they call Tool. Tool's the one who put me onto towing and recovery. He's in the same business, but he's got damn near twenty different locations all over the East Coast."

Calvin nodded. "They're the Valdez boys, right? Macho and Tool?"

Jeff nodded again. "Yep. Them dudes ain't no joke, Calvin. Billionaires, plain and simple. You know Perry's wife is the creator of that *FeFe* clothing line?"

"WHAT!" Katrina shouted.

Whitney's eyes widened. "Hold on . . . you two know the woman that started FeFe Couture? Personally?"

"Not personally," Calvin said. "Just in a round-about way. Her husband and his people, yo . . . they were . . . how should I say it?"

"The Steel City Mafia," Jeff suggested.

Calvin nodded. "Period. That says it all."

"She's agreed to let me showcase her new men's fashion line in my magazine," Whitney said. "I've seen her designs and that girl is dope!"

"She is. She gon' take over the fashion industry completely one day," Katrina added. "I'm beyond proud to see a Black woman's ideas being marketed and sold all over the world."

"We need more of that. Wait and see what I have in store for Ruby," Whitney said with a glint in her eye. "Tyra Banks, Naomi Campbell, and Kylie Jenner are going to beg to meet Ruby, yo!"

Laughter erupted at Whitney's determined look. They knew Whitney was cooking up something good for Ruby. But they didn't know she had more plans in mind for them all.

"Let's just hope we can keep her from going to prison," Katrina said, bringing up Ruby's pending court cases.

"She's good," Calvin said.

They all looked at him quizzically.

"What does that mean?" Whitney asked.

He grinned as Dior stood up on his hind legs, barking to be picked up.

"It means, Ruby is good. It's handled," he said.

"O…kay," Whitney replied, really wanting to ask what that meant but trusting Calvin's word.

"Aww! I love this freakin' dog, yo!" she said as Gucci snored on her lap.

Calvin picked Dior up and gave him a belly rub that made his little legs kick.

"Well, we gon' go ahead and scoot," Jeff said, patting Katrina's thigh. "Let's get outta here, red-head girl."

After hugs and daps, Jeff and Katrina headed to their Trackhawk.

A little while later, two muscular Black men in long-sleeved shirts, bullet-proof vests, jeans, and running shoes walked up to Calvin and Whitney. On instinct, Gucci and Dior stood in front of them, growling.

"Afternoon, officers," Calvin said with a goofy smirk.

The bald cop chuckled. "What's good, big cutty?"

Gucci barked when the man dapped up Calvin.

"Gucci! Relax!" Calvin commanded.

The other officer stood quietly.

Whitney could tell they were cops, but she was puzzled about why they were here.

"What's up, Smooth?" Calvin asked.

Smooth handed him a phone. Calvin's eyebrows furrowed as he looked at it.

"Is that . . ." Whitney began.

"Yep," Calvin said, handing her the phone.

She shook her head after one glance.

"What's the move, big man?" the bald cop asked.

"Keep them clowns on ice," Calvin said. "Baby girl came up outta the coma today."

"We heard. Allahu Akbar," Smooth said. "Get at us when she's ready, my brother."

"I surely will. Thank you both," Calvin said.

The officers nodded at Whitney and left.

"Um . . . baby? What's going on?" Whitney asked.

Calvin grinned. "Justice is sometimes best served . . . cold."

Now Whitney was completely lost.

CHAPTER 26

"Oohh . . . damn! Whoa! Holy shit, Ruby!" Darrell groaned, his head thrown back as Ruby went wild on him, giving him an explicit congratulatory present for the successful deal on the new building.

Leaning back in the front seat of his Range Rover, parked in the newly acquired building's lot, Darrell's toes curled up as Ruby deep-throated him like a pro. Despite it being her first time performing oral sex the night before, she had perfected it. Ruby loved the way he groaned and how his face contorted with pleasure.

On her knees in the seat, her round booty tooted up in the air, Ruby's head bobbed up and down in his lap. She pretended she was Pinky in the porn flick she'd watched for pointers while Darrell was sleeping the night before.

Ruby was shameless in her performance—not because the windows were so tinted or because Bagz and his wife were parked a few hundred feet away, but because she was proud of her man and wanted him to feel how proud she was. And one way to show it was to give him the best head ever, all while he gripped and smacked her juicy curves.

Up in the Cadillac, Bagz was also receiving a congratulatory present from his wife, and judging by the way the Escalade shook, Darrell knew they were going crazy up there too.

Earlier, the real estate agent had brought the keys, the deed, and left with a check for $55,000 from Real Entertainment,

LLC. Darrell and Bagz had plans to renovate the place into a multi-purpose party venue. Seeing the vision, Ruby was as excited as Ericka.

●●●

"Goddamn, Ruby! Wooo! You k-k-killin' me! Shit!" Darrell cursed again.

The engine idled, music playing softly. Adina Howard's *"Freak Like Me"* crooned through the speakers, setting the perfect freaky vibe. Ruby let her inner freak run free and was going for the high score.

"Aaarrghhh . . . shit! I'm about to 'buss!'"

Darrell's back arched as he felt his release approaching. Ruby felt his cock spasming in her mouth, so she turned it up a notch. She used one hand to jerk his shaft while sucking him all the way to the edge. Seconds later, he exploded. Ruby drained him, swallowing every drop before holding him in her hand and looking up with a seductive smile.

"Congratulations, baby," she purred, planting a kiss on his tip.

Darrell felt drained beyond belief. He didn't even have the strength to tuck himself back into his jeans.

Ruby burst out laughing at him.

"It's not funny, yo," Darrell said, though he couldn't help but laugh too. "I can't even move right now. What the hell did you just do to me, girl?"

Sitting back in her seat, Ruby grinned. "I just hit ya' fine-ass with the WOO WOOOO!" she shouted, laughing hysterically.

Darrell laughed so hard his eyes filled with tears. "Wow. Bae, you's a nut, yo. Real rap."

"Oh, you wanna buss another one?" she teased, reaching for him again.

"NO! HOLD UP!" Darrell jumped away, quickly tucking himself back in and zipping up his pants. "I gotta be able to drive, yo! I can't do that if I'm blind!"

Ruby screamed with laughter.

Just then, the Cadillac started up. They looked ahead as Bagz's brake lights flashed before he peeled out of the lot, leaving a trail of rubber and smoke.

"The hell?" Darrell reached for his dashboard screen and called Bagz.

"What up, cutty?" Bagz answered after three rings.

"Aye, yo, you good?" Darrell asked.

"Most definitely. Why you ask?"

"Because you just pulled off like 5-0 was about to swoop in."

"Oh . . . naw . . ." Bagz's Escalade engine roared in the background. "Me and the wife… we gots to get home…right now," he chuckled.

"Oh . . . gotcha, bro. Y'all be safe. See you later, yo."

"Yessiir! Get at me, cutty!" Bagz said, ending the call.

Darrell looked over at Ruby, who was eyeing him hard. "Where you wanna go now, bae?" he asked.

She licked her lips seductively. "To the *top* of the world, so I can try to make you go blind."

●●●

Katrina gasped as she held her new three-and-a-half-month-old male German Rottweiler pup. The beefy little thing had a shiny black coat, and Katrina fell in love the moment he trotted up to her. His puppy dog eyes melted her heart as he looked up at her, practically begging to be picked up. Jeff's friend, City, and his wife, Chardonnay, told Katrina it wasn't the human that chose the pup—it was the pup that chose the human.

Katrina named him Chi-Town, and Jeff loved it. He paid $15,000 for the Von Ruelmann-bloodline pup—a major discount, as Royce K9 didn't sell any dogs for less than $30,000. Chi-Town had already been microchipped, had his shots, and was fully ready to go.

City's twin brothers gave Katrina a kennel cage and iFeeder food and water bowls that could be controlled by app on an iPhone, while City provided a custom name tag, a leather spiked harness, and a matching collar. She also got a portable fold-out doghouse for when she took her pup to Jeff's place.

After Jeff paid in full, City handed over Chi-Town's pedigree papers, showing an extensive family history that made the pup even more valuable.

Leaving Royce K9, Jeff took Katrina to his towing business in New Kensington. Katrina couldn't help but be impressed by all the trucks—everything from one-tons to huge semi-tow trucks that cost half a million dollars each. His company, Steel City Towing & Recovery, had grown into a major business.

The half-acre property also had a big garage with twelve service bays, all occupied with vehicles being repaired. Jeff had taken his woman and her new pup inside of his office. Katrina had been there before, so she knew most of Jeff's employees, and they knew her. Following him, Katrina was led through a hallway that led a private garage area. When she saw the shiny all-black vehicle parked inside, gleaming under the bright lights, she nodded in approval, smitten with it the instant she saw it. It was when Jeff handed her the key fob that she went ape shit with excitement.

•••

"Oh my God! Oh my God! Jeff! Are you for real?" Katrina exclaimed, struggling to wrap her brain around what was happening.

Jeff had just handed her the fob to a brand-new Dodge Durango Hellcat. The SUV had the meanest, most aggressive look she'd ever seen.

"I'm very for real, baby," Jeff said, smiling. "It's yours—bought and paid for. Already insured and ready to drive."

"Holy shit! Holy shit! I have a Hellcat Durango! I have one! I have one! Oh my God!"

Katrina set Chi-Town down and threw her arms around Jeff, squeezing him so tight he thought she might crack his ribs. But her excitement made him ridiculously happy. He figured she'd love the truck, but her reaction blew him away.

"I take it you like it?" he asked with a chuckle, as Chi-Town jumped up and down with her.

"Like it? I LOVE IT! Thank you so much, Jeff! I can't believe it! These things are like a hundred grand!"

Jeff shrugged. "Price didn't matter; your happiness did. And you are very welcome, my love."

He leaned down to kiss her, tasting the cherry lip gloss on her lips. "Oh, I almost forgot—check out the interior. I think you're really gonna love it."

"I already do love it," Katrina said, pressing the fob to unlock the truck. She opened the driver's door and gasped. "Oh my God! Jeff! Really?"

The custom Chicago Bulls interior stunned her. Black leather with red accents, the front seat headrests were embroidered with the jersey numbers of two champion Bulls players: 23 stitched in red on the driver's seat and 33 on the passenger's. Red carpeting, a red suede ceiling, and a custom carbon-fiber dashboard added to the one-of-a-kind exclusivity. A high-end sound system had also been fabricated so she could blast her favorite tracks as she tore up the streets of the Steel City.

"This is amazing! I cannot believe this!" Tears filled her eyes as she turned to Jeff. "Jeff, I . . . I don't know what to say, baby."

"Say, *'I do,'*" he told her with a big smile.

"Huh? I do what?"

Jeff reached into his pocket, then dropped to one knee, pulling out a little suede box.

"AAAHHHH!" Katrina screamed as realization hit her. "OH, MY GOD!"

Chi-Town, thinking Jeff was playing, started jumping on him.

"Katrina. Baby. I love you more than I can describe with any words that exist. Life with you has color and warmth. Without you, it was bleak and cold. I've been waiting for the right moment, and now feels like the time to show you how much I want to spend the rest of my life with you."

He opened the box to reveal a flawless 3-carat diamond engagement ring, its rock surrounded by sparkling baguettes on a platinum band.

"Katrina Renee Rose, will you make me the happiest man on earth and marry me?"

Tears of joy streamed down Katrina's face as she realized there was nothing she wanted more than to be Mrs. Jeffrey Hawkins.

"I WILL! YEEEESSSS! I WILL MARRY YOU, JEFFREY!" she shouted at the top of her lungs.

Jeff was beyond relieved. Though confident in their love, he hadn't been 100% sure she'd say yes. But Katrina wasn't materialistic. The Hellcat truck and diamond ring didn't win her over—her love for him did. And he loved her just as much.

He slid the ring onto her finger before she yanked him off his knee and threw her arms around his neck. Their kiss was passionate, Katrina nearly melting in his arms.

"The ring is so beautiful, baby," Katrina said, gazing at it when they broke apart.

"Not as beautiful as you, Katrina, but it is pretty dope."

She chuckled as Chi-Town nudged her leg. Scooping him up, she raised him high over her head.

"CHIIIIII-TOOOOOWN! MOMMY AND DADDY ARE GETTING MAAAARRIIIIEEEED!" she sang, kissing him on the nose.

"In a few months, you won't be able to pick him up, you know that, right?" Jeff asked.

"Well, until then, I'ma fly him around like he's my little German astronaut," Katrina replied as Chi-Town licked her face.

Jeff laughed. "Let's hop in your new whip and see how fast it goes."

"Ooooo, you ain't said nothing but a word, baby! Let's go!"

●●●

Darrell swung by the PennDOT driver's licensing facility in Penn Hills to get Ruby a driver's license study guide. Learning that she didn't know how to drive, he offered to teach her. They ended up at a massive parking lot in East Hills for her first driving lesson.

Despite the $115,000 price tag on his SUV, Darrell didn't trip. Ruby, though, was a ball of nerves, terrified of wrecking his vehicle. She stuck to the middle of the lot, driving straight and practicing turns to make a rectangle. Darrell tried not to laugh at how tightly she gripped the leather-and-wood steering wheel, but it was too funny. Ruby eventually laughed it off too, and by the end of the lesson, she was proud of herself—and so was Darrell.

Later that evening, Darrell drove Ruby to Monroeville to meet Whitney and Calvin at a tattoo parlor. Ruby had a tattoo session lined up, and after some persuasion, Whitney was getting her first tattoo.

Ruby's tattoo was a tribute to her parents—a portrait so lifelike it looked like someone had taped a photo to her right arm.

Whitney chose to get her zodiac sign tattooed above her right breast. The initial sting bothered her, but Calvin stayed by her side, holding her hand and massaging it. The artist chatted with her the whole time, keeping her calm.

Suddenly, Ruby screamed at the top of her lungs, startling the tattoo artist.

"WHIT'! TRINA AND JEFF ARE GETTING MARRIED, YO! LOOK!" she shouted, showing Whitney a picture message she'd just opened from Katrina.

Whitney gasped at the photo of Jeff hugging Katrina from behind as they leaned against a clean black SUV. Katrina held up her hand, showing off the rock on her finger. Her smile was as big as the diamond.

"Oh my God! Yes! Baby, look!" Whitney showed Calvin the picture.

"That's what I'm talkin' about. Good job, Jeff," he said, grinning.

Darrell joined the celebration. "Yo, y'all should see if Trina would be down for Bagz and me to throw her an engagement party—no charge. And we can do her wedding too."

"She'd love that, Darrell," Whitney said. "Katrina really deserves this. She's one of the nicest women I've ever known, and I'm so damn excited! God, I'm so blessed to have such great friends." Her eyes welled with tears. "I love my sister so much, man."

"We love her too," Calvin said. "We'll make sure Trina and Jeff have the best wedding and honeymoon ever."

"Most definitely," Darrell agreed, pulling out his phone to hit up Bagz. They had some extravaganzas to plan.

CHAPTER 27

After Whitney's new tattoo was finished, the artist applied skin ointment to reduce swelling wrapped her arm in plastic. Thanking the artist, they all left and headed back to the hospital to see Onika.

To their surprise, when they got to her room, the saw the girl was up on her feet, balancing herself on her crutches while a physical therapy nurse walked beside her. Bruce was there too, cheering for her.

Whitney, Katrina, Ruby, Darrell and Calvin cheered her on as well. Onika made it ten feet away from her bed, then ten feet back.

It was obvious she was still in pain—her broken ribs would be the hardest to deal with since only a body brace and pain meds could help.

Katrina and Jeff showed up soon after. Onika was so happy to see that Katrina was engaged that she actually cried tears of joy. It was something that nobody ever thought would come from the feisty little lady, but as Whitney watched Onika and Katrina hug, she saw something had changed inside of Onika. It seemed to her that both Onika and Ruby's near-death experience had done wonders for their character. Whitney grew even more optimistic about Onika's future at that moment. Seeing her reborn right in front of her eyes brought tears to Whitney's own.

Thank you, God. Thank you so much for sparing my little sister. Thank you for guiding Ruby. And thank you so much for putting such a good man in Katrina's life. She deserves the unconditional love that Jeff has been, and will continue giving her, Whitney thought.

She glanced over at Calvin, who was embracing Jeff with a brotherly hug alongside Darrell.

And thank you for putting such good men in all our lives, God. I promise that we will treat them like the kings they are and forever be their queens, she added to the Man above.

•••

The six of them stayed with Onika for as long as the nurse allowed. They shared ice cream with her, and Whitney showed Onika pictures from Ruby's spontaneous photo shoot. Onika was stunned by how gorgeous Ruby looked.

"You are a very beautiful girl, sis," Onika told Ruby. "I wish I could look like that on camera."

"What makes you think you can't?" Katrina asked.

"Because I might look good on the outside, but inside, I'm ugly," Onika said.

"Hey, hey—naw." Bruce took Onika's hand, making her look at him. "You are beautiful inside and out. Yes, you've had a crazy past, but that doesn't mean your future has to be dark. If you want to be that badass Onika you already are, then just do it, like Nike. And I'll be right there to see you blossom into the rare, beautiful rose that no other woman can be."

"Awww!" the three ladies cooed, their hearts melting at Bruce's heartfelt words.

Onika's eyes filled with tears. His words meant so much to her. Bruce had been a great friend during her time in the ICU. He'd forgiven her for the way she'd treated him. And when he showed up with a Bible, ready to teach her about God, she was stunned. Onika had never even seen a Bible before, but some of the verses and stories touched her so deeply that she felt the darkness inside her being replaced with light.

Calvin, Darrell, and Jeff nodded in approval of Bruce. They'd already started rocking with him when they saw how much he genuinely cared for Onika. Now, they saw him as part of the circle—a brother.

"You just tryna get in my pants, Bruce," Onika said, a tear falling down her cheek.

Whitney gasped while Katrina, Ruby, and the guys all chuckled.

"Onika!" Whitney scolded.

"Well, you aren't wearing any pants right now, Onika," Bruce shot back. "So that can't be true."

They all burst into laughter. Even Onika couldn't help but laugh, though it made her ribs hurt.

"Oww! Stooop, Bruce. Don't make me laugh 'cause it hurts when I do."

"I'm sorry, baby. I can't lie, though—I'ma always make you laugh and smile. But I'll hold off until your ribs are better. Then I'ma make you laugh so hard that you pee on yourself."

They erupted in laughter again. Onika laughed so hard she had to hit the pain med button four times to ease the pain.

"Bruuuuuuuuuuce!" she whined, drifting off into a euphoric state from the pain meds.

"Okay, I quit," Bruce said with a mischievous grin. "For now."

Onika raised an eyebrow. "Asshole."

●●●

With plans for a family gathering, the men decided to cook for the ladies. Bruce was invited, but as expected, he turned it down—he didn't want to leave Onika's side. The nurses had gotten so used to him that they allowed him to stay well past visiting hours.

A couple of hours later, everyone met up at Calvin's house. Katrina brought Chi-Town, who instantly befriended Gucci and Dior. Bagz and his wife, Ericka, also showed up and were formally introduced to everyone. Though Whitney and Katrina were meeting Bagz and Ericka for the first time, they instantly approved and welcomed Ericka into their sisterhood.

●●●

Grilled barbecue chicken, bratwurst, burgers, corn on the cob, baked beans, and greens were served with freshly made cornbread. The men worked their magic, creating plates so delicious the ladies joked about needing to hit the gym afterward. Bagz and Ericka brought desserts—cookie pies with icing decorating the edges.

They all gathered in Calvin's spacious lounge, big enough to accommodate everyone, pups included. Conversations flowed effortlessly, covering topics from sports to business, dreams, and future goals. The fun really kicked off when trivia questions started flying.

"Bet you don't get this one," Calvin said to Jeff, who was proving to be a trivia whiz. "What's the difference between a jaguar and a panther?"

Jeff looked at Calvin like he'd just asked an infant to solve algebra. "Bro, are you serious right now? Come on, man!"

"Yup!" Calvin grinned.

Whitney and the girls looked stumped. Darrell had a guess but held back, thinking it might be a trick question.

"Calvin, a jaguar has spots; a panther is all black!" Jeff declared.

"Dammit!" Calvin cursed. He had really thought Jeff wouldn't get it.

"I knew it!" Darrell said, kicking himself for not speaking up.

Ruby started laughing at him.

"Wow . . . that question was cheesy as hell," Whitney said, side-eyeing Calvin.

"Aye, man, real rap—I am thee king of trivia, player!" Jeff boasted, grabbing his cup of wine and taking a sip. "But I got one for you now, though, my man."

"Bring it on, homeboy," Calvin said, ready for whatever Jeff threw at him.

"What is the main difference between a Bentley and a Rolls-Royce, back in the day?"

"Oh, damn . . . I fold," Whitney said, throwing in the towel immediately.

"I'm not even gon' act like I know that one, Jeff," Bagz said. "And I love Bentleys, yo."

"And I love Rolls-Royces, but there's no way I'll get that right," Ericka added.

"I'm out," Ruby said, glancing at Darrell.

Darrell gave it a shot. "Um . . . their hood emblems?"

"EEEEHHHHH!" Jeff made his own buzzer sound. "Nope!" He looked at Calvin. "Come on, big dog. We waitin' on you."

"Why you ain't ask your fiancée?" Calvin asked, shooting Jeff a look.

"Because she don't know."

Katrina shot Jeff a glare. "How you know I don't know?"

He turned to her. "What's the answer, then?"

She shrugged. "I don't know."

"Exactly! Now hush, punk!"

Katrina smacked her lips and reached over to mush Jeff's face.

"Come on, Calvin. What's the answer?" Jeff pushed, sipping his wine again.

Calvin gave it a go. "A Bentley is for a driver; a Rolls-Royce is for people who want to be chauffeured."

"Oooo. Good answer, bro!" Jeff nodded. "But NO! EEEEEHHHHHH!" He burst into a fit of laughter.

246

"What is it, then, Jeff?" Darrell asked.

Everyone stared at Jeff, waiting.

Jeff finally calmed his laughter. "Bentleys had turbocharged engines; Rolls-Royces didn't."

"Oh . . ." Calvin chuckled, while everyone else groaned or shook their heads.

"A'ight, you got that one, Jeff. It's all good, homeboy."

"Hey! I got one!" Ruby suddenly shouted.

"Let's hear it, baby," Darrell said, patting her back.

"Where is Waka Flocka Flame originally from?" Ruby asked, looking around at everyone's confused expressions.

"Uh . . . he's from Atlanta . . . right?" Katrina guessed.

"Nope! EEEEHHHH!" Ruby busted out laughing.

Jeff laughed too. "GET 'EM, GIRL!"

"He's from somewhere in Georgia," Ericka tried.

"Nope!" Ruby shook her head again.

"New York," Bagz answered casually.

"YES!" Ruby cheered.

"Hey! How did you know that?" Ericka asked.

"I watch that *WTF* show, bae," Bagz said. "Waka and Tammy's show."

"Yooo, they are the dopest couple ever! I love them!" Ruby gushed.

"Okay, okay. I got one for y'all," Whitney said with a mischievous grin. "What ethnicity is the actress, Cameron Diaz?"

"Cuban," Ruby answered immediately.

"Hey! That's not fair, Ruby!" Whitney protested. "You're half Cuban, so of course you'd know. Okay, what about . . . the actress/singer Christina Milian?"

"Cuban," Ruby said again, before anyone else could speak.

"RUBY! SHUSH!"

Everyone burst into laughter. Whitney was frustrated, and Ruby just snickered to herself.

"All right! Last one! Ruby, do not answer!" Whitney warned.

"Okay, sis," Ruby said, giggling.

"The actress . . . Eva Mendes . . . what ethnicity is she?"

Ruby pursed her lips, dying to answer.

"I'm gonna take a wild shot," Calvin said. "But . . . Cuban?"

"DAMMIT!" Whitney groaned.

Ruby burst into uncontrollable laughter, nearly falling out of her seat.

CHAPTER 28

The next day, Jeff and Katrina offered to cook a big Sunday breakfast for everyone. By the time the others arrived at Jeff's, the newly engaged lovebirds already had a feast made and ready to be served.

With a cookbook by Ayesha Curry called *The Seasoned Life*, Katrina and her fiancé went about putting together a couple of the delicious recipes the Jamaican-Chinese-Polish-African American basketball wife had in the book.

Katrina started a pot of Ayesha's "Power Coffee," then chopped up apples that would be added with other ingredients to make "Apple-Cinnamon Oatmeal."

Jeff got to work on the "Honey-Pepper Cast-Iron Biscuits," then together, they made "Smoked Salmon Scramble," which was a recipe of scrambled eggs spiced up with sweet corn, smoked salmon, and cherry tomatoes, all coming together to make the most colorful plate of scrambled eggs ever. They also made Ayesha's "Ham and Cheese Waffles."

By the time Whitney, Calvin, Darrell, and Ruby showed up, the food was ready. They ate and were wowed by the food. Whitney was floored by the cooking and asked, "How the heck did y'all come up with these ideas?" Katrina showed her the cookbook by the famed NBA star's wife.

"Oh, I gots to get me a copy!" Whitney said, pulling out her iPhone and going to Amazon to order one right away.

Once they finished eating, they all hopped into their vehicles and went to see Onika.

●●●

As expected, Bruce was there. He was on his MacBook, sitting in the chair next to Onika, who was watching TV. When the crew walked in, they both lit up with excitement.

Onika's doctor gave her the okay to go outside for a little while, but not for long. It was pretty chilly outside; the middle of November on the East Coast was always frigid.

Whitney wheeled her out with everyone in tow. The men walked behind the ladies. Outside, Bruce filled them all in on what he had been working on as far as building his private security firm. Onika chimed in, letting them know how supportive she was of his plans.

They all nodded in approval, digging Bruce's plan and who he planned to offer services to. He talked about his attempts to create a safe haven for battered women, who may or may not have problems with addiction, and how he kept hitting brick walls because of his former job at the nightclub.

"I know a few people who can help out with that, Bruce," Calvin said.

Bruce nodded. "I'd appreciate it, Cal'. For real. To be honest, I agree with the people who turned me down for funding. Their logic was, if I really cared about women in duress, why would I ever have chosen to be a bouncer at a dirty nightclub? To keep it funky, I don't know; it was just a job at the time."

"Don't let that make you feel like your intentions ain't valid, big homie," Darrell said. "Just 'cause somebody don't approve of what we did in the past and thinks we can't do somethin' better for our future, which could help others, don't mean you give up."

Ruby smiled at the wisdom her man just dropped. She put her arm around him and leaned her head against his shoulder.

"Thanks for that, Darrell," Bruce replied, grateful for the encouragement. "I'ma keep hope alive. If I give up, then there'll be one less person out there to help those in need."

"True," Katrina agreed, knowing a thing or two about being a woman who had come from the trenches. "Your dedication is what's gonna make it happen, Bruce. We got your back."

● ● ●

After spending a few hours with Onika, she was getting tired. They took her back to her room. Bruce helped her back into bed. Before leaving her to get some rest, they all took a family photo. Onika was caught in the flick yawning. Whitney said it should be their "photo of the year."

● ● ●

Ruby was excited for her first day at work. She dressed in a dark blue ribbed turtleneck sweater, khaki-colored leggings, and brown Uggs with furry insides. She put her hair into a ponytail and styled her baby hairs with gel, encircling her face and emphasizing her exotic beauty.

Whitney let her drive the BMW truck, riding in the passenger seat to work. Ruby took her time and proved she was ready to go to the DMV and take her computer test to get her permit.

When she pulled into the parking lot, Whitney wished her luck and reminded her to call if she needed anything. Ruby assured her she'd be okay, then headed inside. Whitney watched her go in, just like a mother watching her fourth-grader on the first day of school. She was so proud of Ruby.

Hopping back into her X7i, she rolled through Monroeville, heading east to get to the parkway. She hopped on 376 and made her way downtown to get to work. She had a lot to do and was excited about it all.

●●●

2 Weeks Later—

Katrina arrived at her job, but instead of wearing her uniform, she was carrying it. Inside, a few of her co-workers greeted her, happy that she'd been granted the opportunity to move on to bigger and better things but sad to see such a vibrant part of the team go.

Shamika, Yvette, and Andrea were all bummed out, but they supported their friend's decision to join forces with her fiancé, helping him run his towing and recovery business.

"You better not go more than a day without calling and texting us, yo," Yvette told her as they hugged it out. "Or we comin' lookin' for ya' red-head ass, girl."

Katrina laughed. "I ain't hard to find, wanch."

Shamika had tears in her eyes. "Who's gon' beat up dope-head inmates with me now that you're leavin' us, Trina?"

"Um . . . the same person that been doin' that with you, which was not me," Katrina replied.

"Oh . . . yeah . . . true." Shamika wiped her eyes, then hugged her friend. "Don't be actin' like a stranger, Chicago."

"Naw, joe. I'll stay in touch. I promise."

Andrea hugged Katrina in a sisterly way, wishing her well. "I can't wait to see you walk down the aisle to your man, Trina. You're going to be so beautiful in your dress."

"Thanks, 'Drea. I hope he thinks so, too."

Just then, a huge heavy-set man with steel-gray hair around the sides but bald up top, wire-rimmed glasses, a pressed white shirt, a gold badge, and a taser in a holster walked into the locker area where the ladies were hugging it out.

"Rose," the big man said, his voice so deep he had to talk loud just to be understood. "I hate to lose such a good officer and a good friend, but I hear your new profession's gonna make you rich."

"Maybe," Katrina said with a curt smile and a shrug. "Hard work is what can make anyone rich, Captain Mara," she added, quoting her fiancé.

"Indeed, though I can't say that goes for us uniform-wearin' folk." The captain gave Katrina a friendly hug then. "You make sure you keep in touch so I know how you're doin'. Yinz better not be afraid to stop in and see me either, ya' hear me?"

"I do, sir. I give you my word that I will," Katrina told him.

"Stay blessed and safe, Officer Rose," Captain Mara said. Then, nodding to the two other officers and his sergeant, the big man took his leave.

Katrina said goodbye once more to her friends, then went and turned in her uniform and badge. After saying goodbye to a few more people, she left the Allegheny County Jail for the last time, feeling relieved she no longer had to see so many Black men and women constantly being locked up, stuck in the revolving door.

Outside, posted next to her Hellcat Durango, Jeff waited for her. He was dressed in jeans, a bright neon-green work shirt with *Hawkins Towing & Recovery* on it, and steel-toe boots. The driver's window was down; Chi-Town stood up on the seat and barked out of the window, seeing his human coming back toward them.

"Well, I am officially no longer a correctional officer, babe," she told her fiancé as she approached him.

Chi-Town got so excited he jumped out the window and hopped all around her. Jeff and Katrina chuckled at the black and brown ball of energy.

"You sure this is what you wanna do, love?" Jeff asked, scooping Chi-Town up into his arms.

Katrina nodded. "Yes. I am." She stood on her tiptoes and gave him a kiss. "Joining your team is what I most definitely want to do, Jeffrey. Black royalty is what I want to be, and with you, baby, we are that. Maybe you can even teach me how to drive a tow truck?" she asked, the idea having once crossed her mind when she went on a call with him.

"Now that's a great idea, my love! Ooo, what I wouldn't give to see you behind the wheel of one of my trucks! WOOO! Sexy!" he shouted. "I might even buy you your own! We can paint it pink, too!"

Katrina busted out laughing. "I do not want a pink tow truck, asshole."

"Okay. Whatever color you choose, baby. Just know, you make me sooo very happy, Katrina. I love ya' red-head ass to death, yo!"

He leaned down and planted a kiss on her forehead. Katrina cheesed up hard.

"Let's get on up outta here," he told her, putting Chi-Town back into the SUV. "Gotta get to the shop and get to work; this'll be our first shift together. How does that make you feel?" he asked, opening the driver's door.

"Whole," she told him, taking his hand and getting behind the wheel. "I feel like I finally have what God has been trying to give me for so long."

"Me, too, baby," Jeff said. "Me, too."

●●●

Days Later—

"Heeey! Look at you!" Whitney entered Onika's bedroom to see her up and moving around on her own, with crutches, of course.

Whitney was happy to see the swelling in Onika's face had gone all the way down, and the discoloration of her skin was fading, letting her natural color come back. She looked like she was refilled with life.

"Hey, sis!" Onika replied, smiling as bright as the sun over Los Angeles in July. "I'm freakin' glad to see you, yo! Real rap!"

Whitney hugged the young girl, careful not to squeeze too tight. "Everything okay, baby girl?"

"Of course. Why you ask that?" Onika looked at her with furrowed brows.

"Well . . . because I can't remember ever seeing you so happy . . . at least . . . not for something that was good."

Onika sighed. She knew exactly what Whitney meant. Even though she had come to terms with how crazy her life had been and had moved on with a change of heart, she still had nightmares about all the close encounters where her life could've ended.

"I could be dead right now, yo. I let my anger and frustration from bein' dissed by a married man drive me to allow two guys to feed me drugs and take advantage of me in a sexual way. They took it *waaay* to the left and tried to kill me. I've been raped before, and beat, but it's like . . . this time, something made me wake up and realize life is not a game. You only live once, ya' know?"

Whitney's heart raced. Those words—if she was honest, she never expected them to come from Onika. But hearing them brought tears of joy to her eyes.

Yes! She gets it! She's saved! Thank you, Lord! Thank you, thank you, thank yooouuu! she thought, rejoicing so much she wanted to run up to the roof and scream it to the Man above at the top of her lungs.

"Wow! Onika! I am so happy to hear you say that, sis!" Whitney couldn't help but want to hug her again. "Yes, you're right, too; there's a reason you're alive. God didn't want you up there with him yet. You have more to do down here on earth." She paused, placing a hand on Onika's shoulder. "And if you'd let us, we'll help you in any way we can. We all love you, Onika."

Tears welled up in Onika's eyes. She nodded. "I love y'all, too, Whit'. I'm so sorry for the way I was wildin' out, yo; bein' so stubborn and crazy. I swear to you, I'm changin' my ways. I will never go back to dancin' again, jumpin' around and searchin' for sugar daddies. I don't need that. I want a good life, and I want love. I want a good man that'll cherish me, treat me like a queen, ya' know? Despite my crazy past, I want one who'll love me unconditionally and let me love him unconditionally."

"Bruce?" Whitney asked.

She saw a smile growing on Onika's face at the mention of his name. That told her everything she needed to know.

"He's a good man. He introduced me to God," Onika told her. "At first, I was like, how the hell does *dude* love me? He ain't never even met me, yo!"

Whitney busted out laughing. "No, you didn't say that, Onika! Are you for real?"

"Yeah. I didn't know he was the one who allowed me to be born, or that he's the reason I survived everything I've been through. But as Bruce taught me more, I realized God is also the reason I have all of you in my life."

"Aww! Onika!" Whitney hugged her again. "Oh my God, I just started loving your crazy little ass even more!"

They talked for a while longer until it was time for Whitney to head out.

"You look nice as hell, by the way," Onika said, nodding in approval of Whitney's outfit.

Whitney struck a sexy pose to show off the new white form-fitting *FeFe* dress with black flower prints all over it. The flowy hem stretched down to just above her knees. Around her midsection, she accessorized it with a red YSL belt with a gold buckle, matching her Tiffany & Co. earrings. Accentuating her legs were sheer black pantyhose with rose prints, and on her feet, she wore red six-inch ankle-strapped Yves Saint Laurent pumps with pointed toes and gold heels. Her hair was styled up like she was going to a beauty pageant, and her makeup was simple: red lipstick and black eyeliner.

"Aww, snap! I dun' got that Gabrielle Union up outta you!" Onika teased, as Whitney did a follow-up twirl, then twerked her perky little booty.

"Guuurl, I'm just showin' off what I'm blessed with," Whitney told her, chuckling.

"I ain't mad at you, big sis. How's the . . . uh . . . the UC?" Onika asked.

"I've actually been flare-up free. Calvin went with me for a check-up, and my doctor said it could take up to a year to put me in remission. I was due for another infusion when I went, so I got that taken care of. I just . . . gotta be careful, but all in all, I feel great!"

"That's what I'm talkin' about, yo. Good shit, sis," Onika said, giving her another hug. "So why you dressed all fancy anyway? Not that you ain't always lookin' fly."

"Well, I'm going to a photo shoot for FeFe's new men's fashion line. She let her husband come up with the name: Steel City Billionaire. I actually like it. The shoot's at a truck dealership in Green Tree. The *FeFe* queen herself and her husband will both be there. I'm excited to meet her. It's crazy how small a world it is. Trina's new pup came from a breeding/training business that's partly owned by the woman's husband and his cousins. You ever heard of this group that called themselves the Steel City Mafia?"

Onika's eyes widened as she gasped. "Hell yeah! Yo, them dudes are rich as hell! And they're so connected it ain't even funny! One of 'em is a female, too! She owned that little club that used to be in Homewood, right on the corner of Kelly Street and Brushton. Crazy thing is, she's a white girl, yo!"

Whitney chuckled. "Well, the woman who started *FeFe* is married to one of the Steel City Mafia guys."

"Wooow! Yo, and you're about to meet her! Maan, I wish I could come! Dammit!"

"Don't worry." Whitney gave her a smile. "There'll be plenty of things for you when you're cleared to leave here. That, I promise you, Onika."

She hugged Onika goodbye, kissed her on the forehead, then headed out, hopping into her BMW truck and making her way to the highway.

●●●

"So, Ruby, how are you liking it?" Gordon asked, stopping by Ruby's assigned section for the day: bedroom furniture.

"It's great, sir. I really like being able to guess the preference in style the customers may have when choosing furniture. It's fun," Ruby told him cheerfully.

"It is, right?" Gordon chuckled to himself.

"I've learned that bright and cheery people go for the light-colored sets, and those who have more of a serious personality like the darker-colored sets, like charcoal, black, and grays."

Gordon's smile grew as he listened to her share her discoveries on the dynamics of providing excellent customer service.

"Wow! Ruby, you're so intelligent, and you learn so fast! Good job! You've already sold five bedroom sets today, and the other day, while you were in kitchen appliances, you sold four stoves, three fridges, and six cabinet fixtures! You're amazing! Soon, you're going to be making checks bigger than mine!"

Ruby chuckled. "Thank you, Mr. Gordon. Eighteen dollars an hour plus commission—I've been really liking what I've been seeing deposited into my bank account."

"I bet. How is everything with court?" he then asked.

"My attorney's been negotiating with the state's attorney; they've been warring with each other. To be honest, the lady wants me in prison. She says just because I'm doing good now doesn't excuse my past. I actually agree, but I'm a changed woman, and I don't feel prison is needed. I got it together without going, so why take away what I've been working hard to build if I'm constantly showing how much I deserve a chance?"

Gordon nodded. "I agree with you one hundred percent. If there's anything I can do—write up a letter of character witness for you, or even show up in court on your behalf—please, let me know, and you have my word I'll do so."

Ruby nodded, grateful for his willingness to help.

Gordon took his leave and left Ruby to it, as a couple entered her area. Like a seasoned saleswoman, Ruby got right on it, walking up to them with a bright smile, ready to get another sale under her belt.

●●●

"Ooowee! We got us a big one, baby! Truck accident on the parkway in Green Tree! Let's roll!" Jeff shouted after getting a call from the Pennsylvania state police department, dispatching his company to a major wreck.

Dressed in a bright orange *Hawkins Towing & Recovery* work shirt with reflective safety stripes on the sleeves, durable ladies' Wrangler jeans, and steel-toed boots, Katrina was ready to go. Chi-Town, wearing his harness, hopped up and down, just as eager.

Jeff called his three main guys on his two-way radio, getting them on point. One of them was already a few minutes out from the wreck site since his job was posting up at sections of the highway with the worst rush hour traffic. Another one of his guys had just pulled into the yard in the five-ton flatbed tow truck he drove.

Hurrying out with Katrina and the dog, Jeff led them to the big garage, which housed four brand-new heavy-duty wreckers. The shiny black Kenworth W990 tow truck was a 50-ton wrecker, capable of towing up to 100,000 pounds. It was basically a tow truck built for hauling big commercial vehicles. It cost Jeff half a million dollars, but with the money he could make clearing wrecks involving big trucks or buses, the truck would pay for itself in a year or less.

●●●

Katrina and her pup hopped up inside the luxurious tow truck while Jeff unhooked the engine block heater and the airline that kept air inside the air tank. This allowed him to start the engine and roll out right away, instead of waiting for air pressure to build up for the air brake system to work.

He opened the tall garage door and hopped up inside. Starting the powerful diesel engine, he clutched the 18-speed transmission into gear, released the brakes, and as the door lifted all the way up, he slowly crept out of the garage.

Katrina had never been in such a big truck before. She'd always been a little scared of them; riding next to big rigs on the road, she'd seen some pretty crazy accidents. But being so high up inside one, she felt invincible.

Jeff reached out to the dashboard and hit a switch. The emergency strobe lights on the truck started flashing brightly, warning people to move out of the way. Katrina saw the guy in the five-ton Freightliner flatbed fall in behind them as they exited the yard. They both put their pedals to the metal, speeding toward the parkway.

CHAPTER 29

30 Minutes Earlier—

Whitney sang along with Rihanna's "YOU DA ONE," which played from an XM radio station for Pittsburgh. She cruised along with the steady flow of traffic on the parkway. Ascending up onto 279 to get out to Green Tree, Whitney got onto a double-decker bridge, crossing over the Monongahela River, going towards a narrow two-lane tunnel.

As soon as she got up onto the bridge, Whitney ran into a traffic jam that slowed to a snail's pace. She cursed under her breath but didn't let herself get upset.

"It's still going to be a great day," she told herself. "The shoot is going to go perfectly; I'm going to meet one of the most talented Black fashion designers to come out of Pittsburgh, and then, go see my handsome man. Nothing is going to ruin this day. *Nothing!*"

●●●

Traffic got even worse once she entered the tunnel. Whitney made it to the middle, and everything came to a dead stop. She took a deep breath, keeping calm. Rolling down her window, she could've sworn she heard sirens coming from the other end of the tunnel.

Just then, her music was interrupted by a traffic news update:

"Afternoon, folks! Everybody traveling west toward Green Tree and beyond, you're gonna wanna grab a Snickers. Sorry to rain on your day, but we've got an accident involving a tractor-trailer and three other vehicles. We've got on-the-scene footage from our traffic cams right now, and I'm looking at it. It's bad, but reports of no casualties or serious injuries are something to be happy about. I'll keep you updated on things."

"Crap!" Whitney groaned as the music started playing again.

Suddenly, her stomach started bubbling up. She sat still for a second, thinking it was nothing. But when the bubbling turned into pressure building inside her like her body was a balloon and her gut was full of baking soda and someone poured vinegar on it, Whitney began to panic.

"Oh God, no, no, no, no, no!" Whitney clenched her teeth and dug the heels of her stilettos into the floorboard, squeezing her legs and rear end closed as tight as she could. "What the hell, man! Please, not now!"

Then, remembering what the man on the radio said about it being a while, Whitney cursed. Her bowels filled with more pressure, threatening to burst. She had never before had to go this bad, this fast.

Stuck in gridlock, bumper-to-bumper, with a pickup truck on her left, the tunnel wall on her right, a bus in front of her, and another car behind her, she was boxed in.

"Dammit!" she squealed, feeling herself seconds away from exploding. "No! Nuh-uh! Not today!"

As fast as she could, she threw it into park, grabbed her purse, and jumped over to the passenger seat. She threw the door open, then opened the back passenger door.

Whitney quickly hiked up her dress, yanked her pantyhose and panties down, and squatted next to her SUV just as her bowels began to evacuate.

● ● ●

State police closed down the parkway's east lanes leading from Green Tree to downtown. Jeff and his man in the flatbed flew through the tunnel up the closed lane, arriving at the scene just outside the other end.

"Oh my God," Katrina gasped as she laid eyes on the horrible sight.

She saw the tractor-trailer, coupled to a long dry-van trailer, jackknifed across the westbound lanes, with all the traffic stuck behind it. The front end of one car was trapped under the middle of the trailer; the second's front end was smashed in from slamming into the rear of the trailer, and the third's rear was crushed from the semi rear-ending it.

Up in the sky, Katrina saw the Channel 11 News helicopter hovering over the scene, filming it to keep viewers informed of the accident and the massive traffic jam it caused.

The driver of the one-ton tow truck, who had been closest to the scene when the call came in, was already hooking up to the car that the semi had hit. The driver of the flatbed moved to get the vehicle behind the trailer. Jeff maneuvered the long Kenworth wrecker past the semi and parked in the lane the semi had been traveling in.

Jeff and Katrina put on gloves and high-visibility vests. Chi-Town stayed inside the cab as they got out. The officer commanding the scene came right over to Jeff, already having quite a rapport with him.

"How long you think you'll need to clear the road and get traffic moving again?" the officer asked.

"Fifteen minutes," Jeff told him.

The trooper's eyes went wide. "Fifteen? Are you serious, Jeff?"

"I am, Trooper Jones. You've got the best recovery company in Pittsburgh on scene. Now let us work so we can get traffic rolling."

●●●

In thirteen minutes, after a second one-ton truck showed up and Jeff had the semi cab pulled straight, the cars were towed away. By minute fifteen, the semi was on the side of the highway, on the shoulder, allowing traffic to roll.

As Jeff hooked chains around the front axle of the tractor, after extending the wrecker's stinger lift under it, the trooper walked up to him with a look of true admiration etched on his face. Katrina, holding a bright sign telling traffic to get over so nobody would ride in the lane where Jeff's legs were sticking out from under the truck, silently cheered her fiancé on.

"Jeff! That was fifteen minutes!" Trooper Jones said, still in disbelief. "Most companies can't even move four cars in thirty minutes when there's an accident like this, guy! Yinz are awesome!"

Finished chaining the truck up so he could tow it safely, Jeff slid back out and stood up.

"Well, when *Hawkins Towing and Recovery* is called in, we don't mess around," he told the man.

"I see. I'll do my damndest to make sure all D.O.T. calls go to *Hawkins*, guy! You've earned that!"

The trooper shook Jeff's hand, then Katrina's, before heading over to his cruiser parked in a turnaround space between the center median.

"Good job, baby," Katrina said as they climbed back up into the wrecker's cab, with an excited Chi-Town.

"Thank you, my love. You think you could do that?" Jeff asked, pushing in the air valve knob on the dash to release air into the semi's air brake system so its wheels would roll freely behind him.

"With your teaching, yes, I think I could."

He clutched into low gear and started rolling. His flatbed driver was behind him, blocking traffic in the granny lane so Jeff could get on the road.

With Chi-Town on her lap, Katrina told Jeff, "You are amazing, Jeffrey," as he shifted gears and put the truck's 600-horsepower Cummins engine to work, gaining the momentum needed to ascend the long upgrade they were about to hit heading into Green Tree, with the 70-foot-long semi adding significant weight to the pull.

"Why, thank you, ma'lady," Jeff said, chuckling. "I ain't gon' lie; I had to show off for my future wife a little bit, 'yah mean?"

She laughed. "Well, keep it up, and you might get some booty in yo' office when we get back."

"Oh yeah!" Jeff reached his left hand up and pulled on the air horn cord, blasting the loud horns excitedly. "WOOOO WOOOO! OFFICE SEX, BABY! YEEAAH!"

●●●

Whitney nearly jumped out of her skin when the big tow truck next to her suddenly blasted its loud horn.

"What in the hell is wrong with him?" she asked herself, then mashed the gas to get away from the crazy tow trucker.

Seconds after pulling far ahead, her music cut off, and a call from Katrina came in.

"Heeey, guuuurl!" Whitney answered, happy for the call and even happier that she hadn't ruined her outfit—though somebody would be pretty ticked off when they discovered stuff on their tires.

"Girl, why is you speedin' like that?" Katrina asked.

Whitney looked puzzled. She checked her mirrors but didn't see Katrina's new SUV anywhere.

"How do you know I'm speeding, Trina?"

"I'm in the big tow truck you just passed up."

Whitney glanced in her rearview mirror and saw the tow truck flash its headlights.

"Hold up . . . are you driving that thing?"

"Heeeell no! Girl, I would crash before I even started the engine!"

Whitney busted out laughing.

"Jeff's driving, sis. First day on the job with my baby, and I'm looovin' it!" Katrina added.

"Ask your fiancé why he was blasting that loud horn all up in my ear like that, though," Whitney asked, cresting the lengthy upgrade and approaching her exit.

Whitney suddenly heard Jeff's voice.

"BECAUSE TRINA SAID SHE GON' LEMME HIT—"

"JEFFREY!" Katrina shouted, cutting him off. "Man, the whole world don't need to know, punk! Now shut up and drive!"

Whitney laughed her ass off. "Y'all are too much. Hey, what time you gonna be done?"

"Not sure exactly," Katrina told her. "The shift is from ten a.m. to ten p.m. Accidents happen all day, and Jeff says for some reason, there's always one close to the end of the shift."

"Oh. Well . . . I was gonna see if you wanted to get Ruby from work with me. We've been texting back and forth all day. It sounds like she's having the best day ever."

"Eeeeeeee, joe! Lil' sis makin' a come-up today! Heeeey!" Katrina said, excited to hear Ruby was doing so good.

"Well, I'll talk to you later," Whitney said, exiting off the parkway. "You two be safe, okay?"

"Yup. And you, too," Katrina replied.

"And slow ya' butt down, Whitney! We can't even see you no more, yo!" Jeff chimed in.

"I have a fast vehicle. Sue me. Buh-bye!" Whitney laughed, ending the call.

As she made a left turn onto the road where the hotel for the shoot was, Whitney crossed over a bridge that ran over the highway, catching a glimpse of Jeff and Katrina in that huge truck.

"Well, isn't that crazy? I was just scrollin' through my call log to call you, baby," Calvin said when he answered her call.

"Great minds think alike," Whitney told him, smiling at just the sound of his voice.

"How's your day going, beautiful?" Calvin asked.

"Um . . . eventful," she told him.

"That pause said otherwise . . . what happened?"

Whitney told him about the almost-accident that had nothing to do with the traffic accident.

"Oh wow . . . you are brave . . . and dedicated," Calvin said.

"You can laugh, babe. I know you want to; hell, I laughed when I got back in my seat and saw the guy in the pickup truck next to me lookin' at me like I was crazy."

Calvin busted out laughing then; Whitney laughed, too. In that moment, she realized all her fears about her condition were gone. She had never been able to laugh at it until now. It was because of Calvin. He made her feel like she could laugh it off. Her insecurity was gone! Because of him! She now felt completely comfortable in her own skin because of Calvin Herman. And it was a damn good feeling.

I love this man so much! she thought, coming to a stop at a red light.

"I'm sorry, Whitney. I really ain't laughing at you. I'm picturing the face on the person that didn't know what you were doing, but still, I apologize."

"Don't apologize, Calvin. I just realized something."

"What?"

Whitney smiled to herself. "You complete me."

"And you complete me, baby. I mean that from the bottom of my heart," Calvin told her. "I so badly wish I was mature enough to have said 'screw what everybody was sayin' back then. I wish I would've been the man I am now, back then. You and I would be married with kids already."

"Oh, is that so, Mr. Herman?" she asked, rolling on as the light turned green.

"Yes. Very so, Ms. Wright. I'm so very serious."

"Calvin?"

"Yes? Talk to me."

Arriving at the hotel, Whitney turned into the parking lot and quickly found where her ladies were all parked.

"You there, Whitney?" Calvin asked, thinking the call had dropped.

"Yes. I was parking."

"You called my name like you was about to ask something."

"No. I wasn't gonna ask anything. I was gonna say that I love you," Whitney told him, feeling her heart rate speed up as the words left her mouth.

"You was gon' say it, or you are?"

"I am. Calvin Herman, I am madly in love with you, and I do not care if you aren't. I am, and I'm telling you this because I will not deny my feelings for you."

"Hmm . . . you are madly in love with me, huh? So, what if I'm wildly in love with you? Whose love is stronger?"

"Mine."

Calvin started laughing. "That's not fair."

"Yes, it is. I'm the woman, so it's fair. Deal with it. Ha!"

"Hey, Whitney?" Calvin called.

"Yes, Calvin?"

"I love you, too, baby."

Whitney cheesed up so hard she gave herself chipmunk cheeks. His words were music to her ears.

"Aww! Okay, when I see you later on, I'm gonna do something to you that I've always wanted to try," she teased.

"Oh yeah? Can I get a hint?" he asked.

"Sure. Ice cubes."

"WHOA! OOO OOO!" he shouted.

She cracked up laughing at him. "Calm down. Don't blow one in your boxer briefs; save it for me, okay?"

"Yes. I do not need to go into court and start knocking over coffee cups; the DA would be pissed!"

Whitney screamed out laughing. "Holy cow, yo, you are funny as heck!"

Calvin chuckled. "For you? All day. I love you, and I love sayin' I love you. I can't wait to see you later so I can show you how much I love you."

She felt a flash of heat shoot through her. "Mmmm . . . me neither. See you later, handsome man of mine."

"Yes, you will, beautiful queen of mine," he replied.

CHAPTER 30

Ruby had lunch with her man when he popped up for a surprise visit. He took her to the Evergreen Chinese Buffet just minutes away from her job. They dined on the delicious General Tso's chicken with fried rice and egg rolls. They told each other about their days so far, then after finishing up, Darrell left a nice tip, and they went back out to his Range Rover. Before he dropped her off, they got a lunch time quickie in.

When her shift was over, Ruby came out and saw Whitney waiting for her, the hazard lights blinking as she sat parked in front of the store. Ruby hopped in the front and saw that Whitney had the baby guinea pig on her lap.

"Aww! *Onika*! You came to pick me up from work, too?" Ruby said, reaching over and scooping her squeaking critter up.

Onika stopped squealing and sniffed at her owner. Ruby kissed her nose, then Whitney pulled off. Ruby filled Whitney in on her day, showing her the big commission check she'd been issued with all her sales reflected on it. Whitney then told her about her own day but left out the *tunnel accident* part.

●●●

Four Days Later—
Ruby screamed when she saw the two famous female rappers walk into her job. Amongst the big security guards

encircling them were Whitney and her three right hands—Shaquayla, Riley, and Lanisha.

"Oooo, *Ruuuuuby*! What up, *guuuuurl*!" shouted Cardi B, wearing the sexiest *FeFe* body suit that was all red.

Her hair was spray-painted with crosses in it; fire-engine-red lipstick graced her lips, and she was dripping in diamond jewelry. Excited herself to meet her biggest fan, the notoriously wild Bronx girl had the biggest smile on her face.

Along with the Dominican-Trinidadian beauty was the gorgeous chocolate-brown African American belle, Megan Thee Stallion. The tall statuesque Houston rapper was in a sleek purple suede *FeFe* body-con dress with cheetah spots all over it. It had a scoop neck design and long sleeves that ended in gloves. It looked like it'd been painted on her tall, voluptuous frame. A slit ran from the ankle-length hem all the way up her left leg to the hip. On her feet were matching *FeFe* calf-high stiletto booties. Her eyelids were dusted purple, lined in black, and her lips were glossed with purple lipstick. She, too, rocked expensive diamond jewelry, looking like the elegant Black queen that she had every music-loving female wanting to be.

Ruby was wowed that Cardi B and Megan Thee Stallion were actually in the furniture store she worked in. Inside of her head, she chanted, *OH MY GOD! OH MY GOD! OH MY GOD! OH MY GOOOOOD! YOOOOO, IT'S REALLY THEM! HERE! IN MY STORE! NO FREAKIN' WAY!*

Ruby was ecstatic, to say the least. Whitney saw the look of total shock on her face as other shoppers in the store—many who knew who the two famous women were—all screamed in excitement, as if Beyoncé were the one doing a surprise visit.

"This is crazy! You two are really here! In the store I work at?" Ruby asked as they approached her with their entourage behind them.

"Well, my homegirl Whitney told me at the *FeFe* line photo shoot me 'n' La Stallion baddie gon' be in that my biggest fan was workin' here, so La Cardi had to pump the brakes and come check ya' out! And you's a gorgeous mamita, too, yo! Okkrrrrrr!" Cardi B said, finishing her statement with her famous sound that no other woman in the music game could imitate.

Everyone in the store tried to mimic her sound, even a few men. Cardi B laughed her ass off at the attempts.

"And then," chimed in Megan Thee—*ridiculously gorgeous*—Stallion, "hearin' that you been workin' real hard to get ya' life on track, after hearin' you was headin' right into a brick wall, I wanted to meet you, too. Whit' tells me 'n' Cardi that you doin' real good, got you a good man that loves you unconditionally, so we both felt like we needed to come check ya' out and congratulate you. Ya feel me?"

Ruby nodded. "I do. I had to make the change, or nothin' good was gon' happen for me." She then looked at Whitney, who stood to the side, with an appreciative smile on her face. "My big sis saved my life a while ago, her and my other big sis, even when I didn't deserve it. For what they did for me, to help me get on track, and what they are still doin' for me, I can't mess up. It'll be like spittin' in their faces."

"And you most definitely do not do that to people who are in ya' corner, Ma," said Cardi B. "Girl, you know how crazy life can be. You keep doin' you, though; keep ya' head to the sky, keep ya' loved ones close to you, and keep reachin' for ya' goals. You bein' my biggest fan, you gots to know how many people were doubtin' me before I got on, but look at me now."

"Plugged!" Megan added, giving props where due. "And the haters are now pretendin' to be friends, but she knows who's real and who's plastic."

"And so does Megan," Cardi said. "We both been through a lot before our come-ups, so we tryna set an example for all the ladies out there: Never give up, no matter what. If you want it bad enough, you will get it. That means a good, successful life, enriched with love, good friends, happiness, peace, and MOOOLAAAAH! Okkrrrrr!"

"OOKKRRRRR!" the whole store imitated again.

"I understand exactly what y'all mean, yo. On the real, I will always keep strivin' for higher," Ruby told them. Man! I still can't believe y'all are here!"

"Ya' sistah' Whitney deserves the credit for this, baby girl," Thee Stallion told her, putting an arm around Whitney's shoulders to emphasize her point. "This is a very good person you have in yo' life, Ruby. Don't ever forget that."

Ruby held her right hand up. "I swear it on the lives of my parents, I will never forget, and I will never screw up again."

Ruby's eyes filled with tears just then. She ran to Whitney, overwhelmed with emotions. Whitney's eyes filled up with tears of joy as well. She hugged Ruby tightly in her arms. Every person in the store awed at the picturesque moment.

"I love you so much, big sis!" Ruby sobbed, her head against Whitney's bosom.

"I love you, too, little sis. You make me so proud to call you that," Whitney replied, hugging her so tightly, never wanting to let go.

Shaquayla, Riley, and Lanisha were all in tears as well. They joined in on the embrace, hugging Ruby. Cardi and Thee Stallion then embraced Ruby. The photographers stepped in and took flicks of it all, ready to post everything on social media sites.

To say the least, the appearance of Cardi B and Megan Thee Stallion nearly quadrupled the amount of customers that day when people saw the social media explosion of their presence. Even a few local news channel reporters came out to get coverage.

With Cardi B and Megan Thee Stallion at Ruby's side, she sold so many sets of furniture that half the store was cleared out by the end of her shift.

The massive intake had Ruby's boss wowed by the sales she made. Because of it, he gave her a big raise and a two-week long vacation—though he secretly hoped she wouldn't take a single day off, since she was now known as Cardi B's and Megan Thee Stallion's homegirl that worked in his store.

●●●

The summer was officially gone, and fall seemed to have gone straight to winter. Colder weather, shorter days, and less to do outside had many people experiencing seasonal depression, but the ladies and their men had each other to lean on.

Onika, finally cleared to discharge with a clean bill of health despite her broken leg and ribs, left the hospital with high spirits working miracles inside her every day. Bruce brought her to his house, which was surprisingly lavish. He was prepared to nurse her all the way back to health, physically and mentally.

Ruby's big court date came the second week of October. For it, everyone took off work to be there in support of her. Calvin told them that with the type of judge she had, having all the positive support would help her significantly. Her complete turnaround from crime to leading a good, law-abiding life, with so many people in the courtroom supporting her, would go a long way.

Ruby was shocked beyond belief when Cardi B and Megan Thee Stallion showed up to support her, which brought the paparazzi cameras and news station reporters out.

The judge was surprised to see how many people were there on Ruby's behalf. The DA was also amazed and kept trying to be seen on camera, laying down the law.

When it was all said and done, the state proposed a prison sentence of five years, which made Ruby's heart drop. Calvin argued that while Ruby may have deserved it at the beginning of this, she had done exactly what someone who lived a life of crime should do: change for the better.

When the judge asked if Ruby had anything she wanted to say, she looked back at Whitney, Katrina, and Onika, along with Darrell, Bagz, Jeff, and Bruce. They all gave her reassuring smiles and nodded their heads. She then looked at Calvin. He gave her a nod and then sat in his seat next to her.

Ruby stood and spoke from the heart.

"Your Honor, it's true; at the beginning of this, I deserved to go to prison. I was living recklessly and had no goals or light in my life. I only had darkness. I didn't care; it was about the fast money, living for the next come-up. But then I met my sisters. They saved me from myself, and now, I save me. I've changed from a criminal to a woman with dreams of being someone other young women can look up to."

Whitney and Katrina held hands as they listened to Ruby speak. Onika's eyes filled with tears as she sat in her wheelchair. She was so proud of Ruby and the way she was speaking. It had her wanting to be just like her.

Ruby continued, "I was not, and never will be, perfect, Your Honor, but what I am, and will forever be, is a human that knows right from wrong. All the things I've accomplished over the last few months are very dear to me. I can't picture my life without them now—my career, my family, my friends."

She paused and looked back at Darrell. He smiled at her, giving her a wink. She smiled and wiped away a tear that rolled down her cheek. Turning back to the judge, she continued, "The man that God put in my life, that loves me unconditionally despite my past . . . I couldn't ruin all that. They've taken so much time from their own lives to guide me. I gave them all my word that their time wouldn't be wasted. That promise still stands, and always will. I am sorry for what I did to them and to all the other people I took from. I know sorry doesn't erase it, but all I can do is acknowledge my wrongs, repent, ask for forgiveness, and grow from it."

With that, Ruby sat down. Calvin gave her shoulder a light squeeze, telling her she did a phenomenal job. Everybody else was wowed by her speech; even the DA and the judge were surprised by how sincere she was.

"YOU GO, GUUURL!" shouted the Bronx rapper, clapping for Ruby.

The judge nodded as he took it all in. He looked at the state, then at Calvin.

"Alright. I've made my decision," he said. "Please rise, Ms. Solice."

Ruby and Calvin stood up. Ruby's palms were sweating so hard you'd think she'd dipped them in water.

"Young lady, I hear everything you just said all the time from people who go back out to the streets to do the same exact thing," the judge said, making Ruby grow nervous as hell. "But," he continued, "it makes a very big difference when I actually see the change before sentencing. I must say, you've really turned your life around, and I myself am very proud of you."

Ruby gasped when she heard that. The shock on her face was priceless.

"In so, I will go with the state's recommendation to charge you with only the criminal damage to property, which is a misdemeanor, and sentence you to one year of court supervision. You are ordered to pay a $2,000 fine and are to stay clear of police contact. If you have any police contact, your supervision will be violated, and I will be seeing you again . . . not a good thing. If you successfully complete the supervision, the conviction will be expunged from your record. Are there any questions?"

Too excited to form words, Calvin spoke for Ruby. "No, Your Honor. We thank you and the DA for the leniency displayed here today for Ms. Solice. She will continue growing and traveling on a positive path. I am sure of this."

"Very well. Court is adjourned. You may go, Ms. Solice," the judge told her, then called the next case.

•••

Ruby screamed and hopped up and down excitedly when they all got outside of the courthouse.

"I'M NOT GOING TO PRISON! I'M FREE!"

"Good job, girl!" Megan Thee Stallion said, giving Ruby a congratulatory hug. "Now, you can't have no police contact. You know how easy it is for that."

"Ya' gots to be on ya' square, 'yahm sayin'?" Cardi B chimed in, patting Ruby's back.

"Yes. I know. I'm not messing up this opportunity. I've come too far to do that," Ruby said. She looked at her family and her man. "I promise," she added.

•••

One Month Later—

"Yes! Yes! Beautiful, ladies! Just beautiful!" shouted Pierre as he snapped photo after photo of the two women in *FeFe* Couture.

December had arrived, and Onika and Ruby were rapidly becoming the next big thing in the world of fashion modeling. The shoots they did for the first time together with Cardi B and Megan Thee Stallion in *Steel City Queens* magazine had flown off the shelves and had been plastered all over social media. The solo shoots they did were even hotter. Demands for them to model other high-fashion labels poured in, flooding Whitney's email every day for weeks.

Even on crutches and in a wheelchair, Onika was highly desired in other magazines and was even asked to appear on TV shows like *Tamron Hall, Sherri, J Hudson,* and even

Oprah. Ruby was featured in many tattoo magazines, posing with other tatted-up models and celebrities. She and Onika had become celebrities themselves. Their social media pages had so many followers that veteran runway models were jealous.

Essence, Ebony, XXL, Cosmopolitan, and countless other fashion magazines reached out to Whitney to get Ruby and Onika featured in their spreads. Whitney shared all the requests with the young ladies, and when they agreed, she contacted those who reached out to her and arranged for them to feature her girls—but only for top dollar, paid directly to them.

Ruby and Onika were seeing big checks with lots of zeros rolling in. They were invited to top-model events, fashion shows, and met the biggest celebrities and fashion designers on earth. They were both surprised to see how many Black men and women were in the fashion game now. They prioritized modeling for the cause before anything else.

As Christmas approached, Onika was filled with joy. She had a man now. Bruce had proven to be the man she'd always wanted. He loved her unconditionally and showed it daily. They spent so much time together that it seemed weird when they weren't together.

Bruce was blessed with funding to purchase a building to create a shelter for battered and addicted women. He also received support to help those needing education get into school. He was able to help single mothers feed and clothe their children and get them food stamps, even if they didn't have identification. Housing, transportation, jobs, and most importantly, support that didn't last for just thirty days—Bruce provided each woman with a network of resources to help them get their lives on track, and he didn't make a dime doing it.

His security firm was growing as more businesses hired his services to protect their assets. Soon, he employed over thirty highly skilled security guards who had passed a rigorous ethics and personality course. He did not want any of his people harming anyone because of foolish split-second decisions.

Darrell and Bagz planned Katrina and Jeff's wedding, which was going to be at one of the most beautiful places on earth. Ruby and Darrell had grown so close that talks of marriage were in the air. Whitney and Calvin were so in love that whenever they were with each other—which was all the time—they couldn't keep their hands off each other.

Love was in the air for all of them. They continued taking life one day at a time. Love couldn't and shouldn't be rushed because it takes time to build. Trust went with it, along with being friends. When it finally comes, it could be the best feeling in the world that a human can have.

Love conquers all, and with the right one, nothing can beat you or keep you down. With the right one, you are a team. You keep each other in the game, and even if you lose, you still win because you have each other. No amount of money can buy the happiness that love can provide. And *that*, is facts!

CHAPTER 31

"Ayeeeeee! We in New Yitty, yo! Ooo ooooooo!" Onika shouted, excited as hell as the jumbo jet landed at John F. Kennedy International Airport. "I cannot wait to see what's to the Concrete Jungle, yo!"

Sitting next to her, Bruce chuckled. "You gon' love it, baby. The shoppin', the restaurants, the sights. Yo, we about to have a ball, love," he told her.

Behind them, Whitney and Calvin sat, excited themselves. Calvin was even more excited, though, because of the baby growing inside Whitney's belly. A week ago, she had discovered she was pregnant with his child. He was thrilled knowing that in seven and a half months, he was going to have his first child with the woman he had been in love with since they were kids.

Katrina giggled as her husband rubbed on her belly. Her baby bump was growing with the bundle of joy inside her. She was one month ahead of Whitney in her pregnancy.

The wedding that Darrell and Bagz had planned was held in Negril, Jamaica. They booked an exclusive resort that sat right on the coast, with the clearest blue waters of the Caribbean Sea. It was there that Katrina and Jeff revealed they were having a baby—though their guests would've figured it out when Katrina donned her custom-made, form-fitting Pnina Tornai wedding dress.

The wedding was such a hit that Darrell and Bagz had been receiving nonstop calls to plan weddings all over the country, not just in Pittsburgh.

Ruby had traveled with Darrell to many of the events and ended up becoming a key contributor because of her ideas and her rising status as a fashion celebrity.

Now, being in New York for a big end-of-the-year vacation, Ruby wanted to see all the best places the Big Apple had to offer. Having grown up on the other side of the many bridges linking New York to New Jersey, Ruby realized she had never actually been to New York.

"I wish we could go see what Jay-Z's club is like, bae," she told Darrell as the jet taxied toward the terminal tunnel.

"Next time we come for a trip, if it's at least eight months later, we can," he told her, putting a hand on her belly, rubbing it and smiling, geeked about their child growing inside her. "But best believe, when our son is born, we gonna go all over the world and live one hell of a life. How's that sound? Maybe back to Negril . . . to enjoy the adult beaches?" He wiggled his eyebrows at her, grinning hard.

Ruby started laughing. "Sounds like one more reason to add to the other ones that say why I'm so in love with you, babe. Like, I'm really gonna be a mom, yo. I cannot freaking believe it."

"The way you be havin' morning sickness all day, and you still can't believe there's a baby growin' inside you?"

Ruby laughed again, then mushed him in the face. "I do not be sick all day, Darrell," she told him—then, suddenly hit with that queasy feeling, Ruby clapped a hand over her mouth, shot up from her seat, and ran for the bathroom.

Also there were Bagz and Ericka, and like Whitney and Katrina, Ericka was with child, going on twelve weeks into her pregnancy. Her baby bump was the biggest, and so were her feet.

●●●

They all spent Christmas together.

A house that Calvin owned in the Hamptons housed them all in luxury. Once they settled into the deluxe home, Calvin had a few luxurious SUVs from a car service come pick them up and take them into the city so they could all see Rockefeller Plaza at the most magical time of the year.

The gigantic Christmas tree, which they had only seen on *The Today Show, Good Morning America,* and movies shot in the famous area, was even bigger and grander in person.

Spending a few hours there, they all went ice skating. Onika, still with her leg in a cast, got pushed around on the ice in a special skate-blade-equipped chair by her man. She and Bruce had a ball.

Later on Christmas evening, after a long shopping spree—where they all broke into groups to shop for gifts to exchange—they gathered back at Calvin's home, exchanged presents, and ate a huge Christmas dinner.

The days between Christmas and New Year's Eve were spent exploring as much of New York City as they could.

Then, on New Year's Eve, they all bundled up and were chauffeured back to Times Square to see the ball drop.

The place was packed. Hundreds, maybe thousands of people were there to say goodbye to 2022 and welcome 2023. A few celebrity performances took place. They all felt like they had been taken to a wonderland by God himself.

●●●

"Okay! Here we go! Here we go! Count down, everybody!" Whitney shouted as the brightly lit humongous ball began to descend the tall pole it sat on top of.

Everyone got ready to scream at the tops of their lungs.

"Whitney?" Calvin took his woman by the hand, getting her attention. She looked at him with the most beautiful light in her eyes.

"Yes, my king?" she said, smiling bright.

"I got somethin' I wanna ask you before this ball drops."

Next to them, Darrell took Ruby's hand and pulled her to him, whispering in her ear, "You know I love you, beautiful, right?"

She nodded. "Yes, of course I do, baby. Duh!" she replied playfully.

"I got a question for you, then," Darrell said, glancing at Calvin.

Calvin nodded, then together, they both dug into their pockets and pulled out little ruby-red velvet boxes. At the same exact time, they both dropped to one knee in front of their women.

Thirty seconds on the countdown . . .

Whitney, Ruby, Katrina, Onika, and Ericka all screamed in surprise.

In unison, Calvin and Darrell spoke.

"Whitney Ann Wright, will you—"

"Ruby Baez Solice, will you—"

"YEEEES!" Whitney and Ruby screamed together, overjoyed beyond the moon. "YES! YES! YES! YEEEEESS!"

Fifteen seconds . . .

Everyone erupted in applause, cheering, clapping, whistling, and shouting as the two men opened the boxes, revealing flawless 5-carat VVS diamond engagement rings. Whitney and Ruby gasped at the size of the shiny rocks.

With ten seconds left, Calvin and Darrell hurried to slip the rings onto their women's fingers, then rose to seal their proposals with a kiss.

FIVE! FOUR! THREE! TWO! ONE! the massive crowd chanted. Then the ball touched down and lit up for 2023.

"HAAAAPPYYY NEEEW YEEEAAARR!" New York City screamed out in unison.

Calvin locked lips with his woman, as did Darrell.

Forever, they would be able to say that the very first few seconds of the new year, they kissed their fiancées.

Jeff, Bruce, and Bagz all followed suit, kissing their women as their first act of love in the new year.

When Onika pulled back from Bruce for just a brief second, she looked up at him from her wheelchair.

"When you propose to me, I want a blue diamond. Got it?" she said.

Bruce busted out laughing. "Sounds extremely expensive, my queen. But you worth ten blue diamonds to me. Now stop makin' demands on New Year's Day and gimme some more sugar, yo."

Onika smiled, then yanked him back to her and kissed him with so much love and passion.

She had fallen so deeply in love with Bruce that it brought tears to her eyes. She loved him because he never gave up on her. He endured so much ridicule and negativity from her. But most of all, she loved him because he had taught her how to love herself.

And for that, she couldn't be happier to have such a wonderful man in her life.

"I love you, my strong Black king," she told him when they'd parted lips.

Bruce smiled at her, holding her hand in his. "And I love you, my beautiful Black queen. Forever and ever, I will love you, and cherish you. Thank you, Onika, for giving me the chance to show you that I can love you the way you deserve to be loved, and for loving me the way I've always wanted to be loved."

Onika smiled. "You're welcome. Now stop gettin' all mushy on me and let's enjoy this new life we have with each other."

Bruce nodded in agreement. "Let's."

EPILOGUE

January, 2023—

"Okay, I'm sorry! Calvin! Darrell! Please! I don't want to die! I'm a changed woman, y'all! Please don't kill me!"

Calvin parked his Mercedes truck in the dark circular area of the old auto scrap yard out in McKees Rocks. He and Darrell both looked at Onika, sitting in the back seat of the SUV with tears in her eyes.

"Yo, there is no possible way you seriously think we would let anything happen to you, Onika, especially by our own hands," Calvin said, a puzzled expression on his face.

"What is wrong with you? You buggin' real hard right now," Darrell added, looking at her like she had lost her mind. "Ruby would never let me hear the end of it if somethin' happened to you while you was with me, yo."

Onika looked around. She saw walls of crushed vehicles stacked in a circle. At the opposite end of the entrance was an old yellow car crusher. Parked next to it was a van with no windows. She could see the silhouettes of two figures standing outside the van, waiting for something . . . or someone. It was so dark that only the light from the full moon kept the area from being completely swallowed up by pitch black.

"So . . . so why did y'all bring me here?" Onika asked, wiping the few tears that had fallen from her face.

Calvin then smiled at her. "You'll see, lil' sis. Come on."

He and Darrell got out. Darrell opened the door for her and held her hand as she got out. He grabbed her crutches for her, then he and Calvin led her over to where the two men at the van awaited them.

Onika saw a dark-skinned bald guy with a thick beard. Joining him was a light-skinned guy with a low-trimmed beard. She noticed they were both in black jeans and wore black hoodies, looking like they had more clothes on underneath.

"Good evenin', my brothers and sister," the dark-skinned man said.

"Derrick," Calvin greeted the man, then nodded at the light-skinned one. "Smooth," he said to him.

"As-Salamu Alaikum," Smooth said to Calvin, shaking his hand, then shaking Darrell's. He looked at Onika. "You must be Onika."

She nodded but couldn't form words at the moment.

"Yes. This is our young fair lady who has made a great turnaround in her life," Calvin told them. Then to Onika, he said, "Onika, Derrick and Smooth are here to assist you with a little get-back. I think she deserves a little revenge, right, fellas?"

Darrell put one hand on Onika's shoulder and reminded her that she was safe.

"I concur, good, sir," Derrick said, then he and Smooth went and opened the rear door of the van.

Calvin and Darrell guided Onika to the back of the van. She was sweating bullets as she hobbled around to see what was inside. When she got to the back, Smooth pulled out a big flashlight from the front pocket of his hoodie and shined the light inside.

Onika gasped when she saw the two men who had beaten and violated her, hog-tied with duct tape over their mouths.

"Oh my God!" she shrieked and almost fell off her crutches trying to jump back.

Darrell caught her before she tumbled. "Whoa, whoa, whoa. Relax, lil' sis. You're safe. I swear on my unborn child. They can't hurt you."

Calvin stepped up next to her. From his waistband, he pulled out a big semi-automatic handgun.

"But you can hurt them," he told Onika, holding the gun out to her.

Onika looked at it, then at the two creeps. Their eyes were bugged wide in fear.

"Just so you know," Calvin said, "there will be no murder charges. You got two of Pittsburgh's finest here to let you regain yourself, then they'll make sure these punks are never found."

Onika's eyes went wide when she realized Derrick and Smooth were cops.

"What you gon' do, sis?" Darrell asked her.

She took a deep breath, then started reaching for the gun. The two perverts in the van began crying, their pleas for mercy muffled by the socks in their mouths and the tape over their lips. Their begging fell on deaf ears.

Onika's hand was inches away from the gun when suddenly, she stopped. She quickly drew it back to her body, then shook her head.

"No," she said. "No. I don't want blood on my hands, even if they deserve it. I'm not a killer. I'm a changed woman, and I won't go back to the dark."

Calvin grinned. Despite being a firm believer in 'an eye for an eye,' he was beyond proud of Onika's decision not to take the gun and kill the two rapists. It showed she had truly let it go and moved on. It showed that what they did to her had no hold on her. She was too strong, mentally and spiritually, and held no malice in her heart.

Calvin let the gun fall to his side.

Darrell patted Onika's back, a proud smile forming as he nodded in apprI'moval. Even he didn't think he could've done what she just did, especially if it had happened to his fiancée.

"I'm very proud of you, little mama," Calvin told her. "Real rap, you surprised me."

"Me too, Onika," Darrell added. "Now, you really are ready for life, and all of us are gonna be there for you—and Bruce—no matter what. I promise you that."

Onika nodded, then blew out an exasperated breath of relief. "Can we go now? This place creeps me out."

The men chuckled.

"Yeah, we can go. Let's get on back to our family," Calvin said, then he turned to Derrick. "Make sure the DA hits them with every single charge that meets the criteria, yo."

"You already know, big cutty. They might even meet Big Bubba, who's also a fan of unwanted sexual encounters with poor defenseless punks like them," Derrick said. He and his partner closed the van's doors, closing the darkest chapter in Onika's life so a new, bright one could begin—with the love of her life and her big, happy family.

THE END

Lock Down Publications and Ca$h Presents
Assisted Publishing Packages

Due to an increase in the price of services we have increased our prices. The prices below reflect the price increase as of 11/1/24.

BASIC PACKAGE	UPGRADED PACKAGE
$699	$1000
Editing	Typing
Cover Design	Editing
Formatting	Cover Design
	Formatting
	Upload eBooks to Amazon
	Upload Paperback to Amazon
ADVANCE PACKAGE	**LDP SUPREME PACKAGE**
$1,400	$1,700
Typing	Typing
Editing (line editing/content)	Editing (line editing/content)
Cover Design	Cover Design
Formatting	Formatting
Copyright Registration	Copyright Registration
Proofreading	Proofreading
Upload eBooks to Amazon	Set up Amazon Account
Upload Paperback to Amazon	Upload eBooks to Amazon
	Upload Paperback to Amazon
	Advertise on LDP's Amazon and Facebook Page

***

Other services available upon request.
Additional charges may apply

Lock Down Publications
P.O. Box 944
Stockbridge, GA 30281-9998
Phone: 470 303-9761
Email: lockdownpublications@gmail.com

289

Submission Guideline

Submit the first three chapters of your completed manuscript to ldpsubmissions@gmail.com. In the subject line add **Your Book's Title**. The manuscript must be in a Word Doc file and sent as an attachment. Document should be in Times New Roman, double spaced, and in size 12 font. Also, provide your synopsis and full contact information. If sending multiple submissions, they must each be in a separate email.

Have a story but no way to send it electronically? You can still submit to LDP/Ca$h Presents. Send in the first three chapters, written or typed, of your completed manuscript to:

LDP: Submissions Dept
P.O. Box 944
Stockbridge, GA 30281-9998

DO NOT send original manuscript. Must be a duplicate. Provide your synopsis and a cover letter containing your full contact information.

Thanks for considering LDP and Ca$h Presents.

NEW RELEASES

BLOODLINE OF A SAVAGE 1-3
THESE VICIOUS STREETS 1-3
RELENTLESS GOON 1-3
BY PRINCE A. TAUHID

THE BUTTERFLY MAFIA 1-3
BY FUMIYA PAYNE

A THUG'S STREET PRINCESS 1&2
BY MEESHA

CITY OF SMOKE 3
BY MOLOTTI

GET IT IN SLUGS 1 &2
BY B. STALL

STANDING ON HER BUSINESS 1&2
BY DG SANTANA

STEPPERS 1,2&3
THE REAL BADDIES OF CHI-RAQ
BY KING RIO

THE LANE 1&2
BY KEN-KEN SPENCE

THUG OF SPADES 1&2
LOVE IN THE TRENCHES 2
CORNER BOYS
BY COREY ROBINSON

TIL DEATH 3
BY ARYANNA

CHRISTOPHER "DIESEL" HORNEZES

THE BIRTH OF A GANGSTER 4
BY DELMONT PLAYER

PRODUCT OF THE STREETS 1-3
BY DEMOND "MONEY" ANDERSON

NO TIME FOR ERROR
BY KEESE

MONEY HUNGRY DEMONS 1-2
BY TRANAY ADAMS

HUB CITY MENACE 1-3
BY J. WHITE

A THUGGISH PASSION 1&2
LAND OF DA HOOLIGANZ 1-4
KILLAZ ON STANDBY 1&2
BY IRA B.

FO'EVA ROLLIN 1&2
BY ASSA RAYMOND BAKER

THE LEVEL UP 1&3
BY LUXURY KING

Coming Soon from Lock Down Publications/Ca$h Presents

IF YOU CROSS ME ONCE 6
ANGEL V
By Anthony Fields

A THUGS STREET PRINCESS 3
By Meesha

CORNER BOYS 2
By Corey Robinson

THA TAKEOVER
By Keith Chandler

BETRAYAL OF A G 2
By Ray Vinci

SAVAGE FAMILY EMPIRE 1&2
SOULLESS GOON 1,2&3
THE DIRTY SIDE OF MONEY 1,2&3
By Prince

FOR MY ENEMY'S SAKE
AMBITIONS OF A SLIDER
FRESH OFF DA PORCH
By IRA B.

THE TRUCKLOAD 1-4
TIPPIN' THE SCALES 1-3
BAD BITCHES WIT GUNZ 3
PROBLEM SOLVED 2
By Christopher "Diesel" Hornezes

Available Now

RESTRAINING ORDER 1 & 2
By **CA$H & Coffee**

LOVE KNOWS NO BOUNDARIES 1-3
By **Coffee**

RAISED AS A GOON I, II, III & IV
BRED BY THE SLUMS I, II, III
BLAST FOR ME I & II
ROTTEN TO THE CORE I II III
A BRONX TALE I, II, III
DUFFLE BAG CARTEL I II III IV V VI
HEARTLESS GOON I II III IV V
A SAVAGE DOPEBOY I II
DRUG LORDS I II III
CUTTHROAT MAFIA I II
KING OF THE TRENCHES
By **Ghost**

LAY IT DOWN I & II
LAST OF A DYING BREED I II
BLOOD STAINS OF A SHOTTA I & II III
By **Jamaica**

LOYAL TO THE GAME I II III
LIFE OF SIN I, II III
By **TJ & Jelissa**

IF LOVING HIM IS WRONG…I & II
LOVE ME EVEN WHEN IT HURTS I II III
By **Jelissa**

PUSH IT TO THE LIMIT
By **Bre' Hayes**

THE SINGLE LADIES

BLOODY COMMAS I & II
SKI MASK CARTEL I, II & III
KING OF NEW YORK I II, III IV V
RISE TO POWER I II III
COKE KINGS I II III IV V
BORN HEARTLESS I II III IV
KING OF THE TRAP I II
By **T.J. Edwards**

WHEN THE STREETS CLAP BACK I & II III
THE HEART OF A SAVAGE I II III IV
MONEY MAFIA I II
LOYAL TO THE SOIL I II III
By **Jibril Williams**

A DISTINGUISHED THUG STOLE MY HEART I II & III
LOVE SHOULDN'T HURT I II III IV
RENEGADE BOYS 1-4
PAID IN KARMA 1-3
SAVAGE STORMS 1-3
AN UNFORESEEN LOVE 1-3
BABY, I'M WINTERTIME COLD 1-3
A THUG'S STREET PRINCESS 1&2
By **Meesha**

A GANGSTER'S CODE 1-3
A GANGSTER'S SYN 1-3
THE SAVAGE LIFE 1-3
CHAINED TO THE STREETS 1-3
BLOOD ON THE MONEY 1-3
A GANGSTA'S PAIN 1-3
BEAUTIFUL LIES AND UGLY TRUTHS
CHURCH IN THESE STREETS
By **J-Blunt**

CUM FOR ME 1-8
An LDP Erotica Collaboration

CHRISTOPHER "DIESEL" HORNEZES

BLOOD OF A BOSS 1-5
SHADOWS OF THE GAME
TRAP BASTARD
By **Askari**

THE STREETS BLEED MURDER 1-3
THE HEART OF A GANGSTA 1-3
By **Jerry Jackson**

WHEN A GOOD GIRL GOES BAD
By **Adrienne**

THE COST OF LOYALTY 1-3
By **Kweli**

BRIDE OF A HUSTLA 1-3
THE FETTI GIRLS 1-3
CORRUPTED BY A GANGSTA 1-4
BLINDED BY HIS LOVE
THE PRICE YOU PAY FOR LOVE 1-3
DOPE GIRL MAGIC 1-3
By **Destiny Skai**

A KINGPIN'S AMBITION
A KINGPIN'S AMBITION II
I MURDER FOR THE DOUGH
By **Ambitious**

TRUE SAVAGE 1-7
DOPE BOY MAGIC 1-3
MIDNIGHT CARTEL 1-3
CITY OF KINGZ 1&2
NIGHTMARE ON SILENT AVE
THE PLUG OF LIL MEXICO 1&2
CLASSIC CITY
By **Chris Green**

THE SINGLE LADIES

A GANGSTER'S REVENGE 1-4
THE BOSS MAN'S DAUGHTERS 1-5
A SAVAGE LOVE 1&2
BAE BELONGS TO ME 1&2
A HUSTLER'S DECEIT 1-3
WHAT BAD BITCHES DO 1-3
SOUL OF A MONSTER 1-3
KILL ZONE
A DOPE BOY'S QUEEN 1-3
TIL DEATH 1-3
IMMA DIE BOUT MINE 1-6
DYING FOR LIKES
By **Aryanna**

A DOPEBOY'S PRAYER
By **Eddie "Wolf" Lee**

THE KING CARTEL 1-3
By **Frank Gresham**

THESE NIGGAS AIN'T LOYAL 1-3
By **Nikki Tee**

GANGSTA SHYT 1-3
By **CATO**

THE ULTIMATE BETRAYAL
By **Phoenix**

BOSS'N UP 1-3
By **Royal Nicole**

I LOVE YOU TO DEATH
By **Destiny J**

I RIDE FOR MY HITTA
I STILL RIDE FOR MY HITTA
By **Misty Holt**

CHRISTOPHER "DIESEL" HORNEZES

LOVE & CHASIN' PAPER
By **Qay Crockett**

TO DIE IN VAIN
SINS OF A HUSTLA
By **ASAD**

BROOKLYN HUSTLAZ
By **Boogsy Morina**

BROOKLYN ON LOCK 1 & 2
By **Sonovia**

GANGSTA CITY
By **Teddy Duke**

A DRUG KING AND HIS DIAMOND 1-3
A DOPEMAN'S RICHES
HER MAN, MINE'S TOO 1&2
CASH MONEY HO'S
THE WIFEY I USED TO BE 1&2
PRETTY GIRLS DO NASTY THINGS
By **Nicole Goosby**

LIPSTICK KILLAH 1-3
CRIME OF PASSION 1-3
FRIEND OR FOE 1-3
By **Mimi**

TRAPHOUSE KING 1-3
KINGPIN KILLAZ 1-3
STREET KINGS 1&2
PAID IN BLOOD 1&2
CARTEL KILLAZ 1-3
DOPE GODS 1&2
By **Hood Rich**

THE STREETS ARE CALLING
By **Duquie Wilson**

THE SINGLE LADIES

STEADY MOBBN' 1-3
THE STREETS STAINED MY SOUL 1-3
By **Marcellus Allen**

WHO SHOT YA 1-3
SON OF A DOPE FIEND 1-4
HEAVEN GOT A GHETTO 1&2
SKI MASK MONEY 1&2
By **Renta**

GORILLAZ IN THE BAY 1-4
TEARS OF A GANGSTA 1/&2
3X KRAZY 1&2
STRAIGHT BEAST MODE 1&2
By **DE'KARI**

TRIGGADALE 1-3
MURDA WAS THE CASE 1-3
By **Elijah R. Freeman**

SLAUGHTER GANG 1-3
RUTHLESS HEART 1-3
By **Willie Slaughter**

GOD BLESS THE TRAPPERS 1-3
THESE SCANDALOUS STREETS 1-3
FEAR MY GANGSTA 1-5
THESE STREETS DON'T LOVE NOBODY 1-2
BURY ME A G 1-5
A GANGSTA'S EMPIRE 1-4
THE DOPEMAN'S BODYGAURD 1&2
THE REALEST KILLAZ 1-3
THE LAST OF THE OGS 1-3
By **Tranay Adams**

MARRIED TO A BOSS 1-3
By **Destiny Skai & Chris Green**

CHRISTOPHER "DIESEL" HORNEZES

KINGZ OF THE GAME 1-7
CRIME BOSS 1-4
By **Playa Ray**

FUK SHYT
By **Blakk Diamond**

DON'T F#CK WITH MY HEART 1&2
By **Linnea**

ADDICTED TO THE DRAMA 1-3
IN THE ARM OF HIS BOSS
By **Jamila**

LOYALTY AIN'T PROMISED 1&2
By **Keith Williams**

YAYO 1-4
A SHOOTER'S AMBITION 1&2
BRED IN THE GAME
By **S. Allen**

TRAP GOD 1-3
RICH $AVAGE 1-3
MONEY IN THE GRAVE 1-3
CARTEL MONEY 1&2
By **Martell Troublesome Bolden**

FOREVER GANGSTA 1&2
GLOCKS ON SATIN SHEETS 1&2
By **Adrian Dulan**

TOE TAGZ 1-4
LEVELS TO THIS SHYT 1&2
IT'S JUST ME AND YOU
By **Ah'Million**

THE SINGLE LADIES

KINGPIN DREAMS 1-3
RAN OFF ON DA PLUG
By **Paper Boi Rari**

THE STREETS MADE ME 1-3
By **Larry D. Wright**

CONFESSIONS OF A GANGSTA 1-4
CONFESSIONS OF A JACKBOY 1-3
CONFESSIONS OF A HITMAN
CONFESSIONS OF A DOPE BOY
By **Nicholas Lock**

I'M NOTHING WITHOUT HIS LOVE
SINS OF A THUG
TO THE THUG I LOVED BEFORE
A GANGSTA SAVED XMAS
IN A HUSTLER I TRUST
By **Monet Dragun**

QUIET MONEY 1-3
THUG LIFE 1-3
EXTENDED CLIP 1&2
A GANGSTA'S PARADISE
By **Trai'Quan**

CAUGHT UP IN THE LIFE 1-3
THE STREETS NEVER LET GO 1-3
By **Robert Baptiste**

NEW TO THE GAME 1-3
MONEY, MURDER & MEMORIES 1-3
By **Malik D. Rice**

CREAM 2-3
THE STREETS WILL TALK
By **Yolanda Moore**

CHRISTOPHER "DIESEL" HORNEZES

THE STREETS WILL NEVER CLOSE 1-3
By **K'ajji**

LIFE OF A SAVAGE 1-4
A GANGSTA'S QUR'AN 1-4
MURDA SEASON 1-3
GANGLAND CARTEL 1-3
CHI'RAQ GANGSTAS 1-4
KILLERS ON ELM STREET 1-3
JACK BOYZ N DA BRONX 1-3
A DOPEBOY'S DREAM 1-3
JACK BOYS VS DOPE BOYS 1-3
COKE GIRLZ
COKE BOYS
SOSA GANG 1&2
BRONX SAVAGES
BODYMORE KINGPINS
BLOOD OF A GOON
By **Romell Tukes**

CONCRETE KILLA 1-3
VICIOUS LOYALTY 1-3
BLOODY MONEY BAGS
By **Kingpen**

THE ULTIMATE SACRIFICE 1-6
KHADIFI
IF YOU CROSS ME ONCE 1-3
ANGEL 1-4
IN THE BLINK OF AN EYE
By **Anthony Fields**

THE LIFE OF A HOOD STAR
By **Ca$h & Rashia Wilson**

NIGHTMARES OF A HUSTLA 1-3
BLOOD AND GAMES 1&2
By **King Dream**

THE SINGLE LADIES

GHOST MOB
By **Stilloan Robinson**

HARD AND RUTHLESS 1&2
MOB TOWN 251
THE BILLIONAIRE BENTLEYS 1-3
REAL G'S MOVE IN SILENCE
By **Von Diesel**

MOB TIES 1-7
SOUL OF A HUSTLER, HEART OF A KILLER 1-3
GORILLAZ IN THE TRENCHES
OOPS CRY TOO 1&2
THE DAUGHTER OF A CARTEL BOSS
By **SayNoMore**

BODYMORE MURDERLAND 1-3
THE BIRTH OF A GANGSTER 1-4
By **Delmont Player**

FOR THE LOVE OF A BOSS 1&2
By **C. D. Blue**

KILLA KOUNTY 1-5
TENDER
By **Khufu**

MOBBED UP 1-4
THE BRICK MAN 1-5
THE COCAINE PRINCESS 1-10
STEPPERS 1-3
SUPER GREMLIN 1-4
A GANGSTA'S SON
By **King Rio**

MONEY GAME 1&2
By **Smoove Dolla**

CHRISTOPHER "DIESEL" HORNEZES

A GANGSTA'S KARMA 1-5
By **FLAME**

KING OF THE TRENCHES 1-3
By **GHOST & TRANAY ADAMS**

BAD BITCHES WIT GUNZ 1&2
PROBLEM SOLVED
By **"Christopher Diesel" Hornezes**

QUEEN OF THE ZOO 1&2
By **Black Migo**

GRIMEY WAYS 1-3
BETRAYAL OF A G
By **Ray Vinci**

XMAS WITH AN ATL SHOOTER
By **Ca$h & Destiny Skai**

KING KILLA 1&2
By **Vincent "Vitto" Holloway**

BETRAYAL OF A THUG 1&2
By **Fre$h**

COUNTDOWN OF A KILLA 1&2
SEX, MURDER AND GOD 1&2
GUNS DOWN, BOTTOMS UP 1&2
By Lo-Life

THE MURDER QUEENS 1-7
By **Michael Gallon**

FOR THE LOVE OF BLOOD 1-4
By **Jamel Mitchell**

THE SINGLE LADIES

HOOD CONSIGLIERE 1&2
NO TIME FOR ERROR
By **Keese**

PROTÉGÉ OF A LEGEND 1,2&3
LOVE IN THE TRENCHES 1&2
By **Corey Robinson**

THE PLUG'S RUTHLESS DAUGHTER 1&2
By **Tony Daniels**

BORN IN THE GRAVE 1-3
CRIME PAYS
By **Self Made Tay**

MOAN IN MY MOUTH
By **XTASY**

TORN BETWEEN A GANGSTER AND A GENTLEMAN
By **J-BLUNT & Miss Kim**

LOYALTY IS EVERYTHING 1-3
CITY OF SMOKE 1-3
By **Molotti**

HERE TODAY GONE TOMORROW 1&2
By **Fly Rock**

WOMEN LIE MEN LIE 1-4
FIFTY SHADES OF SNOW 1-3
STACK BEFORE YOU SPLURGE
GIRLS FALL LIKE DOMINOES
NAÏVE TO THE STREETS
By **ROY MILLIGAN**

PILLOW PRINCESS
By **S. Hawkins**

CHRISTOPHER "DIESEL" HORNEZES

THE BUTTERFLY MAFIA 1-3
SALUTE MY SAVAGERY 1&2
By **Fumiya Payne**

THE LANE 1&2
By Ken-Ken Spence

THE PUSSY TRAP 1-5
By **Nene Capri**

DIRTY DNA
By **Blaque**

SANCTIFIED AND HORNY
by **XTASY**

BOOKS BY LDP'S CEO, CA$H

TRUST IN NO MAN
TRUST IN NO MAN 2
TRUST IN NO MAN 3
BONDED BY BLOOD
SHORTY GOT A THUG
THUGS CRY
THUGS CRY 2
THUGS CRY 3
TRUST NO BITCH
TRUST NO BITCH 2
TRUST NO BITCH 3
TIL MY CASKET DROPS
RESTRAINING ORDER
RESTRAINING ORDER 2
IN LOVE WITH A CONVICT
LIFE OF A HOOD STAR
XMAS WITH AN ATL SHOOTER

www.ingramcontent.com/pod-product-compliance
Lightning Source LLC
Chambersburg PA
CBHW051242260626
47162CB00002B/559